P9-CRC-140

A Christmas Promise

Also by Thomas Kinkade and Katherine Spencer in Large Print:

Cape Light
A New Leaf

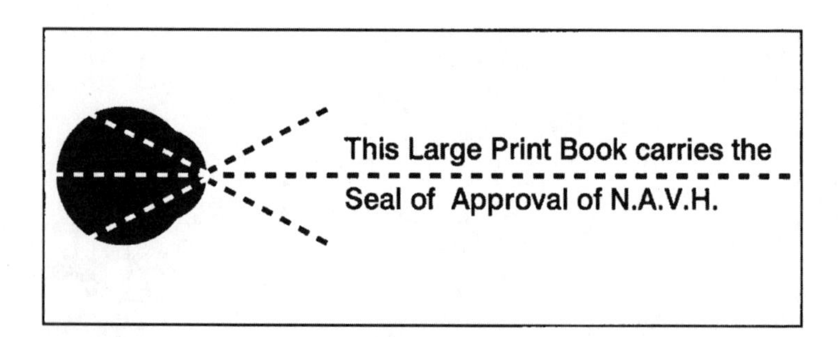

A Cape Light Novel

THOMAS KINKADE
& KATHERINE SPENCER

Thorndike Press • Waterville, Maine

All scripture passages have been quoted from the King James Version of the Bible.

This is a work of fiction. Names, characters, places, and incidents either are the product of the author's imagination or are used fictitiously, and any resemblance to actual persons, living or dead, business establishments, events, or locales is entirely coincidental.

Published in 2005 by arrangement with The Berkley Publishing Group, a division of Penquin Group (USA) Inc.

Thorndike Press® Large Print Americana.

The tree indicium is a trademark of Thorndike Press.

The text of this Large Print edition is unabridged.
Other aspects of the book may vary from the original edition.

Set in 16 pt. Plantin by Elena Picard.

Printed in the United States on permanent paper.

Library of Congress Cataloging-in-Publication Data

Kinkade, Thomas, 1958–
A Christmas promise : a Cape Light novel / Thomas Kinkade & Katherine Spencer.
p. cm.
ISBN 0-7862-7149-3 (lg. print : hc : alk. paper)
1. Cape Light (Imaginary place) — Fiction. 2. City and town life — Fiction. 3. New England — Fiction. 4. Large type books. I. Spencer, Katherine. II. Title.
PS3561.I534C47 2005
813′.54—dc22 2004059812

A Christmas Promise

National Association for Visually Handicapped
serving the partially seeing

As the Founder/CEO of NAVH, the only national health agency solely devoted to those who, although not totally blind, have an eye disease which could lead to serious visual impairment, I am pleased to recognize Thorndike Press* as one of the leading publishers in the large print field.

Founded in 1954 in San Francisco to prepare large print textbooks for partially seeing children, NAVH became the pioneer and standard setting agency in the preparation of large type.

Today, those publishers who meet our standards carry the prestigious "Seal of Approval" indicating high quality large print. We are delighted that Thorndike Press is one of the publishers whose titles meet these standards. We are also pleased to recognize the significant contribution Thorndike Press is making in this important and growing field.

Lorraine H. Marchi, L.H.D.
Founder/CEO
NAVH

* Thorndike Press encompasses the following imprints: Thorndike, Wheeler, Walker and Large Print Press.

DEAR FRIENDS

When I was a child, Christmas was my favorite holiday. The sweet smell of gingerbread cookies baking in the oven, the joyful bells jingling on our front door, the presents piled high under the tree — these were the things I remember fondly from my childhood. Christmas, more than any other holiday, rang with the promise of wonderful things to come.

Christmas continues to be my favorite time of year. During this joyous season, I love to sit by the fireside and reflect on the true meaning of the holiday. Beneath the tinsel and wrapping paper and all the colorful lights, there lies a simple message of God's love for us all.

When I paint my Christmas scenes, I try to capture the beauty of the season and all of its promise. Homes with candlelight shining through the windows, welcoming all who pass by, this glowing light is so poignant — a symbol of warmth and love and rays of hope that shine through the dark of winter.

So come with me this Christmas to Cape Light, a small coastal New England town, and we will visit the glowing homes along the shore. Cape Light is a place where the people celebrate their joys and help each other through their sorrows. Like all towns, Cape Light has people with open hearts and others whose hearts have yet to open. . . .

Let's visit with a young woman named Leigh Baxter, an outsider who comes to Cape Light desperately in need of a haven, and a minister named James Cameron who wonders if he has lost his calling. Let's look in on Sam and Jessica Morgan who, in the midst of holiday celebrations, are facing challenges that will shake their relationship to its core. Let us see how Cape Light bestows on them the true gifts of the season. These are, of course, love and forgiveness and faith, the very gifts that God gave to us on this most joyous of days.

Welcome to Cape Light, where it is my hope that these same gifts will find their way into your heart.

— Thomas Kinkade

Chapter One

James Cameron stepped from the church into the frigid night air. Snowflakes drifted down on his cheeks and hair, melting wet and cold as they landed. He stopped short and took a sharp breath. Then, reaching out, he caught a few and watched as they magically disappeared.

Reverend Ben Lewis lagged a few steps behind, locking the heavy wooden door. "Been a while since you've seen the white stuff, James?"

"More than two years, I guess. It's funny how you forget."

"I forget myself. The first snowfall always catches me by surprise."

Standing side by side, the two men looked out at the village green, already covered by a thick, silvery blanket; the snow-covered branches, hanging heavy and low. Just past the green, the village harbor stretched empty and mysterious as snow drifted down to the dark shifting water. The sight was mesmerizing, and neither man spoke for a long moment.

"It looks like a painting," James said.

"Yes . . . doesn't it? And we know who the artist is without checking the corner for His signature." Ben grinned at his friend and pulled his car keys from a pocket. "Let me give you a lift. You can pick up your car tomorrow."

"That's all right. I'm not going far."

Ben wondered if he should say something more then stopped himself. He knew the visiting minister hadn't driven in weather like this for a long time, at least two years by his own admission. But he also knew how James valued his independence. He resisted all coddling, despite the fact that he was still recuperating from the illness that had demanded a leave from his mission work in Nicaragua.

He'll be all right, Ben reasoned. He'll have to drive in snow sooner or later and probably worse than this flurry once the winter goes into full gear.

"It doesn't usually snow this early up here, does it?" James asked.

"Two weeks before Thanksgiving? No, this is unusual," Ben admitted, though he held back from saying that he was afraid that the mid-November snowfall might betoken a severe winter.

Huddled in their parkas, Ben and James tromped across the green and started up their cars.

James turned the ignition key, sending up a quick prayer as the engine coughed and sputtered before finally turning over. A well-intentioned gift from a church member, the gray hatchback was hardly the newest model in town. But it had good tires and brakes and, so far, a reliable battery. The radio got three stations if you slapped the dashboard. James was grateful for it.

The snow was still soft enough to whisk off with windshield wipers. James found a brush in his trunk and cleared off the rear window. He glanced down the street and saw Ben doing the same. Finally, Ben pulled his car out. He waved through the window, then turned at the first corner he came to, and headed for the parsonage, which was walking distance from the village.

James drove up Main Street, past the shops and restaurants, toward the Beach Road. It was Friday evening, just past ten, but Cape Light had never been a place known for its nightlife, and the snowfall seemed to have made Main Street even more deserted than usual at this time of night. One café near the green, the Beanery, was still open. Farther down, the movie theater marquee was still bright. Since it was Friday night, there was a late show, James recalled. But the rest of the street looked empty and still, the dark storefront windows reflecting a glow from the old-fashioned street lamps that lined the sidewalks.

Main Street had been plowed and sanded, but when he reached the Beach Road he found it slower going. The winding, two-lane route was bordered by trees and narrowed by drifts of snow on either side. James felt his small car swerve as he navigated a tight bend and slowed to a near crawl.

I'd better be careful. I don't want to miss the turn. It's hard enough to find that road in broad daylight. . . .

James had been staying with Vera Plante since September, when he'd arrived in town. A widow living on a small fixed income, Vera made ends meet by renting rooms in her large Victorian-style house. James wouldn't describe it as a boardinghouse, but it wasn't quite a bed-and-breakfast either. Vera did serve her houseguests

— as she preferred to call her paying customers — breakfast and dinner a few days a week, though her schedule was random and her cooking skills questionable. While the house was often full in the summer, James was the only guest at present. He could see that Vera really didn't like sharing her home with strangers and did so only out of necessity. She hid this reluctance under an air of particularity, and he sometimes wondered if even he, a minister and the very model of an ideal boarder, met her high standards.

He spotted a turn coming up on the right but didn't recognize any landmarks. He slowed down, straining to read the sign. Evergreen Way. No, that wasn't it. He wanted Meadowlark Lane. Funny how the snow changed the way things looked, he thought.

James leaned forward, peering at the road through the frost-covered windshield. Chunks of ice clung to the wipers now, streaking the glass and obscuring his view with a frost coating. He reached down and turned up the defroster, but the windshield quickly fogged over and he realized he'd turned the wrong dial. He swiped at the fog with his hand, smearing the glass all over, which helped for a moment then seemed to make matters even worse.

"Now I've done it. . . . Cover your ears, Lord. I'm about to say something really outrageous. . . ."

Then the road took a sudden dip and James put both hands back on the wheel, steering into the turn as he felt the car swerve over an ice patch.

The red taillights of another vehicle suddenly appeared straight ahead. Too close, he realized. He hit the brakes but it was too late. His car skidded forward. He pulled the steering wheel hard to one side, trying to avoid impact, but his brakes had locked. Seconds later, the front fender of the hatchback plowed into the other car's trunk with a dreadful crunch.

"Dear God . . . help me, please," James managed through gritted teeth. Finally, his car slowed and stopped, stuck in a high ridge of snow at the edge of the road.

The other vehicle lurched forward, swerving off the road, then down the snow-covered shoulder. It rolled on slowly for a few feet, finally coming to a stop against a line of bushes and deer fencing.

James felt his seat belt pull taut against his shoulder, pinning him to his seat, and suddenly opened his eyes. He hadn't even realized he had shut them. His hands still gripped the steering wheel, his knuckles white. *I'm not dead* was his first thought. *Thank you,* his second.

He took a deep breath. A spot on top of his leg, just above his knee, throbbed with pain, and he reasoned he must have slammed it into the underside of the dashboard. Other than that, it seemed he was unharmed.

What about the other driver or passengers? He swallowed hard, opened his door, then stumbled through the snow to the other car. Its door hung open and he saw that the other driver was a woman. The air bag had opened and now drooped deflated across her lap.

"Are you all right?"

She stared at him, her large brown eyes reflecting his own sense of shock. "I think so. . . ."

"Are you alone?" Finally reaching the car, he peered in through the door.

She nodded then stared down with a sudden change in her expression that made him afraid she might faint or be sick.

He crouched by the open car door. "Don't try to get up. Take a few deep breaths."

She stared straight ahead then did as he advised. The overhead light in her car revealed wisps of curly brown hair framing a pale face.

"At least I hit something soft and not a tree," she said after a moment.

That was something to be thankful for, he thought.

"My windshield fogged and by the time I saw you, it was too late," he began to explain. "I couldn't stop."

"It wasn't your fault. It's the snow. You couldn't help that."

That was true, James thought. But it was still good of her to say so. A lot of people would be ranting at him right now. Especially considering the condition of her car, which was crunched in accordion-style in the rear and buried hood deep in front.

"Sit tight. I'm going to call the police and get some help."

"The police? Do you really think you have to? Can't we just call a tow truck or something?"

He glanced at her, surprised by her reaction. Beneath her reasonable tone he sensed a certain note of anxiety.

"I mean, we both seem to be fine," she added, "and we'll probably be sitting out here in the cold forever if we have to wait until someone comes."

All that was true. He knew that many

people settled their little fender benders without making official reports. But he wasn't the type to go around the law.

"That's all right; I'll deal with it. You're really supposed to report an accident."

She sat back again and took a breath. "Yes, of course. I just wanted to spare you the bother, that's all."

James watched her face as he took out his cell phone and dialed 911. He had a feeling that calling in the police made her nervous. Maybe she had parking tickets or some other reason to feel anxious about her driving record. People were funny that way. Lots of people who were perfectly law abiding got totally unglued by the mere sight of a uniformed policeman.

She certainly didn't look like a person who had something to hide. Her features were delicate and even, her smooth skin bare of makeup except for a worn dash of lipstick. She wore small pearl earrings and a thin gold watch but no wedding ring, he noticed.

He knew that you couldn't judge a person by his or her appearance. Still, he got a feeling about her just from the way she'd spoken to him, saying the accident wasn't his fault. He tended to trust his impressions. As a minister he was trained to be perceptive, and he'd always had an innate sense of the human heart; all of which made him a good judge of character. But not infallible, he reminded himself.

The 911 operator came on quickly and James explained the situation, estimating their location. "An officer is in the area. He's on his way," the emergency dispatcher said.

James ended the call and turned back to the other driver. She'd pulled on a pair of leather gloves and a stylish wool hat and now sat rubbing her hands together. "Someone will be here in a few minutes," he told her. "The heater is still working in my car. Why don't we wait there?"

"All right." The woman nodded and turned slowly in her seat, preparing to get out of the car. James offered his hand, seeing how the car was sunk so deeply in the snow.

She glanced at him a moment then grabbed his hand and levered herself forward. As she pushed the deflated air bag aside and swung her legs around, James felt his mouth drop open but couldn't stop his reaction.

She was pregnant.

About six months, or maybe more, from the looks of her rounded belly underneath a wraparound wool coat.

"You're . . . expecting?"

She blinked at him and glanced down at her stomach. "Seems so." Her flat, faintly amused tone made him feel embarrassed.

"I'm sorry to sound shocked . . . but you should have told me. Are you sure you're all right? Maybe I should call an ambulance."

Once again, he noticed a wary look in her eyes, but when she spoke her voice was level and calm. "The air bag worked perfectly. I didn't feel a thing. I don't think there's anything to worry about."

She did seem fine and he fervently hoped that was true. Still he felt concerned. "Are you sure? I could come with you if you're concerned about going to the hospital alone."

"Is the hospital far?"

"Well . . . yes. About an hour or so south of here, in Southport."

"Oh . . . that is far. And I would be sitting in some waiting room for hours, I'm sure, since it's not really an emergency. . . ." She stared out at the snow for a moment then turned to him again. "I think I'll just try to see a doctor tomorrow. I'm sure I'm okay, honestly."

Her brown eyes were wide. Her tone,

quiet and persuasive. Still, he worried. If the collision had injured the baby, he'd never forgive himself. But he couldn't force her to go. Perhaps she didn't have insurance and was worried about the cost and that was why she was so reluctant.

"All right. Let me help you to the car at least." He took her arm and helped her through the snow.

Maybe a police officer would persuade her to go to the hospital, James thought. And what was an extremely pregnant woman doing traveling alone on a night like this? That didn't seem right either. But then again, the heavy snow had been a surprise; the forecast had only called for flurries.

When they reached his car he opened the passenger-side door for her. "Have a seat. I'll get the heater going."

She climbed in and he shut the door. Then he got in the driver side and turned the keys, which were still in the ignition. Luckily the car started easily. He turned up the heater and flicked on the emergency flashers. The car had ended up far to one side of the road, out of the way of anyone passing; waiting inside seemed safe. The road was so empty tonight. Nobody had come by yet, he noticed. Most people in this town would stop to help if they saw two stranded cars, even if they didn't know you. Unusual, but that's just the way they were in Cape Light.

"By the way, my name is James Cameron. Reverend Cameron, actually." James turned to his companion and stuck out his hand. She looked surprised by his title then smiled slightly and shook his hand. People were often surprised when he told them what he did for a living. He wasn't sure what they expected a minister to look like, but it certainly wasn't him.

"How do you do, Reverend. I'm Leigh Baxter."

James smiled at her briefly. His usual response would be "nice to meet you" but that seemed inappropriate under the circumstances. Instead, he asked if she was warm enough.

She nodded and he didn't know what else to say. An awkward silence hung between them, and James glanced at his watch. He felt bad for wrecking this woman's car, no matter that it was more the fault of the weather. And she being pregnant to boot.

"Is there anyone you'd like to call? You can use my phone if you like."

She stared at the phone for a moment, as

if tempted, then shook her head. "No, thank you. I have a cell phone in my bag."

"Oh . . . okay." James glanced down the road, wondering when the police would come and wondering about her reply. Why wasn't she calling anyone?

There was no one waiting for her to arrive somewhere? No one who needed to know what had happened to her? He found that curious, then thought maybe she just didn't want to have a private conversation in front of him. That was possible, too.

Red lights flashed in the rearview mirror. He turned to see a blue and white cruiser pull up behind his car. "Looks like the police are here," he said. "Wait here, I'll bring the officer over to speak to you."

James opened his door and climbed out as the uniformed officer tromped toward him through the snow. It was Tucker Tulley, James realized, a member of the church.

"Reverend Cameron! For goodness' sake. I didn't know it was you out here." Officer Tulley picked up his pace, running the last few steps. "Are you all right?"

"I'm fine. The other driver was alone. A woman. She seems to be okay but she's pregnant. Doesn't want to see a doctor, though. Maybe you should ask her again," he added with concern.

"I will," Tucker said. He leaned over to peer into the hatchback. "Officer Tulley, ma'am. I'm just going to take some information and get you out of this weather ASAP."

James heard Leigh murmur a quiet greeting and politely answer Officer Tulley's questions. She fumbled for a while, locating her license and car registration, James noticed, but otherwise seemed perfectly at ease and James wondered if he'd only imagined her anxiety earlier when he'd mentioned the police. Officer Tulley quickly took down his information and arranged for a truck to tow Leigh Baxter's car to a service station in town.

One fender on James's car had a small dent, but he could still drive it. "Can I drop you somewhere?" he asked Leigh.

"I'm not sure . . . is there a motel around here?"

"There's one up on the highway," the police officer answered. "But the roads are getting worse. I don't recommend going all that way out of town." Officer Tulley turned toward James again. "Why don't you take her over to Vera's? She probably won't mind putting Ms. Baxter up for a night."

Contrary to Officer Tulley's optimistic impression, James knew that his landlady probably would mind. She did not like surprises, especially after eleven at night.

Still, it did seem like the best and most logical solution.

"Who's Vera?" Leigh asked. "Is she a friend of yours?"

"In a way. I rent a room in her house. But it's a big place. I'm sure she has room for you."

"I guess that would be all right. If it isn't too much trouble for her," Leigh said.

"She won't like being woken up if she's already gone to bed," James said honestly, "but she'll understand."

Officer Tulley offered to wait for the tow truck. James retrieved two pieces of luggage from the trunk of Leigh's car and stowed them in his backseat. They were leather bags, the expensive kind with designer initials stamped all over them. Incongruous with her well-used-looking car, he thought as he climbed behind the wheel again.

The turn to Vera's house was barely a half mile farther down the road. Meadowlark Lane was unplowed and even harder driving than the Beach Road, and James wondered a few times if he was going to end up in yet another accident before the night was over. But he soon pulled up to Vera's house and maneuvered his car as far up the curving drive as he could manage. He stopped the car with a deep sigh and turned off the engine.

"Well done," Leigh said quietly. She met his glance with a slight smile. He suddenly realized she hadn't said a word for the entire drive and must have been sitting there terrified of what would come next.

"I'm really not a bad driver. You just caught me at a real bad time."

She laughed at him and he realized that his answer did sound funny, though he hadn't meant it that way. He smiled then, too.

It had been a difficult night. He was glad to be home in one piece and able to laugh about the accident. It seemed so basic, so clichéd, but the night's events had served to remind him that we never know what God has in store for us around the next bend in the road. Anything could happen at any moment. One's entire life could change in the blink of an eye, in the time it took to draw a single breath.

He glanced over at Leigh, wondering what she was thinking. She was probably just eager to get in from the cold, he realized.

"Wait right there; I'll help you up to the side door."

James came around to the passenger side and helped Leigh out of the car, then grabbed her bags from the backseat.

Vera always left the light on at the side door that opened to a mudroom and then the kitchen. She kept the large house spotless. If she was still awake, the prospect of melting snow on her clean floors was probably sending her into a tizzy.

Surprisingly, the door swung open as they approached. "Reverend Cameron . . . is that someone with you?" Vera called out. Her voice sounded puzzled and alarmed, and he could barely keep a smile from his face as he imagined her panicked thoughts. Why would her boarder be coming home at this hour . . . with a woman on his arm?

"Yes, Vera. It's me." When he got a bit closer, he added, "I had a little car accident on the Beach Road. This poor lady was my victim. Her car had to be towed, and the motel being so far, I thought maybe she could stay here."

"Oh, dear. What a terrible thing. Thank heavens you're all right." Vera opened the door wider and stepped aside so that Leigh and James could enter. Dressed in her bathrobe and slippers, with a scarf tied around her pin curls, she wielded her beloved sponge mop like an armed guard.

"I hope I'm not putting you out, Mrs. Plante," Leigh said quietly.

James watched Vera stare at Leigh, her expression pinched. He could see that Vera did feel put out but her better nature was battling valiantly, trying to help her live up to the virtues she held so dear. Rather than judging her harshly, James thought she should get extra credit for trying so hard.

Finally, Vera sighed and stepped back. "Well, it is an emergency. We'll have to make do."

James nodded in agreement, relieved that she had not made a fuss.

"Here, give me that wet coat. You're dripping all over the place," Vera said a bit sharply. Leigh just smiled and slipped off her coat then handed it to her hostess. He watched Vera hang the coat, then mop up around their feet. Then James noticed Vera's eyes widen as she realized that Leigh was pregnant.

"Oh! Sit down, dear!" Vera said suddenly. "I mean, sit down on this bench and take off those shoes," she added in a softer tone. "Give them here. I'll put them on the boot tray. They need a bit of newspaper inside to dry them out, too."

"Thank you very much." Leigh watched as Vera expertly stuffed wadded balls of newspaper into her shoes.

James took off his parka, hung it on the coat tree, then added his wet boots to the tray.

Vera instantly began mopping up around his feet again. "What a mess. I don't want anyone to slip. . . ."

"Here, I'll do that." James took the mop. There really wasn't much snow on the floor, but he knew it would make the older woman feel better.

"Can I make you some tea?" Vera asked Leigh kindly. "Or maybe some nice tomato soup and crackers? Are you hungry?"

James suppressed a smile. Vera was clearly moved by Leigh's plight. Tomato soup and crackers was his landlady's notion of a real treat.

"No, thank you." Leigh shook her head and smiled. "I guess I'd just like to get some sleep, if that's okay."

"Yes, of course. It's very late. You must be tired. And what a shock, to have an accident in your condition. Just follow me and I'll find a nice comfortable room for you," Vera promised as she led Leigh upstairs.

James put the mop on its proper hook in

the utility closet and soon followed with Leigh's bags. After mulling aloud a bit, Vera finally picked a room for Leigh on the second floor, toward the back of the house and adjacent to a bathroom.

"I made up the bed fresh this weekend, expecting my sister Bea who's down in Gloucester. Then at the last minute, she canceled on me. But here you are, so it's just as well. Just goes to show, you never know. There's a reason for everything," Vera chatted on as she showed Leigh the room.

Leigh gazed around, taking in the pink flowered wallpaper, matching curtains and quilt, and an oval area rug at her feet, also edged by a border of flowers. A milk-glass lamp sat on a small night table that was covered by a piece of lace-edged linen. Judging from Leigh's clothes and luggage, James had a feeling that Vera's surprise guest was used to finer surroundings, but still she seemed pleased.

"What a pretty room. Your sister missed out," Leigh said.

"Didn't she, though!" Vera shook her head in agreement. "I'll leave a fresh set of towels in the bathroom for you, and that closet is empty if you want to unpack a few things."

"Thanks. I'm sure I'll be very comfortable." Leigh watched James put her bags by a wooden chest at the foot of the bed. "Thanks for bringing up my bags," she said to him.

"That's all right. Good night now." He glanced at Vera, hoping to convey that it was time to leave her newest guest alone.

"I won't wake you for breakfast, though I usually serve at half past seven," Vera added as she followed James out of the room.

"Half past seven sounds fine." James caught Leigh's eye and they shared a brief, secret smile. Leigh bid them both good night again and shut her door.

Alone in the room, Leigh sat on the edge of the high, old-fashioned bed, listening as Vera's scuffling steps retreated to a room nearby. She heard James climb the stairs to the third floor and then his steps echoed down a hallway above.

Her hands moved automatically to her stomach, where she felt the baby's fluttery kicks. She thought again of the accident and the way James had urged her to visit a hospital. She'd come very close to giving in. But it was the same old problem, a choice between two evils: to take a risk with her baby's health . . . or to risk losing her baby altogether.

Showing her fake identification to Officer Tulley had been stressful enough. Going through that a second time in one night, especially in some hospital emergency room, would be pushing the odds. She had to move along as if invisible, without leaving any trail, any imprint, any chance for discovery.

Besides, Leigh had a strong feeling that the baby was just fine. She was almost positive she'd know if something were amiss. Still, as soon as she had a chance she would find a private doctor and make sure, she promised herself.

She rested her hand on her stomach. "You're all right. I know you are," she said softly. "I'd never let anything happen to you. You're all I have. Don't worry. I think we'll be fine here. It feels safe."

It did feel safe. James Cameron and Vera Plante both seemed so trusting; she wasn't worried about them. Though it was disorienting to end up in this strange place. She wasn't even sure where she'd landed. Cape Light, the police officer had said. She hadn't noticed the town on her map. Now she pulled the Massachusetts state map from her bag and studied it again. No

Cape Light; it was just another dot on the shore road she'd chosen in lieu of the highway. Maybe that hadn't been such a smart idea, since at that point the snow was already coming down heavily, but she hadn't been willing to take any chances. She was almost sure a car had been following her from the highway rest stop. So now she was lost and stuck without a car, at least for a day or two. Had she just imagined someone following her? Had it been worth all this trouble?

It was worth whatever it took to get away, an inner voice insisted. Whatever it took to keep her baby safe.

Leigh dug her phone out of her purse and turned it on to check her messages. She found a new one and quickly played it back.

The warm, familiar voice of her friend Alice greeted her. "It's me. I had a call today, your cousin Eileen, in Canada. She said you mustn't go there right now or even call her. A private detective came to her house today. She has no idea how they found her. Martin must have given them an old address book or something, and they're just tracking every single name down at this point. Anyway, she's afraid that her house is being watched now. She was even afraid to call you directly. I feel so badly for you, honey. It seemed like such a good plan. . . ."

Leigh fought down a stab of panic. She'd been counting on Eileen as her haven and Canada as the place where she would safely give birth to and raise her baby.

"I don't know what to say," Alice's distressed voice went on. "Wherever you are, be careful. Call me when you can. I just hope you're all right."

Leigh clicked off the phone, caught in a familiar sense of dread and frustration. She felt like a mouse trapped in a maze: she would come so close to escaping she could practically smell freedom; then she would turn and hit another dead end. She felt tears well up and took a shaky breath. By tomorrow, she would have reached Bar Harbor and boarded the ferry. It just wasn't fair.

What was she going to do now? Martin's investigators were everywhere and sooner or later, he'd bring the police into it. She was almost sure of that. His family liked to keep things quiet, and he rarely went against them. But he must be desperate now, she reasoned, desperate and irrational.

Sometimes she felt desperate, too, almost wishing she could just disappear off the face of the earth. Her life seemed such a mess. Sometimes she didn't think she could ever set it straight again.

But she couldn't think that way, she reminded herself. Not with the baby inside of her, her burden and her joy.

Okay, her plan to stay with Eileen on Prince Edward Island was derailed, but maybe she could still go north. Another route perhaps, to someplace where nobody knew her? Or maybe south again? She had some money from trading in her new car for an old one, but she would need most of it for the baby. She was no longer insured and she knew how many thousands it would cost to have the baby in a hospital, and that was assuming everything went smoothly. She'd gone without eating anything today except a roll and coffee, just to save for gasoline. She had a credit card but couldn't use it. It was just too risky. Her ID didn't even match anymore.

But I'll think of something, Leigh told herself. *Some way around him. Maybe not tonight, but something will come to me.*

It just had to.

She couldn't let him win.

Leigh suddenly felt so tired, weary to her bones, her mind a blank, gray screen. She stretched out on the bed and pulled the quilt up around her shoulders. *I'll just rest for a few minutes,* she told herself. Her head had barely touched the pillow before she fell into a deep, dreamless sleep.

Jessica Morgan stood in the dark, staring out at the falling snow covering the land behind their house. The soft white coating made everything outside look different. That's the way winter was; it changed everything, she thought.

She had imagined her life would be different by now, too. That was the problem. She'd floated through the summer with an image in her head, a vision of how it would be once the holidays came. How happy she and Sam would be, preparing for their baby. But it hadn't turned out that way at all. She had lost the baby in September, just as the nights began to cool and the leaves turned color and dropped to the ground.

Fall had come and gone, and now winter had arrived. But she knew she was not over the shock of her miscarriage.

Jessica tightened the belt on her robe. She touched her stomach, perfectly flat. She should have been . . . what, six months by now? She had pictured herself in maternity outfits and Sam's big shirts around the house. Working on this room, picking out paint and wallpaper, ordering baby furniture. Instead, the room stood empty and bare. Waiting. The way she felt inside.

It wasn't rational but she felt as if she had failed.

Suddenly the holidays loomed up before her, Thanksgiving less than two weeks off and Christmas not far behind. She had no spirit this year for the season. She wished she could hide out somewhere until it was all over. She hadn't felt that way since the year her father died. She couldn't imagine how she would get through it.

"Jess? Are you okay?"

Sam stood in the doorway, staring sleepily at her. She was embarrassed that he had found her here again, but in another way, glad of it.

"I'm all right. I just couldn't sleep."

He walked over to the window and put his arm around her, then gently kissed the top of her head. "Worried about something at work?"

Jessica shook her head, avoiding his gaze. He knew why she came in here all the time when she couldn't sleep. He just didn't want to say.

Sam sighed and pulled her close. "Oh,

sweetie, it's okay. We'll have a baby soon. We need to be patient, that's all."

Jessica pressed her head against his shoulder and nodded. Her throat was too tight to speak. What if they couldn't have a baby? What if it just didn't work out for them? Sometimes that happened to couples. She knew it did. Sam wanted children so badly and she was so afraid she would disappoint him.

"It looks like the snow is stopping," she said finally.

"I hope so. We certainly got enough of it. Guess I'll go dig your mother out tomorrow."

"That's sweet." She leaned up and kissed his cheek. "Not that she'll thank you for it."

Sam laughed. "I'll be lucky if she doesn't call the police and report a burglar."

"Come on, Sam. She's not that bad."

"No comment." Sam leaned back and smiled down at her.

"I guess you could stop by at Dr. Elliot's and see if he needs any help, too," Jessica suggested.

"Don't worry, Ezra is already on my list. I might bring Darrell Lester along. He could help me, maybe earn a few dollars."

"Darrell Lester?" Jessica glanced up at

him. The name didn't ring a bell.

"You know, that kid at New Horizons. The one who made the key chain for me."

"Oh, right . . . sure, I remember." She felt embarrassed for forgetting. Darrell hadn't been at New Horizons very long, but he already had a major case of hero worship for Sam.

It wasn't surprising. Sam was great with kids and a good guy, besides. With his outdoor work slowing down these last few months, he had been spending more time at New Horizons, a learning center for city kids who were at risk: getting into scrapes with the law or having trouble in school or in the foster system. As Jessica recalled, Darrell Lester fell into all three categories. There were so many children with sad stories there. Jessica often thought about volunteering but somehow never got around to it. Sam went regularly, though, helping with schoolwork and teaching woodworking and basic building skills.

Sam was so nonjudgmental, so generous with his time. She admired that about him. Sometimes, though, she wished Sam would be more focused on their own problems, instead of getting so involved with strangers.

Maybe I'm just jealous because I can't dis-

tract myself so easily. Sam's found a way to have kids in his life before we have a baby, but I can't find anything to fill this gaping hole in my heart.

"Ready for bed?" Sam glanced down at her, pulling her a bit closer.

Jessica nodded. "I guess so."

They stood together a moment longer, staring out at the snow. A crescent moon shone brightly through the parting clouds. Jessica saw a star and squeezed her eyes shut, making a quick wish. She glanced up and knew Sam had been watching. He leaned forward and gently kissed her forehead.

"Hope it comes true," he whispered.

Jessica nodded, her head tucked under his chin. *Me, too,* she said inside. *Me, too.*

Chapter Two

James thought he would be the first one up, but as he came down the back stairs that led into the kitchen he heard the women's voices. Leigh stood by the table, fully dressed, setting out mugs and silverware while Vera ransacked a cupboard. Leigh looked up and smiled at him briefly then turned toward Vera again.

"Here it is. I knew I had some." Vera held out an oatmeal box like a hard-won trophy. "Perfect on a snowy morning."

"Just some milk will be fine for me. I can't eat too much in the morning," Leigh said.

Vera frowned sympathetically. "Morning sickness? You're far along for that. I had a terrible case myself with my second child, right up to the finish line. It's a wonder she turned out so big and healthy. She —"

"Is something burning?" James gently interjected.

Vera turned in alarm to the stove. "The milk for the cocoa . . . oh, my gosh. I'm sorry, dear. I'll have to start from scratch."

"That's all right. Cold milk would be fine. In fact, I'd prefer it."

"And I'd be perfectly happy with some cold cereal, Vera. I need to get outside and start digging us out."

"I appreciate your help, Reverend. I used to have a teenager who came around when it snowed, but he's gone off to college now." Vera turned and grabbed another pot, about to start the oatmeal anyway, he noticed. "Quite a bright boy. Hoped to be a doctor, I think. . . ."

Fearing another rambling tale, James jumped right in. "A doctor? Really? He'll be gone a long time then. Is the coffee ready?" he asked hopefully.

"I think so." Leigh smiled at him with quiet understanding. James poured himself a cup and took a seat at the table. "Have you called the service station yet? They probably open early."

Leigh sat down across from him. "No, I haven't tried. I left the phone number upstairs somewhere."

"Harbor Auto, down on Scudder Lane." Vera squinted at the oatmeal box then at her measuring cup.

"That was it, Harbor Auto." Leigh sounded surprised, and Vera laughed.

"Of course that was it. Where else were they going to take your car at that hour? The number's on the bulletin board by the telephone. You can call from down here."

Leigh rose and went to the phone. James started on his cereal. He didn't mean to listen in on her conversation, but it was impossible not to. Besides, he felt responsible for the damage. It was such an old car, she might not have collision coverage. He was wondering how long the repairs would take when Leigh's voice rose on a note of distress.

"But I don't live around here. I can't really wait that long." She paused and briefly turned so that he could see her face. She looked very worried, a deep crease between her brows. "That much? Can't you do it for less? I just need the car up and running. It's really not even worth very much. . . . Yes, I see. I'll wait to hear from you then. Thanks very much," she said slowly, then hung up the phone.

Leigh returned to the table. Her expression was composed, but she seemed suddenly absorbed in the pattern of the tablecloth and he suspected she was trying to mask her distress.

"Listen," he said, "the accident was all my fault. I'll pay for your car, whatever it costs. Don't worry. I have insurance. It should cover most of the damage."

Leigh's gaze rose to meet his. "I appreciate your offer, but insurance companies take so long to settle these things. I really need my car back. The mechanic said it might take a few days, maybe even until next week. He's not sure yet. He may have trouble getting parts since it's so old. He's going to call around and call me back."

Feeling terrible that she was so upset, James began to rack his mind for other options. "Well, let's see. I guess you could have it towed to another shop, maybe up to Newburyport. It's a bigger town than Cape Light. But they might not be able to have it done for you any sooner if it's a matter of finding the right parts."

"Yes, I thought of that, too. I doubt it would help to move the car at this point, though, and it would cost a lot for the tow truck."

"I can rent a car for you," James offered. "The insurance might even cover some of that. Then you could come back and pick up your car when it's done."

"I guess I could do that. But it sounds sort of . . . complicated." Leigh picked up a piece of toast, looked about to eat it, then put it down again. "Besides, what if your insurance company won't cover the cost? I don't want you to spend all that money."

"Don't worry about me. I feel responsible for your predicament. Not only is your car out of commission but you must be inconvenienced, being stuck here. I'd be happy to take you someplace today. Wherever you were going last night, I mean," he added, recalling how he had made the same offer last night but she never said where she was headed.

"Oh . . . well, thanks. That's good to know. I was on my way to see a friend. She lives out on the Cape . . . in Wellfleet. I called her last night and told her what happened. So she knows I'm delayed."

Wellfleet was a distance, but he would have been willing to drive her there if she wanted. It was funny, he thought. She had been driving north, the opposite direction from the Cape. But maybe she had been lost.

"Wellfleet is lovely." Vera came to the table carrying a bowl of lumpy-looking oatmeal. "My late husband, Arnold, had family there. Wonderful oysters. Arnold loved oyster stew, though I haven't made that in years. Easy as pie, once you get them shucked. He was quite handy at that task, believe me, though all thumbs around here for the most part." Vera sat down at the table. "And what about you, dear? Where's your husband? You didn't say."

Vera's tone was polite though pointed. She carefully sprinkled sugar over her oatmeal, waiting for Leigh's reply.

James waited, too. Leigh wasn't wearing a wedding ring, he had noticed. He, too, had wondered about a husband, but it took Vera to plunge right in.

Leigh stared at Vera a moment then looked down at the table. "My husband is dead. He passed away a few months ago very suddenly . . . a heart attack."

James felt leaden inside and saw Vera's bright expression go dark. "I'm sorry," he said. "What a tragic loss for you."

"Oh, my dear. I'm so sorry." Vera put her spoon down and leaned toward Leigh. "Sorry to bring it up. I just wondered, was all. What a heartbreak . . ."

Leigh glanced at both of them. "It was . . . a shock. A great shock. He was only a few years older than me and very healthy. I mean, he seemed to be." She took a deep breath and sat back in her chair. "I'm trying to just think of the baby now."

"Of course you are." Vera touched Leigh lightly on the wrist. "What about family? Isn't there anyone to help you?"

Leigh shook her head. "Not really. I don't have any brothers or sisters, and my parents both passed away. A friend from college invited me to stay with her in Wellfleet until the baby comes. She has a shop and I'm going to help her out for the holidays."

She must need money if she was traveling all the way out to the Cape to work part-time in a shop, James reasoned.

"What did your husband do for a living, dear?" Vera asked.

Leigh paused and looked down at her dish again. James sensed it was difficult for her to answer. "He worked for a textile mill, up in Maine."

"Is that where you're from?" James asked.

Leigh shook her head. "Not exactly. After he died, I moved down to Boston for a new job. . . . But it didn't work out."

"What a shame. He must have been so young. I bet he didn't even have insurance. You don't think of that much at your age. You think you're going to live forever. . . ."

James read the distress on Leigh's face and realized that Vera had struck a nerve. "Is there any more coffee? It's very good.

Did you try a new brand, Vera?"

Vera gave him a curious look then passed him the pot across the table. "Same brand I always use . . . Leigh fixed it though."

"Funny, it tastes different." He glanced at Leigh and could see she was relieved at the sudden shift in conversation.

No husband, no family, at least six months pregnant, and looking for work. She didn't have it easy, did she? Still, she didn't relate this information as if she was looking for sympathy. Quite the opposite, he thought. She seemed reluctant to share the sad details or take him up on any offers of help.

The phone rang and Vera got up to answer it. Left alone with Leigh, James felt he wanted to say something, but he didn't know what more he could offer that wouldn't sound worn and clichéd. More condolences about her husband seemed redundant. Ministers were supposed to be so adept at these moments, but like many people, he often found himself at a loss for truly sincere, honest words when confronted by the enormity of death.

Leigh sat across the table from him, sipping a glass of milk. She somehow looked different to him now than she had the night before. She had faced some rough days, with more ahead, he thought, yet still seemed composed, carrying on, doing what she had to do. He admired that.

"It's for you, Leigh. Harbor Auto again," Vera called out. Leigh rose and went to the phone, and James helped Vera clear the breakfast dishes. Leigh soon returned to the kitchen. James could tell from her expression that the news wasn't good.

"Sounds as if it will take a few days. The mechanic is having trouble finding parts and with the snow and the weekend, everything is slowed down."

"You can stay here then," Vera quickly offered. "That will be fine with me. I'm not expecting any new arrivals."

"Thank you, Vera. I'd appreciate that," Leigh replied. "What is your rate for the room? You never told me."

Vera turned from the sink, holding a scouring pad in one hand and looking flustered. James could see that she was torn. She wanted to let Leigh stay on for free, and yet she depended on the income from her guests to support herself.

"I'll work it out with Vera. Don't worry," James said.

"No, I can't let you do that." Leigh carried her glass to the counter by the sink. "I can pay for myself. I have to —"

“But if I hadn’t smashed up your car, you would already be staying with your friend in Wellfleet. It’s my fault you’re stuck here. You must let me take care of it. I insist.”

Leigh stood staring at him, her lips in a tight line, weighing her pride against her pocketbook, he thought.

“I don’t care who pays, quite frankly. Or even if either of you do, all things considered. The room is sitting up there empty and so far, you eat less than a bird, miss . . . which isn’t good for your condition, I might add.” Vera spoke while leaning over the sink, working on the oatmeal pot with her scrub pad. “And by the way,” she continued before anyone could reply, “if you’re interested in earning a few dollars while you’re stuck in town, I happen to know that Dr. Harding can use a little temporary help. His receptionist took off yesterday on a family emergency. You would have thought her house was on fire. Just picked up her purse and raced out the door. I was sitting right there. She left a big waiting room full of patients. It was bedlam. And I know he’s got the word out, asking if someone can fill in a little.”

“A doctor’s office?” Leigh asked.

“That’s right, Dr. Harding. He came to

town last winter, took over old Dr. Elliot's practice. Nice young man, too."

"I've worked in offices but not as a secretary. . . ."

"All you have to do is answer the phone and keep the appointment book in order. It's not exactly brain surgery — well, not for you, anyhow." Vera shot Leigh a quick grin as she set the pot on the drain board and wiped her hands on a towel. "I can call him for you right now, see what's up."

James watched Leigh curiously. He couldn't tell from her expression what her answer would be. Would she want to take a part-time job in town? Did she need money that badly?

Finally, she shrugged. "I suppose I can go speak to him about it. I did want to visit a doctor today. Just to check on the baby. I'm sure nothing's wrong," she added with a quick glance at James. "But it wouldn't hurt to make sure."

"It wouldn't hurt at all." James had meant to talk to her again about seeing a doctor and was relieved that Leigh brought it up first.

"I'm sure he'll make time to see you," Vera said to Leigh, then left again to call Dr. Harding's office.

Leigh turned to James. "If I get the job,

you'll have to let me pay Vera for the room and board." She was smiling but her voice sounded quite firm and determined.

He couldn't help but smile back. "We'll see."

Vera returned, talking excitedly as she walked back into the kitchen. "Dr. Harding was busy with a patient, but I got Molly Willoughby on the line and she practically jumped out of the phone and hugged me. She said, 'Send her right over. I can't wait to get out of here.' "

"Molly is Dr. Harding's girlfriend. I guess she's in the office, holding down the fort for him this morning," James explained.

He would trust the formidable Molly to hold down any fort, any time. But she did have her own business, and he expected she was eager to get back to it.

"Molly is a dynamo, but she can be a little brusque. I think Leigh will have a more pleasant manner with the patients, don't you?" Vera asked as she began to sweep the kitchen floor.

James laughed. "Probably."

"Thanks for the vote of confidence." Leigh looked surprised but also pleased by the sudden turn of events.

"I have to go over to the church this

morning. I'll drop you on my way. I just need to clean off the car and do some shoveling."

"Okay, if it's not out of your way," Leigh said. "I'll run upstairs and grab my purse."

Vera emptied the dustpan into a trash pail and let the lid fall with a resounding slam. " 'All's well that ends well.' That's what Arnold used to say. He did love his Shakespeare."

More an example of God moving in strange ways, James thought as he pulled on his parka. But he didn't bother to debate the point with Vera.

As James drove toward town he found the Beach Road sanded and easy to drive. The snow-covered road, so treacherous last night, seemed benign, even beautiful, in the brilliant sunshine.

"A big difference from last night," he said to Leigh.

"It's another world," she agreed, glancing out the window. "Look, that must be the place where we had the accident."

James slowed the car, noticing the telltale marks in the snow across the road. His throat tightened for a second, and he felt grateful all over again that no one had been harmed.

"We were lucky," Leigh said quietly. She turned her head away and stared out the window.

"I'm glad you're going to ask Dr. Harding to check the baby," James said honestly. "I could never forgive myself if anything was wrong."

"I'm sure I'm all right. But I guess it is a good idea to check."

He didn't answer, but felt relieved at her reply.

"You're so nice, James. . . . No wonder you're a minister."

"Thanks. I think." He glanced at her and smiled. Her tone had been complimentary but also held a note of wry humor. As if she didn't have a very positive outlook on people.

He soon turned off the Beach Road and came to the edge of town. "Did you get to see the village at all last night?"

Leigh shook her head. "No, I drove off the connector from the highway."

"You wouldn't have seen much with the bad weather anyway. We're coming down Main Street now. That's the movie theater . . . and that's the village hall and police station."

James looked out at Main Street, seeing it the way a stranger might. The town looked magical today, covered in sparkling snow. Most of the storefronts dated back to the 1800s, and some, like Grace Hegman's antique store, the Bramble, were Victorian houses, converted to shops with apartments tucked above. A bit farther down the street, the Cape Light Historical Museum, a stately brick building, stood covered with ivy and a snowy banner that announced the latest exhibit about whaling.

"It really is so pretty here." Leigh turned again, watching out the window. "I'm surprised. . . . I'd never even heard of the place before last night."

"It's a very well kept secret. I've come to think the locals like it that way, too." James glanced at her and grinned.

It was a place out of time, he thought, an ideal pit stop for his recovery, though he sometimes wondered if Cape Light was too relaxing for him, almost too idyllic.

"There's a diner down here on the left," he added, pointing out the Clam Box. "The atmosphere isn't much but the food is pretty good."

James turned and drove down a side street then stopped and parked in front of Dr. Harding's office. "This is it. I'll take you in and introduce you."

"No need. Vera said they're expecting me. I can manage from here." Leigh opened her door and smiled at him. "Thanks for the lift."

"Here's my number. Call me at the church if there's any problem." James fished a card out of his wallet and handed it to her. "Let me know what time you'll be done. I'll give you a ride back."

Leigh looked surprised. "Aren't there any taxis around here?"

"Believe me, I'm more reliable — and cheaper, too."

She sighed and smiled then leaned over the open car door. "All right. I'll let you know. But if I'm going to stay a few days, you'll have to stop treating me like visiting royalty. I'm only pregnant. It's happened to quite a few women before me."

"Okay, I'll try to remember that. Good luck in there."

"Thanks. See you later." She slammed the car door shut and waved briefly at him, then turned and began walking toward the small house that held the doctor's office.

James turned at the corner and headed back down Main Street toward the church. Was he being overly protective? he asked himself. In his years as a missionary, he'd certainly encountered pregnant women in far worse circumstances than Leigh Baxter: malnourished and often diseased, giving birth on dirt floors in huts without running water or any hope of medical assistance.

Still, he felt responsible for Leigh. He couldn't help that. Maybe it was because of the accident or hearing about her husband's death. Maybe it was because she intrigued him.

And of course, being a minister, he couldn't help wondering if God had brought this woman into his life for some reason. He had to help her, he realized, in any way that he could. Even if she were only here for a few days. That was both his calling and his nature.

Leigh paused in the doorway of Dr. Harding's waiting room and took in the scene. It wasn't exactly bedlam, as Vera had described it, but it certainly was busy, with patients of various ages milling about, babies crying, and small children vying for attention.

A woman about her age with dark curly hair sat at a desk on the far side of the room, speaking on the phone in a loud, animated fashion while shuffling through some papers on the desk. The infamous

Molly Willoughby, Leigh assumed. A few people stood near the desk while others sat reading magazines.

For a moment, Leigh felt tempted to turn around and slip back out the door before anyone could notice her. Was it wise to put herself in a place where so many people would see and possibly remember her? Wouldn't it be smarter to just hide out at Vera's house and wait for her car to be repaired?

But before Leigh could decide whether to stay or go, Molly looked up and practically gasped with relief. "Are you Leigh?"

Leigh nodded and before she could answer, Molly ran across the room to greet her. "Thanks so much for coming. I promised Matt — Dr. Harding, I mean — I'd help him today. But I'm catering a wedding tonight and we're nowhere near ready. I've been on the phone all morning with my crew —"

"You're a caterer?"

"Mostly. I have a shop around the corner. Takeout and catering." Molly had led Leigh over to the desk and now motioned for her to sit down. "I'll bring you some lunch. I always bring Matt something on Saturdays. Soup and sandwiches. How's that sound?"

"I'm hungry already," Leigh admitted.

"Amy stashes some pretzels and cheese crackers in the lower right-hand drawer of the desk. Help yourself if you need a snack." Molly pulled the appointment book out from under a sheaf of insurance forms and sat on the edge of the desk. "Here's the book. Basically, all you need to do is figure out who's coming and going and give Matt the files. I already took out most of them. They're in this pile over here. And I made this list. . . . If someone calls to make an appointment, just fill it in as you go along. The spaces have time slots. Ask Nancy or Matt if you're not sure how long he'll need for the visit."

"Nancy?"

"Nancy Malloy, Matt's nurse. Sorry, I almost forgot. They're in with a patient now, giving stitches. They should be done soon."

"That sounds simple enough." Leigh was in awe of the speed at which Molly spoke, her flashing blue eyes, and changing expressions. Molly hadn't even bothered to ask if she actually wanted the job.

Leigh wondered again if she should do it. She certainly needed the money. *This is such an out-of-the-way place,* she reminded herself, *and it will only be for a day or two. It probably doesn't matter if a few more people around here see me. Isn't there some expression about "hiding in plain sight?"*

"It's a snap. You'll be fine." Molly's optimistic words broke into Leigh's wandering thoughts.

Molly quickly reviewed a few more essentials of the job — how to schedule appointments and collect any fees.

"Any questions?" Molly grabbed her coat off the back of Leigh's chair and pulled it on.

Leigh did have a few but could see that Molly was desperate to go, so she simply shook her head. "I think I can manage."

"Of course you can." Molly lightly touched her shoulder, then reached for her handbag on the floor beside the desk. "Vera told me about your car accident. Tough break, but if you're struck with a lemon, make lemonade, right?" Without waiting for Leigh's reply, she added, "Well, see you later. Good luck!"

Before Leigh could say good-bye, Molly was out the door. Leigh turned, noticing a blinking light on the phone. She hit the button and picked up the call.

"Dr. Harding's office. Can I help you?"

The woman on the other end of the line told Leigh about an earache that had kept her up all night. Leigh made some sympathetic sounds and scheduled an appointment for two o'clock. The woman hung up, sounding pleased and grateful.

So far, so good, Leigh thought.

The door to the doctor's office opened and a patient came out followed by a tall, dark-haired man in a lab coat who, Leigh assumed, must be Dr. Harding. His warm smile put her instantly at ease. "You must be Leigh. Thanks for helping out."

"That's all right. Nice to meet you, Dr. Harding."

"Call me Matt. This is Mr. Wilkie. He slipped on the ice this morning," he said, turning to his patient, a middle-aged man with a large bandage on the top of his bald head. "He needs to come back on Tuesday so I can take off that bandage."

"Lucky I'm so hard-headed," Mr. Wilkie mumbled. "At least that's what my wife says."

"Yes, you are lucky." Matt patted his patient's arm and then turned to the exam rooms again.

"Um . . . next Tuesday, let's see." With a small smile, Leigh turned to the proper page in the book and arranged Mr. Wilkie's next visit.

When she looked up, a woman wearing a

nurse's uniform stood by the desk. "I'm Nancy Malloy, Dr. Harding's nurse," the woman said as she reached down for the list of patient names that lay beside the appointment book. "It's wild in here this morning. But it should calm down in an hour or two."

"It does seem busy. It might take me a while to figure out which file is which."

"That's all right. If you have any questions, just let me know."

Nancy was a large woman in her early forties with a wide face and large brown eyes. She had a friendly but no-nonsense air and seemed to Leigh someone who would remain completely calm and focused in any emergency. Her straight, chin-length auburn hair and lack of makeup seemed to suit her efficient manner.

Nancy glanced down the list of names again and called the next patient. Leigh quickly found the right file in the stack Molly had showed her and handed it up to her.

"Thanks, dear." Nancy took the folder and flipped it open. "By the way, we need to take care of a little bookkeeping. I'll need to make a copy of your Social Security card and some photo ID. Your driver's license would be fine." She closed the folder and looked down again.

Leigh felt a tightening in her chest but tried to act unfazed by the request. "Sure . . . I think I have my license with me. . . . I don't know about my Social Security card, though."

"Oh, well, as long as you know the number, I guess that should be all right for today." Nancy turned to follow the patient to the exam room. "We'll take care of it later."

Leigh nodded and turned back to the desk. Of course they would need some identification, even if she only worked here one day. Why hadn't she thought of that this morning before she agreed to let James drive her over here? She considered getting up and walking out but quickly discarded that idea, realizing it was bound to arouse suspicion.

She did have identification. It just wasn't authentic. Though it looked like the real thing — and she had certainly paid dearly for it — she wasn't comfortable showing it around. Last night was the first real test. To her profound relief, Officer Tulley hadn't batted an eye when he checked her license and registration.

It would never have even occurred to her

to get counterfeit anything if it weren't for Alice. Leigh knew she had to change her name in order to hide from Martin, but Alice was the one who'd suggested the false documents. Alice had a nephew who had been in trouble with the law and had what Alice called "contacts." Though reformed, her nephew was happy to offer his felonious knowledge for a worthy cause. Leigh had simply given him money and he had taken care of everything.

The fake ID passed for real with a police officer, Leigh reminded herself, *so it should satisfy Nurse Malloy. If not, I'll need to leave here in a hurry — without a car. No, it won't come to that. I'm just panicking now.*

Leigh put the worrisome thoughts aside, forcing herself to get acquainted with the stacks of files on the desk. She answered the phone and tried her best to help the patients who came to her with questions.

The hours flew by and Leigh found herself so busy she didn't have time to worry about her car, her fake ID, or any of the secret troubles that so often circled her heart and mind like baleful, scavenging birds.

Jessica pushed open the kitchen door with one shoulder, plastic sacks of groceries dangling from each arm. She dropped the grocery bags on the counter and stared around at the messy evidence of Sam's cooking: a Sahara Desert of crumbs drifting across the countertop, a greasy fry pan and spatula, and a half-melted stick of butter on the stove. On the table two empty soup bowls and two plates with crusts of grilled cheese sandwiches lingered alongside an open bag of chocolate cookies.

It didn't take Sherlock Holmes to guess the menu or to discern there had been a guest for lunch. A guest who was probably still here, she realized.

She listened to the quiet in the house. No sound of voices. "Sam? I'm home. . . . Are you around?"

No answer. Then she turned and glanced outside. She saw a sudden movement through the window of the barn where Sam had set up his home workshop.

Jessica slipped on her jacket again and headed out the back door. She walked across the yard, noticing two sets of footprints in the snow, one Sam's size, the other set much smaller.

The door to the barn stood open and she soon heard voices, Sam and a boy. Before she even entered she realized it must be Darrell Lester, the boy from the New Horizons Center. Jessica had been curious to meet him; still, she was surprised that Sam had brought him back to the house for a visit. Well, there were no rules against that sort of thing, she guessed. Somehow, though, she doubted that most of the people in town who volunteered at the center got quite so involved with the kids there.

Jessica stood at the open door a minute. Sam was using a small power tool, a hand-held sander, and Jessica knew he wouldn't hear her over the sound.

A small, dark-haired boy stood by his side, focused on his every word. Sam ran the sander across a piece of wood, then shut it off and handed it to the boy, who seemed hesitant to take over.

"Go ahead, you can do it. This is just practice." Sam's voice was calm and reassuring. "We won't use the good wood until you're ready."

The boy took the sander, turned it on, and made a face. "Man . . . that feels weird. Feels like it's alive or something."

Sam laughed and helped him guide it over the wood. "You can use two hands if you want. That's okay."

Jessica walked over to the workbench and finally caught Sam's eye. "Hi, honey."

He leaned over and kissed her cheek. "How long have you been standing here?"

"Just a little while. How's it going?"

"Good. We were looking for a sled, but Darrell wanted me to show him around the workbench and we got started on a project."

Jessica smiled at Darrell but he avoided her gaze. Dark, with thick curly hair, bright eyes, and a round face, he wasn't quite what she'd pictured from Sam's stories. A husky boy, he looked as if he spent too much time cooped up inside, watching TV. And he was younger than she had imagined, about eight or nine. He definitely seemed young to have been tossed around in the social services system, tossed around and toughened by it, she guessed, like most of the kids that ended up at New Horizons.

"Hi, I'm Jessica, Sam's wife."

She saw the boy glance uncertainly at Sam. Then he ducked his head and nodded at her. "Hi."

"What are you making?"

"Oh . . . nothing. We're just fooling around on some old wood." He looked down and rubbed the toe of his sneaker against the floor. No boots, she noticed, despite the high snow outside. He seemed either shy or annoyed to be interrupted during his shop lesson. Or maybe a bit of both.

"Darrell wants to make a jewelry box for his mom. For a Christmas present. We're going to use this piece of mahogany."

Sam showed Jessica a piece of wood. She really ought to know the difference by now — between pine and walnut and all the rest — but she really didn't. She nodded admiringly and made an effort to sound enthusiastic. "That's going to be great. I bet your mom will love it."

Darrell met her glance for an instant but didn't smile back. She sensed that talking about his mother was sensitive ground and suddenly felt awkward, sure that she had sounded inanely chipper.

Darrell's sullen expression changed as Sam reached across the table and handed him a little cardboard box.

"Hey, buddy. Check this out. I knew I had one of these around for you."

Darrell opened the box and took out a small metal gadget. He looked up at Sam, his brow furrowed. "What is it?"

At first Jessica didn't recognize it either; then she realized it was the inner workings of a music box.

"It plays music. See, here's the key." Sam

found the key at the bottom of the carton and wound it up. He set it back on the workbench and it began to turn. "We can put this in your mom's jewelry box, and it will play music when she opens the lid."

Jessica heard the tinkling notes of "You Are My Sunshine," which always made her smile. She watched Darrell listening, his expression growing brighter.

"Maybe I should just send her that part. I don't know if I can make a whole big box for it."

Sam laughed. "Sure you can. One step at a time."

Darrell didn't look convinced. "Okay. But if it doesn't come out good, I'll give it to my grandma. She likes any old thing I make for her."

Jessica had to smile at his honesty. He wasn't intentionally insulting his grandmother, just stating a fact. At least his grandmother was a nurturing presence in his life. From what he didn't say, though, she sensed that pleasing his mother was something he worried about more. "Maybe after you make the music box for your mom, you could make something just for your grandmother," she suggested.

Darrell gave her a blank look, as if she couldn't possibly say anything that interested him, and Jessica felt herself flush with embarrassment. This was nuts. She was feeling awkward — like she was intruding — in her own home.

Sam didn't seem to notice. "Ready to fire up that sander again?" he asked the boy.

"I guess I'll get back to the house," Jessica said. "I have to unpack the groceries."

"What's for dinner? I thought maybe Darrell could stay and I could bring him back to New Horizons later."

Jessica thought a moment, not really wanting the boy to stay but also not wanting to give in to such uncharitable thoughts. Then she remembered what day it was. "Gee, I don't think that works out, honey. We're going to that play in Newburyport with Suzanne and her boyfriend."

"Oh, right. I completely forgot." Sam shook his head, and she realized he had already invited the boy and was now in a bad spot.

She glanced over at Darrell. He was examining the music box intently, acting as if he wasn't listening to them but not missing a word. She saw the way his shoulders slumped when she announced that he couldn't stay, and she instantly regretted not phrasing her words in a softer way. She might not be exactly comfortable with the boy but she didn't want to hurt him.

"I'm sorry, Darrell," Jessica said. "Maybe we can have you over some other night."

"Sure. We'll figure it out," Sam said.

Darrell stared at her; the bright expression he had worn listening to the music had turned moody and grim again.

"No problem. Whatever," he said. Then he turned and picked up a block of wood, casually smacking it against the workbench, as if to test the sound it would make.

Sam didn't seem to notice.

He's mad at me, disappointed, Jessica thought with dismay. She felt mean-spirited and horrible but didn't know how to change things. She resisted an impulse to run back inside; that would look even worse.

Sam glanced at his watch. "It is getting late. We can work for a while longer, Darrell. Then I have to bring you back."

Darrell didn't look happy to hear that news but seemed resigned. "Can I try the sanding thing again?"

"Sure. Wait here a minute. I'll get some

more scraps to practice on."

Sam walked with Jessica toward the doorway and paused at a large plastic bin full of odd-shaped bits of wood. He pulled out a few small pieces and looked them over.

"I'm sorry," Jessica murmured. "It just didn't work out for tonight."

"It's okay. I'll explain it to him later. How about tomorrow?"

"Lunch after church at my mother's. Emily and Dan are going, too."

"Lucky me. At least we'll be done in time to catch the Patriots game . . . I hope?"

"I hope so, too. Didn't she remind you when you shoveled this morning?"

"We didn't exactly speak. She just gave me one of her regal nods from the window."

Jessica sighed. Her mother was impossible sometimes. She'd nearly boycotted their wedding last year and still acted as if Sam were persona non grata. Sam put up with her valiantly, which was another reason why she loved him so much.

"Maybe Darrell can sit with us in church tomorrow," Sam said.

"He goes to our church?"

"Luke brings some kids there on Sundays, any who want to go. Darrell says his grandmother used to take him sometimes and he wants to try it here tomorrow."

"Oh . . . that's nice." Jessica guessed that Darrell would volunteer to hike barefoot to the North Pole if he knew Sam would be there. But no matter the motivation, the result would be a good one. Their church was full of warm, caring people, and she hoped kids like Darrell Lester would find some comfort there.

"Sure, let him sit with us if he wants to. I don't mind," she said lightly. "Do you want some hot chocolate when you come in?"

"That would be great. We'll be in in about fifteen minutes." Sam smiled and she felt instantly better.

So that's Darrell Lester, she thought as she tromped back to the house. He didn't like her much, it seemed. But she wasn't sure how to take it. Maybe the boy was just shy . . . or moody . . . or doesn't like women, she thought. Many of the New Horizons kids had issues — they'd been abandoned or even abused by parents or foster parents and had trouble making connections.

I shouldn't take this personally, Jessica reminded herself. Besides, the boy was Sam's friend — his little project, it seemed. It didn't matter that much if Darrell liked her, did it?

"Here are a few files that were left in my office. And here's a check for you, Leigh." Dr. Harding stood by the desk and handed her a paycheck for her day's work.

Leigh glanced at it briefly and realized he'd overpaid her. "I think there must be some mistake. Nancy told me —"

"No mistake," he cut in. "I just wanted to give you a little bonus for running in here on such short notice. Molly told me you're only in town for a few days, but do you think you could come back again?"

Leigh sat back and considered the idea. She'd had a tense moment handing Nancy her identification, but that had passed without a hitch so the worst was really over, she reasoned. She would meet a lot of people working here, but the village was so far off the beaten track, it wouldn't be much risk for a few days. And she did need the money for the baby. That point now seemed most pressing.

"I don't think my car will be ready until Wednesday. I can work for you until then if you want."

"That's good news. You did a great job,

too. You have a very nice way with the patients."

Leigh shrugged, feeling self-conscious at his compliment. "I was just trying to be polite."

Nancy Malloy came out of the doctor's office, her coat unbuttoned over her white uniform. "Well, I guess it's a wrap. I hope we didn't burn you out in one day, Leigh."

"I'm okay." Leigh smiled, feeling relieved the day was over.

"How's that baby doing?"

"She's fine." Leigh smiled slightly and touched her stomach. "Dr. Harding checked and everything's okay."

"That's good. I had a feeling it would be. It's a girl, isn't it?"

Leigh nodded. "I had an amnio a few months ago. That's what they told me."

"You're lucky. I'd take a girl over a boy any day. I've got two of each," she added proudly. She checked her watch and hitched her purse up higher on her shoulder. "Time to see what they've been up to all day. When my husband takes over, I'm never sure I'll find the house still standing. Will I be seeing you again?"

Leigh nodded. "I'll be back."

"Good. Nice working with you." She headed toward the door then turned to call over her shoulder, “Good night, Doc.”

“Night, Nancy. See you Monday.”

As Nancy pulled open the door, Leigh glimpsed James standing on the other side. “Sorry, we’re closed for the day,” the nurse told him.

“I’m here to pick someone up.”

Nancy glanced back at Leigh. “Oh, sure. Go on in. She survived.”

“Glad to hear it,” James replied. He walked in and smiled at Leigh then looked up at Dr. Harding. “Hello, Matt. How’s business?”

“Fine, and yours?” he replied with a laugh.

“Slow today. Tomorrow’s my big day.” James glanced at Leigh. “Ready to go?”

“I’m all set.” Leigh put on her coat and grabbed her purse. She felt a little odd having James pick up her like this, as if there were some relationship between them when they were actually strangers. Still, what did it matter? She’d only be in this town a few more days. In a week or two, no one would even remember her, she told herself.

She said good night to Dr. Harding and thanked him again for the check then walked with James to his car, which was parked just outside the office.

"How did it go?" James asked once they were under way.

"Fine. Dr. Harding must have been desperate. He practically paid me double. I'm going back again on Monday. Maybe until my car is done."

James nodded, his gaze fixed on the road. "Sounds good."

"It was very busy in there but interesting." Leigh leaned her head back on the seat and closed her eyes. She had enjoyed dealing with all the different patients during the day. She didn't really think of herself as very social. She was naturally more of a loner, the very definition of one since she'd left Martin. But it was a great relief to be so nonstop busy and distracted.

James went silent, and she could almost guess what he was thinking. "I told the doctor about the accident and he checked the baby. He said the heartbeat was very strong and everything seemed fine."

"Good. I'm glad to hear it." James turned to face her briefly then looked out at the road again. "Thanks."

"Why are you thanking me?"

"Because I was concerned and I appreciate that you followed through," he said simply.

"Oh." He was so straightforward and

open about his feelings. She wasn't used to that, especially coming from a man. It set her off balance.

"I feel better myself. I was just a bit overwhelmed last night," she admitted. *And trying to avoid complications,* she added silently. He glanced at her but didn't say anything.

James turned on the radio, a classical station that was playing a soothing piece Leigh thought she recognized — Bach, maybe, or Vivaldi. They drove the rest of the way to Vera's house without talking, and to Leigh's surprise that felt just fine.

The silence between them was the opposite of the tense, oppressive silences that used to hang between her and Martin, Leigh realized. Those silences made her feel she was sitting on a time bomb that any second, without warning, might explode.

She glanced at James, his gaze fixed on the road. She didn't know him well — she didn't know him at all, in fact — but she somehow felt certain he was never like that.

Vera's house was dark except for a lamp in the front sitting room and lights on in the kitchen. They entered through the side door again and Vera called out to say hello.

"You didn't come back so I figured it must have worked out at Dr. Harding's," she said to Leigh.

"It was all right. I'm going to work there again on Monday."

"A baby needs a lot of things. I'm sure the extra cash will come in handy for you."

Leigh took a glass from the cupboard and filled it with water. She watched Vera snapping the ends off of string beans.

"Dinner will be ready in about half an hour. Are you hungry?"

The cooking smelled tempting but Leigh felt her stomach churn. She didn't feel up to sitting with Vera and James for the next few hours. She was exhausted and liable to slip and say the wrong thing. *It would be safer to stay in my room and read a book or something,* she decided.

"I'm sorry. It smells great but I had a big lunch. Molly Willoughby sent over a huge basket of food from her shop. I guess I overdid it. I think I'll just go up and lie down for a while."

"I've got just the thing for you." Vera reached into a cupboard and pulled out a small round tin. "Ginger tea. Settles your stomach like magic. I'll fix you some and bring it right up."

Leigh was touched by the older woman's concern. Why was everyone around here so kind to her? She was just a stranger.

"Thank you, Vera. You don't have to serve me, I can come down and make some later."

"It's no trouble. You go put your feet up and rest."

Leigh thanked her again then went upstairs to her room and closed her door. She snapped on the small lamp on the bedside table and glanced around the room.

Did I leave my scarf folded on the dresser top that way? she wondered. She didn't think so. She walked over to the dresser and picked up the scarf. *Maybe Vera came in to straighten up . . . or to check up on me.*

Leigh looked around the room again and had the funny feeling her belongings had been touched. She felt a sudden wave of panic, wondering if she had left out anything that might give her away. She quickly sifted through the drawers of clothing and a few personal items she had left on the dresser top: a bracelet, a key ring, and a paperback book. Her heart began to pound as she opened the book and saw her real name written inside the cover.

Had Vera noticed that? But what would it prove? A book could be borrowed or bought secondhand. Leigh sat on the edge of the bed and took a deep breath. She was getting herself into a state over nothing. She was so emotional lately. They said being pregnant did that to you. *And the rest of my life doesn't help either.*

She opened the book again and stared down at the name, her married name. The name of a person from another life, one she couldn't bear to think about. The woman with this name was gone, as good as dead, she realized. Still, she couldn't help feeling a pang of guilt for deceiving Vera and James this way.

But I really have no choice. And there's really no harm to it. I'll be gone in a day or two and they'll never know. It won't make a difference to them one way or the other.

Leigh reached for her purse on the night table and took out her cell phone. She dialed her friend Alice at home, hoping she would be free to talk. The phone rang three times and Leigh's stomach knotted with dread. If the machine clicked on, she would have to hang up. Fortunately, Alice didn't have caller ID.

"Hello?" Alice's familiar voice was instantly comforting.

"It's me," Leigh said. "Are you alone? Can you talk?"

"Thank goodness! I was waiting for you to call. Pete's out, walking the dog, so I can talk for a while," she replied quickly. "I got your message about the car accident. Are you okay?"

"Yes, I'm just fine. The baby is fine, too. Can't say the same for the car, but it should be repaired in a day or two."

"Well, as long as you and the baby are okay, that's all that matters. I looked for that town on the map. I could hardly find it," Alice added. "How in the world did you end up there?"

"Oh, it's a long story. I thought someone was following me so I tried to take a back road instead of the highway. I guess I panicked. I don't even think anyone was really there."

Alice didn't answer at first and her silence made Leigh nervous. "Well, you can't be too careful. I'm sure you're disappointed that Canada didn't work out, but maybe it's all for the best."

"If Martin had someone watching my cousin's house, I guess it is." Leigh tried to sound resigned about that disappointment, but heard her own bitterness.

"Oh, I know it's frustrating for you, honey. But don't give up. . . . Listen, there's a lot going on at the office." Alice was not only Leigh's dear friend, she was Martin's assistant. Ever since Leigh had fled her marriage, Alice had voluntarily been her spy. "The company's in trouble. They announced some layoffs this week, and Martin might be investigated for mishandling company funds."

"Investigated? By whom?"

"The state attorney general's office. He's tried to keep a lid on it, but the word is getting out. Something about falsifying the books. From what I can tell, he presented inflated profits going into that merger. Meanwhile, he was having trouble meeting the payroll and paying taxes."

Leigh had mixed feelings about that. She hated to think of employees being laid off for her husband's greed. Then again, if Martin was in trouble, that might bode well for her.

"And that's not all," Alice continued, "I overheard something else last night — more to do with you. Everyone else had gone and he must have thought he was alone, so he was on the phone with the door open. He's definitely hired a new detective, and this one seems a little sharper than the last guy. He found your car. Boy, were you smart not to buy another one at the same lot. I think he's still looking for you in Boston, so that's good news. But sooner or later, he's bound to figure out you've left town."

Leigh felt her stomach drop, as if she were standing in an elevator that had missed a few floors. Needing cash, she'd sold her expensive foreign car at a small car lot on the outskirts of Boston. She knew she wasn't getting full value but it was a quick deal, with few questions asked. She hadn't meant to cover her trail on purpose; she simply hadn't trusted the used cars for sale there so she had gone to another lot to buy a cheaper replacement car.

"I guess someone was going to find the car sooner or later. But I've been very careful. I don't think I've left much of a trail — unless he's using bloodhounds." Leigh tried hard for a light tone but her joke fell flat.

"I'm sure you've been careful. But these guys are relentless. Especially . . . Martin." Alice seemed hesitant to even say the name of Leigh's ex-husband. "If it came down to bloodhounds, he'd pay for the best. Whatever money can buy. You know that."

"Yeah." Leigh felt tears of hopelessness well up behind her eyes and tried hard not to cry, not with Alice still on the line.

"You okay?"

"I was just thinking . . . maybe I should give up. I'm so tired of this, Alice. It's so hard. I just want to have my baby and have a real life again."

"Oh, sweetie. Please don't say that. I know it seems bad right now, but you're doing the right thing. Really." Alice paused and Leigh could almost feel her sympathy and concern coming through the line like waves of energy. "You know what I think?" Alice asked without waiting for a reply. "This car accident was a blessing in disguise. That town is the perfect hiding place. I've never even heard of it."

Leigh took a deep, steadying breath. "It is very . . . tucked away. And it's pretty, too. You should see it. It's like a postcard or something."

"It's more than tucked away, it's practically invisible. I think you should stay there and sit tight, maybe even until the baby comes. Meanwhile, I'll let you know what's happening on this end. As best as I can, of course."

"Thanks, Alice. Thanks for everything. I don't know what I'd do without you," Leigh said honestly. She felt a new wave of emotion well up.

"I'm here for you, dear. You're going to make it, too. Do you need any money? I can wire some on Monday." Leigh was touched by Alice's offer. She had already borrowed more than she knew her friend could afford to lend.

"I'm okay, really. I've even found a temporary job here, a receptionist at a doctor's office."

"That was fast work. See, I told you this was meant to be."

A soft tap on the door made Leigh sit up sharply.

"Leigh? I have your tea," Vera called from the other side of the door.

"I'll be right there," Leigh called back. She turned to the phone again. "Someone's here. I've got to go," she whispered. She heard her friend's quick farewell, then clicked off the phone and quickly pulled open the bedroom door.

Vera stood holding a tray with a teapot, a cup, and a plate of plain crackers. "I hope I didn't wake you. I knocked and then I thought, oh, maybe she's sleeping, I shouldn't disturb her —"

"No, not at all. I wasn't asleep." Leigh took the tray and placed it on the dresser. "I don't think I've ever had ginger tea. It smells good."

"I always made it for my kids. Works in a flash. If you feel hungry later, there'll be leftovers from dinner in the refrigerator. Just help yourself."

"Thank you, Vera. And thanks again for the tea."

"No trouble." Vera started to turn away, then paused. "By the way, Reverend James and I will be going to church tomorrow morning if you'd like to join us. We usually leave here around half past ten."

The invitation caught Leigh by surprise. She hadn't been to church in years or even thought about going. "Um . . . thanks for asking but I think I'll just stay in tomorrow morning, sleep late if I can."

Vera nodded agreeably. "Yes, of course, dear. You need your rest. I just thought I'd let you know."

Vera turned toward the staircase and disappeared. Leigh went back into her bedroom and closed the door again.

She poured herself a cup of ginger tea and took a testing sip. It tasted good, spicy but not sharp, and a few sips later she felt her stomach settling. She wondered why she had never had ginger tea before. She smiled to herself. It suddenly seemed perfectly logical, almost inevitable, that she would discover this miracle cure in this remote, picturesque place.

Maybe Alice was right. Maybe she had

stumbled on a safe haven here. Maybe being stranded in Cape Light was a blessing in disguise.

Chapter Three

Jessica hated being late for church. She could tell from the number of cars parked around the church and the sight of the closed arched wooden doors that the service had already started.

Sam gripped her hand and quickened his pace. "It's my fault. I shouldn't have begged you for those pancakes."

"I wanted them, too." It was true; plus, facing lunch at her mother's house, where the portions were notoriously spare, Jessica knew her husband needed something substantial to start the day.

Sam held the heavy door open for her and they slipped into the vestibule. Inside, the congregation was standing, singing a hymn led by the choir. At least they hadn't missed much, she thought.

With his hand lightly touching the small of her back, Sam led her through the side door into the sanctuary. "There are some seats on the left," Sam whispered. Jessica spotted a space on the aisle in a middle row and slid in. She slipped off her coat, grabbed a hymnal, and held it out for Sam to share. As they started to sing she heard someone quietly call, "Hey, Sam! Over here!"

She turned to see Darrell Lester seated across the aisle a few rows behind them. Sam turned, too. He smiled and nodded at the boy. That seemed to be all the encouragement Darrell needed. He quickly left his seat and came over. "I was waiting for you. We're going to sit together, right?" Darrell whispered eagerly.

Jessica felt Sam nudge her to move in and make room. "Sure thing. You sit right here," he said quietly.

Jessica shifted over and Sam held the hymnal out to Darrell so they could share. Darrell held up his side, Jessica noticed, but didn't sing. He kept glancing up at Sam, who had a deep, impressive voice and wasn't shy about singing in church. Jessica found another book and quickly looked for the page, but by the time she found it the hymn was over.

Settling into her seat, Jessica looked around the pews for her family. She soon spotted her mother sitting in her usual place, front and center, alongside her older sister, Emily, and Emily's fiancé, Dan Forbes. Jessica found it secretly amusing that Dan, the former newspaper publisher and avowed skeptic, was now a regular at the Sunday service. But perhaps he just came to help with their mother and to stay on Lillian's good side, Jessica thought. Although Dan's prominent background made him a far more acceptable son-in-law than Sam had ever been, that still didn't prevent Lillian from subjecting him to her barbs.

As if sensing Jessica's thoughts, her mother slowly turned and met her younger daughter's gaze. She nodded slightly in greeting, then her cool, gray gaze took in Sam, and finally, Darrell Lester, which caused her eyes to widen and her eyebrows to arch. She stared at Jessica again, pursed her lips in what could only be displeasure, and turned to face forward.

Jessica felt a small knot of tension in her stomach. Of course there would be questions later. "Who in the world was that strange child sitting with you? One of those troublesome boys from that center?" her mother would say.

The unavoidable comments would rub Sam the wrong way. *And I'll be right in the middle of it, as always,* Jessica thought. Not that it was any of her mother's business if Sam let a kid from New Horizons sit with him in church. It was just that her mother had a true genius for making tempests out of molehills . . . or whatever the expression was.

Jessica looked up, realizing her thoughts had wandered. The service had begun, and Reverend Ben was making this week's announcements. ". . . And in two weeks, on November thirtieth, we'll be celebrating the first Sunday of Advent. Though it's far too soon to start hearing Christmas music in shopping malls, it's certainly not too early for us to begin work on our holiday projects.

"Particularly, the Christmas Fair, which will be held over two days this year, starting on Friday, December nineteenth. As most of you know, the fair is a big fund-raiser for the church. The proceeds are an important part of our budget. While I know this is a hectic time of year, if we each donate some hours and effort, we're bound to have a successful event. The sign-up sheets are out in the hallway. I'm sure everyone can find a job they're suited for, from making floral arrangements to cleanup crew —"

"And if you don't see anything you want

to do, come see me. I'll put you to work."

All eyes turned to Sophie Potter, who half-stood in her seat then sat down again at the urging of her granddaughter, Miranda.

"Sorry, Reverend," Sophie added in a meeker tone.

"Not a problem," Reverend Ben said easily. "Sophie is in charge of the fair this year . . . in case any of you haven't guessed. Sounds like we got the right woman for the job."

The comment drew some laughter, and he paused and smiled. Jessica wasn't surprised to hear that Sophie was going to organize the fair this year, even though Sophie had lost her beloved husband, Gus, only last spring. It wasn't that she didn't still mourn Gus, Jessica knew. Sophie simply believed that the best way to honor Gus's memory was to keep active and contribute what she could for as long as she could.

"Last, but not least, is our annual outreach to the Helping Hands Mission," Reverend Ben continued in a more serious tone. "This year we have the honor and pleasure of having Reverend Cameron, the mission director, visiting us and serving as our assistant pastor. In the coming weeks, he'll be talking to us more about the mission and the latest developments there."

Jessica saw Reverend Cameron sitting in the front row near the pulpit. She hadn't spoken with him much since he had arrived in Cape Light earlier in the fall, though she enjoyed his sermons on the weeks he stepped in for Reverend Ben. Jessica admired the work he did with the mission. She could barely imagine the degree of personal sacrifice and hardship he seemed to so willingly embrace. Yet his personality gave no hint of that. James Cameron was bright and humorous, clearly committed to his work but not weighed down by his calling.

It took a special kind of person to be so selfless, Jessica thought, so empathetic. She thought of herself as a good person with good intentions most of the time. But she knew she didn't have whatever it took to make that kind of effort. Sam was more the type. He didn't seem to notice a person's "container" — the type of clothes someone wore, their age or profession, their status or lack of it. He looked to the light inside a person, the spirit common to everyone. Which was probably why her husband had so many friends . . . and such a motley crew of them.

She glanced at Sam and the boy seated beside him. Darrell had made a paper airplane out of the church bulletin and was now tugging on Sam's sleeve, trying to show it off. Sam looked down, smiled gently, and shook his head. Then Jessica saw him whisper something in Darrell's ear. Darrell nodded and put the plane down carefully between them.

At least he's not going to launch it out over the pews, she thought. *With my luck, it would probably hit Mother right in the head.*

It was soon time for the children to go to Sunday school. Darrell left with the others without complaint. Jessica felt relieved. Although she couldn't pin down the what or why of it, something about the boy unsettled her. Maybe it was because he wasn't very friendly to her. He hadn't even spared her a glance this morning. No matter, she told herself. It's great if Sam can help him while he's here.

After the service Jessica and Sam walked out to the vestibule, where Jessica looked around for her mother and sister. She saw them some distance back, coming out of the sanctuary. Dan was the easiest to spot, standing head and shoulders above the crowd.

"I guess I should wait for my mother and

Emily. I'm not sure what time she expects us."

"I hope we don't get stuck there all day. The Patriots are playing San Diego. I really want to catch some of the game."

"Just tell me one thing, honey. Will there ever be a weekend when you *don't* want to watch some part of some game?" The Patriots, the Celtics, the Red Sox — in the short time they'd been together, Jessica had quickly learned there was a sport for all seasons.

Sam caught her eye and laughed but didn't attempt to deny it. "There's Luke. I need to talk to him. I'll be right back." He grinned at her again and walked over to talk to his friend.

She'd married a charming man, that was the problem. All he had to do was look into her eyes and turn up the wattage on that smile of his and she forgot what day it was. *I still fall for it, too. After almost a full year of marriage. I guess that's a good sign,* Jessica thought with a secret grin. *My mother was definitely wrong about my choice of husbands.*

"There you are. We tried to save a seat for you but you came in quite late, I noticed."

Jessica turned to find her mother

wearing one of her many annoyed expressions.

"We weren't that late, Mother. We didn't even miss the announcements." Jessica forced a bright note into her tone. It must be hard to be Lillian Warwick, she thought. The world was just so irritating, in a conspiracy to frustrate her at every turn.

"Mother, please. Does it really matter?" Emily gave Jessica a sympathetic glance and leaned over to kiss her cheek. "Nice service, wasn't it?"

"I didn't notice anything unusual about it. Seemed rather mundane if you ask me." Lillian offered her critique without waiting for Jessica to reply. "Who was that little boy sitting next to Sam? They seemed very cozy."

"Oh, just a boy from New Horizons. Sam's been volunteering out there, teaching woodworking and doing some tutoring and sports." Jessica felt her mother's cold stare but didn't meet her eye.

"Is he really? Good for him." Emily sounded genuinely impressed. "I've been thinking of doing that myself one of these days. When things slow down a bit."

"When you give up being mayor, you mean?" Lillian said.

"I'm not giving it up, Mother. I'm only

taking a honeymoon trip."

"A rather extended one, I'd say. I'm surprised the town council lets you get away with that. I only hope Dan doesn't expect you to give up your career and run off to live on some tropical island." Lillian sniffed and shook her head. "Such a silly fantasy for a grown man."

Everyone in town knew that Dan Forbes, a dedicated sailor, had long planned an extended sail through the Caribbean once he retired from the newspaper. Emily's appearance in his life had slowed down the schedule. Though his long-awaited solo adventure had unexpectedly turned into a honeymoon, he was still determined to carry out his plan.

"Maybe I should give you a grass skirt for your trousseau." Lillian persisted when her first barb brought no reaction.

"I think she would look cute in a grass skirt. She certainly has the legs for it." Dan came up behind Emily and kissed her on the cheek. Jessica thought it was sweet the way her older sister actually blushed.

"There you are. I thought we'd lost you, too," Lillian said to Dan.

"You can't shake me that easily, Lillian. I'm going to be around for a while." Dan gave his future mother-in-law a calm smile.

"I stopped to talk to Reverend Cameron. He's an interesting guy. He would make a nice feature for the paper."

"There's a good idea — if you know someone who writes for the paper." Emily glanced up at Dan and squeezed his arm. "You have a book to write, remember?"

"Right, the book. Thanks for reminding me." Dan nodded dutifully.

Dan had been running the paper for so long that it was hard for him to stop looking at the world in terms of what made a good story. But Jessica knew he was in the middle of writing a book about the town's history, and the couple couldn't get married and sail off into the sunset until the first draft was at the publisher's.

"It's a good idea for Sara, I meant." Dan turned to Lillian with a hopeful look. "Is she coming by this afternoon?"

Sara Franklin was Emily's daughter by her first husband, Tim Sutton, a local fisherman. Emily had defied her parents and run away from home just after high school to marry him. The young couple lived on the Maryland shore for two happy years until Tim died in a car accident. Grieving, eight months pregnant, and completely alone, Emily called her mother. Lillian agreed to help her reprobate daughter but with a terrible condition: she insisted that Emily give up the baby for adoption.

Sick and vulnerable and convinced she had no other recourse, Emily finally agreed. She returned home and went to college, taking up her life, as if marriage and motherhood had never happened. But Jessica knew how her older sister had suffered silently, living a half life, never able to maintain a real relationship, steeped in regret and self-reproach for having given up her daughter.

Emily had searched for Sara without success. Then about a year ago, Sara had come to Cape Light searching for her birth mother and had finally introduced herself to Emily. Jessica had seen her sister's life completely changed and Emily's spirit renewed in a way she'd never dreamed possible.

Luckily, Sara liked the town enough to stay on and she found a job on the *Messenger*, the newspaper Dan's family had founded, which was now run by his daughter, Lindsay.

Jessica hoped Sara was coming today. Though Lillian feigned indifference, it was clear that she actually delighted in her only granddaughter. Sara seemed to have a mysterious gift for getting along with

Lillian that had completely eluded Emily and Jessica.

"Sara Franklin may deign to arrive after lunch, with her boyfriend, Luke," Lillian said. "But only for dessert. She has some previous engagements, something more important than visiting her grandmother."

Lillian pulled her gloves from her handbag then closed it with a loud snap. "Well, let's not stand around here all day. I need to get back to the house for our lunch, Emily."

"Yes, of course, Mother."

"Do you need any help?" Jessica asked her sister.

"There's not much to do. All the food is ready. I just have to set the table. Where's Sam?"

"I don't know. He was talking to Luke McAllister," Jessica answered as she looked around for her husband. "I don't see him now."

"Well, he can't have gone too far. Come along whenever you find him."

Jessica watched her family depart through the church's front doors. When she turned again she spotted Sam coming toward her, along with Reverend Ben and Darrell.

Reverend Ben greeted her with a smile.

"I hope we haven't kept you waiting long. Sam's friend wanted to see how the organ worked, so I gave him a special tour."

"That was nice of you, Reverend. Did you get to try it?" she asked Darrell.

"A little. I didn't hit too hard though. I didn't want to break it."

"Of course not." She smiled at him again, but the boy wouldn't meet her eye.

He'd spoken to her quickly, she noticed, then stared down at the floor. Jessica wondered if she'd said something wrong, something that had sounded unintentionally accusatory. But she hadn't. He was just touchy — around her, at any rate.

"Darrell loves music. He wants to learn to play the piano." Sam placed his hand on Darrell's shoulder.

Jessica just smiled. She didn't know what to say. Would it even be kind to encourage him? What were the chances of a boy like Darrell getting the opportunity to learn to play the piano? Who would pay for the lessons? Where would he practice? Learning to play an instrument seemed such a simple thing; most kids she knew took it for granted. But for a boy like Darrell, it wouldn't be so simple, she realized.

"So, where are you off to today? Doing anything special?" Reverend Ben asked.

"We're having lunch at my mother's house. In fact, we should probably go. I want to help Emily set things up." Jessica glanced at her watch then at her husband. "Where's Luke? He must be looking for Darrell."

"It's all right." Something in Sam's tone made her wary. "He'll pick up Darrell later . . . at your mother's."

"At my mother's?" Jessica heard the harsh note in her voice and felt embarrassed in front of Darrell and Reverend Ben.

"Luke said he was going over there later with Sara."

Luke and Sara had been going out for several months. Of course he'd be coming over to Lillian's with her today. But how did that add up to Darrell coming along with them?

"You mean Darrell is coming with us?" Jessica asked in a deliberately milder tone.

"Well, he asked if he could visit with us a little longer today, and I thought it would be okay to bring him with us. I mean, it's only lunch. Luke thought it was a great idea."

Jessica felt her cheeks growing warm with embarrassment and annoyance. What could Sam be thinking? He knew it was anything but a great idea. He knew her mother hated surprise guests. She practically hated *any* guests, surprise or otherwise. But Jessica couldn't argue about it, not in front of Reverend Ben and Darrell. For one thing, she didn't want to hurt the boy's feelings again.

Finally, she drew in a breath and forced a small smile. "Sure, it's only lunch. I'm sure there's plenty. Darrell might get a little bored with only grown-ups to talk to, though," she added.

Darrell looked up at her. "Sam's not a grown-up. I mean, not like in a bad way."

Jessica just stared at him a moment. "I definitely agree with the first part." She glanced up at Sam and he gave her a relieved look. He knew he was safe, for a while at least.

"We'd better get going, I guess." Sam held out his hand to the minister. "See you, Reverend."

"See you, Sam. Have a good day, Jessica." Reverend Ben nodded encouragingly at the boy. "Good-bye, young man. I hope to see you again."

"Count on it," Darrell said, making both Sam and the minister smile.

Jessica, however, was stonily silent as they walked to the car and got in. She sat without saying a word all the way to her mother's house.

Darrell was the first one out of the car when Sam parked in front of Lillian's.

"Hey." Sam reached over and gently touched Jessica's cheek. "It's going to be okay," he said softly.

It's going to be a disaster, Jessica wanted to respond, but all she said was, "I hope you're right."

They both got out of the car to find Darrell standing perfectly still. He seemed hesitant to go any farther.

"What's the matter, pal? Feel okay?" Sam stared down at Darrell curiously.

Darrell looked up at him and then back at the imposing three-story Victorian. "We're going in there?"

Sam nodded. "Sure, that's where Jessica's mother lives."

"Is it haunted?" His voice trembled with fear. "It looks like a haunted house."

Sam grinned and glanced at Jessica, who was frowning at the house, realizing that the boy had a point. The house was the kind of Victorian relic Darrell had likely only seen in the movies: a three-story mansard-roofed structure, charcoal gray with faded white trim and black shutters. On this overcast, chilly winter day, she had to admit, it did look like something out of an Edward Gorey cartoon.

"No, it's not haunted. Now come on, Darrell. We're late," Sam coaxed him. "Aren't you hungry?"

Darrell nodded and took Sam's hand in a firm grip.

"The house is just old and needs to be painted. There's nothing to be frightened of," Jessica said as they started up the walk.

Darrell glanced at her but didn't reply. Jessica felt the old familiar tension in her stomach as they climbed the steps to the porch. There were ghosts here, she knew very well. But not the kind that would matter to Darrell or even Sam. Ghosts from her family's past, denied by everyone, but still lingering in the shadows.

At the front door, before they could stop him, Darrell reached up and pressed the doorbell three times. Jessica blanched; her mother would hate that.

"Calm down," Sam whispered in her ear. "It'll be fine."

"No, it won't," she insisted quietly. "And you're going to explain it to her."

The door swung open. Jessica was relieved to see her sister, not her mother, standing there. Emily took them in with a welcoming smile that did not falter for an instant as it landed on Darrell, who stood beside Sam.

"Come on in. You've brought your friend from church, I see." She stepped aside to let them enter then held out her hand to Darrell. "Hi. I'm Emily Warwick."

Darrell looked confused for a moment then shook Emily's hand. "Hi. I'm Darrell."

Sam put his hand on Darrell's shoulder. "Emily is Jessica's sister. She's also the mayor of Cape Light."

Darrell stared up at Emily and gave a short nod. "Cool," he said.

"Did you hear that? I'm finally cool. I like this boy already." Emily smiled, looking pleased with the compliment.

Jessica nearly laughed then, but she was distracted by the sound of her mother approaching from the living room.

"Are you coming in or has the party moved out to the foyer?"

Lillian walked slowly toward them. She was using her cane, which meant her hip was acting up. Since she almost always refused to take her pain medication, this did not bode well, Jessica thought.

"Hello, Mother. These are for you." Jessica kissed her mother's cheek and handed her a bouquet of long white flowers, one of her mother's favorites.

"Calla lilies . . . how clever of you." Lillian looked over the flowers at Darrell Lester. "Are you trying to distract me from something?"

Sam placed a protective hand on Darrell's shoulder. "This is Darrell Lester, Lillian. He's visiting with us for the afternoon. Luke McAllister said he'd be dropping by later with Sara and would pick up Darrell then."

"Luke McAllister. Of course, he would have something to do with this. I don't know why you encourage that romance, Emily. Sara could do much better than that fellow."

Emily shrugged. "Sara has her own mind. You know that. Besides, what's wrong with Luke? I like him very much and I think he's well suited to her."

"This is neither the time nor the place to get into that topic. But remind me to take it up with you sometime." Lillian released one of her trademark sighs of indignation then moved with a crablike motion back toward the living room. "Come along. I've waited long enough for my lunch. I can feel my blood sugar taking a swan dive. I don't know why I bother to organize these family get-togethers. Everyone's on their own schedule. Nobody really wants to come visit me. . . ."

Behind their mother's back, Emily rolled her eyes and Jessica nearly laughed out loud. Sam and Darrell lingered a moment in the foyer and Jessica turned to see what they were up to.

Darrell was staring up at the high ceiling and the long, zigzagging staircase. "That old lady, she really lives here? All by herself?"

"She does indeed."

"It looks like a hotel or something in here. I bet you could fit, like, ten families in all those rooms up there."

"It doesn't seem fair, does it?" Jessica heard her husband reply.

Darrell shrugged in answer. As if he'd already learned the world was not fair, especially when it came to some people having and some not having.

A hard lesson to learn when you're that young, Jessica thought. She felt suddenly embarrassed by her mother's big empty house, all the antiques, paintings, and expensive bric-a-brac. Ten families could probably put this space to good use, she thought, ten families Darrell knew.

Jessica helped her sister set an extra

place for Darrell, then carry bowls and platters from the kitchen while their mother enthroned herself at the head of the long dining room table and directed traffic.

"No, Dan, don't sit there. You go here, next to me. I'll put Emily next to you and Jessica in the place across." She fixed Sam with a disapproving glare. "You may take that seat down there, Sam, and put the boy at the corner. Less likely to interrupt at that end," she said to Dan.

Jessica saw her husband give her mother a look, but he didn't say anything. He'll deserve to watch his football game this afternoon, Jessica thought, the whole interminable twelve hours of it.

Her mother picked up her linen napkin and spread it across her lap. "Why don't you say grace, Jessica?"

"All right." Jessica glanced around the table then bowed her head. "Dear heavenly Father, thank you for gathering us today around this table and for the food we are about to share. Thank you for our many blessings, and help us to be mindful of them. Amen."

"And thank heaven that Sam's sister is such a wonderful cook. There's roasted potatoes, butternut squash, sweet peas, and

Cornish game hens with herb and chestnut stuffing." Emily lifted the bowl of potatoes and passed them to her mother.

"The meal is all from her shop? I thought you made it." Lillian eyed the potatoes suspiciously.

Dan laughed. "Emily has many fine qualities, Lillian, but you should know by now that culinary talent is definitely not one of them. Once she got all these little chickens home from the market, she'd be more likely to line them up and call a meeting than cook them."

Sam and Jessica exchanged a glance and both of them broke out laughing. The image was just so perfectly Emily.

"Hey, I'm not that bad." Emily stared at her fiancé, managing a moment's indignation before giving in to laughter.

Unsmiling, Lillian took a spoonful of potatoes and passed the dish to Dan. "Is that why you haven't set a wedding date? Wary of her cooking?"

"Mother, please . . ." Emily still looked amused, but Jessica could tell from her sister's tone that Lillian was once again pushing buttons.

Jessica focused on the far end of the table where Sam was filling Darrell's plate. Darrell didn't look that interested in the food. He was sliding a teaspoon around his place setting, weaving it in and out of the china and crystal glasses, as if it were a little vehicle on an obstacle course.

Jessica stared hard at Sam, trying to signal a warning of imminent danger. She didn't even want to imagine the scene if Darrell tipped over one of her mother's Waterford goblets.

"Well, I was just wondering." Lillian gave an innocent shrug and stabbed her fork into a pile of peas. "I thought long engagements had gone out of fashion. Especially for people your age. Then there's that trip you've been planning. I can't imagine what you're both waiting for. Unless of course, there are some problems?"

Emily and Dan had been engaged since May, about six months. Not really long at all, Jessica thought. But she, too, was starting to wonder why they hadn't set a date.

Dan smiled at his future mother-in-law and said smoothly, "There aren't any problems, Lillian. Don't get your hopes up."

Sam started to laugh again but with his mouth full, nearly choked. Darrell jumped up at once and began pounding him on the back. "Are you okay, Sam? Do you need the Heimlich maneuver? I can do it to you. I saw it on TV."

Darrell tried to grab Sam from behind but Sam peeled him off with one hand, as if dislodging a small, affectionate pet. "That's all right. . . . I'm okay," he sputtered. He took a sip of water. "Something must have gone down the wrong way."

"It's your sister's cooking. Too many spices. I can't see how she stays in business." Lillian sat back in her seat and set her fork on the side of the plate, as if she suddenly found the meal inedible.

Jessica hated it when her mother criticized Molly. Though Sam had never said so, she knew it hurt his feelings. Besides, the criticism was completely unwarranted; Molly was an incredible cook.

Now that the emergency was over, Darrell had returned to playing with his flatware again, Jessica noticed, though Sam leaned over twice to discourage him. He had made a seesaw-type lever of the sterling silver fork and spoon. He suddenly brought his fist down on the knife's handle, launching the fork into the air. It landed on the floor with a resounding clatter. *Oh, great,* Jessica thought as Sam gave Darrell a stern look then leaned over to search for the fork.

Before her mother could comment, Jessica loudly continued the conversation.

"I think the food tastes great. I love the stuffing. Maybe Molly will give me the recipe for Thanksgiving."

"Yes, very tasty," Dan agreed.

Emily shrugged. "She must be doing something right. The shop is so busy you can hardly get waited on."

Lillian was half listening to their conversation and half watching the far end of the table. She pinned Sam with a stare as he sat up again and straightened the napkin on his lap.

"Where's the boy? Did you lose him under there?"

Sam looked around. Jessica could see he was baffled to find Darrell's chair empty. "Here was right here a minute ago. . . ."

"For heaven's sake! What was that?" Lillian pressed her hand to her chest and jumped out of her seat, as if poked by a cattle prod.

Jessica heard Darrell's laughter under the table and instantly knew what had happened.

Sam leaned over. "Darrell, come out from under the table. That's not a place to play."

Jessica thought Darrell would emerge at the head of the table, somewhere near her mother, but she suddenly felt something scurry past her legs and realized he'd wisely decided it would be best to come out near Sam.

Sam helped him up and brushed off his clothes. "You shouldn't have gone under the table. That's not polite."

"I was looking for my spoon."

"Well, I found it. Now, say excuse me and we'll go wash your hands."

"Excuse me," Darrell mumbled.

"That's all right. See you later." Emily smiled at him, clearly amused. "I'll bring out dessert."

"Dessert? Do you think a child should be rewarded for such behavior? I can see you've never been a parent." Lillian took her seat again and the table went silent.

It was true that Emily had never raised a child, but that was mainly because her mother had robbed her of the opportunity. Though her sister had sorted out this long-buried issue and more or less forgiven Lillian, Jessica could tell that the comment still stung. And she could tell from Dan's expression that he was keenly aware of it.

"Little boys will crawl under tables, Lillian," he said evenly. "That's one of the things they do best. Having raised one, I do know. So let's not make a federal case of it."

Dan's tone was firm and Jessica saw her mother shrink back in her seat. She also saw a flash of gratitude in her sister's blue eyes.

Lillian made a huffing sound, regaining her composure. "I suppose you can clear the dishes, Jessica. I don't think anyone has any appetite left, after that episode."

Jessica glanced around. It did look as if everyone had finished eating, though she was sure Darrell going under the table had little to do with that. She rose and began to collect the dishes.

"Let me help you." Emily rose, too.

"That's not necessary. Jessica can manage. You did everything else." Lillian pinned her older daughter with a stare. "Besides, I'd like to get back to your wedding plans. Or lack of them."

Emily sat down again and gave Jessica a secret look as she brushed past. From the kitchen, Jessica could hear her mother begin her interrogation.

"With all the commotion around here today you never actually answered my question."

"What commotion?" Emily's counter question was designed to distract and get her mother off the point; Jessica recognized it as one of Emily's favorite tactics.

Dan spoke up. "We haven't set a wedding date yet, Lillian, for a perfectly good reason. We can't agree on what type of wedding we should have. I want something small, quick, simple. Emily seems to have her heart set on a more lavish affair."

"I never said lavish. I'm hardly the lavish type, Dan. You know that by now."

Jessica could tell from the pitch of her sister's voice that the topic was a thorny one. Emily had mentioned the problem to her once or twice in the past few weeks, and she had assumed they would work it out, as most couples do. But Dan was very set in his ways, and Emily was very independent and accustomed to being in charge — a combination that did not favor compromise.

"Maybe lavish is not quite the right word," Dan allowed. "But something more elaborate than I feel is necessary. Would you call that a fair assessment?"

"Elaborate? That sounds as if we're picking out a chandelier. I just know more people around here than you do."

"I ran the newspaper for over twenty years, dear. How could you possibly know more people than I do?" Dan's voice was cajoling yet held a tense edge.

"Maybe that's not the right way to put it,

then. I only mean that of the large group of people we both know, I'd like to have more of them sharing our wedding day."

Jessica entered the room and removed a few more dirty dishes just in time to see her mother tap her empty water goblet with a teaspoon. It made a delicate ringing sound, as if signaling the end of a round between two high-class boxers.

"Time. Time out." Lillian glanced from Dan to Emily, positively enjoying the confrontation. "Why don't you get married here, in this house? That will solve everything, don't you think?"

Jessica couldn't see how the offer, though surprisingly generous, would solve the problem. It would only generate new ones. She watched Emily and Dan gaze at each other across the table, communicating silently.

"Thank you, Mother. That's very nice of you to offer . . . but I don't think we'll need to have it here."

"Really? And why not?" Lillian sat up straight in her chair, looking insulted. "A wedding at home is always more intimate and personal. Far more tasteful than some . . . drafty, tacky restaurant. It was good enough for your engagement party," she reminded them.

"That was different," Emily replied.

Dan looked down at the table and fiddled with his napkin. Finally, he looked up again. "We're just not sure what we want to do, Lillian. We need a little time to work this out."

"You do want to marry her, don't you? Are you getting cold feet?"

"Mother, really!" Emily's cheeks were flushed, and Jessica was certain she was angry, maybe also embarrassed.

Dan laughed. "Don't be ridiculous. I love her madly. I'd get married tonight if she'd agree to it."

"Elope, you mean? Heaven forbid! You won't pull that again on me, will you? I'd never survive it." Lillian pressed a hand to her heart, her eyes wide with shock.

"Calm down, Mother," Emily said, sounding weary. "We're not going to elope. Dan was just . . . making a point."

"I was totally serious. But don't worry, Lillian. I can't persuade her to run off with me. She's too busy — too many meetings to attend."

"Thank heaven for small favors," Lillian grumbled.

Jessica slipped into the kitchen with the remainder of the dinner dishes. After loading them into the dishwasher, she located a bag of ground coffee in the freezer and then began the search for Lillian's coffeemaker.

Sam entered the kitchen from the hallway just as Jessica was switching on the coffeepot.

"Have you seen Darrell around?" he asked a little too casually.

"No, I thought he was with you."

"He sort of disappeared on me. I thought he must have come down here."

"Sam, you shouldn't let him just wander around the house like that. He could get into trouble. He could hurt himself."

"I know that," Sam insisted. "We were just upstairs, walking around a little. I thought it would be good to let him stretch his legs. I turned the game on in the spare bedroom to check the score, and he disappeared. Are you sure he didn't come down here?"

"I haven't seen him. Maybe he crawled under the table again." Jessica leaned over, trying to see under the table through the kitchen doorway. She didn't see Darrell there.

She tried to ignore a rising sense of alarm. After all, Darrell wasn't going to get lost inside the house. But she didn't like the idea of him roaming around alone, able to get into all kinds of mischief — able to break any number of her mother's fragile, irreplaceable treasures.

"I don't see him." She glanced at Sam, trying to hold on to her temper.

"I guess I'll go back upstairs and take another look around." He looked a bit unnerved, too, she noticed. Not a good sign.

"What's going on in there? What's all that whispering about?" Her mother's shrill voice caught Jessica off guard.

"Everything's fine."

"Then why are you whispering?" Lillian demanded. "Did something break? Some of my stemware?"

Not yet, Jessica nearly answered aloud. She glanced at Sam and could tell they were both thinking the same thing.

Suddenly, a strange cry broke through the silence, a mixture of both terror and delight that reminded Jessica of the way people yell on a roller coaster. And in the background, there was an odd bumping noise, like a suitcase tossed down the steps. Everyone stood stone still for an instant then ran toward the noise, which seemed to be coming from the foyer. Lillian, moving as quickly as her bad hip would allow, brought up the rear.

Before they reached the foyer, Jessica

heard the sounds again: the muffled, bumping noise and the roller-coaster scream.

Then came a loud crash, the sound of breaking glass, and a different kind of crying. Real crying, with tears.

Chapter Four

"Darrell, are you okay? What happened in here?" Sam reached the boy first, with Jessica close behind him. Darrell was sprawled facedown on the floor of the foyer. He lifted his head and Jessica saw blood stream out of his nose.

Sam quickly pulled a hankie from his pocket and covered Darrell's nose and mouth. "Just sit up slowly and lean your head back." Sam turned quickly to the rest of them. "Can somebody bring some ice, please?"

Jessica suddenly realized that she, Emily, and Dan were all just standing there, frozen in place.

"I'll get it." Dan ran back to the kitchen while Darrell tilted his head back, as Sam had instructed. The wadded-up hankie covered most of his face and all Jessica could see were his dark eyes, wide with fear and glossy with tears.

One of her mother's Persian wool area rugs, which usually covered a stretch of the second-floor hallway, was crumpled up beneath him. Jessica wondered how it had ended up downstairs.

"Is he hurt — other than his nose, I mean?" Jessica asked Sam.

Darrell shook his head as best he could. "I'm okay," he mumbled from under the hankie. Sam checked him anyway for broken bones, but there didn't seem to be any serious damage.

Except for one small item, Jessica realized. An antique Oriental bean jar, prized for its unusual ceramic finish, now lay in shards, scattered like pieces of jigsaw puzzle across the foyer floor.

Dan returned with a plastic bag of ice and handed it down. Sam pulled the hankie away and replaced it with the ice bag. Darrell winced but didn't say anything.

"What in heaven's name is going on here?" Jessica turned to see her mother standing in the doorway, her face ashen white.

Lillian looked down at Sam and Darrell. Then Jessica saw her gaze shift to the blue shards of pottery.

"My bean jar! It's demolished! That

piece has been in our family for over a hundred years!"

She tottered precariously on her cane, her hand pressed to her throat as if she couldn't breathe. Jessica was afraid she was about to faint — or maybe even have another stroke — and started toward her. But Emily and Dan reached her first, each grabbing an arm to hold her upright.

"Come back into the living room, Mother." Emily's tone was quiet but persuasive. "You need to sit down."

Lillian let herself be led away from the demolition site, her voice carrying clearly. "I loved that jar. It's positively irreplaceable. It was a wedding gift to my great-grandmother."

"Yes, it was a lovely piece," Emily agreed. "But you have so many lovely things, you can find something else to put there. You probably won't even miss it."

"Don't tell me I won't miss it! I most certainly will. They showed a jar just like that last week on that rambling antiques show. It was worth a bloody fortune. That awful little boy! I knew he'd do something like this. I knew it from the moment I set eyes on him. A little rabble rouser. Like the rest of those . . . those delinquents at that rehabilitation farm —"

"Mother, please. Control yourself. He's right outside —"

"Don't tell me to control myself! What do I care if he hears me? Who invited him here today anyway? I certainly did not!"

"Lillian, please calm down. Do you want your pills?" Dan asked.

Her mother's voice finally grew softer but Jessica didn't need to hear more. She walked over to Sam, still crouched near Darrell and holding the ice pack to the boy's nose. "Is he okay?"

"I think so. Just shook up." Sam looked at Darrell again. "What happened? What were you doing in here?"

"Nothing."

"Nothing doesn't break stuff and give you a bloody nose," Sam pointed out.

Darrell stared at Sam, his eyes wide with fear. Jessica could see he was struggling, wanting to confide in Sam, but afraid.

"Don't worry. Just tell me the truth and it will be okay. No one is going to hurt you." Sam touched the boy's shoulder. "I promise."

Darrell took the ice pack off his face. His nose was red and his upper lip a little swollen. He wiped his eyes with the back of his sleeve. "I didn't mean to break anything. I was just playing, fooling around."

Sam nodded at him. "Playing with the rug?"

"Yeah, with the rug. I was sliding on it in the hallway. Then I tried it on the stairs. Like a snowboard."

Jessica blinked in astonishment, picturing Darrell's inventive game. "You rode down the stairs on the Persian rug?"

Darrell finally looked at her and shrugged. "It was really fun . . . until I came down too fast and wiped out."

"Until you slid into the wall and knocked the jar over, you mean?" Sam's voice was firm but quiet.

Darrell nodded, looking scared again. "I didn't mean to. I didn't even see it. I'm really sorry. Will you tell that lady Lillian I'm sorry?"

Sam sighed and stood up. "I think you should tell her yourself."

"Do I have to?" Darrell look terrified and Jessica sympathized.

"Yes, Darrell, you do. But first I want you to go upstairs, wash your face, and tuck your shirt in. Then come back downstairs and we'll go talk to her."

"Okay." Darrell slowly stood up, his head hanging.

"And take the rug with you and put it back where you found it."

"Sure, Sam." Darrell gathered the rug in his arms and headed for the staircase.

Jessica felt what she recognized as an uncharitable surge of righteousness. She had known from the start that bringing Darrell to Lillian's was a terrible idea. But she also couldn't help marveling at the way Sam handled the boy's misbehavior. He'd been calm but firm, making his point without flying off the handle. *He'll be a great father someday,* she thought. *Someday soon, I hope. Maybe then he'll no longer need a surrogate kid.*

Sam watched Darrell climb the long stairway then turned to her. "I guess I'll clean up this mess. Should I save the pieces?"

"Probably . . . though there's really no point to it."

He gathered up more of the jagged pieces, his expression grim. "I'm sorry. I should have kept a better eye on him."

"Obviously."

"It could have been worse. I mean, he could have broken his neck pulling a stunt like that."

"Yes, it's lucky he wasn't really hurt." Jessica knew her tone sounded curt but she couldn't help it. "Honestly, Sam. I knew something like this was going to happen.

You never should have brought him here."

Sam looked up at her, his eyes narrowed. "I was trying to give him a nice day, an afternoon away from the center when he could have some companionship and attention. Was that so wrong?"

"Of course not. But clearly he has some behavior problems. He doesn't know how to act appropriately in any place other than a playground or a gymnasium."

"Jessica, come one. You're not being fair. You sound just like your mother," he muttered.

Jessica felt her face redden. It was true. She did sound like her mother, and the realization made her even more annoyed at Sam and Darrell and the entire unnecessary situation.

"Maybe for once in her life my mother is right," she said. "Let Darrell apologize and we'll go. We can drop him at the center on the way home. Luke will understand."

Sam stared at her a moment. "Okay. I'll go upstairs and get him."

Jessica knelt down to see if there were any shards they had missed. She heard a sound at the top of the staircase and realized Darrell was on his way down again. She looked up at him, wondering if he'd heard her. She couldn't tell. He just looked terribly unhappy. Which was not the point of the day at all.

She suddenly felt embarrassed by her outburst, then angry that she should be embarrassed at all. She wasn't the one who went snowboarding down the staircase.

She got to her feet as Sam joined the boy at the bottom of the staircase. Sam glanced at her then back at Darrell. He seemed to be waiting for her to say something. Jessica honestly wanted to but couldn't think of what to say. Should she be apologizing when Darrell was the one who had behaved so badly? That didn't feel right, though neither did berating him. She didn't want Darrell to feel worse; she just wanted this whole uncomfortable situation to go away.

Finally, when it became clear that she wasn't going to say anything, Sam took Darrell's hand and led him toward the living room. "Let's go tell Lillian you're sorry and say good-bye."

Darrell nodded, looking contrite. "Okay, I will."

Left alone in the foyer, Jessica saw another piece of the bean jar near her foot and picked it up. She didn't want to be mad at Sam. It wasn't entirely his fault. But she had tried to tell him that bringing

Darrell here was a recipe for disaster. Why hadn't he just listened to her? Sometimes Sam's good intentions were such a blind spot.

Now she had Sam and Darrell and Lillian mad at her. It just didn't seem fair.

Leigh sat with Vera in the small front parlor, the Sunday paper spread out on her lap. She scanned the headlines, unable to focus on a single article. She hadn't slept well the night before, disturbed by her conversation with Alice. Now she felt too drowsy to concentrate on anything other than the clicking rhythm of Vera's knitting needles. Vera was working at an impressive pace, she noticed. It was one of the few times Leigh had ever seen the older woman refrain from conversation.

Leigh put down her paper and watched. "What are you making?"

"A cardigan, for my granddaughter, cable-knit. I have to keep careful count of the stitches." Vera glanced up and smiled. "Do you knit, Leigh?"

"I never learned how. I sew a little," she added, hesitant to reveal even the most minor detail about herself.

"I could teach you if you like. It passes the time in the winter around here. Of course, you'll have your hands full once the baby comes."

"I'm sure I will." Leigh glanced at the paper, wanting to change the subject. "Do your grandchildren live nearby?"

"Not far. Down in Hamilton. There's my latest picture, up on the mantel."

Leigh rose and picked up the framed photograph. The children were adorable, a girl with long wavy blond hair, missing her front teeth, and a boy, who looked a bit older. They were playing in a pile of leaves with a big yellow dog, their two parents in the background.

"They're beautiful," Leigh murmured. *A perfect, happy family. Hardly the picture of my future,* she realized sadly.

"They look cute, but don't get fooled. Those two can be a handful." Vera shook her head and turned her work over.

Leigh smiled at that frank comment, though the thought that her own child would be growing up without grandparents made her spirits sink again. She sat down and picked up another section of the *Boston Globe,* the business news. She turned to the second page and her gaze fastened on a headline and the familiar names in the article beneath. She felt her breath catch in her throat. She glanced at

Vera, who was counting stitches again, her lips moving soundlessly while she scanned her handiwork.

Leigh quietly tore off the article and slipped it in her pocket. Then she sat back and took a deep breath, trying to collect herself.

Vera glanced at her. "Are you feeling all right, dear? You look a little . . . peaked."

"I'm okay. I think I ate too much lunch. Everything was very good."

Vera looked back at her knitting. "Glad you enjoyed it."

Leigh stared down at the newspaper, pretending to read while her thoughts scattered in a thousand directions. She didn't even realize that James had come into the room until he stood right next to her chair.

He had changed from the suit and tie he wore for church that morning into jeans and a heavy gray turtleneck, with a dark green parka over it. He was also toting a strange object over his shoulder that she couldn't make out at first. She smiled as she realized it could only be a set of bagpipes.

"You're going down to the beach with those pipes again?" Vera shook her head. "I don't think that's such a good idea."

Leigh noticed James flush a bit, as if

Vera's comment had embarrassed him, though she didn't understand exactly why.

"Vera, please . . . you don't have to worry about me."

"I don't?" She made a hurrumphing sound as she pulled more yarn from the ball in her lap. "Excuse me, then. But I think somebody ought to."

"I feel great," James said. "Besides, I can use the fresh air."

Leigh put the paper aside and looked up at him. "Would you mind if I came with you? I'd love to see the beach. Isn't there a famous lighthouse there?"

"I don't know if it's famous, but it's very pretty." James smiled at her. "Get your things. I'm in no rush."

"You're both crazy, if you ask me. The beach, at this time of year? I bet there's no one out there but Digger Hegman."

Leigh didn't understand the reference but it made James laugh. "Yes, he probably will be." He turned to Leigh. "Digger is an old fisherman, a former clammer and lobster man. He's failing now, but no one can seem to keep him away from the shore when it's low tide."

"Digger's half daft. A person ought to have better sense is my point." The older woman cast Leigh a disapproving look, thinking about her pregnancy, Leigh guessed. But she really did need to get out. If she sat here much longer, she'd go crazy, too.

Leigh rose abruptly. "If I get too cold, I'll wait in the car."

"Suit yourself." Vera shrugged. "There are some extra gloves and scarves in the mudroom."

Leigh dressed quickly in all her heaviest clothes and two pairs of gloves. She laughed as James helped her into his car. "I hope I don't fall on my back in this outfit. I'll get stuck, like a turtle."

"Don't worry, I'll roll you over. Just give me a signal or something." He glanced at her, his blue eyes flashing with good humor as he started up the car. "You should have brought some earmuffs. Or at least some cotton for your ears."

"Because of the wind?"

"I meant my playing. Most people don't like the sound of bagpipes."

"I like the bagpipes." He glanced at her doubtfully. "Honestly, I really do."

"Well, you're not like most people, then. But I already knew that."

It was a nice compliment but she didn't know what to say. He smiled again, his eyes fixed on the road. He had a strong profile, she thought, a long straight nose and even features. Tiny lines crinkled attractively at the corners of his eyes. She hadn't noticed that before.

Leigh realized she was staring at him and deliberately turned her attention to the scenery. They were driving on the same winding road that led to town — the Beach Road, she thought it was called. But she noticed that James turned in the opposite direction this time.

"What made you take up the bagpipes?"

"It was more like who. A music teacher at school. He was a piper and insisted I learn to carry on 'our proud heritage, laddie.' " James spoke the last few words in a perfect Scottish brogue. "He gave me lessons every Friday afternoon, free of charge — while I was itching to get out and play baseball with the other kids." James laughed to himself, remembering. "He was an excellent piper. I'd love to watch him in parades in our town. I think he must have marched until he was over eighty."

Leigh smiled at him. "Did you grow up in New England?"

He nodded. "In Essex, not far from here."

They reached the beach and James

pulled into the big, nearly empty parking lot. It took Leigh a bit of effort to lever herself out of the car, but once she stood up and looked out at the water, she was transfixed. The day was surprisingly mild, the bright sun melting away most of the snow.

The sun was still bright and the sky was clear, turning the ocean a deep shade of blue. The waves were high, laced with frothy caps, curling to great heights and crashing with a booming sound against the long, flat shoreline.

Down on the beach, Leigh saw the distant figure of an old man digging in the sand. A big yellow dog ran around in circles, racing between the man and a woman, who sat some distance away on a driftwood log.

"Is that the old fisherman you and Vera were talking about? Down there with the dog?"

James followed her gaze and smiled. "Yes, that's Digger, and that's his daughter Grace there on the log. She has to watch him all the time now. He's become quite senile."

"Oh, that's too bad."

"Yes, it is sad. . . . But it's really been quite beautiful to see how all of their friends in town and at the church have gotten together to help out."

Leigh nodded, glancing again at the trio, who had moved even farther down the shoreline. A community showing concern was a lovely idea, but Leigh was fairly certain James was exaggerating. She chalked it up to his being a minister. He probably liked to think things like that could happen, the way they did in the movies. But not in real life, she reminded herself. In real life, it was hard to find even one person to really help you.

She took a deep breath and glanced out at the ocean again. "It's beautiful here. It takes your breath away."

"It does, doesn't it? It makes me feel good instantly." James had come around to her side, carrying his pipes. "That's the Durham Light, down there." He pointed down the shoreline to an old stone lighthouse, set high on a rocky jetty. "The local populace is quite proud of it. I think the light has some kind of special antique lens."

"Can we go see it?"

"We might get too cold walking but let's try."

Leigh hesitated as she saw that to get onto the beach, they had to cross a high mound of snow.

James held out his hand to her. "I've got you. Don't worry."

She put her gloved hand in his. Moving slowly and concentrating on each step, she began to clamber over the hard-packed snow. She almost slipped once but James steadied her, and they made it over the slippery mound without incident. When they at last stood on the beach, she stopped and let out a long breath.

He flashed her another brilliant smile and released her hand. "Not bad for a pregnant turtle."

"Thanks, I think." She smiled, pushing aside a strand of hair that had blown across her eyes.

She still wasn't used to wearing her hair so short. She had cut it herself, hastily snipping it in the bathroom the night she left Boston. Martin had liked her hair blond, but she'd stopped highlighting it once they'd separated and now it was back to its natural color, which she liked much better.

They walked toward the shoreline and James stopped a minute to sling his pipes over his shoulder. He glanced at her as he brought the mouthpiece to his lips. "Here it comes. Don't say I didn't warn you."

He puffed out his cheeks and let loose an

earsplitting blast, then another, the opening notes of a tune. Leigh resisted a strong impulse to cover her ears.

James began walking along and she fell into step beside him. He played a few more notes then suddenly stopped, turning to face her.

"What's the matter?"

He shook his head, trying not to laugh. "It's nothing . . . just the look on your face." He met her eye and she had to laugh, too.

"I'm sorry . . . it's nice, really. I'm just not used to it at such close range, I guess."

"Of course not. Listen, you walk on ahead. I'll stay here and practice a little. Then I'll catch up with you."

"You don't have to do that. We can walk together."

"This will be better for me, too," he assured her. "I don't usually play for an audience. Besides, it might be harmful to the baby. They say unborn children can hear all kinds of sounds. I don't want to traumatize her and make her end up hating music."

She knew he was partly joking, but once again, she was surprised by his thoughtfulness, his awareness and consideration for the feelings of others.

"I'm sure the baby is in no danger of that," Leigh told him, smiling. "But all right. I'll meet you at the lighthouse, then."

She turned and walked along the shoreline, mindful of keeping her booted feet out of the foam. A few moments later, she heard James start up again, behind her. At a distance the sound was much easier to take, even enjoyable. She didn't recognize the tune but it was lilting and upbeat, not slow and mournful like some of the Scottish airs.

Leigh fixed her sight on the rolling waves, walking in time to their rhythm. A few gulls and smaller birds ran along the wet sand, pecking at bits of shells and seaweed each time a new wave rushed to shore. She loved the beach, no matter what time of the year. The vast space of sea and sky made her heart feel open and even hopeful. The ceaseless ebb and flow of the waves soothed her jagged nerves, and the sound of the pipes mixing with the waves was almost magical. Martin didn't like the beach and she hadn't seen the ocean much while they were married. Now she realized how much she had missed it.

She saw the lighthouse up ahead, painted white with bands of red. It had been built on a rocky hill, with a small stone cottage nearby. Even from a distance, she could see that it was quite old. The light on top seemed to be working, though it was only late afternoon and not dark enough to see it clearly. From time to time, she did notice a brief flash.

That's about right for me. I never get any brilliant, dazzling signals. Just a flash here and there, signaling I might *be on the right track.*

Though the lighthouse hadn't seemed that far at first, she could see that it was still some distance off and she already felt tired. Trudging along the sand in her heavy boots was an effort. She glanced over her shoulder and saw that James was getting closer. She stopped to watch him walk slowly along the shoreline, seeming lost in his music.

Deciding to wait for James to catch up, Leigh sat down on a big driftwood log. She felt so far away in this place, far away from her past life and the troubles that still hounded her. Who would ever find her here? It did seem safe. And all that really mattered now was that she keep the baby safe from Martin.

Leigh shook her head. On the face of it, it seemed morally wrong somehow — having to keep a child from her own father.

But Leigh knew that she could never risk subjecting a child to her ex-husband's rages.

Leigh put a hand on top of her belly. "Don't worry," she whispered. "I'll find a safe place for us. And I'll never let him come close to you, even if I have to fight him to my last breath."

She remembered the newspaper article stashed in her pocket. With James still a good distance down the beach, she decided it was safe to take it out and read it closely. She had only had a chance to quickly scan it in Vera's living room, but even that brief glance had confirmed what Alice had told her the night before.

GARRET MILLS CUTS 200 JOBS, the headline boldly stated. Leigh bent closer and eagerly read the rest.

> Garret Mills, the largest employer in Brighton, New Hampshire, announced that 200 factory jobs will be terminated as of December 1. This latest and most dramatic cost-cutting measure seems to support growing rumors of serious financial problems at the textile mill, one of the largest and oldest in New England. A proposed merger with Martex, due to be completed this month, soured when Garret Mills came under scrutiny

by the state attorney general in a preliminary investigation of the firm's accounting procedures. Investigators suspect that company principals conspired to falsify records to show inflated profits. The volatile, erratic behavior of CEO Martin Garret III, grandson of the company's founder, has also been a red flag to potential investors. Arrested twice in the last three years while driving under the influence, Garret was also charged with spousal abuse during divorce proceedings last year. When asked to comment, Garret flatly denied any connection between his personal life and current company woes. He also added, "We are cooperating fully with the investigation and have no doubt that the firm will be found innocent of any wrongdoing."

Just seeing Martin's name in print gave Leigh a chill. Reading the quote, she could almost hear his voice. Who would ever suspect, hearing that rational, oh-so-respectable tone, that he could so easily lose all control? Like Dr. Jekyll and Mr. Hyde, turning from a button-down executive into an out-of-control monster in the blink of an eye.

Maybe the world at large was finally getting wise to him, Leigh realized. He couldn't hide that side of himself forever. His self-destructive nature was starting to contaminate everything he touched. She had little doubt that he had falsified accounts to promote the merger. He never flinched at cheating. He was bitterly contemptuous of people, especially those who trusted him most. In his twisted, grandiose self-vision, he probably felt entitled to take unfair advantage.

Leigh read the last few lines again, hoping with all her heart that Martin's dire problems would distract him from searching for her. But he was obsessive. He hated to lose. He might well hang on to the very end. She could never be sure.

Leigh crumpled up the paper and stuck it in her jacket pocket as she realized James was only a few yards away.

He was walking toward her, breathing heavily as if he'd just been running. He lifted his hand and smiled, but when he slipped off the pipes and plunked down next to her, his ruddy complexion looked ashen. She watched him open his jacket and wipe sweat from his brow. She recalled Vera's questions and concern just before they'd left and how James had brushed it off. Leigh hadn't thought anything of it at the time, assuming it was just the older woman's usual coddling. But maybe there was some reason.

"Are you all right, James?" she asked quietly.

"Just winded from playing and walking at the same time. I'm out of shape. Been lying around ever since I got here, like a big fat house cat."

His self-mocking image made her smile, yet she sensed an underlying seriousness.

"Since you came to Cape Light?" she asked. "I assumed that you've been living here awhile."

"I came to Cape Light in September," James said. "I've been working at a mission in Central America for almost ten years now. But I had to come back to the States . . . for health reasons."

Leigh could see it wasn't easy for him to talk about this and wondered if maybe she should stop asking personal questions.

"Don't worry. I'm not dying and it's not contagious." James glanced at her, his somber tone cast off and his usual good-natured humor returning.

"Oh . . . I wasn't thinking about that."

"I'm just teasing you, Leigh. Some people get awfully nervous when they hear you're sick. Now you're thinking, *I wonder what he has,* only you're too polite to ask." Leigh smiled self-consciously; she had been thinking just that very thing. Before she could admit it, he said, "I have malaria, a particularly drug-resistant strain. It's partly my own fault. I got lax about taking the pills that ward it off. I'd been down there so long, I got complacent, I guess . . . and now I'm paying for it."

"That's too bad. But you seem very healthy. I would have never guessed. You must be getting better."

"I am. At least I think so, though my doctors and I disagree on that point. The infection is under control but it never really leaves your body. And I have some complications since I waited so long to come up here for better treatment."

James took a breath, staring straight out at the sea. Leigh felt both sympathy and admiration for this man. He had serious problems in his life, just as she did, and yet he always managed to act cheerful and upbeat. And he had a gift for reaching out to others; he had asked her a lot about herself these past few days while she had asked him next to nothing. *He must think I'm completely self-centered,* she thought.

"I don't know much about missions,"

she admitted. "What's it like? What kind of work do you do there?"

"Hard work most of the time, but good work." He glanced at her, the start of a smile in his eyes. "It's just helping people who don't have much. When I was in the seminary I went there for a visit. Back then I never guessed my calling would be in a foreign mission. But I was very moved — inspired, really — to return. I've studied engineering, too, so that's come in handy," he said lightly.

"And you've been there ten years?"

"Yep, just about that. I've been the director of Helping Hands for the past five. It's hard to believe it's been that long. The time has passed so quickly for me. We've dug wells, built a school and houses and a medical clinic. . . ."

"Wow. That's amazing. You must be very proud." James was so modest. She'd had no idea he'd done so much with his life. He had impressed her as a good person from the start, but now her image of him took on new dimensions.

"I am proud. We've done good work — with God's help, of course — but there's still so much more to be done. We were just getting under way expanding the clinic when I left. Here, where life is so comfortable, it's hard to believe that so many people in this world live without the most basic needs being met: enough food to eat and clean water to drink, clothing for their children, medicine —" He stopped, as if afraid he had said too much.

Leigh was again at a loss for words. She felt a pang of guilt, knowing that she had never given much thought to the kind of people James was talking about.

"You sound eager to get back," she said at last.

"I am. I love visiting this church and the people around here, but I feel as if I'm goofing off."

From the little she knew about him, Leigh guessed that James worked hard wherever he was, giving the most he could to any situation.

"After ten years, it sounds as if you deserve a few months off."

"That's one way of looking at it, I guess. I do love what I do there, so it doesn't seem a hardship to me."

"But enjoying yourself does?" she teased him.

"Hmm . . . there's a tough question." His dark blue eyes twinkled. "Not today it doesn't, being here with you."

His compliment made her self-conscious. Was he attracted to her or just being nice again? She couldn't see how he could be interested in her, a totally pregnant turtle. Besides, she told herself, he was probably involved with someone. And that someone was undoubtedly more spiritual, a woman who shared his interests and idealism.

Why not? He was intelligent, warm, kind, and had a sharp sense of humor. And he was quite good looking, too, she decided. It was funny how she hadn't really noticed that before. In his quiet way, James Cameron was sort of a catch.

Leigh shook her head, wondering at the strange turn of her thoughts. What did it matter if James Cameron liked her? Or if he had a string of girlfriends? It was so entirely irrelevant to the life-on-the-run that she seemed to have fallen into.

"How did you end up here?" she asked, determined to stop considering romantic possibilities. "I mean, at this church during your leave?"

"This congregation has always had a special relationship with the mission," James explained. "We're supported by a wide range of donors but Bible Community Church sort of adopted us. They're the ones who always come through. They have a real interest in and commitment to what goes on there. I think it's because the minister who founded Helping Hands grew up in Cape Light. He was part of this congregation as a boy."

"Oh, I see." She didn't really. She didn't understand much about missions or churches or how they fit together. "And you grew up around here, too? In Essex, you just told me, right?"

"That's right." He nodded, looking pleased that she remembered. "But I don't have many connections around here anymore."

"Did your family move away?" Leigh noticed an odd look on his face and wondered if she'd asked too personal a question.

"Oh . . . you might say that. I grew up in an orphanage. I've lost touch with most of the boys I knew there, though I still write to the minister and some of the teachers who ran the place."

"I'm sorry. I shouldn't have pried," Leigh said, realizing that her question brought back unhappy memories for him. Even though her own childhood had been difficult, it wasn't nearly as sad. Still, she could relate to his feeling of being alone with few connections.

James brushed off her apology. "It wasn't a bad childhood. The teachers and counselors at the orphanage were kind, for the most part. And now I think of the church and the people at the mission as my family, so I've more than made up for the one I lacked growing up."

Leigh had to smile, surprised at how he was able to turn an awkward moment into something brighter.

"How about you, Leigh? Did you grow up in a big family?"

"No, not at all. It was just me and my mom. My father died when I was about five — a car accident. My mother loved him very much. She never wanted to remarry. She died about five years ago, still living in Ohio, where I grew up. I really miss her," Leigh added honestly.

"Sorry to hear that. Were you very close?"

Leigh nodded. "Yes, we were. She really encouraged me and tried to help me in any way she could. It was hard for her to send me east to college, but she thought it would be best for me, so she did. I didn't see her much once I moved to New England. I regret that. I came to go to school and ended up staying."

"What did you study?" he asked curiously.

"Fine art. I wanted to be a painter . . . but that didn't work out."

He didn't respond at first; instead he seemed to study her with a thoughtful expression.

"You're still young. You have lots of time to pursue it."

"Theoretically, I suppose. Once the baby comes, though, I doubt I'll be doing much artwork. . . . Maybe when *she* goes off to college."

His mouth tilted up in a charming half smile. "Don't wait that long."

She smiled back, then stared out at the ocean, suddenly realizing that she had told him a lot about herself, a lot that was actually true. How had that happened? She hadn't meant to. It was just that easy way he had of talking and asking questions that had caught her off guard.

I'll have to be more careful in the future or I'll wind up giving myself away.

"When will you go back to the mission?" she asked, wanting to turn the conversation back to him. "Do you know?"

He shrugged and sighed. "Soon, I hope. I wanted to get back for the holidays, but I don't have a doctor's stamp of approval yet. We never know what God has in mind, do we? I guess He has the final say."

"Is that what it is?" she asked softly. Her own life had taken so many unexpected twists and turns. Whether you wanted to call it fate or destiny or the hand of God, it didn't much matter. It still seemed undeniably true that she had very limited control over the shape of her life. Yet, she didn't feel able to share all that with James — not now, probably never.

James picked up a handful of sand and let it sift slowly through his fingers. Leigh watched it fall, reminded of watching sand in an hourglass. When he spoke again, his voice was brighter, more upbeat.

"A friend of mine once told me that life is like booking a hotel room over the Internet. You have this false sense of confidence that you know what you're getting, but once you get there it's always different from what you expected." He grinned. "I've never booked a hotel room over the Internet, but I still found it an amusing way to look at things."

"It is." Leigh found herself smiling again, too. She hoped he'd be able to return to his mission soon. It seemed so important to him.

Where would she be by then? Long gone from this place. She suddenly felt uneasy, drawing so close to him, talking about such personal matters. What was the point? In a few days, she'd be gone and they'd never see each other again.

She turned and looked down the beach. "Look at the light. You can really see it now."

The sun had started to set in the winter sky, and the thin beam from the lighthouse was clearly visible, sweeping over the beach and rolling sea.

"It's beautiful, isn't it?" James said. "Lighthouses seem so charming to us now — quaint, scenic relics of another era. But in the days before radio and electronic signals, they were critical to life up here. Keeping the light was an important job. That beam must have guided thousands and saved countless lives at sea."

"Probably," Leigh agreed, looking back at the light. "But it must have been lonely living there in the winter, even if you had a family."

"Ideal if you play the bagpipes, though. Especially rather badly." She could see from his expression he was teasing her again. "But I know what you mean. You'd need to be a certain kind of person. Still, everyone has their talents." He smiled at her. "You never told me what you do for a living, Leigh. I mean, what you did in

Boston before you left to see your friend in Wellfleet. Is it some kind of work related to your art?"

Leigh felt her mouth go dry. She hated lying to him. She felt so comfortable talking with him like this, and he was so trusting. *But I can't help it. I can't tell him the truth.*

She shrugged her shoulders and pulled out her gloves. "No, not at all," she lied. "I was never able to make a living with art. I just did . . . this and that. I worked in stores and offices, whatever I could find."

Before James could ask any more questions, a sudden puff of wind whipped off her hat. Leigh felt her short curls blowing around her face as she stood up and saw the wool hat tumbling down the beach. James jumped up and took after it.

She watched him chase it along the sand, the wind jerking it out of his reach a few times just as he made a grab for it. Then finally, the hat landed in a tall clump of beach grass and stuck there.

James plucked it out and started back to her. She could see that he was breathing heavily again.

"Here you go." He brushed off some sand and handed it back. "That's a nice hat. It suits you."

Once again she didn't know how to respond to his compliment. "Thanks. Sorry to make you chase after it. The wind picked up a lot. I didn't even notice." She tried to put her hat back on, but it was an impossible task as her thick hair seemed to be blowing wildly in every direction.

"Would you like me to hold your hat while you fix your hair?"

"Um, no . . . no, thanks." She quickly bunched up her hat and stuck it in her pocket. "My hair is so thick. It's such a nuisance sometimes."

"It's a beautiful nuisance then."

Leigh glanced up at him, and a certain look in his eyes surprised her. It had been a long time since a man had looked at her that way. She had to admit, it did her ego good, but she felt awkward again. Maybe she was just imagining it.

Feeling self-conscious, she looked away, back up at the lighthouse again.

"I'm sorry, James. I don't think I can make it the rest of the way. It feels too cold now that the sun is going down."

The temperature had dropped, but that wasn't the real reason she said she didn't want to stay. She knew she had to bring the outing to a close.

In his own quiet way he's dangerous to me.

So no matter how kind or charming he is, I can't let myself get too close.

"That's okay," he quickly agreed. He leaned over and picked up his pipes, taking one last long look at the ocean.

Maybe I've saved him the trouble of admitting he feels too tired for the rest of the walk, she thought.

"We'll come back another day and do it, okay?"

She nodded and stuck her hands in her pockets as they began the slow trek back over the sand. "Sure. Another day."

Jessica set some dishes and napkins on the table. She checked the oven but the pizza didn't seem hot enough yet. That was the problem with living so far from town. When you ordered takeout it inevitably arrived cold, that is, if the restaurant would even deign to deliver.

Sam walked in from the TV room and set an empty glass in the sink. He had been watching football all afternoon, ever since they had come home from her mother's house. They had barely spoken. Which was just as well, Jessica thought, since he still seemed a bit moody.

But someone has to bring up the subject of Darrell, she thought, *so it might as well be me.*

"I've been thinking about the bean jar," she started off slowly. "I guess we'll have to pay for it, though I doubt it's worth nearly as much as Mother claims."

Sam sat at the table and opened the newspaper, barely glancing at her. "That's okay. Just write her a check."

If only it was that easy, Jessica thought. If only handing her mother a check would buy her silence. Jessica anticipated hearing recriminations over this for years to come.

"You know my mother. She might not take the money, just to prove her point."

"What point is that?"

"That the jar was irreplaceable." *And that we should have never brought Darrell to her house, uninvited . . . and unwanted.* Jessica thought the words but didn't dare say them aloud.

"I know it was valuable, but I don't understand the big fuss. It was just . . . a ceramic vase. She has a million of them."

"Maybe I could look for one like it at antique dealers. Or maybe I'll find one on the Internet. People say you can find all sorts of things at those auction sites."

"Whatever." Sam shook his head. "If your mother had half a heart, she wouldn't make such a big deal about it. Darrell apologized to her. And she just sat there like a fire-breathing dragon."

"Well, what did you expect her to do?"

"She could have said 'Thanks' or 'I accept your apology.' Or even 'Okay.' It wasn't easy for him to face her like that. I know how a kid's mind works at that age. He wanted to just cut and run, but he stuck it out and took his medicine. I don't think she sent him the right message. She could have been more gracious. Then he would have learned a real lesson."

"Sam, really. This is my mother we're talking about. Besides, she had every right to be upset. He went through her house like wrecking crew —"

"He broke a bean jar, Jessica. It wasn't the end of the world. Meanwhile, she said some very harsh things about him. You did, too," he pointed out honestly. "And I saw his expression. What Lillian said hurt his feelings. Frankly, I think that's far more important than some stupid vase. If you ask me, she was the one who owed him the apology."

Jessica swallowed hard. She'd heard what her mother had said, too. It was hard to defend her and equally hard to defend herself, too. Impossible, actually.

But on the other hand, that didn't let Darrell off the hook in her book. Nor did it mean that they weren't obligated to make some amends.

"What my mother said was wrong," Jessica admitted. "And what I said was wrong, too. I guess I just lost my temper. And I thought Darrell was upstairs. I never thought he'd hear me."

Sam just raised a dark, skeptical eyebrow.

"And that was after he acted out," she plunged on. "My mother was so upset. I didn't know what to do. . . ."

Sam glanced at her and shook his head. "I know you were upset. I hate to see your mother get to you like that, Jess. But honestly, all things considered, I thought Darrell's behavior was pretty good."

"Pretty good?"

"Think about it. Where is this kid coming from? His mother is a drug addict, in and out of rehab. He's never even met his father. He's been shifted around, living in foster homes, sometimes even in shelters with his mother. He's never once finished a grade in the same school, Luke told me. So considering all that, I can understand why he doesn't have very good table manners. Can you?"

Jessica felt her heart sink. Sam's tone was quiet but censuring.

"Yes . . . yes, of course I can. I know he's had a terrible time. He wouldn't be at New Horizons otherwise." She ran her hand through her hair and sighed. Once again, she was caught like a deer in the headlights, between her mother's imperious demands and her husband's big-hearted principles.

She let out a long breath, feeling guilty for not having more sympathy for Darrell, for failing to show more charity and compassion, for not having more control over her own emotions.

"You're right, of course." He was, too, though sometimes her mother's demands clouded her vision and it took her a while to see her way clear.

"Thank you." Sam nodded but didn't quite look at her. She could see he was still fired up but probably willing to drop the subject if she did. Still, she couldn't quite let it go, not when everything about Darrell Lester made her so uncomfortable.

"He doesn't seem to like me much. Today I just made it worse."

"Who, Darrell?" Sam seemed surprised by her observation, though she thought it was perfectly obvious. "Don't worry. He likes you."

"I'm not worried about it. I've just noticed it, that's all." Jessica opened the oven again and took out the pizza. She placed it in the middle of the table and served herself a slice. "Maybe he doesn't want to share you with anyone."

"Come on, you're being silly. He just needs to get to know you better. He's a great kid, honestly."

"If you say so. You know him a lot better than I do. How long is he staying at New Horizons?"

"I'm not sure. Until January, I think."

It wasn't all that long, Jessica told herself. She would manage to stick it out. The boy was important to Sam, for some reason she couldn't quite understand. Maybe he was a substitute, a way for Sam to deal with his own disappointment about not having a child of their own yet. She knew Sam loved her. They were best friends, as well as man and wife. But there were some things she knew he didn't share with her, and those feelings were part of it.

Maybe by the time Darrell leaves I'll be pregnant, Jessica thought hopefully. It was possible.

When the pizza was finished there wasn't much to clean up. They worked together, clearing the table and cleaning up the kitchen.

Sam turned on the dishwasher and dimmed the kitchen light. "Man, I'm beat. I'm working in Gloucester tomorrow. I'll probably be home late."

"Gloucester? But we have a doctor's appointment. It's with that new specialist in Southport. Did you forget?"

"Gee . . . I guess it slipped my mind." Sam paused, looking abashed, even in the dim light. "What time were we supposed to be there?"

"Four-thirty. We need to get there a little earlier to fill out some forms."

He was quiet for a moment, and she wondered if he was going to ask her to cancel the appointment. Had he given up on their having a baby? He glanced at her, then touched her shoulder. "Four-thirty. No problem. Just write down the address. I'll be there."

Jessica stepped closer and quickly hugged him. She realized that tears had welled up in her eyes and hoped that Sam hadn't noticed. "Okay, I will. I'll leave it on the kitchen table. Thanks."

He put his arms around her and gave her a tight hug back. Jessica squeezed her eyes closed; after the day's tension it felt so good to be back in his arms.

"You don't need to thank me, sweetheart. We're in this together. I want a baby as much as you do."

Jessica didn't answer. She knew how much Sam wanted a child. That made it easier for her . . . and harder sometimes, too.

Chapter Five

Leigh walked to Harbor Auto on Thursday during her lunch hour. Art Kroger, the mechanic there, had called the day before to say her car would be ready by noon.

"What do you think?" Art asked as she looked over the car.

"Oh, it looks great." It did look fine, as good as ever. But Leigh realized she had mixed emotions. She'd been so eager to have the car finished, and now that it was ready, she wasn't nearly so eager to leave town.

"It's running good, too. You don't have to worry. Of course, if there's any problem, let us know."

"Thanks, but I'm probably leaving here tomorrow."

"Oh, sure. That's right." He nodded and handed her the keys. "Well, you have a good trip."

Leigh smiled at him. "Aren't you forgetting something?" When he stared back blankly, she added, "You never gave me the bill, Mr. Kroger."

"Oh, that's been taken care of. Reverend Cameron stopped in last night, took care of everything. I thought you knew."

Leigh took a breath, feeling surprised. "No . . . I didn't."

She and James had already talked this over. She knew that his insurance wouldn't cover all of the repairs. She had told him she wanted to pay some share, but he had never given her a firm answer about it one way or the other. Now she knew why. James had been harboring a secret plan to swoop in and pay for everything.

"I guess I'll have to speak with him about it."

"Yeah, I guess so." Art Kroger looked puzzled as he helped her into her car and waved good-bye.

Leigh pulled out of the station and drove past the harbor. She spotted the church at the far end of the village green and considered stopping there to speak to James, but she didn't have enough time. She needed to get back to Dr. Harding's office. Even though it was her last day, she didn't want to leave on a bad note; she knew Nancy Malloy was watching the reception area and was eager to get out herself.

When Leigh walked into the office she found Nancy seated at the front desk, handing a file to Dr. Harding.

"How's your car? Is it all fixed now?" Dr. Harding asked.

"Good as new . . . well, I bought it secondhand, so it's good as used, I guess."

Nancy chuckled as she stood up to get her coat. The office was in one of its temporary lulls. The waiting room stood empty, and there didn't appear to be anyone in the exam room either.

Leigh stopped at one of the lamp tables and straightened a pile of magazines.

"We'll be sorry to see you go, Leigh. Any chance we could persuade you to stay a little longer?"

Leigh looked up at Dr. Harding, surprised at the request.

"Amy Mueller, my regular receptionist, just called. She needs to stay with her family a few weeks longer and says she can't come back now until after the holidays," he explained.

"Gee . . . I'm not really sure." Leigh mulled over the possibility. Should she stay here? Working those extra few weeks until the baby was born would help her limited finances.

She had sold her fancy car, the one Martin had given her, for a fairly large sum. But then she'd had to buy a car, something safe enough for the baby. A good car, even used, wasn't cheap. She still had some money left over, of course. But without health insurance she knew having the baby would deplete another large chunk. And then she would need some money to set up another apartment, for a security deposit and rent and furniture. And she still had several weeks until the baby came. She was using money every day just to live. She'd even put off doctor visits in order to save, though she knew it wasn't very wise. If she started on the road again, she would be using up the small gain she had made so far, and she wasn't likely to find another job so easily.

Still, was she safe here? That was the big question. There had been no further news from Alice about Martin's attempts to find her. Alice suspected he was distracted by his business problems, but she couldn't say for sure if he had given up his search. Nobody could.

Leigh sighed, weighing the pros and cons. She felt both Dr. Harding and Nancy watching her, waiting for her answer.

"I'll give you a raise. How's that sound?"

Dr. Harding grinned, and Leigh wondered if he thought she was hesitating on purpose.

"Don't be silly. The salary is fine." Leigh thought he was already paying her very generously, probably out of relief at finding some reliable help in his emergency or maybe because he felt sorry for her. "It's just that this offer is a surprise," she explained. "I'm not sure what to do."

Nancy gave Leigh an encouraging look. "I hope you'll stay, Leigh. For one thing, you're so organized. Those temps from the agency are so scatterbrained sometimes. They come in for a day and mess up everything."

Leigh felt honored to have earned the highly efficient Nancy's approval but couldn't really let that factor into her decision. "Can I think it over and tell you at the end of the day?"

"Excellent idea. Think it over," Dr. Harding said, turning back toward his office. "Just don't forget my offer to raise your salary."

Leigh nodded. It was hard to imagine a nicer place to work or a more considerate boss. She glanced down at her ever-expanding stomach. *What do you think, baby?* she asked silently. *Can we risk it?*

* * *

James returned to Vera's house on Thursday night and pulled his car up the long gravel driveway, parking behind Leigh's tan compact. He shut off the engine and stared at Leigh's car, feeling wistful. The shop had told him that the repairs were done and Leigh had picked up the car earlier in the day.

But maybe I was secretly hoping for some other delay. If her car is here, she'll be gone soon, he reasoned. *Probably not tonight — it's late to start the drive out to Cape Cod — but tomorrow or the day after.*

James walked slowly up the path to the side door, toward the warm yellow light shining in the kitchen window. He saw Vera there, making dinner. Leigh stood beside her, helping, as she usually did, a patient audience for Vera's scattered conversation.

Vera will miss her. Then he caught himself. *I guess I'll miss her, too.*

He hadn't realized that. Or hadn't wanted to face it. *She's only been here a few days, not even a week, but I will miss her.* Their walk on the beach had changed something. Though she never completely let down her guard, she seemed more relaxed with him these past few days. He wondered if she was always so reserved or if that held-back quality was connected to her husband's death. She had such a heavy load to bear and did it without complaint. He had hoped to help her more somehow — as a friend. *As a Christian,* he told himself.

And she'll need a lot of help once her baby comes. I hope her friend in Wellfleet is up to the job. I'll ask her to keep in touch, just in case. I'll still want to know how she's doing.

James let himself into the mudroom and slipped off his coat.

"Is that you, James?" he heard Vera call in her singsong voice. "We've been waiting for you."

James felt himself smiling despite his downcast mood. Of course it was him. Who else would it be?

"I'm sorry I'm late. I was held up at church."

As he walked into the kitchen he saw Leigh first, arranging some flowers in a dark blue glass jug. She had a certain way of doing things, he noticed, a creative touch. He hadn't been surprised when she told him she once wanted to be an artist.

She glanced over her shoulder and smiled at him. "Aren't these pretty? Molly Willoughby gave them to me. She had some left over from a party."

"Put those on the table, dear. Perfect for our celebration."

Vera picked a lid up off a pot and stirred something inside. "Leigh got her car back."

"Yes, I noticed. It looks good." James took a seat at the table, willing himself to sound composed.

Obviously, Leigh's departure wasn't a big deal to Vera. A celebration, she called it? Maybe she was trying to put an upbeat face on the situation. Leigh must be happy to be leaving, he realized.

Leigh set the jug of flowers in the middle of the table and took a seat across from him. The steamy kitchen had made her hair even curlier, he noticed, with thick, tight curls falling over her forehead and framing her face. She had a lovely face, oval-shaped with clear skin and dark eyes. A small dimple marked her chin; he had never noticed that before. He felt now as if he needed to study her, commit her image to memory. Then he realized he must be staring.

He picked up the newspaper from the chair and snapped it open. "Maybe you should drive your car around a day or two and test it out. You don't want to get stuck somewhere on the way to Wellfleet."

"She's not going to Cape Cod. At least not yet." Vera stood at the head of the table, obviously pleased to deliver her announcement.

Behind the shield of the opened newspaper, James felt his heart take a joyous, if disbelieving, leap. How could she be staying? Had he misunderstood something?

He slowly put the paper down and glanced at Leigh, but it was Vera who continued to explain. "Dr. Harding's receptionist can't come back until after the holidays, so he asked Leigh to stay until then."

"I thought about it awhile and decided I should." Leigh looked down at the table and smoothed the cloth under her hand. "For one thing, I'd like to pay you and Vera back for all the kindness you've shown me the last few days. And I want to pay for my share of the car repairs."

She fixed him with a stern look, and he couldn't help but answer with a smile. He'd known she would be annoyed when she found out he had paid the bill.

"Don't be silly. You don't have to worry about that, I've already told you."

"Don't worry about me, either." Vera

put in. "You need all your money for the baby now."

That was certainly true, James thought. He had been trying not to pry, but as far as he could tell, Leigh didn't seem to be in any way prepared for the child's arrival.

"What about your friend?" he asked.

Leigh looked confused at the question. "Oh . . . my friend in Wellfleet, you mean? She was actually relieved to hear I was going to stay. Her mother was in the hospital and is getting out later this week. My friend will be caring for her while she recovers. As it turns out, if I had made it there last week, I would be a major unwanted guest right now."

James couldn't believe the surge of happiness that filled him. It was as if someone had just turned on the lights in a dark room.

"Well, you're wanted here." Vera touched Leigh's shoulder as she carried a bowl to the table. "It's funny the way things work out. I think the good Lord wanted Leigh to end up right here all along. Don't you, Reverend James?"

Those were his very thoughts, though he didn't feel as free as Vera did to share them.

"That might be." He glanced across the

table and smiled at Leigh. "Now we'll have another chance to try that hike to the lighthouse."

"Before I get too huge, you mean," she added with a laugh.

James laughed, too, then realized that if Leigh stayed until the holidays, she would most likely have her baby in Cape Light. That was an awesome thought. He would get to see the baby. He felt unaccountably happy about that, too.

The night of the accident, when he first heard Leigh's story, he had felt that perhaps she came into his life so he could help her. James realized now that he had been given a second chance. Grateful, he resolved that this time he wouldn't waste it. He would make a better effort to really help her and her child. Maybe that was God's plan, after all.

"You need to hold the paddle lower, honey. Swing across your body."

Jessica sighed and blew a strand of hair out of her eyes. She tried again, swinging wildly and missing the ball by a mile. She couldn't help it. She had never played racquetball before. Well, maybe once, and she had hated it equally then. The only reason she had come along on this outing to

Sports Zone was because Sam asked her to.

Behind her she could hear Darrell snickering. Sam glanced over his shoulder and gave the boy a warning look. Then he picked up the small blue racquetball, which seemed to bounce as if it had supernatural properties whenever she touched it though it was totally tame in his hands.

"Okay, Jess. Let me show you one more time."

Jessica waved her racquet at him. "That's all right. You just go ahead. I'll try to hit it if it whizzes by."

"Okay. Let's play." Sam turned and served the ball. She knew he was holding back, trying to serve gently for her sake, but the ball still eluded her. She swatted her paddle and missed again, feeling foolish but trying to hide it.

Behind her, she could hear Darrell's sneakers squeaking on the polished wooden floor as he ran and dove for the ball. He dipped down and whacked it, nearly falling on the floor with his effort.

He looked so thrilled to make contact, Jessica had to smile at the sight of his face.

The ball pinged off the ceiling and then the wall. Jessica felt as if she were trapped inside a pinball machine as she tried to follow it.

"Get ready, Jess. That's yours. Here it comes . . . ," Sam coached her.

"All right. I've got it. . . ." Jessica ran toward the ball but totally mistimed her swing. Once again, her paddle swished through thin air while the ball dribbled off in another direction entirely.

"Oh, man . . ." Darrell tried to keep the volley going, but the ball had lost its momentum and rolled weakly toward him. He picked it up, looking frustrated. Jessica could see the boy wanted to play at a much more vigorous pace than she was capable of. They had taken him here as a special treat and now, thanks to Jessica, he was clearly being robbed of his fun. "Can I serve this time?" he asked Sam.

Before Sam could answer, Jessica said, "Why don't you come up here and take my place? You guys can play one on one. I think I need a little break."

Sam looked at her curiously. "We just started playing. Do you feel okay?"

"I'm fine, really." Jessica headed for the camouflaged door in the far corner of the court. She couldn't help but notice how Darrell suddenly perked up.

Jessica found her gym bag outside the court's door and pulled out a bottle of water. This morning when Sam had suggested this outing, she tried to tell him that Sports Zone was not her zone. But Sam, in his charming way, had cajoled her into coming.

Now she watched Sam and Darrell through the window, going full out as the little blue ball ricocheted madly around the room. Darrell made a tough point and they whooped and hollered, playing their hearts out.

Sam's point in getting her to come along, of course, was to bring her and Darrell together on neutral ground, to show her that the boy wasn't the "horrid little creature" her mother thought he was.

Despite Sunday's misadventure, Jessica didn't think badly of Darrell. But apparently, it wasn't enough to accept him from a distance. For reasons she still didn't understand, Sam seemed determined that she and Darrell really get along.

Sam stepped out of the court just as she drained her water bottle. "Why don't you come back in? You play with Darrell. I'll sit out."

Jessica glanced at the boy. He rarely spoke to her directly, but she had become expert at translating his eloquent facial expressions. He looked as if Sam had just suggested a lunch of spinach and sautéed liver.

"I don't think —" she began.

But Sam wasn't giving up. "Come on, Jess. Show the kid your stuff. Don't wimp out on me."

She met her husband's dark eyes and read his unspoken message. She had retreated to the sidelines and he wanted her to try again. To make contact with the ball — and the kid.

She took a breath and picked up her paddle. *I can do this,* she told herself. *So what if I look like a chicken running around with her head cut off? It's just a game, for goodness' sake. And he's just a little boy.*

"Okay. I'll play," she agreed.

Sam leaned forward, kissed her cheek quickly, and murmured, "You're an angel."

"Don't you forget it," she replied as she stepped back into the court. Darrell stared at her with a neutral expression as she said, "Why don't we just hit around a little? We don't have to play a real game. You want to serve first?"

Her young opponent seemed pleased by the suggestion. "Cool. Ready?"

To Darrell's credit, he didn't try to kill the ball and humiliate her totally. The ball bounded just ahead of her and she ran toward it. Luck was with her. Jessica managed to stand in the right place at the right time. She held out her racquet, made contact, and the ball gently bounced toward Darrell again, an easy shot for him to return.

They volleyed back and forth for a while. Jessica felt some of her tennis skills finally kicking in and was able to keep up without too much trouble. *Gee, I'm practically enjoying this,* she thought. She smiled over at Darrell, but his expression was serious, his playing intense despite the nongame.

Was he trying to show off for Sam? she wondered. The boy seemed to feel he was in some sort of competition with her for Sam's attention. But that's just because he's had so little, she reminded herself. He doesn't know that with someone like Sam, there's always enough to go around.

The ball whizzed past her and she realized she had lost focus. "I didn't even see that one. Good shot, Darrell."

She picked up the ball and glanced at her partner. He returned a grudging smile, looking pleased with himself.

She served the ball again, trying her best to keep the ball in play. *If Darrell enjoys himself out here with me, he might like me a little better,* she thought. *Maybe it will even make up a bit for the way I lost my temper on Sunday.* She wanted to apologize to him for that but so far hadn't found the chance.

They rallied a while longer before Sam called, "Time to wrap it up."

"Already?" Jessica looked at the clock, surprised to see their court time was almost up.

Sam came onto the court. "Hey, great game, guys. You were both awesome." He walked over to Darrell and put his arm around his shoulder. "Why don't we have some lunch and see what we want to do next?"

"Those minicars look cool," Darrell said as they started toward the food court.

"Yeah, they do look fun," Sam agreed.

Jessica walked behind, feeling like a third wheel again and not quite sure if Sam's plan for a day of fun and bonding was really working. Her racquetball rally with Darrell went as well as it could, but it hadn't really changed anything between them.

The dining area, called Munchie Zone, was in the center of the sports complex. Sam found them a table from which they could view several different activity areas: basketball, floor hockey, volleyball, and a corner where there seemed to be a massive water balloon fight in progress.

"What would you like to eat?" Sam asked her.

"Anything . . . I don't care. A salad or something?"

He rolled his eyes. Okay, so he wasn't going to find a salad here, not even a deep-fried one. "How about pizza or a hot dog?" he suggested.

"A hot dog would be okay. And a diet cola," Jessica turned to Darrell. "How about you, Darrell? What would you like for lunch?"

"Pizza and coke," he answered quickly.

"You got it," Sam told him. "The line doesn't look too bad; I'll be right back."

Darrell looked suddenly alarmed and glanced from Sam to Jessica. "Can I come with you? I could help you carry stuff."

Sam considered the offer a moment. "I can handle it. You wait here with Jessica."

Darrell looked unhappy at the answer but sank back into his seat. He sighed and stared out at the nearby basketball court, his chin resting in his hand. Jessica felt distinctly snubbed. Darrell obviously didn't want to sit alone with her, not even for as long as it might take for Sam to buy a few hot dogs and sodas.

Hey, I'm good with kids, she reminded herself. *Molly's girls adore me. I can win this kid over. He's not such a tough customer.* Jessica caught his eye across the table and smiled. He didn't smile back, but at least he stopped ignoring her.

"So . . . how's it going at New Horizons, Darrell? Do you like it there?"

He shrugged. "It's okay. They make us work a lot — schoolwork and homework. We help make the food, clean up the dishes. Stuff like that."

"Sounds like you do work hard."

"I'm only there because if I didn't go, I'd have to be in jail instead."

"Is that so?"

He nodded. "Absolutely. The policeman put the handcuffs right on me. Just like you see on TV."

"Wow . . . that must have been scary for you."

"I wasn't scared," he insisted. "I said, 'Go ahead. Lock me up. I'm not scared of you.' "

Jessica suppressed a smile, sure he was trying to act tough, to show off for her. He had a wonderful imagination, that was for sure. She knew for a fact that though this story was true of some other kids there, usually older, it wasn't Darrell's at all. He'd been suspended for truancy, caught wandering around Boston alone when he should have been in school. He may have been caught stealing some food from a convenience store. Jessica wasn't sure. Sam had said his mother was in a drug rehab program, and the social services agency had sent him to New Horizons instead of foster care.

"I guess you miss the city and your family."

He shrugged again. "My mother . . . she's sick. She's not home anyway right now."

"I hope she gets better real soon and you can be with her again."

Darrell's face took on a thoughtful expression. "Yeah, me too." Suddenly, he stared up at her. "Why are you saying all this stuff to me? You don't even know my mother."

Jessica felt stung but she also saw that he had a point. She shouldn't have gotten so personal so quickly. He was upset about his mother and maybe even ashamed of her situation, and Jessica, who barely knew him, had no right to pry.

"That's true. I don't know your mother," she said slowly. "But I know you, and —"

Darrell shook his head. "You don't know me. You don't even like me."

"I do like you," she insisted. "I like you very much."

Was that true? she asked herself. She

didn't feel close to the boy, and she was fairly certain he didn't care much for her. Mostly, she felt sorry for him.

"It's okay. You don't have to lie to me. I heard what you said at your mother's house when I went upstairs to wash up. When you thought I couldn't hear."

Jessica felt her cheeks flush with shame. "I was upset, Darrell," she admitted. "I really didn't mean it, honestly . . . I just lost my temper, I guess. I've been meaning to apologize to you, but I didn't know how to bring it up." Her excuse sounded weak, and she had an awful feeling that she had just made everything worse.

He gave another of his shrugs and stared out at the basketball players again. "Lots of grown-ups think I'm bad. You don't have to act all nice and lie about it just because Sam is around."

Jessica started to reply then stopped. She felt painted neatly into a corner. No matter what she said now, he'd argue with her. No matter what she did today, she couldn't seem to get it right.

Sam suddenly appeared beside the table; he set down the loaded tray and took a seat. "Sorry that took so long. There was this guy in front of me ordering about a hundred hamburgers."

He handed out the paper plates of food, seeming not to notice that Jessica and Darrell were so quiet. Jessica stared down at a cold, partially cooked hot dog on a stiff-looking roll. It didn't matter; her appetite had already vanished.

"I took another look at the minicars. They do look cool. They really move, too." Sam's voice was bright and excited, just like another kid. "How about we do those next?"

Darrell chewed his pizza with a thoughtful expression. He looked up at Sam and then at Jessica. In his dark eyes, Jessica could see a question. He was wondering now if she was going to tell Sam what he had said.

She sighed and took a sip of her drink. She wasn't sure what to do. She told Sam just about everything. On the other hand, she didn't want to seem as if she could only see negative traits in the boy. Sam would just remind her how tough Darrell had it and how that was why he acted the way he did, all of which was true.

She did feel sorry for him. And she did *want* to like him. She couldn't help it if he didn't like her. How could she be friends with him if he wouldn't let her?

"What do you think, Jess? The line

doesn't look that long right now."

Sam's voice broke into her wandering thoughts and Jessica blinked. "Gee . . . I don't know. They seem sort of noisy."

"You didn't eat your hot dog. Should I get you something else?" Sam looked at her with concern.

"Oh, no, thanks. Why don't you and Darrell try the cars? I think I'm going to head home. The racquetball was more of workout than I'm used to, and that new medicine I'm taking makes me feel tired."

The specialist they saw in Southport had prescribed some pills he hoped would help her get pregnant. Jessica had only been taking them a few days and they did make her tired; she wasn't lying about that. Luckily, she had needed to do some errands this morning while Sam picked up Darrell, so they came in two cars.

"All right. I'll meet you at home then." Sam still looked worried. "Do you want me to drive you back?"

"I'm just a little tired. I'm fine to drive home," she assured him. Though she was touched by Sam's concern, she didn't want him to cut short his outing with Darrell on her account. That would undoubtedly breed even more resentment from the boy, and things were already tense enough.

Jessica got up from her chair and picked up her bag. She kissed Sam on the cheek and patted his shoulder.

"Have fun in the cars. I think you'd better drive, Darrell. Sam gets a little wild in those rides," she added, trying to part on a light note.

"I will if he lets me." Darrell's expression was solemn as they parted, and Jessica felt a twinge of sadness, though she wasn't sure why.

Out in the parking lot, the bright sunlight and relative quiet was a welcome relief to the dim, raucous interior of the Sports Zone. Jessica felt instantly calmer and more clearheaded as she started up her car and pulled away.

She felt relieved but also a bit guilty for abandoning the outing halfway. Sam would just have to understand. She had come along as he'd asked and done her best. The boy just didn't like her. She couldn't seem to do anything right where Darrell was concerned. Some things just weren't meant to be.

Chapter Six

Leigh had pretended to be asleep when Vera knocked on her bedroom door earlier that morning. Now she sat on the edge of her bed, fully dressed, carefully calculating how long it would be before both Vera and James left for the Sunday church service.

James never mentioned a word about church to her. But she knew that Vera would coax her again to come along, and she wanted to avoid the conversation.

At a quarter to eleven, Leigh walked down to the kitchen, expecting the house to be empty. She was surprised to hear Vera in the hallway on the phone.

"What do you mean, you can't pick me up until twelve?" Vera sounded nervous and frazzled. "That won't do at all. . . . Well, I've already called that outfit. They won't send a taxi way out here. . . ."

Leigh glanced down the hallway, and Vera quickly turned toward her as she hung up the phone.

"Oh, you're up, dear. I didn't want to wake you, but my car won't start and James left so early for church today. Could you possibly give me a lift into town?"

Finding an appropriate break in Vera's rambling request, Leigh quickly answered, "I can drive you to church, Vera. It's no problem."

"Would you? I'd appreciate that so much. I didn't want to put you out . . . but it is sort of an emergency. It's my turn to bring some cakes and things for the coffee hour. You hate to disappoint people once you make a promise."

Vera was dressed in her coat, hat, and gloves, her bag hooked over her arm. Leigh noticed three foil-covered trays on the kitchen counter and a pleasant, cinnamony scent hanging in the air. She didn't know what time the service started but guessed it must be very soon.

"I'll just grab a glass of orange juice and we can go. I can get some breakfast in town."

Vera watched as she poured the juice and drank it down. "There's always a lovely coffee hour after the service — so much to eat, you won't even want lunch. And James is going to speak today about his mission. It should be very interesting."

Leigh set the dirty glass in the dishwasher, avoiding Vera's searching gaze. "I'm sure it will be. Let me run up and get my bag. I'll be right down."

Up in her room, Leigh found her purse, then paused at the mirror to add a dash of lipstick. She didn't want to go to the church service, but she thought she still ought to look presentable. It was such a small town, faces were already starting to look familiar.

She helped Vera carry the cake pans out to her car and they started off for the village.

"I need to stay at church today for a few hours after the service, so you'll have to fend for yourself at lunchtime. Maybe even dinner, too. I'll probably come back exhausted. The Christmas Fair committee is meeting and I always get roped into doing more than I intend. But it's all for a good cause. I may not have much, compared to some people, but I count my blessings. . . ."

They were driving down Main Street now. Leigh had taken a few walks during her lunch hour to explore the village, so she knew where to find the church. It was really a beautiful little church, she thought, set on the end of the long village green, which was filled with tall trees and bordered on one side by the town's harbor.

"Here we are," Leigh said. "You're not late at all. There are still some people going in. Shall I drop you off in front?"

Though she usually didn't mind Vera's rambling monologues, Leigh was looking forward to being on her own for a cup of decaf coffee and a pile of the Sunday newspapers.

"Yes, right in front would be fine, dear. Oh, the cakes. I almost forgot." Vera glanced at Leigh with another worried look. "Could you help me carry in the pans? It will only take a minute. You'll need to park, though. Look, there's a space." Vera pointed to a nearby parking space that had just become empty.

"Yes, I see it." Leigh put her blinker on and steered her car into the space.

With Vera carrying two of the pans and Leigh holding the third, they proceeded into the church. A woman about Vera's age approached them. She had a friendly, round moon face and wore a coil of white hair on her head that still held a tinge of a former strawberry-blond hue.

"Here, let me help you, Vera. I'll take that back to the kitchen." She reached over and took one of Vera's cake pans. "You'll be at the meeting later, won't you?"

"Yes, of course I will. Sophie, this is Leigh Baxter. She's staying with me awhile. She works in Dr. Harding's office."

The woman smiled and Leigh realized her face was familiar, though she couldn't quite recall her name.

"I'm Sophie Potter," she introduced herself. "I think we met in the doctor's office, though I had a dreadful cold that day and you probably were just trying not to get sneezed on."

Leigh smiled back. "I remember. How are you?"

"Just fine, thanks. Here, let me take your pan, too. Why don't you two get your seats? I think Reverend Ben might even start on time today." Chuckling at her own joke, Sophie swept off to a different part of the church.

"I should get a seat. I'll hang up my coat later." Vera started toward the door to the sanctuary.

"Okay, I'll see you tonight." Leigh headed back in the direction of the vestibule, intending to leave, but she felt someone touch her arm. She turned to see Molly Willoughby.

"Hi, Leigh. Want to sit with us? I think

there's still room in our row. It's a full house today with Reverend Cameron speaking."

Leigh hesitated, wondering if she should stay to hear James. Everyone seemed so excited about it. And he'd been so kind to her. It would seem rude now to run out, especially when she didn't really have anything better to do. Besides, she was genuinely interested in hearing more about his work.

She glanced around for Vera and saw that she was talking to another friend. "I came with Vera but it looks like she's busy. I'll catch up with her later, I guess."

Leigh followed Molly into the sanctuary, where someone handed her a program. The man smiled knowingly at her and she suddenly recognized him, the police officer who had taken the report the night of her accident. Tucker . . . something?

She followed Molly up the side aisle and soon spotted Molly's two girls, Lauren and Jill, who often stopped by the office. They were sitting beside Dr. Harding and his daughter Amanda, whom she also knew by now.

"Look who I found," Molly whispered happily to the group.

"Hi, Leigh. Good to see you," Matt Harding said.

"Leigh! What are you doing here?" Jill's frank question made her mother cringe but Leigh had to grin. It was a good question. She wasn't quite sure herself how she'd wound up here this morning.

"Just scoot over and make some room, please, Jill. And give Leigh your hymnal. You can share with your sister."

Whenever Leigh heard what Molly called her "Commander Mommy" voice she was totally in awe. Mentally, she took notes. She had learned that Molly had more or less raised her girls without her ex-husband's help. Leigh only hoped that she would do as well as a single parent. She was sure it wouldn't be easy.

Settling back in her seat, Leigh glanced around. The church was just as pretty inside as out, simple but elegant and old-fashioned, with cream-colored walls, polished oak pews, and tall stained-glass windows that filtered the light in hues of rose and gold. She saw James sitting in a front row, to the side of the pulpit. Another minister with spectacles and a beard sat beside him. Reverend Lewis, she thought. She'd heard a lot about him from James and Vera, but so far they hadn't met.

James seemed different somehow. She realized it was because he was wearing a long white vestment. It was a bit of a shock to see him in his "work clothes." He didn't make much of being a minister and most of the time she thought of him as just a regular person. Now he seemed to have a kind of solemn authority.

He dispelled that impression at once, smiling as he met her eye and looking surprised but pleased to see her there. She smiled back, but quickly looked away.

The choir sang a hymn to start the service. Leigh spotted Sophie Potter in the second row and a tall young woman with striking looks standing beside her. The resemblance was so strong, Leigh thought they had to be related. She recalled Vera saying Sophie had been recently widowed and that a granddaughter was living with her now. Leigh felt satisfied for a moment at having made the connection, as if fitting a piece into a large puzzle. Then she caught herself, taken aback by how well and quickly she was getting to know the people in this small community.

It's just the job at the doctor's office, she told herself. *I see so many people there every day. It doesn't mean anything. I'm sure I'll forget all about them soon after I go. And they'll forget me.*

Reverend Lewis stepped up to the pulpit

and began to address the congregation. He covered some announcements about church activities, giving special emphasis to the meeting Vera had mentioned. The church Christmas Fair didn't sound like much to Leigh, but it was obviously an important matter here.

Leigh couldn't bear thinking about Christmas. It brought up so many unhappy memories. Even good memories of holidays she spent as a child with her mother seemed bittersweet now. The last few years of her life had soured everything for her.

The service went by quickly with rounds of hymns and prayer, and then Reverend Lewis was introducing James.

"As the holidays draw near, we think of the Helping Hands Mission and our annual outreach to that special community," he began. "Since the mission was started in Nicaragua over fifty years ago, by a minister who formerly headed this congregation, Bible Community Church has maintained a close and special relationship with Helping Hands. The mission is now blessed to have Reverend James Cameron as their director, and for the past few months, we've all shared in that blessing while Reverend Cameron has visited here with us. I've asked him to give us an update on the mission this morning and on the work going on there."

Leigh sat up a bit taller as James came to the pulpit and took Reverend Lewis's place. He looked out over the congregation with his usual warm, easy smile; he might have been saying good morning to her over the breakfast table. Leigh didn't know what she expected but this was not quite it. He seemed so relaxed, so casual, even though he'd now stepped into such a formal, spiritual role.

"I want to thank Reverend Ben for that gracious introduction. I'm not sure I've entirely been a blessing to him, since it seems we both prefer the same section of the morning paper each day." His joke made Leigh smile and drew a few laughs from his audience. "This congregation has been so generous to Helping Hands Mission. Not just at Christmastime, but throughout the year. Yet I don't think that you fully understand what your gifts mean to the people in our community and those who come to us for help. Your donations have provided the simple necessities like nutritious food, blankets, and clothing. Immunization for children who now will live without threat from the most serious childhood diseases, like measles and polio. The schoolbooks that help both children and adults learn to read, or the tools they need to farm their land, or raise livestock, and have a self-sufficient life.

"I do want to update you with specifics, and I have a detailed talk scheduled for this evening, complete with pictures of our school, the new water treatment facility we built last year, and the expansion to our medical clinic which is now under way.

"But when I considered what I really wanted to say to you this morning, I thought about so many of my friends at the mission who came to me and asked me to convey their thanks and tell you their stories, so you could understand how your gifts have truly transformed their lives.

"First, there's Azura Esteban. She's a young woman, still in her early twenties. She gave birth to three children, each of whom died during their first year of life —"

Leigh shuddered inwardly. What if she lost her baby that way? She didn't know what she would do. How did any woman survive that?

"Though our immunization program has helped lower the infant mortality rate, unfortunately it's still quite common for children to die before they reach school age.

Finally, Azura had a fourth child, but that baby became ill with pneumonia. Azura brought her to our mission clinic for treatment, where, by the grace of God, the child was saved.

"That was six years ago. Azura's daughter has grown healthy and strong and now attends our mission school. She tells me she wants to be a doctor someday and help people in her village. I pray that this will be so."

James spoke simply, without any deliberate drama, but his words were powerful and held Leigh and everyone around her riveted.

"There are many stories that don't have happy endings," he went on. "There are many who come to us who are beyond help in this mortal life. All we can do is provide comfort, support their faith, and help them pass on in dignity. There are many who need help beyond our limited resources. Though we'll never be able to solve every problem that comes our way, our goal is to ever expand our reach.

"Above all, I think the greatest gift our mission gives is hope, a light where there was only darkness. And the gift grows tenfold and tenfold again because those whom we help reach out and lift up others, like a handful of seeds tossed on the earth that grow into a garden. That remarkable transformation is God's miracle, the way He takes our small gifts and uses them for His great purposes.

"So please remember that beyond the immediate aid of a hot meal or some new clothes, your gift to our mission gives hope and inspires faith. It's God's love, working through all of us, passed on and on in an endless chain. The impact is immeasurable, and very often, lifesaving."

The congregation was silent. Leigh felt a bit stunned and saddened. It was hard to imagine people who had so little in their lives and struggled so hard just to survive. You knew that people lived at such a desperate level of existence but you didn't want to think about it. It was like passing an accident on the highway; you might glance at it quickly but you just couldn't focus on the gruesome details for very long. It was too disturbing, too upsetting. Most people felt helpless to do anything about such overwhelming problems.

But James had dedicated his life to solving those problems and willingly lived in those conditions, day in and day out. Leigh had always been impressed by him, by his kindness and intellect. This morning, though, she had seen him in a whole different light. He seemed not simply nice or kind but strong and courageous, daring to do difficult, often heartbreaking work.

Martin pretended to be strong, flaunting his wealth and ordering people around like the imperious ruler of a little kingdom. But he was weak, a coward, crippled by his insecurities. He was the very antithesis of James.

Maybe that's what she was doing here, Leigh reflected, recalling Jill's forthright question. God wanted her to hear James talk, to see that there were some truly good people in the world. Not everyone was as small and self-serving as her former husband and his family.

And maybe to see her own self-centeredness, too. She had woken up that morning and hid out in her room from poor Vera. She had been feeling sorry for herself, thinking her life was so difficult. Now it seemed easy in comparison. Yes, she had her problems, plenty of them. But she still had food to eat, a roof over her head, and money in her pocket. She had her health and when the time came she would provide for her baby. She decided she would make a donation today to the mission. She didn't have much money but she had enough.

James's talk had been disturbing but also inspiring. *If people with so little means and so little hope can make their way, so can I. It does take some hope and faith, though,* she thought. She'd been so short on both for so long, like a car running on empty.

The service ended and Leigh was swept along by the crowd leaving the sanctuary, down the main aisle to the doors that opened to the vestibule. Molly glanced over her shoulder and met Leigh's eye. "Just follow along. We won't lose you."

Leigh soon found herself face-to-face with Reverend Lewis. He held out his hand to her, his blue eyes sparkling behind his gold-rimmed spectacles. "Nice to see you this morning. Welcome to Bible Community Church."

"This is Leigh Baxter." James leaned over Reverend Lewis's shoulder, speaking before Leigh could reply. "She's the woman I ran into on the Beach Road."

"Oh, yes, I remember. James tells me you've taken a job and decided to stay in town."

"It's a beautiful town." Leigh forced a smile. News certainly traveled fast around here. She glanced at James, wondering what else he had said about her. "The job is only temporary, until Dr. Harding's secretary comes back."

Reverend Lewis smiled again. "I hope you enjoy it here, no matter how long."

"Thank you, Reverend. I enjoyed the service," she added.

"Good. Maybe we'll see you again."

"Maybe . . ." Leigh's voice drifted off. She didn't want to lie, but she didn't know what else to say. She wasn't much of a churchgoer, not since she was a little girl and her mother used to take her. When she went to college she fell out of the habit.

The line ahead of her moved forward, and she found herself facing James. He held out his hand and she shook it. It seemed a funny thing to do, considering they saw each other all the time.

His grip on her hand was warm and strong. "It's good to see you this morning, Leigh. I was so surprised when I looked out and saw you sitting there."

He was also so honest about his feelings. As usual, it caught her off guard.

"Vera had trouble starting her car so I gave her a lift. Your talk was very interesting . . . and very moving," she admitted. "I'd really like to hear more about the mission sometime."

"Anytime at all. I have some photographs back at the house. I can show you some of my friends, the ones I spoke about."

"I'd like that." Leigh suddenly realized that she was holding up the line. "Well . . . I'd better catch up with Vera."

"Okay. See you." James watched for a moment as she walked away.

Leigh glanced around for Vera but ended up meeting Molly again. "Have you seen Vera?" Leigh asked her.

Molly quickly scanned the crowd. "She must have gone to the Christmas Fair meeting."

"Can you show me where it is? I just want to let her know I'm leaving." Leigh knew she could probably ask Molly to convey the message, but she wanted to make sure Vera had a ride home.

"I think they're meeting in the all-purpose room. It's this way." Molly led Jessica through the church and then through a set of double doors.

The big room looked exactly the way it sounded, Leigh thought. There were folding tables with cake and coffee on one end, a piano in one corner, and long drapes over one wall, concealing storage and possibly a small stage. The polished wood floor could have been either a basketball court or a dance floor.

Most of the congregation was now gathered here, talking and laughing, with children who had just come from Sunday school chasing each other around the big space.

"I see Vera back there with Sophie Potter." Molly directed Leigh to a group at the far end of the room that was gathered around a square table. As Leigh began to walk toward them Molly touched her arm again. "Oh, wait. Here comes my big lug of a brother. I want to introduce you."

Molly's brother was a big man but not quite what Leigh would call a lug. His striking good looks and brilliant smile were distinctly unluglike. A very pretty woman walked beside him, also greeting Molly with a smile. Leigh assumed she must be Jessica, Sam's wife, whom Molly had mentioned.

Molly quickly introduced Leigh to the couple, extravagantly praising her work at Dr. Harding's office. "It was like a miracle, I mean it. She just dropped in out of the blue and saved the day. I think she's even better with the patients than Amy. But don't tell Amy I said that — if she ever comes back, that is."

Jessica met Leigh's eyes and smiled, then

her gaze wandered lower, taking in her pregnancy, unmistakable beneath Leigh's sweater. For just a moment Leigh thought she saw the woman's clear blue eyes cloud over with a troubled expression.

"Amy will be back," Leigh said. "I just spoke to her on Tuesday."

"We'll see. She's always been a little flaky." Molly shook her head and turned her attention to her brother. "Are you going to Mom and Dad's for Thanksgiving? Mom said she wasn't sure."

"Gee, I guess I forgot to call her. Sure, we'll be there." Sam said.

Leigh noticed Jessica glance at her husband then back at Molly. "Will there be a big crowd?"

"Just the usual suspects — five hundred adults and ten million kids. I'm doing some of the cooking so that should help her out a little."

"I can bring something. I'll call your mom tonight and see what she needs."

"Holiday prep talk. I don't think I'm ready for this yet. You'll have to excuse me." Sam gave them a charming grin as he headed toward the coffee table.

"He won't mind eating the dinner though. Just for that, no dessert," Molly called after him.

Jessica took a sip of her coffee. "When are you due, Leigh?" she asked.

"In about six weeks. January fifth."

"You'll probably be late," Molly predicted. "Or early, depending. They actually don't know, which is what you really need to remember. Which reminds me of this joke: A woman asks her doctor, 'Should I have a baby after thirty-five?' And he says, 'Thirty-five children are probably enough, don't you think?' "

Leigh laughed but noticed Jessica's smile seemed halfhearted.

"By the way, since you are sticking around for a while, have you found an obstetrician?" Molly asked her.

Leigh had thought about that the other day when she told Dr. Harding she would stay. She was due for a checkup and didn't want to miss the visit. "I've been meaning to ask Matt for a recommendation but haven't gotten around to it. Do you know someone?"

"I have a great doctor for you. She's just down in Hamilton. Matt thinks very highly of her, too. Here." Molly took a pen and a small notepad from her purse and scribbled the doctor's name on it, then handed it to Leigh.

"Great, I'll call her this week." Leigh was

grateful for the recommendation but noticed that Jessica had grown very quiet. Perhaps she felt left out of the conversation, Leigh thought, hoping she hadn't been rude. "Well, I'd better catch up with Vera," she said. "I just want to make sure she has a ride."

"Oh, I can take her. We live out on the Beach Road. I have to pass the turn to her house on my way." Jessica finished her coffee and tossed the cup in a nearby trash can. "I ought to be back there myself. They're going to send someone after me in a minute."

"You're sure it's not any trouble?" Leigh asked.

"Not at all. It was nice to finally meet you, Leigh. Good luck with your baby." Jessica lightly touched Leigh's arm and her eyes held a sincere, caring light.

"My brother and sister-in-law are trying to start a family," Molly whispered as Jessica headed back to the Christmas Fair meeting. "They're having some problems though."

"Oh, that's too bad." That explained Jessica's interest in her pregnancy, Leigh thought. It also made her mindful of her own blessings, for the second time that day. At least her pregnancy was going well so far, and soon she would have her very own baby. "I hope it works out for them."

"Me, too." Molly sighed. "I'd better go round up my gang. Enjoy your day off. I'll be in the library, doing homework projects. Ah, the joys of motherhood." Molly rolled her eyes. "See what you have to look forward to?"

Leigh couldn't help laughing at her. "I do. See you."

Molly ran off to look for her family, and Leigh slipped on her coat and headed out of the gathering. As she walked toward her car, she realized that she felt suddenly lonely; she was almost sorry to go. She nearly turned back, thinking she would sit in on the meeting and wait for Vera. How long could it take?

Then she stopped herself. She didn't understand what was going on with her today. All this time, she had been waiting for the chance to slip away and have some time alone. Now she wanted to go back inside?

No, she shouldn't do that. She pulled open the car door and got inside, then started up the engine and pulled away from the church. She wasn't sure where she should go, back to the house again? Or maybe out to the beach? It was a sunny, calm day, and she was dressed for cold weather. Maybe the fresh air would help clear her head. She wished that James was around to walk with her, then stopped herself again.

She knew that when you were pregnant you had to expect mood swings. Maybe that was it. Or maybe it was that everyone at the church had been so warm and welcoming. The whole morning had been a little overwhelming. Still, the last thing she needed was a bout of self-pity.

Okay, so I'm feeling a little low and lonely. It's only normal, considering what I'm going through. Living under a fake identity doesn't exactly lend itself to close friendships. She touched her stomach gently and murmured, "But you're worth it all. So if I stay on here for the next few weeks, I can't let myself get too close to anyone — no matter how tempting or harmless it may seem." *I could let my guard down for one minute and lose everything.*

On Sunday night it was Sam's turn to cook. Jessica sat on a tall stool by the stove and watched him cut an onion into thick chunks as he started to make steak and stir-fried vegetables.

Everybody in Sam's family seemed to know how to cook. Not surprising, since his father was a professional chef.

"Can I help with anything?" she asked.

"Just sit there and look pretty. That helps." He glanced over his shoulder and grinned at her, and she smiled back.

"I spoke to your mother this afternoon and told her we were coming for Thanksgiving. She sounds as if everything is under control. I don't know how she manages with all those people in that tiny house. She's planning on *two* turkeys. Big ones, too."

Sam laughed and stirred something sizzling around in the big metal wok. "She always makes two birds, Jess. I'm surprised she isn't going for three. It got pretty ugly when they ran out of drumsticks last year."

He was joking, of course. But with six sisters and brothers, even if only half of his clan and their children came, there was always a houseful and the table could get pretty raucous.

"You can buy drumsticks separately. Maybe I should cook some here and bring them. Your mom asked me to make cranberry sauce. I think I'll need a gallon of it."

"Sounds about right. Every holiday my parents get in a lather about not having enough food. Then there's always way too much. The real question is, what are we going to do with all the leftovers my mother will try to send home with us?"

"I'm sure you'll think of something," Jessica said. She liked her in-laws very much; she had never found their generosity hard to take. There were other aspects of the Morgan family gatherings, though, that were difficult for her. Harder and harder, it seemed.

"I don't know, Sam. I'm sorry to sound like such a downer, but I'm sort of dreading the holiday. It's hard for me, being around all your sisters and brothers and all their kids." She waited, watching his expression change, seeing that he was starting to understand. "I know that everyone feels sorry for me about the miscarriage, and they're either giving me these long sympathetic looks or pulling me aside to get a progress report."

Sam nodded and cast her an understanding look. "I know. I get the same thing, in a way. They mean well. But they're all too nosy sometimes."

"Sometimes?" Jessica's expression made him smile again. She tried to smile, too. It was better than crying, which was what she really felt like doing.

Her mood was just out of control today. Maybe it was the medication she'd been taking. Meeting Leigh Baxter in church today had set her off track, too. She couldn't help thinking about Leigh's due date. Her baby's due date had been exactly one month after: February fifth.

Sam walked over to her and put his hands on her shoulders. "Honey, don't worry. We're going to have a family. The doctor said our chances are good, very good."

Jessica sighed. "He didn't say very good. Just good was all. What else could he say?"

Sam leaned over and kissed her forehead. "Please don't worry like this, Jess. I know it's tough right now, but let's try to be more patient."

"I am trying. It's just — hard."

"I know. It's hard for me too. But we're making some progress with this new doctor, I think. Hey, Reverend Cameron asked me to read in church next week. You know what my verse is going to be?"

Jessica shook her head, unsure of whether this little tangent had anything to do with their conversation. "What is it?"

" 'Ask, and it shall be given you; seek, and ye shall find; knock, and it shall be opened unto you.' " Sam smiled at her. "It felt like more than a coincidence when Reverend Cameron told me. It felt like . . .

like a message or something, about you and me. That we're on the right track and we have to be hopeful."

She nodded, knowing he was right. The verse lifted her spirits, too.

"I think part of it is, Jess, that we have to keep an open mind. I mean, sometimes the Lord sends us what we asked for, but it isn't exactly what we had in mind." He paused and rubbed her shoulders a bit. "I mean . . . if we try and try and try and still can't have a baby, maybe we ought to consider adoption. Don't you think?"

Jessica could see that it was hard for Sam to talk about this with her, and she could tell from his tone that it had probably been on his mind for some time.

"I don't know," she said truthfully. "Right now, I just want to see if I can have our own baby. I want the experience of being pregnant and giving birth, Sam. That might be hard for you to understand, being a man. But it's very important to me. I'm not thinking of giving up so soon and adopting."

"Sure, I understand. I'm not giving up either, honey. I was just trying to say there are other things we can think of. If the pills you're taking don't work, there are plenty of other ways to increase our chances. The doctor offered a lot of alternatives."

"Yes . . . he did." Jessica nodded, whisking her moist eyes with the back of her hand. The list of infertility treatments he had given them seemed long and — if she was perfectly honest about it — quite daunting. She truly hoped she and Sam would not need to work their way down the long list of treatments. She wanted a baby in the worst way . . . but she wasn't really sure how much anticipation and disappointment she could endure.

"It's just that I love you so much, Jess. I hate to see you unhappy." He put his arms around her and kissed her then touched her cheek with his hand. "It's going to be okay, I promise."

Jessica stared into her husband's eyes for a moment and tried to smile. She knew he couldn't really promise her that but thought it was very sweet of him to try.

Finally, Sam returned to the counter. He flipped a red pepper on the cutting board and began cutting long thin strips. Jessica picked up a Christmas catalog and thumbed through the pages. Each photo seemed to show an athletic, all-American family dressed in stylish outdoor wear, with ruddy cheeks, windblown hair, and golden retrievers prancing at their heels as they strolled through snowy woods or decorated Christmas trees.

Jessica suddenly wished she could step into the pages, as if through a magic glass, and be part of that perfectly color-coordinated world where problems like infertility didn't exist. She'd be happy to be a mother to any one of those pretty children. If only you *could* order a baby from a catalog . . .

"Listen, Jess, I wanted to ask you something. I thought on Thanksgiving we could bring Darrell with us to my parents' house. Luke said some of the other kids at the center are going to different homes around the village for the holiday, but so far, Darrell hasn't been invited anywhere."

I'm not surprised, either was her first thought. Then she caught herself, ashamed of her response. When she didn't answer, Sam glanced over his shoulder at her.

She avoided his questioning look. "Gee . . . I don't know. I'm not so sure that's a good idea. I mean, considering the way he acted at my mother's house . . ."

Sam had his back to her now, but she could see the tense set of his shoulders as he kept slicing. "We had a good talk about that. I think Darrell understands now that what he did was wrong. I think we should give him another chance, to show that we trust him to behave himself."

That you trust him, you mean, Jessica wanted to say.

"I'm sorry, Sam. I just don't think it's a good idea. What if he disrupts the whole party? What if he fights with the other kids? You'll have to watch him every minute. It could spoil our entire day."

Sam pushed the pile of chopped vegetables to one side of the cutting board and turned to face her.

"I know this will be inconvenient. I know I'll have to keep an eye on him, and it might not be the most relaxing Thanksgiving of my life. But it will be worth it to me, Jessica, because I think I'll be giving Darrell a great day, maybe the best holiday he's ever had." Sam's tone softened and he grinned. "It will certainly be the most food he's ever seen on a table at one time. What better time to share what we have and show him what a real family is like? Isn't Thanksgiving the perfect day for that?"

Jessica met his gaze then looked away. Why was it that every time they talked about Darrell, she wound up feeling selfish and mean-spirited and Sam sounded like a finalist for the Nobel Peace Prize? She slipped off her stool and walked across the room to stand opposite him.

"I know what you're saying is true," she said. "But think about it a minute. Is it really the right thing to do? Darrell might enjoy himself for the day and then end up feeling even worse about his life, seeing everything he's missing out on. I mean, it builds up his hopes, his expectations. Is it fair for you to get so involved with him when it can't lead anywhere?"

Sam crossed his arms over his chest. "Why can't it lead anywhere?"

Jessica felt flustered by his reply. Was he saying that he wanted them to be even more involved with Darrell?

She took a breath and tried to speak calmly. "I thought we were starting our own family, Sam, not adopting or becoming foster parents. Besides, we don't even know what his situation is. Maybe his living arrangements after New Horizons are already settled."

Sam stared at her with a moody expression. "Maybe they are. I'll have to talk to Luke about it. He can tell me."

Jessica had no reply to that. How had they even gotten started on this topic? Now she had opened up an entirely new can of worms.

Sam scooped the cut vegetables into the wok and added a jolt of soy sauce. "Why don't you set the table and we'll eat? I'm starving."

"Fine." She rose and pulled some dishes from the cabinet, glad to concentrate on something other than these worrisome issues. She and Sam were clearly at odds when it came to the questions of Darrell Lester and adopting a baby. She knew adoption or fostering were perfect solutions for some couples, but she couldn't get her mind around either one of them yet. If ever.

Chapter Seven

"James? You don't look well. Is everything all right?"

James looked up from his desk and found Ben standing beside him. He had been so lost in thought, he hadn't even heard the older minister approach.

Ben wasn't usually around on Monday mornings. That was his time to visit older members of the congregation who were in a nearby nursing home. James hesitated then realized it might be a good thing that Ben had changed his schedule today. He did need someone to talk to.

"I've had some bad news about the mission," James admitted. "I got a fax this morning. There are some serious problems with the clinic expansion. They haven't been working for the past three weeks . . . but no one wanted to worry me."

Ben took a seat in a leather armchair in front of the desk. "That is bad news.

What's the issue? Is there a problem with the plans?"

"I only wish. I could fix plans from here. It's something I can't manage so easily at this distance. There's some dispute between the builder we've hired and the local authorities. They can shut you down sometimes for no reason at all. It's just the way the government works there. I've always been good at navigating my way around the bureaucrats and their demands. I've been there so long, I've gotten to know a lot of people who can help us. Sometimes it takes me a while, but I usually find the right door to knock on."

"What about the people on your staff that you left in charge? Can't you tell them who to call or visit?"

"I guess they tried — or they wouldn't have brought me in on it. I've been gone for almost three months. The political scene there changes quickly. The same bureaucrats who controlled things when I left might not have any influence now."

"I see. That does sound tricky," Ben agreed.

"I've been on the phone for hours, and I've accomplished exactly nothing. I don't know who to call or fax or harangue next." James pushed aside a pile of papers in frustration. "The building is at a crucial stage. They have to get the roof on and the walls up before the bad weather hits again or all that effort and money will be lost. The place will be washed away."

He sat back in his chair and looked up at Ben. "I need to get back there right away. They need my help."

Ben took a long breath. "I know the situation sounds very serious, James. But physically, do you really think you're ready to go back?"

James gazed out the window as he said, "Yes, I am. I feel fine. Better every day."

"When was the last time you checked in with a doctor?"

James shrugged. "Oh, I don't know. A few weeks ago, I suppose."

"I remember. More like September, just before you got here. That wasn't very good news, as I recall."

"Doctors don't know everything, Ben. That specialist would be happy if I didn't go back to Nicaragua at all."

Ben's tone was grave. "He's a very well known specialist. Maybe you shouldn't brush off his opinion so quickly. I've seen you looking tired lately, James. I know you try to hide it from us, but I think you've been rushing yourself to recover. Or at least, to convince everyone that you have. I don't think you're ready to go back — not even for an emergency."

James picked up a glass paperweight and examined it, as if it might hold the solutions to his problems. Ben's response wasn't the one he had been hoping for; in fact, it just seemed to make everything worse. Still, he had to give Ben credit for his honesty. "Well . . . what can I say? I appreciate your advice, Ben. I just don't happen to agree with it."

"I'm saying this as your friend, James, because I care about you. We all do. I know you set high ideals for yourself and I admire that. But you're not . . . Super Minister."

James felt himself cracking a smile despite his low spirits. "I'm not?"

"Sorry to disappoint you, but no. Don't try to leap off any tall buildings while you're in town either. That's my second bit of advice."

Ben sat back in his chair and slipped off his glasses. He carefully cleaned them on a handkerchief.

"What do you suggest? I just sit here and let the construction site crumble?"

"Of course not. But I do think you could have a little more faith in the people you've left in charge. Give them some guidance, some suggestions. See what they can do." Ben put his glasses back on and pushed the frames up the ridge of his small, straight nose.

"I simply don't think you need to rush back to the mission yet. Not when I consider the gamble you'd be taking — with your recovery, your future health, maybe even your life."

The heavy words were hard to accept, but James knew what Ben said was true.

Ben rose and pushed the chair aside. "Will you at least think about it a little more?"

James nodded. "Yes, of course I will."

"And will you see a doctor and check your progress?" Ben's tone was quieter but still firm.

James felt backed into a corner. He didn't want to lie or mislead Ben, but he dreaded visiting a doctor again. He wasn't sure what he would do if he were told his condition hadn't improved.

Finally, under Ben's uncompromising gaze, he relented. "I guess I should. Maybe I'll just check in with Matt Harding here in town, see what he thinks."

"That's a good idea. Let me know how it turns out." Ben stood by the doorway. "Is there anything I can do for you — anything at all I can do to help?"

James shook his head. "No, but thanks for listening. And for the advice," he added. "Though it wasn't what I wanted to hear."

Ben smiled gently at him. "I know. But what are friends for?"

The Clam Box was packed with its usual lunchtime crowd. Jessica glanced around quickly. She saw Tucker Tulley at the counter, eating a bowl of soup and chatting with Charlie Bates, the diner's owner, while he flipped burgers on the grill.

At a table in the front, Reverend Ben was having lunch with Digger Hegman. Both men said hello, though Jessica wasn't entirely sure if Digger always remembered who she was these days.

Finally, she spotted Emily seated at a booth near the back. Although they both worked on Main Street, with Jessica at the bank and Emily in the village hall, they rarely got together for lunch. But this morning, Emily had called sounding cheerful. Her usual Tuesday afternoon meeting had been canceled and she wanted to take Jessica out for lunch.

Jessica always found the Clam Box an

odd choice for her sister's favorite restaurant. Charlie Bates was Emily's archrival and most outspoken critic, using his lunch counter as a soapbox for his political rants. But Jessica knew that in her quiet, dignified way, her sister was a fighter. In fact, she had started to believe that Emily enjoyed coming here just to show Charlie she wasn't afraid of him and didn't care a whit what he said about her.

"You got here early. I'm in shock," Jessica teased, referring to her sister's well-earned reputation for always being late. Jessica slipped her suede jacket over the back of her chair and sat down. "This must be important."

"Good news. Dan and I figured out our wedding." Emily sat back and beamed, as if she had just announced the discovery of a cure for the common cold.

"That is news. Will there be a parade down Main Street?"

"Seems like there should be after all this haggling, doesn't it?" Emily picked up a cracker from a basket on the table and took a bite. "Dan won't agree to anything nearly that grand, though." She laughed. "I know it sounds sort of 'Duh . . . so what's the problem?' But what we finally agreed to is just a medium, low-key sort of gathering, like a cocktail party with a very strict limit on the guest list."

"A strict limit?" Jessica knew her sister. That stipulation was going to be a tough one. "How many?"

Emily sighed. "Don't ask. It's impossible. I'm trying to convince Dan that there are some people in town I have to invite just to be polite, knowing they won't come —"

"Did you say polite — or political?"

"I said *polite,*" Emily affirmed with a laughing glint in her eye. "He doesn't get the concept."

"Maybe he'll come around once you show him the list. Have you figured out a date?"

"Not yet. Very soon, though. That was another stipulation. The only way I got him to go along with it was by promising I could pull it together before our trip." Emily sighed. "Who can plan a nice wedding in that amount of time? It's just insane."

Jessica patted her sister's hand. "I think it's sweet that he's so eager to marry you and whisk you off to a tropical island. It's very romantic."

"Yes, it is, isn't it?" Emily smiled again, her eyes getting a little dreamy looking, Jessica thought with amusement; that was so unlike her no-nonsense older sister.

"Dan can be very romantic, but don't let it get around. He likes everyone to think he's a real curmudgeon."

"Don't worry. I wouldn't want to ruin his image. So where do you want to have the party? The Pequot Inn is charming. I think they even have a private room upstairs with a fireplace."

"That is a pretty place. But I go to so many political functions there. It would just feel like another Rotary Club meeting to me." Emily slipped on her reading glasses and scanned the menu.

"How about having it at our house? I know Sam wouldn't mind. He'd love the idea."

Emily looked up and smiled at her. "You're so sweet. . . . You'd really do that for me?"

"Of course I would. I'd love to." Preparing for Emily's wedding would also provide the perfect distraction from her babymaking worries, Jessica realized. "It would be fun."

"I love your house. It would be perfect if I can keep the guest list down. I'm going to ask Molly if she can cater it for us. I was afraid she'd refuse if the party was at Mother's."

Jessica answered Emily's grin. Emily's

engagement party had been held at their mother's house and Molly had catered it, battling with Lillian every inch of the way. Molly had come through gallantly, but Jessica doubted her sister-in-law would agree to repeat that experience.

Lucy Bates appeared at the table. "Good to see you, ladies. Want to hear the specials?"

"I think we're set," Jessica said.

"Just what I like: decisive customers." She laughed and pulled her order pad out of her apron pocket.

Jessica ordered her usual, a turkey sandwich on rye. Lucy nodded. "No pickle, extra cole slaw."

"You got it." Jessica smiled up at her. Lucy was so upbeat and friendly, the complete opposite of her husband. It amazed Jessica that the two had remained married all these years, though everyone knew Lucy had already left Charlie once.

Emily started off ordering the fried clam roll, then deducted the roll and finally ended up with a salad.

"Lucy, order up. What are you doing over there, having a coffee klatch?"

Lucy glanced over her shoulder at her husband, who glowered at her from his post at the grill. She turned back to Jessica and Emily, rolling her eyes. "It's called being pleasant to the customers," she mumbled under her breath.

"Be right back with your order," she added as she scurried away.

Once Lucy left, Emily said, "That's another thing. I don't even have time to lose a few pounds."

"Don't be silly. You look great."

"I'm well past forty and I'll have to wear a bathing suit *in February.* And gravity isn't doing me any favors, either."

Jessica laughed. "You'll be alone on a tropical island with a man who adores you. Just wear one of those wrap things over your suit. He'll think you look exotic."

"Words of wisdom from a happily married woman." Emily grinned and picked up another cracker. "So, how are things? What's new?"

"Oh, nothing much." Jessica shrugged but could tell from Emily's discerning gaze her sister wasn't buying it. "We went to a new doctor last week. He put me on some pills he says should help."

"That's encouraging."

"I guess so. I don't want to get my hopes up, though."

"How's Sam? Does he feel discouraged, too?"

"Somewhat. But not as much as I do. He has Darrell to distract him now, which is good in some ways and not so good in others."

Emily looked curiously at her as she slipped off her reading glasses. "I can see the benefits of it. Sam has so much, well, love to give. New Horizons is lucky to have him there, and Darrell is lucky Sam's singled him out. But what's the bad side? Do you feel Sam's not giving you enough attention?"

It was hard to admit but perhaps that was part of her problem, Jessica realized. But it wasn't all of it. "I'm not really sure," she said honestly. "Maybe it's that I lost the baby and" — her voice faltered but she forced herself to continue — "and the next thing I know, Sam's bonding with this kid and bringing him into our lives and expecting me to care about him. And he never even asked me." She pressed a hand over her mouth, appalled by the resentment in her own voice. "You must think I'm a horrible person and —"

"I have never thought anything of the sort," Emily said firmly, "and I've known you since you were born. Jess, what you just said — it's not unreasonable that you're upset. Have you told Sam this stuff?"

Jessica shook her head and swallowed hard. "No. I just figured it out. All I've known is that I've been uncomfortable with Darrell, and I couldn't understand why. He's really not a bad kid. It just seems that ever since Sam took him under his wing, there's been all this tension. Sam really wants us to get along. He even tried taking us all out for a day at this indoor sports complex — which to me was an automatic migraine." Emily gave her sister a sympathetic glance, and Jessica went on. "I really have tried to get along with Darrell, despite what happened at Mother's house. But I can't seem to do anything right around him. The boy just doesn't like me, and Sam can't see it. If anything, he thinks it's my fault."

Emily sighed. "That's pretty hard. Especially when you're both so focused on this pregnancy issue."

"I think it's great for Sam to help Darrell," Jessica finished, her voice growing steadier as the situation finally became clear to her. "But maybe it's also a way for Sam to avoid worrying about our problem."

Emily took a sip of her coffee. "Do you think it will help you get pregnant faster if you're both worrying?"

"No, of course not." Jessica tucked a loose strand of her long hair behind her ear. "But we just don't seem to be on the same track anymore about all this stuff. The other day, we somehow got onto the topic of adoption, which I suppose is an option if all else fails. But I'm not ready to consider that yet. Then, a few minutes later, Sam is talking about taking in Darrell as a foster child. It's like some huge snowball heading down a big hill at me and I can't do anything to stop it. When I try to be honest with Sam about it, I sound like a heartless, selfish monster. Is it wrong to just want my own baby right now?"

Emily's expression softened. "There's nothing in the world wrong with that, Jess. And you're the last person I'd call a heartless monster. Sam knows that. He loves you very much." Emily sat back in her seat. "You're in a tough spot. Maybe you should just wait and see. You never know. You might start to like Darrell better and see what Sam sees in him. Or maybe you'll get pregnant and Sam will get more focused on you and his own baby."

Jessica nodded. "Yes, I've thought of all that. I guess I will have to wait."

She sat back, feeling curiously lighter.

She was glad she had confided in her sister and aired her feelings honestly — more honestly than she could with Sam right now. Although she knew that nothing had actually been solved and the question of taking Darrell in remained, at least she wasn't so confused about it anymore.

Lucy returned with their dishes and Emily began talking of other things, lighter matters than wedding planning and pregnancy problems.

Emily was relating some annoying incident from a town council meeting when her expression suddenly brightened. She sat up and waved to someone up front and Jessica turned to see her niece Sara walking toward them. Sara's long dark hair was pulled back in a ponytail, and her cheeks were flushed from the cold outside. She wore a navy blue peacoat, her leather knapsack slung over one shoulder.

"Hi, honey. What a nice surprise." Emily stood up and quickly kissed Sara's cheek, then slid over in the booth to make room for her.

"I called you back and your secretary said you were probably still here. Sorry I couldn't make it for lunch. I wouldn't mind some dessert, though, if you're going to hang out longer."

"I'd like some, too, now that you mention it." Jessica glanced around for Lucy. "But your mom's on a diet."

Sara turned and gave Emily a look that Jessica identified as pure Emily. Sometimes their resemblance was so strong, Jessica couldn't believe it. Though Sara had her father's coloring, she definitely had her mother's eyes and many of her expressions.

"You don't need a diet, Emily. For goodness' sake."

"I absolutely do. For the wedding. It's a tradition."

Sara looked surprised. "Don't tell me. Have you and Dan finally set a date? Can I have an exclusive for the paper?"

"Not exactly, but we're making progress. . . . And no need to be snide."

Sara glanced at Jessica and shook her head, trying hard to keep a straight face. "I didn't mean to tease you but honestly, I'm starting to worry. I almost agree with Lillian. Don't you dare tell her I said so, though."

Jessica and Emily laughed, and Emily put her arm around Sara's shoulder. "Don't worry, honey. We definitely won't."

"Well, what do you think, Doc?" James sat on the edge of the examining table and slowly buttoned his shirt.

Matt Harding's expression hadn't been very encouraging throughout the examination and now, as the final verdict was about to be delivered, he looked even grimmer.

Matt sat in a chair at a small wooden desk and looked over his notes. "I wish I could give you better news, James," he began, and James felt his heart fall. "But it doesn't seem to me that you've improved very much at all from your last visit to a doctor. Your blood test wasn't very good and your kidney function is still impaired. Frankly, from what you've told me — and I doubt you've told me everything — I'm surprised that you're able to manage working at the church."

James rubbed his forehead with his hand. "I must feel a lot better than those tests indicate or —"

"Or you're just a stubborn Scotsman," Matt finished for him.

"That too." James slipped off the table and picked up his sports coat from the back of a chair.

"I'm not a specialist in malaria and its complications. But from what I can see and what I know about your mission, I wouldn't advise you to return there yet."

"Isn't there something more you could

give me, to speed things up?"

Matt glanced at the chart again and shook his head. "I think we're doing all we can medically. Your body needs more time to build up strength and rebuild your immune system. Your vital organs are working hard, too hard sometimes. You're in danger of a relapse and vulnerable to any kind of bug that comes along, some that I don't even know the names of."

James didn't answer. He'd expected better news — well, perhaps *wished* for better news was more honest. He still had his bad days, feeling weak and feverish despite the medication. Often it was just his willpower that kept him moving. But he didn't think he could wait for an entirely clean bill of health to return to the mission. That day seemed as far off as ever.

The two men stood facing each other and James could see that Matt Harding, too, had found their meeting difficult.

James held out his hand to bid Matt good-bye. "Well, thanks for seeing me on such short notice."

"You can call me anytime, you know that." Matt shook his hand and sighed. "I'm sorry I couldn't give you better news, James. As I said, I'm not an expert. You might want to get another opinion from that infectious disease specialist in Boston."

"Maybe I will. Thanks again."

James had been the last patient of the day, and the waiting room was empty when he came out. His exam had taken a long time and though she was free to go, Leigh decided to wait for him. She smiled when she saw him; his answering smile was faint.

"How did it go?"

"More or less what I expected." By now she knew him well enough to tell that he was trying to be offhand about the exam, but it hadn't been good news. She could see he was disappointed, and she felt badly for him.

"Do you need to make another appointment?" she asked politely.

He glanced at his watch then back at her. "No . . . I don't. Have you been waiting here all this time just to ask me that?"

"Of course not. I just needed to work a little later, clear some things off my desk." She had stayed late to talk to him but didn't want to admit it. "They're going to light the Christmas tree in town tonight. Molly told me about it. She says it's fun. Are you going?"

"Oh . . . the tree. I almost forgot. . . . I

don't know." He gazed down at her. "I'm feeling a little tired. I might just head home."

Leigh had half a mind to say the same. She wasn't in the mood for Christmas this year and didn't need any large-scale reminders, like a giant outdoor tree and a high school chorus singing carols. But the look on James's face changed her mind. He was always so kind to her; she could put her feelings aside tonight and try to cheer him up.

"Don't go home yet, James. Come with me and see the tree. It won't take very long. I bet it looks pretty set up in that park, near the harbor."

He looked surprised at her invitation. Very surprised, she thought, still wondering if he would say yes. Then he smiled, a real smile this time, making her glad she had gone out on a limb and asked him.

"Sure, I'll go with you. I haven't seen a tree lighting for years. It might be fun."

Once outside, they decided to walk down Main Street to the green, rather than take a car. There wouldn't be any parking left, James thought, and Leigh wanted the exercise after sitting all day.

They reached the area set up for the tree lighting and found a huge crowd already gathered.

"Looks like every seat is filled. I didn't think we were late." She glanced at James, who was still scanning the rows for some empty seats.

"There must be someone here who'll give up a seat for a very pregnant lady."

"No, don't be silly. Besides, then we wouldn't see it together. That's not the idea." It wasn't her idea, at any rate. "Let's just walk up front and stand on the side."

James considered her suggestion a moment. "I think I know a good place — if someone hasn't already claimed it before us."

He grabbed her hand, catching her off guard, and led her away from the crowd into the green.

Leigh followed James down a gravel path and past a stone monument. On the other side of the monument, she saw a high stone retaining wall, exactly in line with the big tree and the chorus risers.

Leigh gazed at the wall and then at James. "Perfect. If you have a crane in your pocket to lift me up there."

James laughed at her. "Come along, O ye of little faith." They followed another path that led to a flight of stone steps, and when they reached the top Leigh could see that they were now above the monument, looking down.

"Here, let me help you sit down," James said, holding her hand again as she lowered herself onto the wall. "Are you all right up here?" he asked with concern. "Maybe this wasn't such a good idea, after all."

"I'm fine." Leigh sat back, swinging her legs a bit over the edge. "I just hope no one mistakes me for Humpty Dumpty."

"No chance." He shook his head and grinned at her.

"Wow, what a view." Leigh stared out, amazed at her bird's-eye perspective of the harbor and green. "Look at the sunset. I didn't really notice it before."

The sun was low in the sky, casting the horizon in a rosy hue, with large blue-gray and lavender clouds puffing up behind it, the colors reflected in the dark harbor. As they watched in silence a few radiant golden beams arched up, like final, silent bursts of a fireworks show.

"It's a beautiful night. It was a good idea to come. Thanks for persuading me." James glanced down at her and smiled.

"I'm glad you decided to. I don't think I would have come to watch it alone," she said honestly.

A town official welcomed everyone and the chorus sang a few familiar holiday songs. Leigh enjoyed watching the show from a distance, away from the crowd with everything in miniature, though she wasn't sure quite why. Maybe because she was a loner at heart, always feeling on the outside, looking in. She glanced at James, who also seemed at ease in this secluded perch. She wondered if he was more like her than she had first thought.

No, of course not. He was a minister; he loved working with people. Hadn't he once told her he considered the church his family? They were very different that way.

Emily Warwick, the town's mayor, spoke for a moment. Leigh had not yet met her, but Molly Willoughby seemed to know her well and sometimes mentioned her in passing. She kept her remarks light and brief, just right, Leigh thought.

Emily announced it was time to light the tree and started a countdown. The audience quickly joined in, their voices growing louder and louder. Leigh watched silently. Then beside her, she heard James counting. ". . . Seven. Six. Five . . ."

She joined in. ". . . Three. Two. One!"

She stared out at the tree and watched the lights flicker a moment then go on fully. She suddenly realized James was holding her hand again — for no real reason, unless he thought she was so excited she was liable to slip off her seat. But she did like the feeling of his large, warm hand surrounding hers. She couldn't deny that. Not even to herself.

He turned and smiled at her. "I think Santa's arrival is next on the program. Want to stay?"

Leigh shook her head. "If we leave now, we'll beat the rush."

"Good idea." James helped her stand up and they left the green, heading back to Main Street. Leigh heard a siren and they paused at a corner as a fire truck slowly rolled by. Santa was in the front seat, waving wildly while his elf helpers tossed out candy canes to the crowd. James reached out and caught one, then handed it to her with a gallant flourish.

"Here you go. That's for the baby." He grinned at his own joke, and she was glad to see him looking cheerful again.

"Thanks. But I have a firm rule about candy so close to dinner."

"Very wise. Why don't we grab a bite to eat somewhere? Are you hungry? I don't think Vera's home tonight so it won't spoil her plans."

Leigh recalled that Vera had said she would be out and wouldn't be serving dinner. But she hadn't expected to eat with James. It wasn't why she'd invited him to the tree lighting.

This was starting to feel like a regular date, she thought with alarm.

Then she caught sight of her reflection in a store window — mainly, her very pregnant tummy — and reminded herself she had nothing to worry about on that score. She didn't feel very attractive these days; she couldn't even imagine anyone being interested in her that way. James was just being friendly.

"Sure. Where shall we go?"

"How about the Clam Box?" James pointed to the diner just across the street. "Have you tried it yet?"

"One of my favorite lunch spots. The waitress already knows my name."

"Lucy Bates? She makes it a point to know everyone. She could run for mayor if Emily Warwick ever steps down. Though I understand that's her husband Charlie's fondest ambition."

Leigh had met Charlie, too, but wasn't very impressed. The brief moments of interaction she'd seen between Lucy and her husband had left her ill at ease, bringing on a wave of her own bad memories. If she ever got to know Lucy better, maybe she would have an honest talk with her about the dangers of putting up with someone like Charlie.

But she wasn't going to be around here that long, Leigh reminded herself. She might get to know people by name and even be friendly, but that wasn't the same as making real connections and true friends.

Except maybe for James, she realized as he held open the diner door for her. James was in a different category, maybe because of the way they'd met or simply because of his caring, disarming personality. Even so, she couldn't let their relationship go very far. She suddenly felt a little sad about that, and a little guilty.

James suggested a table by the window. The restaurant was nearly empty, with only a few other customers. Leigh slipped off her coat and placed it on the chair behind her. Lucy Bates stood behind the counter, leaning over a thick book. She hadn't lifted her head at the sound of the jingling bell over the door, or even seemed to notice when they entered. Holding a yellow highlighter in one hand, she practically pounced on the page and began underlining text.

"Lucy is trying to finish her college degree," James explained quietly. "She wants to be a nurse."

"That's wonderful. That must be hard while working here."

"Yes, it is. But she's a hard worker and very persistent. I think I've come to see that, more than anything, persistence is the key if you're trying to accomplish something. And faith, of course."

"That's probably true." Leigh thought of her own life, what she'd been through lately. She had only escaped her nightmarish marriage by sheer force of will and that's what still kept her going: her will to protect her baby.

"Oh . . . for goodness' sake. I'm so sorry." Lucy looked dismayed as she rushed over to the table with two menus. "I hope you weren't waiting long? Hello, Leigh. Hello, Reverend James."

"Hello, Lucy. We just walked in, honestly. How are you tonight? Catching up on schoolwork?"

"Aren't I always?" Lucy shook her head and smiled. "I have midterms next week and a bunch of papers due. And of course, one of the boys is sick with the flu. But we're still running a diner here."

Lucy quickly took down their orders and ran off to the kitchen. James watched her go, smiling ruefully. "I don't know how she does it. I wish I had half her energy."

His wistful words reminded Leigh of his health problems. He had brushed off her questions at the doctor's office. Maybe he would open up more now.

"I was wondering, James, were you in Dr. Harding's office for a checkup today — or was there some specific reason?"

He seemed startled by her question and didn't answer right away. "It was a checkup, more or less. I've been meaning to stop by and see him for a while." He paused and fiddled with a spoon on the table. "Something came up this week at the mission, a pretty big problem. I was thinking I ought to go back right away. But I needed to get an update on my condition first. Ben thought so, anyway."

Leigh felt a small jolt as she took in his reply. He had been thinking of leaving here, just like that? She knew he didn't plan on staying in Cape Light for very long, but she had always assumed she would be the first to go. The idea of staying on without James around seemed unthinkable. Like finding herself stranded on a desert island.

"So . . . what have you decided?" she asked carefully.

He glanced up at her, his blue eyes looking dark and shadowed. "I'm going to stay a while longer. Seems I really have to. At least Matt Harding thinks so. I'm going to see a specialist in Boston, though, just to get a better idea of what's going on and find out if there's anything more I can do to speed up my recovery."

"That makes sense." Leigh sat back in her seat and stared out the window. She took a breath. So he wasn't leaving, after all. Thank goodness, she thought. Then she wondered at her own reaction.

Well . . . I just like him, as a friend, she reasoned. *He's so easy to talk to. I'm so emotional these days, up and down. And he's so steady and reassuring to be around. It doesn't mean anything.*

"This whole malaria thing is really frustrating. Well, it was this week anyway."

The tone of his voice caught her attention. She'd rarely heard him sound so upset. Here she was, lost in her own feelings and he had a real problem to talk about. He was always so good at listening to her. She ought to be here for him now.

"What was going on at the mission? Why did you want to go back?"

James briefly explained the situation to her. "I've always been the intermediary between the mission and the local authorities and politicians. At times it can be critical to say just the right thing to just the right person. It's not as if I don't trust anyone else to do it . . . but in a way, I guess I don't."

"So you felt you had to go back to work things out, so that the project wouldn't be ruined by the delay?"

"I was ready to run off on Monday, as soon as I got the fax. But Ben made me slow down and think it over."

"I'm glad he did," Leigh said impulsively. Then she wished she could take back the words. James met her gaze, staring at her across the table. She couldn't quite read the expression on his face, but she felt embarrassed by her rash admission.

"I mean, from what Dr. Harding said, it sounds as if it isn't really safe yet for you to return."

James didn't answer at first. "Seems so," he said finally.

"Here you go." Lucy set their dinners on the table. "Enjoy! And just holler if you need anything more," she added before dashing away again.

Leigh squirted some ketchup on her hamburger and cut it in half. "What's happening at the mission now? Has there been any progress?"

"I got a fax late this afternoon, before I left my office. It looks as if things will work out. Construction could start again as soon as tomorrow."

"Well, that's good news. You must be very relieved."

"To be honest, yes . . . and no. I was happy, of course, to hear the work would start again and the building wouldn't be ruined by the delay. On the other hand, I have to admit, it's hard to hear that you aren't nearly as indispensable as you think."

He was laughing at himself, but Leigh could see that his admission hurt a bit.

"From the little you've told me, James, it sounds as if you're the cornerstone of that place. I think it's to your credit that work can go on without you. When a person is a good leader there isn't mass confusion if they walk out the door for a few minutes. People on your staff know what to do because you've taught them well and helped them develop their own judgment and abilities."

He gave her a questioning look, and she again wondered if she had said too much. But all he said was, "I've really encouraged the people I work with to be self-sufficient and use their own judgment. Right now, I guess I'm like a parent who sees that his children don't need him anymore and feels . . . superfluous."

She considered his words for a moment. "That's not what it sounds like to me."

"What do you mean?"

"Well . . . I really don't know anything about mission work, at least nothing more than what you've told me. But perhaps your role is done there and it's time to start something new, to go where another community needs you more."

He stared out the window and shook his head. "I originally went to Helping Hands as a seminary student, for a few weeks during a summer vacation. But by the end of my first day I knew I would be back. Once I started working there, I never pictured myself anywhere else."

Leigh had never heard anyone sound so certain of anything. It was so different from her own life, which seemed like the fault line of an earthquake, always about to open into a chasm beneath her. She couldn't seem to get a grip on anything solid or permanent. She had married a man she thought she loved only to find out he was someone else entirely. She didn't even trust her judgment anymore.

There was only one thing she felt completely sure about in her life: her love for her baby. That was her touchstone, the center of reality.

"That must be a wonderful thing," she said, "to feel so sure of what you're doing and where you belong."

"Yes, it is." He turned to look at her again. "It always has been — until I had to come back here. I guess I'm starting to see it differently now. Maybe it's like you said. Maybe my work there is done. Maybe God wants me to pray outside the box?"

Leigh had to smile at his choice of words. "I guess you'll just have to see."

They sat and ate, not talking. James finished his burger, then sipped his coffee, looking thoughtful. At last he said, "What are your plans, Leigh? I mean, after you have the baby."

"Oh . . . I don't know. I don't have a real plan," she said honestly. "I might go stay with my friend in Wellfleet for a while, if she has room for me by then."

The truth of the matter was that there was no friend in Wellfleet. There was no friend anywhere to run to. Ever since the plan to stay with her cousin Eileen in Canada had fallen through, Leigh had been trying to figure out the next step. She considered driving down to Florida or Texas or maybe even Mexico. But she was too low on money to get far. Now it seemed safer to hide out here for a while.

James didn't say anything. His quiet, appraising look was unsettling to her. She didn't want him to ask any more personal questions. He was getting too close and she was afraid she might tell him the truth about herself. Would he be sympathetic and understanding? she wondered. Or would he be angry about the way she had deceived him, deceived everyone she met in this town? She felt so guilty, she could hardly bear to look at him.

Lucy arrived and cleared away their plates. "How about some dessert? We have some good pies tonight — apple crumb, pecan, and pumpkin, which I highly recommend. I've already had two slices," she admitted with a grin.

"I'll try the pumpkin, with a big glob of cream on top, please. How about you, Leigh? You can't let me do this alone."

"The pumpkin sounds good. And more tea when you have a chance?"

Lucy jotted down the order and soon returned with their servings of pie. Leigh took a small testing bite and then closed her eyes to savor the spicy flavor. "I do love pumpkin pie. I've never understood why you only find it at Thanksgiving."

"Me, neither," James agreed heartily as he took a large bite. "Maybe we can start some sort of movement, the pumpkin-pie-all-year-long advocacy group."

"Good idea. We'll need a catchier name, though, don't you think?"

"I'm just an idea man. I'm not very good with marketing."

He smiled at her, his blue eyes flashing. Leigh had to force herself to look away; he really looked so attractive to her at times.

"I can't believe it's nearly Thanksgiving. Only two days away," he said. "Do you have any plans for the holiday?"

"Not really. Molly Willoughby asked if I wanted to go to her parents' house. She'll be there with her girls and Matt Harding, and his daughter Amanda. I thought it was very nice of her to invite me."

"Yes, very considerate. Is that what you plan to do, then?" he persisted.

She looked up and met his eyes. She couldn't lie to him about this, too. Besides, he would find out the truth easily enough. "Well, I'm not sure. I appreciate Molly asking me, but it sounds as if it will be a very big crowd there. She has such a large family. I'm not sure I'd feel comfortable with all those strangers."

"I know what you mean." James nodded. "Would you like to come with me to Reverend Lewis's house? There won't be many people there, just Ben; his wife, Carolyn; their son, Mark; their daughter, Rachel; and her husband, Jack. Oh, and they have a little boy, William. He'll be one in January."

Leigh was surprised by the invitation. Vera was going to her daughter's house and Leigh had expected to be alone and make the best of her solitude. "That's a lovely invitation, James, but I don't want to impose."

"Don't worry about Ben and Carolyn. I've already asked them. They'd love to have you, really." She tried to avoid his gaze, but couldn't quite. "It's not good to be alone on a holiday, Leigh. Especially with all you've been through this past year," he added quietly.

She wondered for a second what he meant. Had he somehow guessed the truth about her? Then she realized he meant the story she'd told him — that her husband had died. She felt overwhelmed for a moment, wondering how she was able to fool him so well. It just wasn't right.

"I didn't mean to upset you," he said.

"No . . . it's not that. I'm not upset, honestly." She took a breath and tried to get control of her emotions.

"I hope not, and I hope you'll think it over. You'd actually be doing me a favor, you know. I think the Lewises are wonderful people, but it's hard to be the only nonfamily member at a gathering like that. If you come, at least I'll have some company. I won't be the only outsider, I mean."

He cast her a warm smile and she couldn't help smiling back. Leave it to James to frame the question in a way that made it look as if she would be helping *him*. She could suddenly imagine him talking circles around bureaucrats.

"All right, I'll think about it."

"Good." He sat back, looking calm and satisfied.

Lucy stopped by. "Can I get you folks anything else?"

"I think we're fine. The pie was great, by the way."

"I thought you'd like it." Lucy set the check on the table and James quickly picked it up.

"You don't have to treat me, James. I should be taking you out." Leigh took out her wallet and pulled out some bills.

"You'll do nothing of the kind. Besides, I owe you for the therapy session."

"The therapy?"

"For listening to my woes . . . and cheering me up."

Leigh felt her cheeks color from his compliment. She didn't deserve his gratitude. "Don't be silly. That was nothing."

"It was something to me." He was smiling, as usual, but his tone was very serious.

Leigh didn't know what to say. "You're very welcome. Thanks for dinner."

"My pleasure." He rose and held out her coat to help her. She slipped into it, suddenly aware of his nearness.

They walked outside and down Main Street, where their cars were both parked near Dr. Harding's office. "You could leave your car if you like, and I'll give you a lift to town tomorrow," James offered.

"No, thanks. I'll drive myself home."

"All right. I'll wait and follow you, though."

Leigh got into her car, smiling to herself. She had tried to tell James not to fuss over her, but he couldn't seem to stop himself. It was just his way.

She turned off Main Street and onto the

Beach Road. The lights of James's car reflected in her rearview mirror, following her, just as he'd promised.

I have feelings for him, Leigh realized, *good and serious feelings. Feelings that scare me if I let myself dwell on them too long.*

There was no sense in thinking about James, she reminded herself. Soon they would each leave Cape Light and go their separate ways.

Nothing could ever come of it.

Chapter Eight

Thanksgiving Day at her in-laws' house was just as Jessica expected: cheerful and crowded, with music playing in one room and the TV blasting a football game in another. Every room was filled with guests; a folding chair or snack table was squeezed into every corner space. Jessica had no idea how they would all manage to fit at the table, though it stretched from the Morgans' small dining room out into the living room and even made an L-shaped turn, to avoid the piano.

It was the same at every holiday she spent here. It seemed like utter chaos, with adults charging about with platters and steaming pots, and children chasing each other through the narrow hall. But it all fell into place eventually. Even magically, it seemed.

She drifted into the kitchen, wondering if she could help. Molly and Sam's mother,

Marie, stood at the stove, debating the best way to roast a turkey. "I know what they say in cooking school, but I've been cooking our turkeys for over thirty years, honey. Don't you think that by now I know how to do it?"

"I know, Mom, and they always come out great. I'm just saying there's more than one way to do it, that's all."

Molly turned to Jessica and rolled her eyes. Jessica noticed that even the indomitable Molly didn't bother to argue with Marie.

Molly's younger sister Lisa sat at the kitchen table, feeding one of her twins. The baby was about six months old, a beautiful little girl with a round face and a pink button nose.

Just the way she'd imagined her own baby would look. The one she lost.

"She's getting so big," Jessica said softly, trying to sound bright and positive, despite her own wrenching emotions.

"Isn't she?" Lisa answered without looking up. She kept offering the bottle, and the baby kept turning her head away. "She's so fussy today. Must be all the excitement. The slightest change in routine throws them off." Lisa sighed and glanced up at Jessica. "Just wait. You'll see," she promised.

Jessica forced a smile. "I hope so."

She knew her sister-in-law meant well but the comment still stung. People didn't realize how it could hurt to be around children when you were longing for your own. Why was it so easy for some women and so hard for her? It just didn't seem fair. Lisa hadn't even been trying to start a family when she ended up with twins.

Jessica shook off the feeling. She didn't want to mope the whole day. She went to stand near her mother-in-law and finally caught Marie's attention. "Can I help with anything?"

"Oh, well, let's see . . . can you take this tray into the TV room? I fixed some special snacks for the kids."

Molly leaned over her shoulder and appraised the tray of tiny hot dogs and miniature pizza rounds. "Oh, Mom, you spoil them with all that junk food."

"Oh, hush. It's their holiday, too, you know. What are grandmas for?"

"Exactly," Jessica replied. She took the tray and slipped out of the fray, then worked her way through the clusters of guests and finally reached the TV room without spilling anything.

Another large group was gathered in front of the television, mostly male

Morgans: Sam's dad, his sons and sons-in-law, and a few boyfriends of the unmarried daughters. They were watching a football game while assorted children played board games on the rug. Through the glass sliders, she spotted a group in the back-yard playing touch football. Darrell was one of the kids out there, she noticed. Then she saw that Sam was playing, too, and keeping the action from getting too out of hand.

She watched for a moment, realizing that Darrell wasn't acting any wilder or more mischievous than any of the other boys. She thought again of her mother's house. It had been hard for him there, surrounded by adults and Lillian's fragile knickknacks. The place was almost a museum.

Sam spotted her and took a break from the game. He stepped inside and put an arm around her. "Did I see you carrying some food in here, or was that just a mirage?"

"There was some on that tray about five seconds ago . . . but I think it's mostly gone." The crestfallen look on his face made her laugh. "Don't worry. Your mom has enough to feed an army. I don't think you'll starve today."

"You don't understand, it's survival of

the fittest in this family." Sam reached across his brother and beat him to the last mini hot dog. His brother Paul, who had been best man at their wedding, glanced up at Sam with a startled look.

"Sorry, I need my protein. Those kids are running me into the ground."

Paul laughed. "I'll come out and help you. That kid Darrell looks pretty good. Is that the boy from New Horizons that you told me about?"

Sam suddenly looked a little uneasy. "Yeah, it is. We've been spending a lot of time with him lately."

"That's really nice of you guys. He seems like a good kid. Are you trying to adopt him or something?"

Paul's question was innocent enough, but it still made Jessica do a double take. She shot Sam a questioning look. Exactly what was he telling his family about Darrell?

Sam kept his eyes on his brother. "We're looking into it. Being his foster parents, I mean."

He finally looked at Jessica but she was so angry at him, she couldn't speak.

They had never agreed on anything. They'd barely discussed it. But now was neither the time nor the place.

She shot him a scathing look and picked up the empty tray. "I'd better go back and help your mom. I think dinner's almost ready."

"About time! I'm starved," Paul said, oblivious to the tension.

Sam just looked at her wordlessly. He had to know that she was upset. Maybe he, too, thought it best to save the conversation until they were alone.

Sam rubbed his chin. "I guess I'll go out and round up the kids and get them to wash their hands before they sit down."

"You do that." Her tone was sharper than she intended but she couldn't help it.

She turned and headed for the kitchen, hoping she could drum up a better mood to get her through the rest of the day.

Leigh noticed the number of cars in the driveway and guessed that she and James were the last to arrive. James had picked up a pie at Molly's shop and she was holding a bouquet of flowers.

They stood on the doorstep side by side. Leigh felt a little nervous as James rang the doorbell. She wondered again if coming here had been the right thing to do and wondered now why she hadn't made some excuse to stay home alone.

Anyone spotting them there would mistake them for a couple, she realized. Of course they weren't. Just two loose ends, finding a place to spend the holiday. Together.

Suddenly the door opened and Carolyn Lewis appeared. "Welcome, welcome. Come right in," she said brightly.

James stepped aside to let Leigh enter first. The house seemed cozy and warm compared to the crisp fall weather outside. Her senses were overwhelmed by wonderful cooking smells: turkey and sweet potatoes roasting and sweet scents of desserts. From some distant room, she heard the soft notes of classical music.

"Come on in out of that cold weather. They're saying we might get a little snow flurry tonight, though I hope not. I like my Christmas white, but Thanksgiving seems rushing it."

Carolyn's smile was wide and warm. She spoke with a slight southern accent, Leigh realized. She could also hear an occasional slur in her words, the only remaining trace of her stroke. Leigh had heard that Carolyn had been in a life-threatening coma last January just as her daughter was rushed to the hospital to give birth to her grandson. But both women had pulled through valiantly, and Carolyn had made an amazing recovery.

James kissed Carolyn on the cheek, wishing her a happy holiday, then helped Leigh off with her coat. Reverend Ben walked in from the living room, nearly shouting his greeting.

"There you are! Happy Thanksgiving, James. So good to see you today." Ben leaned forward and gave James a hug. He turned to Leigh, beaming a welcome as warm as his wife's and folding the hand she offered in both of his.

"Hello again, Leigh. We're so happy you could join us."

"Thank you for having me," Leigh said.

"Our pleasure. My wife's made us an enormous dinner. We needed more customers. I hope you're up to the challenge."

"I'll try my best." She smiled at him, feeling at ease already.

"There's a good attitude. We'll have to work on James, though. We need to fatten him up a bit, don't you think?"

"Thanks a lot. What am I, a Christmas goose?" James's expression was comically indignant and Leigh laughed.

James glanced down at Leigh, who stood close beside him in the small foyer. Their eyes met, sharing the good humor, and he was glad he had persuaded her to come with him here.

As Ben and Carolyn led them into the living room James stepped aside to let Leigh go first, noticing the golden lights in her rich brown hair. She wore a navy blue dress with gold buttons, very stylish, he thought, despite her pregnancy. He knew by now that she felt self-conscious about the changes in her body, but he thought she was beautiful. She had a natural, unassuming type of beauty, the kind that takes time to really see.

Her cheeks were still rosy from the cold air outside and her eyes bright, as she took a seat on the long couch. James quickly sat beside her. So she wouldn't feel adrift in this sea of new faces, he told himself, though he knew very well it was also because he liked to be near her.

Ben's son, Mark, and son-in-law, Jack Anderson, were seated across from each other, a chessboard set up between them on the coffee table. They both looked up to say hello, and James introduced Leigh.

He glanced over the board. Only a few pieces were left standing. "Who's winning?"

"I am." Both men spoke at the same time then laughed at each other, though neither took his eyes away from the battlefield.

"Why don't you play the winner, James?" Mark reached out and moved a pawn one space forward.

"Sure, but I'm not great at chess."

"That's all right, neither is Mark." Jack slid his bishop forward, took the pawn, and sat back. "Check."

Mark looked distressed. He hadn't seen that coming.

"Here's someone who'd like to play," Ben announced.

James followed Ben's gaze and saw Ben's daughter, Rachel, coming into the room, bent over almost double as she held up the two tiny hands of her ten-month-old son, William.

"Here he comes. Don't say I didn't warn you. . . ."

William was dressed in miniature blue corduroy pants, small black boots, and a green-and-blue-striped rugby shirt.

"Hey, buddy. Come to your uncle Mark. Help me out here. This is an emergency."

James watched as Rachel led the baby over. He glanced at Leigh, who looked enthralled. "He's totally adorable," she said quietly.

"Isn't he?" James agreed, mesmerized by

the sight of the tiny person.

Rachel popped her head up and smiled. "Thanks. I can't wait until he starts walking. My back can't take much more of this."

Carolyn followed close behind. She was holding a wooden spoon and wore an apron tied over her dress. "You say that now. Just wait. He'll be into everything once he's roaming around on his own."

William had finally reached the chess table where Mark and Jack beamed down at him.

"Let him go a sec, honey. Let's see if he can stand."

Rachel carefully released William's tiny hands, one by one. He looked perplexed a moment and stared up at her, holding on to the edge of the coffee table for dear life, James thought.

"You're okay, honey. You can do it," his mother coaxed.

"Look at that big boy." Jack's voice was full of pride. The baby responded happily; he looked up at his father with a laughing gurgle. Then he let go of the table and moved toward Jack with an awkward step.

Suddenly the chess table caught his attention. He quickly turned to face it, reached out, and grabbed for everything in sight.

"William! For goodness' sake!" Jack leaped up and scooped up his son just as the toddler began to sway, heading for a fall along with the cascade of chess pieces. "Did you have to do that, honey? Daddy was finally going to beat your uncle Mark. I've waited years for this!"

"Way to go, Willie-boy." Mark reached up and patted his nephew's diapered bottom. "I knew you'd come through for me."

"See, I told you." Carolyn laughed, shaking her head at her grandson. "Well, I guess the chess game is over. You can all come in to dinner."

Ben showed them to their seats, and James was relieved to see he and Leigh were seated side by side. Then he felt a little odd, realizing that the Lewises were treating them very much like a couple. Was it just his imagination? He had spoken with Ben about Leigh a few times since she arrived in town. Ben knew very well that she and James were merely friends, thrown together by circumstances. He had told Ben plainly enough that as much as he admired Leigh, he simply wanted to help her while she was in town.

Still, his host and hostess continued to give him knowing looks, and there was nothing James could do about it. He glanced at Leigh, who was now helping Carolyn light the candles on the table. *Well, there are worse things people could think about me than to assume I claim a special place in this woman's life,* he decided.

"It's so nice to have you all here today," Ben said when everyone was seated. "We all have so much to be thankful for: our health, our family, our friends." His gaze came to rest on James. "I was wondering if you'd care to say the blessing for us today, James?"

"I'd be honored," James replied.

Around the table, everyone bowed their heads and held hands. James was keenly aware of holding Leigh's smooth hand in his own. He thought for a moment about what he might say.

"Thank you, Lord, for bringing us together today, to share in this wonderful meal and to share in all the love and good feeling within these walls. Please keep us mindful of our duty to share our bounty with those less fortunate, not just today, but every day. Please help us to be thankful and aware of our many blessings today and throughout the year to come. Amen."

"Amen." Ben raised his head. "That was perfect, thank you. Though I might ask the Lord to help us be mindful of both the blessings that are obvious to us — and those that might come in disguise." He pinned James with his sharp blue eyes, then stood to carve the turkey that Carolyn had set before him. "You've outdone yourself, dear. This looks too beautiful to eat."

Bowls of vegetables, stuffing, cranberry sauce, and two kinds of potatoes were passed as Ben filled everyone's plate with a portion of turkey. The family banter continued, interspersed with compliments on the food, which was amazing, James thought. Or maybe it had simply been too long since he'd been back for this most all-American holiday.

Rachel sat on Leigh's other side, with the baby's high chair to her right at the end of the table. James was glad to see Rachel engage Leigh in conversation, asking about her work at Dr. Harding's office and how she liked Cape Light, and about her pregnancy.

"Come to think of it, I have tons of things I can give you for the baby. William got so many clothes, he didn't get to wear half of them. And it's not all blue. Most of the things are for a boy or a girl," she added.

Leigh smiled. "I won't mind dressing my daughter in blue once in a while. I don't think of colors as strictly for boys or girls."

"I totally agree," Rachel said. "Some people get so silly about things like that. . . ."

Carolyn needed some help in the kitchen and Leigh started to rise. "Oh, no, you sit. I can go," Rachel said. She had William on her lap, though, and he didn't want to go back into his high chair. "Jack, can you take the baby?"

"I can take him. Give him here." Leigh smiled and held out her arms to William, and he went to her willingly.

Rachel stood by and watched a moment. "Are you sure you're all right?"

"We'll be fine. I need the practice," Leigh replied.

Rachel bent down to retrieve a small stuffed giraffe from underneath the table. "Okay, just call if you need me."

James pulled his seat a little closer and draped his arm around the back of Leigh's chair, so that William wouldn't wiggle away and fall between them.

William grabbed a silver spoon from the table, banged it on the tablecloth, then put it in his mouth. James quickly cleared away anything potentially dangerous within his reach.

"If we're not careful, he might try one of those stunts, where the magician pulls the tablecloth off the table with all the dishes still on."

"Oh, I hope not." Leigh gave a short laugh and glanced at him just for a second before focusing back on William.

James smiled again, watching her, and got the oddest rush of feeling. What if she were his wife and this was their son? Then he wondered where the strange question had come from. It was this house maybe, so filled with family warmth and the love the Lewises shared for each other.

Though James always assumed he would marry someday, he never seemed to make the time or space for it in his life. His commitment to the mission was all-consuming. It fulfilled him, gave his life structure and meaning and a deep spiritual dimension. Perhaps it was the most obvious truth in the world, but it now occurred to him that family life was rich and meaningful, too. Was there a more profound or more spiritual experience than raising a child? Watching Leigh amuse William while he sat on her lap, James didn't think so.

The mission and the church were his

family. Hadn't he told Leigh that when they first met? Yet now, that didn't seem enough. He had deep connections but no one truly intimate to share his life, no partner whose life was entwined with his through love and children and the many vital threads that married couples shared.

Maybe the problems at the mission had set off this chain of thoughts. First had come the unsettling realization that he wasn't indispensable. His presence was valued and respected but not essential. Even his calling as a minister was not quite as he had always pictured it. His work was important, but it didn't take the place of having a family. It wasn't supposed to, he realized as he watched Ben sitting at the head of the table, the patriarch of this warm, loving clan. James admired Ben, his experience and wisdom, the way he had with people. Now he wondered if Ben was perhaps a better minister in some ways, because his life experience had been made richer by marriage and children.

Rachel returned and reached down to take William off Leigh's lap. "Come here, big guy. Time for a nap, I hope."

Leigh looked at James and raised an eyebrow. "He doesn't look very sleepy, does he?"

"Not at all. But they have certain schedules, I understand."

"Yes, I've been reading about that. It's not as easy as it looks."

He sensed a note of worry beneath her joking tone. He gave her shoulder a light squeeze. "Don't worry, you'll be a great mother. You're a natural. I can see it already."

"Thanks." She glanced up at him and smiled slightly. He was suddenly aware that he still sat with his arm around her chair. Around her shoulder now, actually. But Leigh didn't seem uncomfortable with this closeness and he didn't move away.

What about Leigh? he thought, gazing down at her.

Could he love her?

She had already touched his heart in a certain way he had never quite known before. But was that love or just a kind of empathy? The two of them were so different, on completely different paths it seemed. Whenever he thought of the woman he might someday marry, it was someone who shared his commitment to the church and who would embrace mission life. Leigh didn't seem to fit either of those images. But maybe there were other things that were more important, things he'd had little experience with and didn't even expect.

"This is the last of it. Do we have any more bags?" Sam dropped his rake and pulled a pair of work gloves from his back pocket. Jessica found a box of plastic lawn bags and pulled out one more. It felt good to get outside and do some hard work after all the eating and lying about she had done yesterday at Sam's parents' house. She needed to stretch her muscles and clear her head in the fresh air.

She snapped open the bag and began stuffing the raked leaves inside. "I still need to put those bulbs in. They say Thanksgiving is the absolute latest you can plant them."

"We can do it tomorrow. They'll still sprout." He leaned over and scooped up an armful of leaves. Then he paused and pushed up the sleeve of his fleece pullover to check his watch.

"I want to get over to the center this afternoon. I promised Luke and the kids I'd come by for some basketball."

"Basketball, today? I thought we were going to do yard work."

"We've been raking for hours, Jess. It's almost three o'clock. You must be ready for a break, too."

Jessica stood up and picked a few leaves off her sweater. "You just saw Darrell yesterday, Sam."

"What's Darrell got to do with it? I promised Luke I'd help him coach the kids."

"All right. You're just going there to help coach. . . . But I want to talk to you about something that happened yesterday. I just didn't get the chance . . ."

Sam shoved more leaves into the bag. "Something about Darrell, you mean?"

"Nothing he did, nothing like that. . . . I'm upset with you for telling your brother that we're taking Darrell in as a foster child."

Sam stood up and stared at her, clearly surprised by her outburst. "I said we were looking into it. And I only said that when Paul asked me, point-blank."

"Telling Paul is like broadcasting it worldwide."

"Maybe, but I still don't see the problem."

I'm not thinking about taking Darrell in. You are, she wanted to say.

But that response was far too harsh. It would only make everything worse, she thought.

Jessica chose her words carefully. "I

would just like to talk it through more before we start telling people we're considering it. I don't even know Darrell that well yet."

"And you still don't really like him, right?" he finished for her.

"I didn't say that." Jessica crossed her arms over her chest. Now that they had stopped working she was chilly. "I actually like him a little better than before. He was pretty good at your parents' house. You must have had a talk with him or something."

"I did. But it wasn't just that. Darrell felt more comfortable at my folks' house than he did at your mother's, calmer and more accepted probably. And there were plenty of kids there to play with, so that helped a lot."

"That's what it looked like to me, too." She kicked at the leaves with the toe of her sneaker, sending a few into the air and watching them float down.

"You were nicer to him, too, I noticed."

Jessica didn't look up at him. "Well, he was nicer to me. He didn't play any tricks on me or crawl under the table."

"I laid down the law about that." Sam crouched down and started working on the leaves again, stuffing handfuls in a steady rhythm into the open bag. Jessica stood watching him, her thoughts on the boy.

Darrell had been awed by the Morgan gathering, and she had found herself touched by that. It was clear to her now that Darrell had been raised with very little: tenuous family connections, sparse emotional support, and few material comforts.

"I saw him break the wishbone with your father," she said, her voice a little softer. "How did he get that job?"

"My dad always pulls one kid's name out of a hat. We did it that way when we were kids, too."

"Darrell was the lucky winner. I didn't realize."

"That day he was."

Jessica bent down and helped again. The bag was almost full, and she used her hands to compress the leaves. "Have you spoken to Luke about him yet?"

"I asked him to find out if Darrell will be available for fostering. He might tell me more today. He thinks it's possible."

"But he doesn't know for sure?"

"No, not for sure."

Sam picked up the bag, pulled the ties, and sealed it. "Why don't we call it a day?"

Jessica nodded to a smaller pile of leaves

on the other side of the yard. "I want to clean those up, but why don't you get going? It is getting late."

"I can help you finish."

"No, it's all right. I can manage." She stopped and faced him. "I don't want you to hate me over this, Sam, but I need to be honest. If we're going to do something as major as fostering a kid, I need you to talk to me about it first. And now that it's come up, I'm not sure I can be a good parent to Darrell. Maybe it's just a bad time for me, and I'm too stressed about getting pregnant or something. I don't want to disappoint you . . . but I'm just not ready for it."

She watched Sam take a breath. He started to move toward her, then stopped. "Okay. Well. At least you're being up front with me, Jess. It's important that we know where we stand on this."

Though he would never admit it to her, she could tell from the sound of his voice and the look on his face that he was crushed. She didn't regret being honest with him — that was necessary — but she didn't feel good about hurting him either. It left her feeling bleak and hollow inside.

Sam rubbed his chin. "So the idea of taking in Darrell is closed for good?"

She could say yes, end this discussion once and for all, but the moment she thought about doing that the bleak feeling inside got worse.

"Maybe we can think about it some more," she allowed.

"Can I talk to Luke? It might not even be possible, you know."

She nodded quickly. "Sure. Let's see what Luke finds out. I guess I'm curious now myself."

That much was true. If Luke were to say that Darrell had already been placed in foster care, then there wouldn't be much of an issue here. *And I'd be off the hook, in a way,* Jessica realized.

"Okay. I'll be back around five." Sam leaned over and kissed her cheek. "Is that good?"

"That's fine." Jessica forced a small smile.

She watched Sam walk heavily across their property, then climb into his truck and drive away. She leaned on the rake, feeling as if she might suddenly cry.

She looked up at the darkening sky and the web of bare branches above, then pressed her fingers to her eyes.

Dear Lord, this is so hard for me. I'm sorry I can't seem to love this boy the way Sam does.

It doesn't seem right to take him if I feel the way I do, but I also can't bear hurting Sam. I don't know what to do. Please show me some way through this. Please let this question pass.

Leigh often had trouble sleeping, getting comfortable with the weight of the baby inside her and with her many worries flocking around her bed once the lights were out. Sunday nights, for some reason, seemed particularly hard, and tonight was no different. It was worse, in fact, since something she had eaten for dinner wasn't settling quite right.

She pulled on her robe and crept down the stairs, planning to make some more of Vera's foolproof remedy, the ginger tea. But at the end of the staircase she saw all the lights in the kitchen still on.

In the kitchen, Leigh found Vera standing at the table, her eyes downcast.

"Vera? Are you all right?"

Vera nodded her head vigorously but couldn't answer. Her mouth was filled with straight pins.

That's the first I've ever seen her at a loss for words, Leigh thought with merry affection. She noticed scraps of cloth on the table, satiny white stuff and some other type of fabric that appeared to be fake fur. In her right hand, Vera was holding a long pair of shears at an odd angle, looking as if she was afraid of it.

She put the shears down and took the pins from between her lips. "Would you look at this mess? Such a waste of good material . . . I'll be so embarrassed."

She shook her head sadly, and Leigh suddenly saw that this was no laughing matter; Vera was truly dismayed.

"What is it? What's the matter?" Leigh stepped beside her and surveyed the table. "Are you trying to make something?"

"Costumes for the pageant. I don't know how I got stuck with the job. I told the committee I'm all thumbs when it comes to sewing. But they insisted it would be easy. 'Just cut it and pin it, then bring it in to the meeting and we'll all help you sew,' they said." Vera shook her head. "Well, it's well past midnight, I'm almost asleep on my feet, and I've cut this stuff out all wrong and have no idea how to get it together and —"

"Don't give up yet." Leigh patted Vera's arm, which felt thin and fragile as a bird's through her flannel robe. "It may not be as bad as you think." She picked up some pieces of the white material and held them in the air. "Is this supposed to be some type of tunic?"

"Angel's clothes. This fur stuff is for the shepherd and maybe the kids who play the animals, too. I got it all mixed up."

Leigh studied the chaotic array of fabric, notions, and tissue-paper pattern pieces that covered the table. "Do you have a picture or something?"

At the counter Vera showed Leigh the pictures of the costumes that had come with the patterns. "Then I have all these measurements of the children in Sunday school. So you need to adjust, but I wasn't sure which lines to follow, once I started snipping."

"I see. . . . Well, I think I could do something with this. It won't look exactly like the pictures, though."

Vera's expression grew a hundred watts brighter. "Could you, dear? You told me you knew how to sew, but I didn't want to bother you. I thought it was beyond all hope, quite frankly."

"Not at all. I think I can make something angel-like out of it. When is your meeting?"

"Tomorrow night, down at the church."

"So we have some time, then. Dr. Harding goes to Southport Hospital on

Monday afternoons for his rounds. So I can help you some more tomorrow, when I get home."

"Bless you!" Vera leaned over and gave her a quick, tight hug. Then she hopped across the kitchen and grabbed the teakettle off the dish drainer. "I'll make some tea. Or would you prefer some hot cocoa or warm milk maybe?"

"Some ginger tea would be perfect. I couldn't sleep and I was coming down to make some."

"The good Lord answered my prayers and sent you down. That's what happened."

Leigh smiled to herself as she made a rough sketch on the back of the pattern package and then sorted through the pieces of material. She doubted that God had sent her down to the kitchen tonight — it was more like her secret worries and upset stomach — but she didn't bother to debate Vera about it.

Chapter Nine

No matter how many times Sam passed the sign that said NEW HORIZONS, he would always think of the place as the Cranberry Cottages. Some of the old cottages were still standing, now renovated as sleeping quarters for the students and counselors. Luke McAllister had bought the property on a whim, simply because he'd spent summers at the place as a boy and it brought back fond memories.

Luke had been at loose ends back then, with the rest of his life ahead of him and no clear plan. Injuries from a shooting had forced him to quit the Boston police force and left him bitter and scarred, inside and out. The town had been deeply divided when he announced his intentions to build a rehabilitation center for troubled city kids. Many in town had wanted him to take his "troublemakers" and ideals elsewhere. They tried to drive him out, but Luke had stuck with his plan.

Sam was one of those who had taken Luke's side, and one of the only workmen in town willing to help him renovate and put up the new buildings that now held classrooms, offices, and a gym.

Once the center opened, Sam kept coming back, New Horizons' on-call Mr. Fix-it. Gradually, that role expanded to volunteer counselor and sports coach. It wasn't always easy to connect with these kids — some had real issues and seemed unreachable — and it wasn't always clear that the help he offered made any difference. But he tried to keep in mind what Luke had once told him: "Even if one little thing you say or do reaches one kid, that's enough. You've changed someone's life, and that's a lot."

Sam hadn't come today to change anyone's life around. He was here to repair a broken gutter. He also hoped to ask Luke whether he had found about more about Darrell's situation with foster care. Sam had never gotten a chance to mention it last Friday when he came to coach basketball. Or maybe, he reflected, his conversation with Jessica that afternoon had made him hesitate to bring it up.

Sam felt caught. He thought Darrell was a terrific kid in a terrible situation. He wanted to help him, but now he was worried about where that help might lead. What if it all just added up to another disappointment for the boy? He prayed to heaven that wouldn't be so.

The truth was, the situation wasn't looking good. Jessica still hadn't really warmed to Darrell, and Sam couldn't blame her. She wanted a baby, their own child. He did, too. But he had gotten so involved with Darrell, he was just seeing it from a completely different angle. The look on her face Friday when she admitted her real feelings had finally broken through. He was just starting to understand her side of it.

And he finally realized he couldn't ignore it anymore — or hold out great hopes that it would change.

Still, he wanted to talk to Luke and find out what he could. Jessica thought it was okay to go ahead that much at least.

He found himself on a path leading to the main building, where Luke's office was located. Then he spotted some kids playing soccer on the nearby athletic field. Except for himself, Sam had never known a guy less suited to sitting behind a desk than Luke. He knew there was a good chance he would find his friend outside, watching the game or maybe even kicking the ball around.

Sure enough, Luke stood with a whistle around his neck, watching from the sidelines. He saw Sam and grinned.

"Hey, Sam. Want to play? The red team could use a sub."

Sam shook his head. "I'm here to work, remember?"

"Oh, right. The gutter. It's the one on the back of the building, just over my office window. Need me to go with you?"

"I can find it. . . . Listen, I was wondering if you learned anything more about Darrell. Is he going into foster care when he leaves here?"

"Oh, right." Luke nodded. "I'm sorry I didn't get back to you on that. I called the social worker who's dealing with the family and basically, the situation is still undecided. It sounds as if Darrell's mother has more or less faced the fact that she can't take care of him right now. She's thinking about signing him into foster care, but she hasn't gone through with it yet."

"Oh . . . I see." It wasn't the answer Sam had hoped for, but it wasn't the worst. "Wasn't there a grandmother or a neighbor taking care of him too? How do they fit into the picture?"

"There's a grandmother but she's not well. The boy is a little too much for her to handle. She could possibly apply for custody, but the social worker doesn't think she will. There was also a neighbor who got involved with him, but she has children of her own to care for. Darrell and her son are friends, and she was just trying to help out."

"Darrell told me about the neighbor," Sam said. "He talks to his buddy on the phone a lot. He hasn't heard much from his mother lately, though, and I know that's hard for him. He tries to understand, saying she's sick and needs to get better before he can go home again."

"That's one way to look at it. The least painful for him, I guess." Luke stared out at the soccer players, his arms crossed over his chest. "His mother has a serious problem. She's in and out of rehab. It's hard to give a child up to foster care. I don't know if I could do it. But the counselor working with her thinks that's what Darrell needs right now — some stability, a real home life. Even being here a few weeks has helped him. You've helped him, Sam."

Sam shrugged. "Darrell is special. We just seemed to click."

"Well, there's no doubt you'd be a great guardian for him. I've already told the social worker about you, and I'll be the first one to help you fill out the forms to apply. But what about Jessica? How does she feel about the situation?"

Sam dug his hands into his pockets. He didn't know how to answer. He knew it might hurt his chances, but he had to be honest about it, especially with Luke.

"Jessica and I are still talking this over. She's very focused on getting pregnant and having a baby. I'm afraid the whole idea just sort of sideswiped her. She and Darrell haven't really gotten to know each other that well, either. I'd love to say they get along great, but it just hasn't worked out that way . . . so far."

Luke considered his words. "I'm sorry to hear that. It won't really work if you're not both willing — more than willing, I'd say."

"I know." Sam nodded. "I haven't given up hope yet, though."

"I hope not. There's a lot of ball game left, pal. Darrell is scheduled to be here until January. A lot could happen by then."

Sam felt grateful for his friend's encouragement. That was one thing he had always liked about Luke — he wasn't a quitter. Sam knew he wasn't a quitter, either. He wouldn't give up on Darrell. He wouldn't turn into another grown-up who abandoned him. He knew it was hard for Jessica, but he prayed that by some small miracle, she would come around to the idea.

Emily couldn't help feeling a little wary as she entered her living room, where Dan sat on her couch, her two cats snuggled on either side of him like fur bookends. Dan seemed oblivious to the cats as he stared down at a yellow legal pad with a grim expression. His pencil was poised just above the paper, swooping down every few seconds to jot a note or two. He was reviewing the guest list she had made for their wedding, as if it were copy about to run on the front page of the *New York Times.* She loved him to the stars, but when he got into this cranky editor mode it made her sort of crazy. Besides, she'd had a wretched day at the village hall, trying to get a squabbling committee to agree on the size of new street signs. She had left her office at six, with the debate still raging, only to find that Dan was set on coming over to discuss the wedding list. It was a Monday in spades.

She watched him a moment then went to

tend the fire. She poked the logs around, making them spark, and tossed on another log. She started back to the couch but didn't sit down.

"Do you want some more coffee or something?"

"I'm fine." The pencil swooped; another guest knocked off the list — or, at least, put into the doubtful category.

"I'm sorry, Dan. . . . I know it looks like a lot of people. But half of them probably won't even come."

"Then why invite them at all?"

Emily sighed. They had been through this so many times. Why couldn't he understand?

"I have to," she said, enunciating every word. "If we're inviting certain people that we do want, then we really have to invite other people that maybe we don't want or we'll end up insulting them."

"If we don't really want them at our wedding, why would we care if they're insulted?"

"Dan, come on. This always happens with a big party."

"That very well might be true, dear. But I recall a certain person who agreed in this very room — on this very couch, no less — that she would keep the guest list down to fifty." He held up the pad and flipped the sheets of names. "This is not fifty guests, Emily. It's more like five hundred."

She cringed and looked away. "It's actually a hundred and twenty-three."

"And that's not even counting our immediate families, who are the only people I really want or need to be with us in the first place. That would be seven, a perfect number. My two kids and son-in-law, Jessica and Sam, Sara and your mother."

"Sara would want to bring Luke."

"All right, Luke is invited, too. I have no problem with that."

"What about Betty?" she asked quietly, mentioning her best friend. "I can't leave Betty out. And she'll probably want to bring a date along."

Dan glanced at her over the edge of his glasses. "Okay, Betty Bowman and date. Counting us, that's still only twelve. We could all sit at the same table in some nice restaurant."

"Just a little gathering at a restaurant? That's all you want to do for our wedding? That doesn't sound like . . . like much of a celebration to me."

She hadn't meant to sound so forlorn, but their wedding was supposed to be the happiest day of their lives . . . well, one of the happiest at any rate.

"Oh, Emily, please. Don't look at me like that. Please?" Dan stood up, took her hand, and led her back to the couch. For a moment they just sat watching the fire, leaning into each other in contented silence.

"I don't want you to be unhappy, sweetheart," Dan finally said. "But we just can't seem to find a common ground. We agreed on a medium-sized party, and you make up a guest list suitable for the inaugural ball." He leafed through the pages on the pad and she finally had to laugh.

"All right . . . maybe I did get a little carried away," Emily said. "But I knew you'd do a real hatchet job. I had to overcompensate."

"Oh, that was just a trick then?"

"Not really. But if we don't decide on something soon, we'll have to push back the date of the trip, and I know you don't want to do that."

He looked alarmed now, sitting up straight. "We can't change the trip, honey. You know that. I've got the boat all lined up. Those weeks are the only time it's available until next fall and it's all paid for. At least our honeymoon is planned."

"And you've done a great job of it," she admitted.

She had to give him credit. While she muddled over the wedding arrangements, coming up so far with zilch, Dan had figured out their entire six-week trip. *Then again, he's been planning a trip like this for years and only had to make a few adjustments to accommodate me, his unexpected traveling companion,* she thought. They would fly to St. Martin and pick up the sailboat Dan was renting from a friend. The thirty-five-foot, three-mast boat was quite beautiful but looked like a lot to handle. Dan had been teaching her how to sail and promised she would be able to sail it herself before their trip was through.

It was going to be a perfect trip, a perfect adventure to start their married life together, she thought. If only they could get through the getting married part. . . .

"Which is why you should let me plan the wedding, too." Dan drew close and whispered the last words, tickling her ear. "Why don't we just elope? Then we can have the big party you seem so set on in the spring when we get back."

Emily settled against him, resting her head on his shoulder. "Oh . . . I don't know. That might work. I would hate to hurt everyone's feelings, though. Like Jessica and Sara and your kids, I mean.

They might feel left out."

"And your mother will be apoplectic. You forgot to mention that."

"That, too." She glanced at him and grinned. The thought had crossed her mind, of course, but it seemed so obvious it didn't bear mentioning.

"Will you at least think about it? Won't it be great to finally be married? Isn't that what we really both want?"

Marriage to Dan was exactly what she wanted. She had waited a long time to meet someone like him. She had thought she would never marry again or have anyone to share her life. Their love was a precious gift, a true blessing. She had to focus on that, she reminded herself, instead of on how and when and where they would celebrate.

"All right, I'll think about it," she agreed. "It would certainly cut down on the list making."

She pushed the legal pad aside and it fell on the floor. Dan watched her, looking very pleased by the gesture. "That's the spirit. I knew you'd see this my way sooner or later."

Then he pulled her close for a deep, warm kiss, and Emily decided she didn't want to think about party planning any more. She was going to like being married to Dan. She just had to keep focusing on their future. This wedding glitch would sort itself out one way or another.

"Thank you so much for coming, dear. I know it's an inconvenience, but you've done such a beautiful job with the costumes, and I really didn't think I could show the ladies how it's all supposed to fit together on my own."

"That's all right, Vera. I understand." Leigh glanced at Vera seated beside her in the car, nervously twisting her gloves.

Just as she promised, Leigh had worked on the costumes and changed the design to compensate for the mistakes Vera had made cutting the fabric. Leigh had drawn sketches of how the costumes would now look and written out instructions for the sewing, but at the last minute Vera got nervous about showing her group the revised designs. More than nervous, actually; Vera was more like terrified.

She had practically begged Leigh to come along, and Leigh found she couldn't refuse — which didn't really make Vera any calmer. Now she rubbed energetically at a speck of dirt on Leigh's dashboard.

"They've always done it just the same

way for so many years. I hope no one is upset." Vera turned to Leigh again. "Not that what you've done isn't lovely. It's even nicer, I think, but some of the women on these committees can be very particular."

Leigh smiled to herself, guiding the car into a parking spot. The church committee didn't faze her — she had certainly faced down far worse — though she doubted they were half as intimidating as her landlady seemed to think. Besides, what did she care what the women thought of her? She might not even be around for the Christmas Fair. In the meantime, though, she could lend Vera some support. Leigh felt as if she owed it to her.

They started toward the church, each carrying shopping bags with the costume pieces.

"Into the lion's den," Vera murmured. "At least I brought a coffee cake."

Leigh only laughed. Vera always seemed to have a coffee cake handy.

A short time later, Vera was slicing up her cake and basking in the rave reviews. The group of women had looked wary as she confessed to botching the fabric cutting. But once she passed around Leigh's sketches and showed them a sewed-up sample of one of the costumes, their expressions had changed from apprehension to delight.

"This is absolutely exquisite. It looks like it belongs in a Broadway show." Sophie Potter held up the angel costume and spun it around, showing it off from different angles. "I don't think we've ever had anything nicer."

"Look at the sheep's outfit. I love the little ears." Carolyn Lewis held up the headpiece Leigh had made for the manger sheep. She smiled at Leigh. "Where did you learn to sew like this, Leigh? Have you worked in the fashion industry?"

"No . . . not exactly." Leigh paused, unsure of how to answer without an outright lie. "My mother taught me. I've just always had a knack for it."

Rachel Anderson stood near her mother, admiring the tulle sash Leigh had fashioned for a belt on the angel tunic. "This is so cute. You must be making things for your baby."

"I haven't had a chance," Leigh said honestly. "I don't have a sewing machine handy."

"I can loan you mine, dear. It's only a little portable, but it should be fine for baby clothes." Carolyn hung the angel costume on a hanger again, taking great care.

"I'll ask Ben to bring it over to Vera's house for you."

Leigh was surprised and moved by her generosity. Rachel had already given her several boxes of clothes and linens, most of the items brand new. She did need more things for the baby, though. She would buy most of the clothes, of course. But she had always imagined making some special things if she ever had a child. Still, she couldn't accept Carolyn's offer. She didn't feel right, not when she was lying to her — lying to them all.

"That's nice of you, Carolyn, but I don't know. The noise might bother James and Vera —"

"It wouldn't bother me at all." Vera appeared carrying plates of her cake, which she proceeded to hand out. "You can set it up in the living room if you like. James won't hear a thing up on the third floor."

"If you had a machine handy, maybe you could help us a little more, Leigh?" Sophie's voice was both hesitant and coaxing. "We're so shorthanded on a sewing crew this year. I know you're not a church member . . . but it would be a great favor to us. We would appreciate it so much."

Leigh felt herself the focus of the small

cluster of women, all gazing at her, all waiting for her reply. The attention made her nervous. Her first impulse was to say she couldn't help and give some plausible excuse.

Then she thought of Vera and James and how kind they had been to her. The church was important to them both, certainly to James. She would be helping both of them in a way if she helped these women. Perhaps the gesture would help them think a little better of her when she was gone. And the truth was, she didn't have anything better to do at night than sit in her room reading or in the living room listening to Vera's knitting needles. Sewing, which she loved, would be a welcome distraction.

"I guess I could help you if you really need me to," she said finally.

Sophie clapped her hands together. "Oh, we need you, dear. I think you were heaven sent." Leigh found her choice of words amusing. Hadn't Vera said almost the same thing when she had shown up in the kitchen Sunday night? "I have some more fabric to give you for costumes for the wise men and the shepherd —"

"I bet you could help with some of the items we're making to sell at the fair, too," Carolyn added. "Table runners and aprons, that sort of thing. We sold a ton of them last year and hoped to do even better this year. I can show you what we have so far. Maybe you'll have some new ideas for us, though."

"I bet she will. She's so artistic." Vera beamed at her.

All the praise and attention was embarrassing, but Leigh's protests — she really didn't want them to get their expectations up — fell on deaf ears. It seemed settled that she was the newly crowned sewing authority.

When the meeting ended, Leigh found herself carrying out several more shopping bags of fabric than she and Vera had come in with. She now had enough sewing projects to keep her busy for weeks. How had that happened? She had only meant to stay for a few minutes, to help Vera explain the new costumes.

This town was a strange place, she decided. She had tried her best to stay aloof and uninvolved, but something about the people here kept drawing her in.

Vera sat beside her in the car, looking far calmer than she had on the ride over. She smiled and gently shook her head. "Dear me, one thing leads to another, doesn't it?"

"It does around here." Leigh gave a

short, amazed laugh. She could tell that Vera didn't understand her little joke, but it was too difficult to explain.

It was nearly eleven when they arrived back at Vera's house. Vera wanted to catch up on some knitting and watch the news. Leigh went straight up to her room. She clicked on the light on her bedside table and carefully shut her door.

Taking her phone out of her purse, she checked her messages. One from Alice. She had just spoken to Alice last night. The situation was status quo then. Now Leigh wondered if there had been some sudden change. She hoped Martin's business problems had gotten even worse, so much so that he couldn't spare the time to pursue her.

But maybe it was bad news, a change that shifted things the other way. Maybe she would need to leave here right away.

She dialed the replay code and strained to hear Alice's soft tone. "Hi, honey, it's me. I have some news for you. He fired the detective. It was one of his fits. He practically threw the poor man right out of the office. I don't think he's found anyone else yet. The bills go through me and these PIs always want something up front to start. The layoffs and investigation have been distracting. He had to turn over some records this week. I thought he was going to lose it. That's when he fired the guy, took it all out on him, I guess. So much going on. All the better, right?

"You sounded good the other night. Sounds as if you've met some good people down there. God is watching over you, honey." Alice's voice sounded a little husky, as though she felt overwhelmed. She was such a good friend. She worried so much. Leigh wished she could tell her again she was all right. "Okay, don't mind me. Sit tight. I'll call if I hear anything."

Leigh glanced at the clock. It was too late to call back. She would try Alice tomorrow, first thing.

She got ready for bed and shut off the light, letting the idea sink in that for the first time in a long while, she wasn't being hunted down, with someone liable to spring out at her from any shadow and drag her back to her ex-husband.

It was hard to believe it might really be over. *But I can't get too excited yet,* she told herself. *He might be hiring someone new, any day, someone even better.* Still, it was tempting to hope he had given up the chase for good. Couldn't that happen someday?

Leigh closed her eyes, pressing her hands on her stomach, aware of the new life inside her. She felt the oddest impulse to pray, though she hadn't for such a long time.

Dear God, thanks for the good news I heard tonight from Alice. Thanks for this safe place I've found. Please watch over us, especially my baby. Please help me to protect her, no matter what . . . and when the time does come for me to leave here, she added, *please don't let James and Vera think too badly of me.*

That last request might be unreasonable, she realized. She had deliberately deceived everyone; sooner or later, they were bound to find out.

But maybe she would never be forced to leave Cape Light, Leigh thought. Maybe she had stumbled into the place where she was meant to be, just as Vera had said. Did things like that really happen to people? It was a pleasant thought. Pleasant enough to lull her into the first peaceful sleep she'd had in months.

Jessica stood up from her seat as the choir began the final hymn. "This Is the Day" was one of her favorites, but she listened impatiently, eager for the service to end. She knew the thought was irreverent, but instead of the lyrics recalling the Scripture, all she could think was "this is the day" she'd planned to start her Christmas shopping, a full-scale attack at the mall. There were only three more weeks left, more or less, and she usually had more done by now.

She glanced over at Sam and Darrell, sharing a hymnal. Sam's hand rested casually on the boy's shoulder. She didn't mind that Darrell had asked to sit with them again, but she hoped Sam didn't plan on spending the day with him. She needed help to pick things out for his family; there were so many Morgans and so little time. Taking Darrell along would be a major distraction. He would just get bored and antsy and they would probably wind up in a bowling alley or at a skating rink. And she wouldn't get anything done.

The hymn ended and Reverend Ben delivered his final words of blessing. Jessica followed Sam and Darrell out of the sanctuary. There was such a long line waiting to stop and chat with Reverend Ben, she felt impatient.

"I'll go get our coats," she whispered to Sam. "I'll meet you out front."

"Okay. I won't be long."

Jessica left the sanctuary from the side

door, then gathered up the coats from the hooks near the all-purpose room. She navigated through a swarm of friends and fellow committee members, carefully avoiding anything more than a quick greeting. The last thing she needed was to be lured back for yet another Christmas Fair meeting.

A few minutes later, she found Sam again. She was relieved to see him standing with Luke McAllister. Darrell was no longer in sight.

But as she drew closer Jessica could tell that the two men were discussing something serious. Sam's expression looked grim. He barely noticed when she came to stand beside him.

". . . But when did this happen? I mean, she can't just make a phone call and yank him out of here." Sam sounded shocked and angry.

"I'm sorry, Sam. She's his mother. She can do whatever she wants . . . well, practically."

Sam looked shaken; Jessica could tell it was hard for him to speak. She turned to Luke. "What's happened? Has something happened to Darrell?"

"His mother is taking him out of the program," Luke explained. "She's decided she wants him back."

"Just like that?"

"Just like that. The social worker called me yesterday. I'm driving him down to Boston this afternoon."

Jessica didn't know what to say. The news solved her problem, instantly. Yet, to her surprise, it was also disturbing. She felt so bad for Sam. And for Darrell, too. The poor kid was being tossed around like a piece of baggage. No wonder he acted defensive at times.

"That's too bad. I mean, he seemed to be doing so well here."

"Yes, he was — mostly due to your husband's interest in him."

Sam finally snapped out of his daze. "But his mother, how can she care for him? I thought the social worker said she wasn't able to right now."

"She agreed to go into rehab again and do what she has to do. They're going to live with Darrell's grandmother for now. The social worker has approved the plan. So his mother will get another chance."

Sam took a breath. Jessica saw how hard it was for him to take this all in, and her heart went out to him. "Does Darrell know?"

"I told him last night."

"I'm surprised he didn't say anything to me. I mean, this morning during the service."

Luke shrugged. "I guess it may have been too hard for him to tell you." Luke paused, considering what to say next. "Darrell misses his mother and grandmother. He's happy about going back to them. He was worried about you, though, Sam."

"About me?" Sam nearly laughed but it was a sad sound.

"He knew you would be sad to see him go." Luke stood by quietly, concern in his eyes as he watched his friend.

Sam's dark head was bowed, as if he had just taken a blow. Jessica reached out and touched his arm, but Sam didn't seem to notice the gesture.

"Can he at least spend some time with us?" Sam asked Luke. "A few hours? I'll drive him to the city myself."

Luke considered the idea a moment. "Sure, I think that will be okay. I'll take him back to Boston, though. I have some business at the main office tomorrow morning. Can you get him back by four o'clock?"

"Absolutely." Sam glanced at Jessica. Did he think she was going to object?

"We'll do something special with him — take him out to a video arcade or something," she suggested. "Isn't that what kids his age like to do?"

"That would be a treat . . . if you don't mind a funny ringing sound in your ears for a few days afterward." Luke smiled knowingly at her. He had been inside a few video arcades lately, she gathered.

Sam looked surprised but pleased by her suggestion. "We'll do some shopping, too," he added. "He needs some things before he goes."

Yes, they ought to buy him some new clothes. That was the least they could do. Still, Jessica's good feelings about these generous impulses felt tainted, mixed with a vaguely guilty feeling. She had gotten her way, and now she felt ashamed that she had wished him away.

Well, she couldn't help what had happened. The boy's mother wanted him back. She had her rights as his parent and no one could stand in her way. Hadn't Luke just said that?

They found Darrell waiting outside on the green, playing tag with the other kids and two counselors. He acted a bit shy with Sam at first, Jessica thought. Until he realized that Sam wasn't mad at him for keeping his sudden departure a secret.

"Don't be crazy, Darrell. Why would I get mad at you for that? I'm just surprised. It's sort of sudden," Sam admitted. "Luke said it was okay if you wanted to hang out with us today. We thought we might try that video arcade near the mall and then find you some new clothes and things to take home with you. What do you think? Want to come with us?"

Darrell's eyes grew wide and bright. "Are you fooling me?"

"No, I'm not joking." Sam rested a hand on Darrell's shoulder. "Come with us. We're going to have a good day, a real blowout, okay?"

Darrell looked incredulous but followed. He paused abruptly and looked at Jessica, checking to see if maybe she was going to be the one to pop this happy bubble.

She smiled at him, feeling wistful and not understanding her reaction at all. "Hey, the arcade was my idea. I ought to get some credit, please."

"Oh, boy, now I know I'm dreaming," Darrell said.

Sam burst out laughing and mussed the boy's hair with his hand. He glanced over his shoulder at Jessica, to see if she shared in the joke. She smiled, despite herself. *I guess I deserved that,* she thought.

The day went by quickly. The arcade was as noisy, overwhelming, and insane as she expected. Sam and Darrell seemed enthralled, however, taking in a simulated jet, a NASCAR race through a field of volcanoes, and a deep-space clone adventure all in the first fifteen minutes.

Jessica tried to keep up with the score but couldn't follow any of it. She turned over her Christmas list and made another, of items she thought Darrell might need, clothing mostly — though she was sure Sam would find time to hit a toy store or two.

There was a quick lunch break — Darrell's favorite, pizza — then off to the mall, where Sam swept them through the boys' department, having Darrell choose jeans, shirts, sweaters, and even underwear. They shopped for new sneakers and snow boots. Sam took great care choosing a thick, warm jacket, too.

"It's going to be a cold winter," he kept saying. "I think you need a jacket with down inside, something with a hood that keeps the wind out."

Darrell tried on the jackets Sam offered, very agreeable about colors and styles. He was in a happy daze. "Tell the truth," he said to Jessica as Sam paid for the jacket. "Am I on one of those TV shows where you've won some big super prize, but you don't see the hidden camera?"

Jessica couldn't quite tell if he was kidding or not. She shook her head. "It's sort of Christmas coming early," she explained.

"I never saw this much stuff for Christmas. Not under ten Christmas trees." His tone rang with disbelief at his good fortune.

"It's all for you, pal," Sam assured him.

Their last stop was a toy store. Darrell had begun dragging a bit but suddenly got a second wind. Sam had also been looking a little less cheerful at the last store, Leigh noticed, possibly realizing that the hours were slipping by. But at the toy store, his spirits picked up considerably, too.

"Well, here we are. Let's do it," he said to Darrell. Sam glanced at his watch and then at Jessica. "It's nearly three. We don't have much time left." His voice was even but she could see the sadness building in his eyes.

"Why don't I wait out here with the bags?" she suggested. "That way you guys won't be loaded down."

"Okay, thanks." Sam nodded at her, appreciating the gesture.

"Yeah, thanks," Darrell said for about the hundredth time that day. Then he smiled at her, too, as Sam took his hand and led him into the store.

If only this kid had acted half as reasonable for the past few weeks, maybe I would have reacted differently. Jessica shook her head and found a spot on a nearby bench, dropping the many packages around her feet. *Then again, what difference would that have made? His mother would have wanted him back anyway. Sam and I would have both ended up disappointed.*

When Sam and Darrell emerged from the toy store twenty-five minutes later, they had so many bags that Jessica and Darrell had to wait by the entrance to the mall while Sam brought the car around.

Darrell was very quiet as they headed back to New Horizons. But it wasn't the angry kind of quiet that Jessica had experienced with him before. He kept glancing at her shyly, as if he wanted to talk, but didn't know what to say. He seemed sad, she thought, despite his bounty of gifts. The manic shopping spree had been a distraction for all of them, she realized, but now the truth was setting in.

It was already growing dark as they turned toward Cape Light. Sam tried to keep up a conversation but Jessica could tell his light tone was forced. Darrell answered in monosyllables, seeming lost in thought as he stared out the car window at the lights on the highway.

Luke was waiting outside when they reached New Horizons. He and Sam transferred the packages from Jessica's car to his SUV. Darrell went inside to say good-bye to some of the kids and counselors. He came out carrying a black duffle bag. Jessica could see he'd been crying.

"I guess I'm ready," he said.

"Okay. You guys say good-bye," Luke told him. "I'll start the car."

It was thoughtful of Luke to give them some privacy, Jessica thought. Standing near Sam, she felt that she too was an intruder on this scene. She stepped back, giving him some space.

Sam crouched down, putting his face at Darrell's level. "You take care of yourself, okay? We don't have to make a big deal out of this. We're going to keep in touch. Maybe I can come into the city sometime and take you to a ball game or something."

Darrell nodded solemnly. "Sure. That would be cool."

He had his head down and Jessica thought he was about to walk away. Then he suddenly dropped his bag and flung his arms around Sam's shoulders.

Sam looked overwhelmed. Jessica could see his dark eyes getting glassy. "Hey . . . hey, pal. It's okay. Everything's going to be okay. You're going home to see your mom and your grandma. They've really missed you. I know it's hard to go but once you get home, you'll feel better."

Darrell just stood hugging Sam as Sam hugged him back. Then Jessica heard the boy take a long shaky breath. Slowly, he stepped back.

"I'm going to miss you, Sam."

"I'm going to miss you, too." Jessica could hear her husband's strained tone, forcing his voice to sound bright when he was clearly on the edge of tears.

"Thanks again for all the stuff. Nobody's ever been so nice to me. You're the best, man. I'll never forget you."

Sam didn't answer for a moment. "I'll never forget you, Darrell. I mean that."

Sam looked so grief-stricken, Jessica could hardly stand. Darrell turned to her then. "Bye, Jessica. Thanks for all the clothes and stuff, too."

She nodded. "Sure thing." Their gifts didn't seem like so much suddenly, just the things that most kids she knew were given as necessities and totally took for granted.

"You take care, Darrell. I hope everything works out for you."

"Thanks. Me, too," he said.

Sam opened the door to Luke's truck and helped Darrell in, checking the seatbelt twice.

They said good-bye again and Darrell shut the door. As Luke began to pull away Jessica saw Darrell wave through the window. She waved back. Sam didn't, though. He just stood watching the truck until it disappeared out of the parking area.

He turned to her finally. "Let's go, I guess."

She nodded and followed him to their car.

Once they were on the road, she felt as if she had to say something. He looked so bleak, retreating into some dark, painful place. "He's a good kid, Sam. I really do hope everything works out for him."

Sam glanced at her. "I hope so, too."

Jessica glanced out the window, her throat growing suddenly tight. She felt sad, too, surprisingly sad. When had she started to care about the boy? It was all so sudden, so unexpected, though she wondered if it would have been any easier if they'd had some warning. Probably not.

It was so ironic, Jessica realized. She never expected that she would grow so attached to Darrell. She never expected that his sudden departure would be a problem.

She didn't feel as bad as Sam, of course. His heart was broken. But as surprising as it seemed, her heart was a little broken now, too.

Chapter Ten

"Why is it that every time someone in this town shouts 'Rummage Sale!' you two dash into my house, like two barbarians on a shopping spree?"

Enthroned in her wingback chair, Lillian Warwick punctuated her words with emphatic thumps of her cane. Emily glanced at her sister, who hid a grin behind an empty cardboard carton.

"I knew something was up. Since when do the two of you ever come here to see me?"

"Oh, Mother. We come all week long."

"Not for dinner on a Tuesday. Not the two of you together. Not for the sheer pleasure of my company."

"It's for the Christmas Fair, Mother. You signed up to donate," Jessica reminded her.

"I remember no such thing." Lillian turned to Emily. "Did you forge my signature?"

"Of course not. We were at coffee hour a few weeks ago, and Sophie Potter came by with a list. Don't you remember?"

"Was that what I signed up for? I thought I was ordering poinsettia plants."

"I think you signed up for that, too."

"That's it, then. There's been a misunderstanding. I think you should run along, find some other house to ransack."

Emily ignored her, scanning the room for possible contributions. Their mother was the undisputed knickknack queen. The mantel, bookcases, and china cabinets were stocked with rummage-worthy items. But just when you thought you'd found a dusty, forgotten trinket she would never miss, Lillian suddenly decided it was her absolute favorite, a precious necessity.

Jessica put the carton on a library table along with a pile of newspapers. "Where shall we start?" she asked brightly.

"In your own house, if you know what's good for you!"

"Mother, be reasonable," Emily said. "You have so much stuff here, things you'll never use in a hundred years. Those china birds, all these old books — it's all going to a good cause."

"Yes, yes, I know. The problem with you girls is that you have no sentimental attachment to things. You would just put it all out on the street if I let you. What's the difference? You probably will anyway when I die."

Emily rolled her eyes and glanced at her sister. "You've guessed our secret plan again, Mother. A combo garage sale and wake to commemorate your passing."

"Very witty, Emily. I'm very amused." Lillian sniffed and drew a lace-trimmed hankie from the pocket of her cardigan.

"I would think that you and your sister would value some of these items as mementos of our family. Those old books, for instance. Some are rare editions, first printings, and quite valuable. I've set aside a few for Sara and planned to give you some, too. Your fiancé might appreciate them, even you don't. . . . You are still marrying Dan Forbes, aren't you?"

"Of course I am." Emily watched her mother's slow, careful pace across the room, wondering if it was the right time to disclose her plans. Too bad her mother wasn't still sitting down.

"We haven't heard much about it lately. Have you set a date? Or will I simply receive my invitation in the mail and find out the specifics with the rest of the guests?"

Jessica seemed interested now as well.

Emily felt them both waiting for her answer.

"Well . . . Dan and I talked it over some more and we've decided on a very small affair. Just the immediate family and dinner or lunch at a nice restaurant afterward. Something very simple and uncomplicated."

Emily could see that Jessica was surprised to hear about the revised plans but was trying not to show it. Emily had meant to tell her about the change, but it was just last night that she had agreed to keep the wedding as small as Dan wanted.

"That sounds nice. Very . . . intimate," Jessica said cheerfully. "Why go crazy planning a big party? You have so many other things to think about right now —"

"Yes, keep it simple, Emily. We all know you have *such* a busy schedule." Her mother's tone was chiding. "Will the ceremony be performed during a lunch hour? Or right at your desk?"

"Mother, you're being silly now." Emily sat down on the couch. She could see that her plan to forage here for the rummage sale had hit a major snag.

"I'm being silly? You're being absurd. The last I heard, it was going to be a medium-sized gathering with a cocktail party, at your sister's house out there in the woods."

Had she told her mother about that phase of the planning? Emily recalled that she had and regretted it now.

"The guest list just got too long," she explained. "We couldn't seem to trim it. And Dan doesn't want a big party."

"Yes, I remember. He has this aversion to talking to people — funny trait for a former reporter. Meanwhile, he gives your situation no consideration. You still have a position in this town, a reputation," her mother reminded her. "You can't get married in secret, as if you're ashamed of the match or are too socially inept to plan a decent party. The next thing you'll tell me is that we're all going to meet at the Clam Box, for fried fish sandwiches."

"*Perfect.* Why didn't I think of that?" Emily smiled at her own joke, though she noticed her mother did not join in. "We still haven't booked the restaurant. Maybe Charlie Bates has the date open."

"Always a comedienne, aren't you?" Lillian shook her head and sat back down on her chair again.

Her mother had gone off on a tangent, which was really no surprise. The problem was, she wasn't entirely wrong.

Though Emily had agreed to go forward with the minimalist wedding Dan preferred, she knew in her heart it was not what she really wanted. She glanced at Jessica, who had come over now, too, to sit with them. She was sure her sister somehow sensed this but wouldn't give her away here in front of their mother.

"If this is what they both want, Mother, then that's what they should have. We should all attend and enjoy ourselves." Jessica sent Emily a sympathetic look. "You can always have a big party later when you get back from your trip."

"That's what Dan said. We think that might be easier. We'll have more time to plan something nice. We don't really have enough time to plan a big wedding now, and we can't delay the trip."

Emily noticed a small china dish on the lamp table. She picked it up and turned it over to check its pedigree. Her mother leaned forward with surprising speed and snatched it from her hand.

"The trip, the trip, the trip!" Her mother sat back in her seat with a long, dramatic sigh. "Well, maybe you should get married on that ship. The captain can perform the ceremony. You don't need us there."

"Mother, you know that's not the kind of

sailing trip we're going on. There won't be any captain, except for Dan."

"That's just the problem." Lillian thumped with her cane again. "You defer to him too much. It's a very bad precedent to set, believe me. It's probably your age. You're afraid to stand up for yourself, afraid you'll scare him off —"

"Mother! What in the world are you going on about?" Jessica demanded.

"All things considered, I never thought your sister would marry again, did you?"

Emily could see that Jessica was about to defend her, and she quickly jumped in. "I've been single a long time; there's no denying it. But marriage is all about compromise. Dan and I are very eager to start a life together. I think we've figured out that the way we get married isn't that important to us. As long as we have our family with us to celebrate, we know it will be a perfect day."

"Of course it will. Just tell me if there's anything at all you want me to do, Emily." Jessica gave their mother a stern look, defying her to continue the argument.

Lillian sighed and settled back in her seat, like an old queen who has been overruled by her advisors. She turned the china dish over in her hands and slipped on her glasses to take a closer look. “Lenox . . . hmm. Not bad but fairly mundane. I suppose you can have it for your good cause . . . and some of those books, too, though I need to check the copyright before you cart them off.” She thrust the dish toward Emily without meeting her eye. “Don’t you dare touch the china closet in the dining room.”

“We won’t, Mother. Don’t worry.” Emily came to her feet and shot Jessica a look; it was time to gather what they could before their mother changed her mind again.

She hadn’t planned on announcing her wedding plans tonight. But now that it had all come out, Emily felt relieved. Maybe a small wedding wasn’t exactly what she wanted, but Dan was right: it was the logical, sensible solution. Once she’d agreed, he seemed so happy and relieved. That was the important thing . . . wasn’t it?

Leigh forced herself to hold on until the waiting room was empty. She swallowed hard and took a deep breath. She had been trying all day to ignore her discomfort, telling herself she was just tired and feeling the symptoms of a late-term pregnancy. But she couldn’t ignore it any longer. Something just wasn’t right.

"Nancy?" Leigh waved the nurse over and tried not to sound alarmed. "Could you watch the desk for a few minutes?"

Nancy had been standing at the nearby counter, filling out a chart. She stepped over and looked down at Leigh, her expression concerned. "You don't look so good. What's up?"

Leigh shrugged. "I'm not sure. I've just been so tired all day. A little dizzy, too . . . and now I seem to have cramps."

"Any bleeding?"

Leigh shook her head. "I don't think so."

"Here, let me help you to an exam room. You lie down and rest and I'll get Dr. Harding."

"All right. Thanks," Leigh added as she leaned on Nancy's strong arm for support.

"It's probably nothing, but I want to check your blood pressure and temperature. Dr. Harding will come listen to the baby's heartbeat. You do have an ob-gyn around here, don't you?"

Leigh nodded. "Dr. Olin, in Hamilton."

"She's good, one of the best around." Nancy helped Leigh lie down on a cot in one of the exam rooms, then felt Leigh's forehead with her hand.

Leigh's fears were beginning to get the best of her. "I hope there's nothing wrong with the baby. Do you think it's something bad, Nancy?"

"Well, you look like you're retaining water and you might have a temperature. I'll check in a second. You just rest a minute. Don't worry, I'll be right back with Dr. Harding," she said in a gentle tone. Leigh noticed Nancy had not answered her question.

Left alone in the dimly lit room, Leigh tried to close her eyes, but another cramp came and she curled her knees closer to her chest, feeling a sudden wave of panic.

Please God, don't let there be anything wrong with the baby. If I lose her this way, I don't know what I'll do. . . .

"I would take her myself but I can't leave the office."

"I understand." James glanced at Matt, unable to focus completely on what the doctor had just said. He paused in the waiting room and looked around for Leigh. "I'm glad you called me. Where is she?"

"She's back here resting." Matt started toward the exam rooms and James followed.

Of course she was lying down. She felt sick. She wouldn't be sitting at the desk taking phone calls. He had to pull himself together. He didn't want to look panicked. That wouldn't do her any good right now.

He was normally so calm and collected in an emergency. He had faced down some real calamities at the mission — fires, hurricanes, scores of medical emergencies. He didn't understand his reaction today. Maybe it was the malaria that was causing him to feel so easily shaken — or maybe it was his feelings for Leigh and her baby.

Matt knocked softly, then opened the door to a small exam room. "Leigh, it's just me. James is here. He's going to take you to your obstetrician. I've called her and told her what's going on."

Leigh was lying down on a leather cot. She had her eyes shut tightly, as if against pain. At the sound of Matt's voice she opened her eyes and looked up, clearly surprised to see him.

"James? I thought Matt called Vera."

"She was out and I picked up the phone." He sat by her bed and pulled his chair closer. He had an urge to take her hand but that didn't seem right somehow. She looked so pale, her eyes ringed by dark shadows. She turned her head but didn't try to sit up, and that worried him.

"How do you feel?" he asked.

"Not so good. Matt thinks I should get a

sonogram right away."

"Yes, he explained all that to me." He reached out impulsively and stroked her soft curly hair. She glanced at him with a question in her eyes but didn't move away. "Where's your doctor, Leigh? Is she far?"

"Just in Hamilton." She turned her head away. "I'm scared, James."

"Of course you are. Anyone would be. But I'll be right there with you, Leigh. It doesn't have to be bad news. Matt said it could be something very ordinary. We just need to find out for sure."

She took a breath and nodded then levered herself to a sitting position.

"Are you ready to go?" he asked quietly.

"I just need my shoes."

He handed her the shoes, then helped her up from the cot. She walked unsteadily, leaning on his arm as they left the room. In the reception area he helped her into her coat.

Nancy Malloy cast them a sympathetic glance as they passed the front desk. "You hang in there, Leigh. Let us know what's happening."

Leigh nodded and tried to smile, but James could see it was an effort for her.

Matt followed them out to the car. "Call

me as soon as you know what's going on, okay?"

James nodded. "We will. Thanks again, Matt."

Leigh, lying down across the backseat, barely said a word as he drove. James thought it was just as well. He was secretly so nervous he needed all his wits to concentrate on the road. He was glad to be with Leigh in her moment of need, but he also dreaded the possibility that it might truly be bad news. Staring out at the highway, he said a silent prayer. *Please help Leigh's baby, Lord. Please let this just be a false alarm. Please have mercy on both of them.*

They soon reached Hamilton, where Leigh showed him the way to her doctor's office, located in an office building just off Main Street.

There was only one other patient waiting, a young woman who sat reading a magazine with a baby on the cover. The nurse at the reception desk recognized Leigh and was expecting her. She ushered them back to a darkened room and helped Leigh up on the exam table.

James watched her take Leigh's temperature and then her blood pressure. She glanced over her shoulder at James. "Are you a relative?"

James was startled by the question and shook his head. "Just a friend," he said quickly.

She must have wanted to ask if I was the father, he realized. He certainly felt as anxious as one.

He glanced at Leigh, noticing again how nervous she looked. He wanted to step closer and at least hold her hand. But the nurse was in the way.

The nurse put her blood-pressure kit away. "I'm going to get her ready for the sonogram now."

Now what? James wondered. Did Leigh want him to stay or would he be intruding if he suggested it?

"Can he stay? . . . I mean, if he wants to?" Leigh asked.

"Sure. It's up to you."

"I'd like to stay," he said, meeting Leigh's gaze. She nodded and he could see that she really did want him there.

The nurse snapped open a paper gown, which she placed over Leigh's lap. Then she lifted Leigh's sweater a few inches to smear some clear gel over her stomach.

The door opened a few minutes later, and a woman in a long white lab coat came in. James knew she had to be Helen Olin, Leigh's doctor. Tall and slim, with short dark hair, she looked about forty or so. Her expression was serious but when she met Leigh's gaze it softened with concern.

"Hello, Leigh. What's going on?"

"Nothing good." Leigh sighed. "This is Reverend Cameron, a friend of mine."

The doctor glanced at James and said hello. If she was curious about his relationship to Leigh, she didn't show it.

She asked Leigh some questions about her symptoms then listened to the baby's heartbeat with her stethoscope. James thought the doctor looked worried.

Finally, Dr. Olin sat beside Leigh on the opposite side of the table from James and started the sonogram. "Okay, let's take a look," she said quietly.

James stared at the small black TV screen. It looked as if it was transmitting images from outer space. Suddenly, he saw the unmistakable outline of a baby. The fetus was curled into itself, yet each of its parts was remarkably distinct. He looked down at Leigh and grabbed her hand. She didn't pull her gaze away from the screen but gave his fingers a hard squeeze.

"Is she all right? Can you tell?" Leigh's voice was quavering.

Dr. Olin didn't answer right away, and he felt himself holding his breath. *Please*

God, let her say it's okay. I'd give anything not to hear bad news right now. . . .

Finally, the doctor glanced up them and smiled. "Yes, everything looks good. Just let me take a few more pictures. Then I'll need to give you a quick exam."

James felt his body sag with relief. He glanced down at Leigh and rubbed her shoulder with his free hand. "She's beautiful," he whispered. "She looks just like you."

Leigh laughed quietly but when she gazed up at him, she had tears in her eyes. "Oh, you can't tell anything like that from these pictures. As long as she's okay, that's enough for me."

James closed his eyes a moment. "Thank God," he said softly.

"Yes . . . thank you, God." Leigh's tone was surprisingly solemn, and he saw that her eyes were closed as well.

James left the examining room and sat in the waiting area. Five, ten, fifteen minutes passed. Did exams typically take this long? He hoped everything was all right. He tried to distract himself by reading a news magazine. As he flipped through the pages, a photo caught his eye. The picture showed a village of huts in some impoverished, tropical locale. A dark-skinned boy with large eyes and a pathetically thin body stared up at him. It could have been a photo from his own mission, and James felt a jolt inside, as if a slack line hooked to some bit of hardware inside him had suddenly been jerked tight.

He realized how far that distant life had drifted away from him today. He suddenly felt guilty and ashamed of himself. How could he forget so easily? So much was waiting there for him, so many people who relied on him, so many plans for the mission's future. That was his real life. This place was just a rest stop.

But Leigh and her baby were important, too, another part of him insisted. He had an obligation, a duty, to help them, too. It was more than duty, that dry, bloodless word. He still felt some intimation that God had brought him into Leigh's life for a reason. And even beyond that feeling, he *wanted* to be here for her. He was happy he had answered the phone instead of Vera and had the chance to take care of her. He hoped she would let him do even more.

James closed the magazine and put it aside, then stood up and paced around the small room. He didn't know what was happening to himself lately. One minute, he was chomping at the bit to get back to the mission; and the next, imagining a life here, staying with Leigh and helping her raise her baby.

Ridiculous ideas. He'd been idle too long. His brain was turning to marshmallow. She thought of him as a friend, sure, but she had never indicated that she felt anything more. She was still getting over her husband's death and dealing with her pregnancy. A new relationship was probably the last thing on her mind.

And we're so different, he thought. *I'm not the type of man she would get involved with, anyway.*

A door opened and Leigh walked into the waiting area. She smiled at him. "I just need to make another appointment and we can go."

"All right." He stood waiting for her, and then they walked out to the car, where he helped her into the front seat.

"What did the doctor tell you? Did she know what happened?"

"She said it was something called preeclampsia, a very mild case. It used to be called toxemia, I think, too. They really don't know what causes it, though it's most common with first pregnancies. It seems the mother's body is just overworked. There's not too much you can do for it. It can become worse, but Dr. Olin doesn't think I need to worry about that right now. She told me to rest and stay off my feet for a few days. I feel bad for Dr. Harding, though. Tomorrow is Saturday, his busiest day."

James began driving back to Cape Light. "Matt wouldn't want you working if your doctor told you to rest, Leigh. You have to do what she says. Think of the baby."

Leigh stared at him, wide-eyed, clearly surprised by his tone, which was far sterner than he intended. He'd overreacted.

"I'm sorry," James said quickly. "I have no right to tell you what to do. I'm just worried about you. We're lucky everything turned out okay."

There, he had done it again. He said "we're lucky," as if he had some real place in her life. He glanced at her, expecting her to say something, to set him straight.

Leigh stared out her window, and he felt her hand cover his on the seat between them. "It *was* frightening," she said at last. "Thank you for bringing me to the doctor and for staying with me."

James took her hand and brought it to his lips. It was not exactly what a friend would do, he knew. But he couldn't help it. And he couldn't take the gesture back once it was done.

Leigh looked a bit surprised but didn't seem to mind. She kept hold of his hand, watching out her window at the passing scenery.

It suddenly seemed clear to him. He knew what he had to do now. He needed to stay and help Leigh — at least until she had the baby. The mission would have to get along without him a few weeks longer.

"I'm going to keep helping you, Leigh, you and the baby."

Leigh hesitated a moment before saying, "I appreciate your friendship, James. But you don't have to make any promises to me."

"I know I don't have to. It's what I want to do." He kept his eyes straight ahead, almost afraid to look at her again — afraid of what he'd see, her beauty and strength and vulnerability.

He didn't understand his own motives entirely, just this compelling need to stand by her, to help her if he could. It just seemed the right thing, the only thing, to do.

"I've always liked this place." Emily sat back in her chair and looked out at the Newburyport Harbor. It was Saturday afternoon and the restaurant wasn't even half full. She and Dan had walked in without a reservation and been shown an excellent table right at the window.

"It's such a beautiful view," she said, looking out at the whitecaps on the water.

"And the food is good, too. This chowder is perfect, hardly any potatoes."

"That's impressive." They hadn't been together that long, but Emily already knew how Dan hated too many potatoes in his chowder. Too much celery was an even greater affront.

He put the cup aside and touched his mouth with his napkin. "I think this would be an excellent choice for the reception. It's a pretty place, fancy enough but not too formal."

In Emily's mind their planned post-nuptial get-together for a dozen guests could hardly be called a reception, but she didn't want to sound negative. The restaurant was a viable suggestion, and she knew Dan was trying to please her.

"Would they let us have that little private room on the side or would we have to take a regular table? They might not let us have it," she continued, answering her own question. "We're only twelve."

They had decided to invite Dr. Elliot, a

close friend of Emily's family, which brought the list up to an even dozen since Betty wasn't bringing an escort. But still, Emily didn't think it was enough to rate the private space in such a fancy restaurant.

"No harm in asking." Dan smiled at her amiably. "If it's not in use, they might not mind."

"It would be nice to have it there, so people can get up and walk around. Maybe they have some minimum number," she mused. "We can always invite Reverend Ben and Carolyn. Since he's performing the ceremony, we probably should."

"Just to be polite, you mean?"

"Not just that. I love the Lewises. Reverend Ben's been a great help to me."

Dan leaned forward and touched her hand. "I was just teasing, honey."

Emily tried to smile but didn't feel cheered by his gentle joke. "I don't know what to do about Harriet DeSoto." Emily picked up her fork and took a bite of her salad. Harriet, the town clerk, was not exactly a close friend but had always been a loyal political ally. Emily didn't want to hurt her feelings — or alienate her. "She overheard me talking about the wedding on the phone the other day, and I know she thinks she's going to be invited."

"Just tell her it's only close family."

Emily shook her head and speared a tomato on her fork. "Harriet knows Betty is invited and she assumes she will be, too. Of course, Betty is my oldest friend from high school, so it's completely different. But Harriet is close, too, in a way. We've been through a lot in the office and through two campaigns."

Dan massaged his forehead. "Emily . . . are you trying to tell me something?"

Emily looked up at him. "What do you mean?"

"Emily, don't give me those . . . those big baby blues." He was trying to sound stern, but she could tell her baby blues were indeed working on him.

"You aren't really happy with this small wedding idea, are you?" She started to reply but he interrupted her. "Come on now, be honest. We're going to be married a long time. We have to be honest with each other."

She put down her fork and looked straight at him. "Okay, then no, Dan. I'm really not —"

"I knew it."

"It's not that I don't agree with you, honestly. I do think a small wedding is the easiest and most sensible solution. And I know we don't have any time left at all and can't change our trip."

"But?"

"But it's not the way I want to celebrate getting married to you. It just doesn't feel right to me. Does that make any sense?"

He stared at her a moment, then reached over and touched her cheek with his hand. "I can tell that you're not that happy about it. That means something to me. If you're not happy, Emily, we just have to think this thing through again."

"Dan, that's sweet, but we've already gone over all the options. I told you a small wedding was okay, and I'll stick to it."

"Well, the problem is, I can't do it that way now, knowing you're unhappy about it. You seem to be forgetting something."

"Which is?"

"I love you. I want to see my beautiful bride radiant with smiles on her wedding day."

She grinned at him. "Well, when you put it that way, I guess I can give in. But what about you? I feel the same way. We can't do something that you're going to feel glum about."

"I'll never feel glum getting married to you, silly."

"You know what I mean."

Dan tilted back on his chair, and Emily spotted an unusual glimmer in his eyes. "Well, I do have an idea. I wasn't going to say anything since we finally seemed settled. But since we're not as settled as I thought . . . I don't know about this idea of mine, though. It's a bit outlandish."

Emily's curiosity was piqued. "Sounds interesting. Will it work for you?"

"In a strange way . . . yes."

"Well, tell me about it!"

Emily leaned closer and Dan described his inspiration. It was completely outlandish, but it definitely appealed to her. The more she heard, the more she liked — and the more she thought it could be exactly the solution they had been looking for.

"Jess? Are you ready? You'd better hurry up or we're going to miss the movie."

Jessica heard Sam calling from the foot of the stairs. She ran to the bedroom door and poked her head out. "I'll be right down. Just a minute . . ."

She took a breath, stared at the white plastic stick in her hand, and quickly whispered a prayer. "Thank you, Lord. Thank you. Thank you. Thank you. . . ."

"Jess? I'm going outside. I'll warm up the truck."

"Wait, Sam . . ." Jessica raced down the hallway, swung around the banister, and flew down the stairs.

Sam stood in the small foyer staring at her. "Are you okay?. You're not even dressed yet. If you're tired from those pills again, we can stay home. . . ."

"Me? I'm great. I'm not tired at all." She took a breath and swallowed hard. "I think I'm pregnant."

Sam stared at her and blinked, his expression frozen in utter shock. Then his words spilled out in a rush. "You do? I mean, you are? I mean, you know for sure? Or you just think you might be?"

She held up the white plastic stick. "See? The dot is blue. That means baby in progress."

He took the stick in his hand and examined it. "This tells for sure?"

"Ninety-nine percent accuracy, that's what the box says. I used about five of them. Blue all the way."

She watched his face melt into a delirious smile. "Baby in progress . . . yes!" He hugged her, lifting her up off her feet, then suddenly put her down again, looking worried. "Is that okay? I didn't hurt you or anything, did I?"

"No, silly." She laughed at him and hugged him back.

"Come on, let's sit down. I'm sort of in shock," he confessed. He took her by the hand and led her into the living room, where they sat together on the couch. He pulled her close and she rested her head on his chest.

"Happy?" he asked quietly.

She laughed. "What do you think? More like delirious."

"You got your Christmas wish, Jess. Now I don't have to worry so much about what to buy you."

"You're off the hook on that one." She lifted her head and glanced at him. "Are you happy?"

"Me? I'm over the top, honey. I didn't think it would happen again so fast. Like I said, I'm sort of in shock." He paused and she felt him take a deep breath and heard his strong, steady heartbeat under her cheek. "Did you call the doctor yet?"

She laughed at his overly concerned tone. "I just found out two minutes ago. When would I have called the doctor?"

"Oh. Right. You'd better call first thing on Monday. He'll probably want to see you."

"Yes, I will," she promised. "But let's not tell anyone right away, okay?"

He tipped his head to look at her. "Are you worried something might go wrong?"

She nodded. "I guess so. I mean, I felt so excited the first time. I didn't even think anything bad could happen, and then when it did . . . I guess I'd rather wait a week or two until we tell everyone. Let me see what the doctor says."

"Sure, honey. I understand. It will just be our secret for a while." He hugged her close and stroked her hair. "I think everything is going to be fine this time. I just have a good feeling."

"I do, too." Jessica forced her voice to sound more positive than she really felt. She had her worries, but anyone who had been through a miscarriage would. Her doctor had already told her that the chances for a second pregnancy to work out were very good. She had gotten pregnant, that was the main thing.

"I'm going to try not to worry. I'm just incredibly thankful," she confessed.

"I know what you mean. Now we have something to really celebrate." He kissed her brow and held her close again. "Why don't we decorate our tree tomorrow after church? We can put it up in the afternoon."

"Sure, that would be fun, but I thought you had to go into the shop tomorrow."

"Oh, that can wait. I'd much rather spend the day with you."

Jessica didn't reply. She knew she didn't have to. She held Sam close and felt her eyes drifting closed. She had felt so sleepy the last week or two, she probably wouldn't have even made it through the movie.

She was glad that Sam wanted to decorate their Christmas tree tomorrow. They had bought it that morning, but when they got it home, Sam said he wasn't in the mood to set it up, which wasn't like him. Sam was usually completely into Christmas, especially trimming the tree and decorating the house. This year, though, he didn't seem nearly as interested.

It had only been a week since Darrell had left town and Jessica knew Sam was still thinking about him, feeling the loss keenly. He hadn't been back to the New Horizons Center all week, but that was to be expected, too, she thought. She was sure Luke would understand if Sam took a break from his volunteer work.

Maybe now that she was pregnant, it would be easier for Sam to get past missing Darrell. If anything could put the situation into perspective, expecting their own baby had to be it, right?

She certainly hoped so.

Chapter Eleven

"This one says 'Eggnog set. Music box. Elvis Santa.' " James stood in the doorway to the living room, holding a cardboard box he had carried down from the attic.

Vera walked over and peered at the label. "Those are just extras. I'll open it later."

"I think it's the last of it, then. I'll just run up and take one more look around." He smiled briefly at Leigh, then headed back up to the attic.

James must have made about a hundred trips so far up from the living room to the attic. He didn't seemed tired, though. Just the opposite, Leigh thought. His eyes were bright and his cheeks ruddy, as if he'd been outdoors, walking on the beach. He didn't talk about his illness much, but she could see how pale and worn he looked some days. He must be getting better, she thought. Either that, or he really liked Christmas.

"Well, let's get started. I'll get the lights

going." Vera stood on a stool, draping a string of lights on the branches.

Leigh noticed her tip precariously and jumped up to help her. "Here, let me get the other end. Where do you want it?"

"Any place that looks empty." Huffing a bit, Vera stepped down and regarded her handiwork. "It's a good tree, has a nice full shape. I hate a tree that's too round or too skinny. This one is just right."

"Yes, it's very pretty." Leigh nodded and sat on the couch again, watching Vera kneel among the boxes, carefully unwrapping the ornaments.

"Oh, here's a beauty, my hummingbird. See, it's even got little feathers for the wings. My granddaughter Meg gave me that one. She knows I have those feeders by the kitchen window so I can watch the birds while I'm washing the dishes."

Leigh smiled at the story but didn't answer. She really wasn't in the mood to decorate anyone's tree but had been swept into the project by the others. She was just waiting for the right moment to make an excuse and slip off upstairs.

Christmas didn't mean much to her anymore. Even in this picturesque little town, where the streets and shop windows were so beautifully decorated, Leigh couldn't muster any enthusiasm for the holiday. She didn't have anyone to get gifts for this year. Maybe she would pick up something small for James and Vera, but she still felt so distant from it all.

Why did people say the holidays brought out the best in everyone? It seemed to Leigh they often brought out the worst: fighting for parking spaces, snapping at sales clerks, being brainwashed by TV advertisements.

It was the season when tensions in her disastrous marriage had always reached a pitch. That's what she remembered most now about Christmas. How her husband would fly into his rages then try to bribe his way back into her good graces with expensive presents. Last year it had been a fur coat and diamond earrings — things she had never asked for, never really wanted. That's what all the lights and decorations and songs on the radio reminded her of. She wished it wasn't so but she couldn't change it.

Was she the only one who saw it all with such jaded eyes? Christmas was a vast marketing conspiracy, designed to get the public to spend, spend, spend. As if you could buy that fantasy feeling of warmth and belonging, of perfect family harmony and goodwill to all. Those were the golden virtues of Christmas she had learned as a child. She knew now that was all a fairy tale, as enticing to believe in as Santa Claus — and just as unreal.

"I'm feeling a little tired. I thought I'd rest upstairs awhile." Leigh started to leave but met James coming into the room with another box.

"Why don't you rest right here?" he asked. "Just sit and watch. I'm not very good at this. You can warn me if I'm hanging all the ornaments on one side."

"You can probably manage without me —" she began.

"Oh, Leigh, don't go up yet," Vera chimed in. "You're so good at decorating things. Just give us a little help here and there."

There was something in James's eyes that made her not want to disappoint him. Besides, she couldn't imagine Vera giving up.

"Okay, I'll stay for a little while." She shrugged and sat back on the couch again. "Can I hand you the ornaments or something?"

"That's a good idea. We'll make an assembly line." Vera got up on the stool again. "Where should we start?"

Leigh noticed an interesting-looking box and pushed the tissue paper aside. "How about these angels? They'd look good near the top."

"Yes, perfect. See, I knew you'd have good ideas." James smiled at her. She could tell he was pleased that she had stayed to help.

"I'll get to work on the fire." He stood at the hearth and rolled up the sleeves of his denim shirt. She watched him toss the logs into the hearth and add bits of kindling. Despite his slim build, his shoulders and arms were quite muscular, she noticed. He had mentioned that a lot of the work at the mission was hard, physical labor, which probably accounted for his build — and his taste in clothes.

He didn't dress like a minister or look like one — or even behave the way she thought ministers behaved, Leigh mused as she fastened hooks to Christmas balls. Sometimes she totally forgot what James did for a living, but his actions and words so often reflected his kindness and rich spirit, she never forgot for very long.

They worked on the tree together for a while, with Vera and James hanging ornaments and Leigh directing. When Vera went into the kitchen to make popcorn,

Leigh and James finished up; all the ornaments were on the tree except the treetop angel.

James put the box with the angel aside. "I'll save this for Vera. She might have some special feeling about it."

Vera walked in the room with a tray. "That's all right. Let Leigh do the angel. She didn't get to do any of the ornaments."

"She'll have to get up on the stool. I don't know." James cast Leigh a worried look.

Leigh got up from the couch and smoothed out her dress. For some reason she did want to place the angel on the treetop. She wasn't quite sure why. Maybe because it was always her job when she was growing up. Even if their tree was tall, her mother would somehow manage to lift her up high enough.

"I can do it. I'll be all right."

James looked surprised at her eager reply. "Okay. Let me help you though. I'll put the stool here." He moved the small wooden steps closer to the tree. "Hold on to my shoulder for balance, okay?"

"Don't worry. I'll be very careful." Leigh climbed up the steps, holding the angel in one hand and holding on to James's solid shoulder with the other. The tree wasn't too tall and she easily reached over and slipped the cloth and papier-mâché angel over the top.

"There, how does that look? Is it straight?"

"Just right. That angel looks just like you, Leigh, with her brown curly hair and all. Don't you think, James?"

"Yes, definitely." James grinned up at her, and Leigh couldn't quite tell if he was teasing or not.

The phone was ringing and Vera ran off to answer it. "That's my sister Bea," she called over her shoulder. "This could take a while. . . ."

Leigh was relieved to see Vera go. Some angel. If they only knew the truth about her. The compliment made her embarrassed and distracted. She couldn't even look at James as she started down the steps.

"Oops . . . oh, my . . ." Leigh felt herself tilt off balance, but James caught her in a strong embrace. She turned to find she had her arm around his shoulder and his face was very close to hers.

"I'm sorry." Her voice came out in a whisper.

"That's okay. That's what I'm here for."

His tone was hushed and husky. She knew she ought to let go of him, but she didn't pull away. He held her gaze for a long moment, then leaned his head closer and kissed her, a deep kiss that was warm and soulful.

Finally, he pulled his head back. He looked dazed and surprised. Leigh was sure her expression was identical. Her heart was racing and the room seemed to spin.

They stared at each other in shock for a moment and then both quickly looked away.

"Um . . . let me help you down. Would you like some of this hot chocolate? I think Vera has some tea here, too."

He sounded nervous and self-conscious and didn't look at her as he took a mug of tea. She sat on the couch, wordlessly.

She felt self-conscious, too. But she didn't feel sorry he had kissed her. She hadn't even realized it until now, but for a long time she had been wanting him to do just that.

James sat down near her and looked up at the tree.

"It's been awhile since I decorated a real Christmas tree," he said after a moment. "I guess the smell of the pine is what I like best . . . and I like sitting down and admiring it afterward."

Leigh had to smile. She started to relax again. "I like that part, too. What did you do at the mission? Did you decorate at all?"

"We had an artificial tree. And we would hang decorations on a palm tree or a big bush. It's not that I don't enjoy Christmas there, but it's different. This is more the kind of Christmas I grew up with."

His tone was wistful, she noticed with surprise. It was the first time he had ever said anything even vaguely negative about living at the mission.

She picked up a mug of hot chocolate and sat back again. "I'm not really in the mood for the holidays this year. It just seems like an ordeal."

She stopped herself. She hadn't meant to be that honest. But then James still believed she had recently lost her husband. He would assume she was talking about that.

The sympathy in his eyes confirmed her guess. He nodded, his expression more serious. "The holidays create a lot of pressure for people. There are such high expectations to feel happy. And if you don't, you sit around wondering, What's wrong with me? Why don't I feel like everyone else?"

That was exactly the way she felt. He understood perfectly.

"But just think of it, Leigh. This year you're going to get an amazing gift. It's going to change your feelings about the holidays forever. Now you can look forward to celebrating Christmas with your little girl and making happy memories for her."

Leigh knew what he said was true. She couldn't dwell on the past. She had to look to the future and try to picture a good life for herself and her baby. Things seemed bleak right now, but she could get through it. She had to.

"I guess holidays are hard for anyone who's alone," she allowed. "Once I have the baby, though, I won't feel that way anymore."

"You're not alone, Leigh," James said. "There are so many people here who care about you. I know you've only been in Cape Light a short time and you still feel like a stranger. But believe me, you've won a lot of friends."

I am a stranger, she wanted to say. *You don't even know my real name.* She met his gaze and quickly looked away.

"Okay," he said, "you want a list?"

"A list?"

"Well, there's me and Vera, obviously. But also Matt Harding and Nancy Malloy, Molly Willoughby and her girls, and Ben and Carolyn Lewis and Rachel Anderson. Not to mention Sophie Potter and all the ladies at church who think you're a genius with a sewing machine," he teased. "I could probably name more. Do you want me to?"

"You don't have to. . . . I see what you mean." She shook her head shyly and turned to watch the fire. She felt James's arm around her shoulder, urging her closer, and she leaned her head on his shoulder.

They sat there quietly for a long time. Then Leigh said, "You're number one."

"Number one?"

"Number one on my list." Leigh lifted her head slightly to look at him. "Of friends. I know I keep repeating myself, but you keep on helping me. I need to thank you for that."

"I already told you, I help you because I want to, because you're important to me —" He stopped midsentence. She waited to hear what he would say next, unconsciously holding her breath. "I care about you, Leigh. I care very much."

"I care about you, too." Her words were so soft, she wondered if he even heard them. But then she felt his cheek against her hair and she knew he had.

Leigh found herself blinking back tears. *It's being pregnant that's making me so emotional,* she reminded herself. *I normally don't cry, no matter what.*

She hid her face from James, her head tucked under his chin. His softly spoken admission had made her feel so happy, so . . . secure. He hadn't said much but it was enough, more than she deserved. She really couldn't handle anything more than that. She had been here over a month now. Every instinct told her that soon she would have to leave or risk being found by one of Martin's detectives. She wanted to stay at least until the baby was born, but she doubted she had that long.

She would miss James so much. In such a short time, he had become so important to her. She had done the thing she had promised herself she wouldn't do. She had made connections here, and it would hurt so much when she had to go.

Could she tell James the truth about her past? Could she trust him with her secret? Part of her wished she could tell him everything right now. More than once she had imagined confiding in him and James understanding, believing her, and seeing at once that she'd never meant any harm. Sometimes, though, she pictured him angry and hurt. He would turn away, hating her.

It was such a huge risk — not only the risk that he might not keep her secret, but the risk of losing his respect and affection, their special connection, which now seemed even more precious to her.

She heard Vera's footsteps approaching from the hallway and realized James must have heard, too. Without exchanging a word, they drew apart. Like two teenagers, Leigh thought, feeling herself blush.

"Here's the popcorn," Vera announced. "Sorry I took so long. Ever since Bea got that low-rate long distance, I can't get her off the phone."

Vera put a bowl of popcorn on the coffee table and began gathering the empty boxes. She hadn't noticed anything between them, Leigh realized.

James rose and went over to the hearth to tend the fire. The logs crackled and popped, and Leigh watched a shower of sparks fly up the chimney.

Just the way she felt inside, Leigh

thought. Her happiness, just as temporal and elusive.

They had been invited to a Christmas party at the New Horizons Center. It was Tuesday night, a little more than a week before Christmas. Jessica probably wouldn't have been invited at all if not for Sam's work there, but here she was, she thought, driving down the Beach Road on a cold, dark night, on her way to the party all alone.

She had come home early from work and packed up the food she made the night before, a baked ham, potato salad, and a tray of chocolate chip cookies. It looked like a lot, but she was sure it wouldn't go very far in that crowd. She remembered Darrell's enormous boy-sized appetite the times they had taken him out, and a certain wistful sadness washed through her. The feeling no longer took her by surprise; she felt it often lately, and she knew now that Sam wasn't the only one with unresolved feelings about the boy. It just seemed her own feelings had shown up a little too late.

While she was packing the food, Sam had come home, saying he felt sick, probably a cold coming on. He'd been working outside all day and felt chilled and achy and already had the sniffles. But Sam usually carried on no matter what, even when he should have been in bed. Jessica hadn't argued when he said he wanted to stay home. Everything connected with the subject of New Horizons and Darrell Lester still seemed a sensitive topic between them.

He had helped her carry the food to the car and she'd promised to come back early. It seemed ironic to her now, as she turned up the drive to the center, that she would turn out to be the one going and Sam would stay in. But things worked out strangely sometimes, didn't they?

Jessica found the party set up in the main building, in a big room that doubled as gym and auditorium. There was a huge Christmas tree by the door, decorated with colorful paper chains and handmade ornaments of all shapes and sizes. Some were in the shape of large stars that held framed photos of the kids at the center.

It wasn't the fanciest or most stylish tree, but Jessica found that of all the trees she had seen this year, it gave her the nicest feeling.

She looked around and realized she was early. The room was nearly empty, except for some adults and students setting up.

She noticed Luke nearby and he quickly walked over to greet her.

"Jessica, Merry Christmas!" He leaned over and kissed her cheek. "Here, let me take that from you." He took the tray of cookies and placed it on a table.

"There's more in the car, a ham and potato salad. I'll be right back," Jessica said.

"I'll help you. Lead the way." Luke pushed open the swinging door and they walked together along the gravel path. "Where's Sam? Is he coming straight from work?"

"Sam's not feeling well. He came home with a bad cold and wanted to stay in tonight. He said to tell you he was sorry he couldn't make it."

Luke considered her news with a thoughtful expression. "I'm sorry too. I was looking forward to seeing him. He hasn't been around much lately."

Jessica felt awkward. "Yes, I know. . . . He often plans to come, but I guess he doesn't get here." Jessica stuck her hands in her pockets. The sky was clear and a light breeze tossed the bare branches of the trees overhead. "He doesn't talk about it, but I know he still feels bad about Darrell."

"Has he spoken to him at all, do you know?"

"I don't think so. Sam said he wanted to wait a week or two before he called — to give Darrell time to settle in with his family again."

She secretly thought Sam needed some time, too, so that the feelings weren't so fresh and raw.

"Are you still in touch with Darrell?" she asked. "We bought him a Christmas present — well, a few presents. I wasn't sure where to send them."

That was all true. She had planned to ask for Darrell's address tonight, but now she found she was actually eager to hear news of the boy. She had been thinking about him a lot lately, wondering how his life was working out, if he was being properly looked after and encouraged — if he was really being cared for.

Maybe being pregnant had made her more sentimental or simply more empathetic to Darrell's plight. She wasn't quite sure what had happened, but she seemed to see things differently now, wishing she had been kinder to him when she had the chance.

They had reached her car but Jessica didn't open it. Luke dug his hands in his pockets. It was a cold night and he had come out in only a sweater and sports jacket. He didn't seemed mindful of the cold, though, as much as unsure of what he wanted to say.

"Listen . . . I guess this is sort of privileged information, but I was going to tell Sam tonight, so I guess I can talk to you about it, Jessica."

Jessica felt instantly alarmed. "Did something happen to Darrell? Is he all right?"

Luke touched her arm. "He's all right. It's just that the plan for him to go back home isn't working out. I heard today from one of the social workers that his mother disappeared again. He's living with his grandmother, but she's not sure she can handle the responsibility. He might end up in foster care, after all."

"Oh . . . dear. That's too bad."

The news seemed stunning. Jessica was having trouble taking it in. It made her feel confused — and sad for Darrell.

Then suddenly, happy, too. As if some precious item she had given up for lost had suddenly reappeared.

"It is sad. The kid can't seem to get a break."

Jessica looked up at Luke. "Can you find out more? I mean, could Sam and I apply to be his foster parents?" The idea was impulsive but the moment she spoke it aloud, it felt right.

Luke's dark eyebrows rose in surprise. "Are you sure you really want to do that?"

Jessica nodded. "Yes, I am. Being around Darrell was hard for me at first, I guess Sam told you. But . . . something's changed, Luke. I feel different now. Sam and I need to talk about it some more, I suppose, but I would like to look into it, see what we need to do. I don't want to tell Sam anything, though, unless it's really possible."

"I know what you mean. Sam doesn't need to have his heart broken twice over this." Luke touched her arm lightly. "I'll look into it and call you at the office. How does that sound?"

"That sounds perfect. I'll be waiting to hear from you."

Luke gave her a knowing smile. She sensed that he wanted this to work out for them but was wary of being too optimistic.

Jessica opened the trunk and gave him the rest of the food. Luke encouraged her to return to the party, but she was eager to get back home. Even if she couldn't tell Sam the news, she just wanted to be with him.

Jessica drove home down the dark, quiet

road. It was a clear, starry night. A bright crescent moon glowed behind the bare trees, lighting her way. She still couldn't quite believe what Luke had told her. She felt nearly overwhelmed to hear about this turn of events and so happy to have the possibility of a second chance. But was she really feeling happy for herself or for Sam?

No, she realized, it wasn't just for Sam. She knew if that were the case, her reaction would have been, *Oh, no, if Sam finds out, he'll want to take Darrell in and I just don't want that.*

She honestly didn't feel that way at all anymore. Something inside her had changed; at some moment when she hadn't even been paying attention, some door inside her heart had opened to the boy. Maybe because she was going to have a baby of her own now, she saw things differently, felt willing and able to include Darrell in her life with Sam.

That could happen, couldn't it? Wasn't that the miracle of love the Scriptures were always teaching about?

Jessica walked into the darkened house and up to the bedroom. Sam was asleep, an open book resting on his chest. She put the book away and turned off the light. She wished she could wake him and tell him about Darrell. Instead, she just stood looking down at him in the dark, thinking how much she loved him, how much she learned from him.

Jessica closed her eyes and said a silent prayer.

Dear God, please give us a second chance with Darrell. Please help us bring him into our family and please help me be the loving parent he needs right now. I'm sure you already know that Sam will be.

James sat on a bench in the village green, huddled into his coat, hugging himself for warmth. It was a bright, clear day, the sunlight deceptive — strong enough to bother his eyes but not lending much warmth. The harbor was frozen solid, a few old boats stuck in the ice, looking trapped and beyond repair. Which was very much the way he felt right now.

He knew he ought to either get back to work or go get some lunch, but he couldn't seem to rouse himself. He considered returning to Vera's house and getting back into bed instead. It was one of his tired days when he pushed himself along by sheer will and his favorite theory: If he forced himself to do what he should be doing, then he couldn't possibly be as unwell as the doctors claimed.

But yesterday's visit to the specialist in Boston had brought more bad news, and this morning he saw his theory crumbling under the weight of it.

A gull swooped down from the sky and perched on the hull of one of the boats trapped in the ice. James watched the bird peer around, toss its head, and fly away again, eager to move on to a place with better pickings.

The sight made his spirits dip even lower; he wished he were the bird but knew full well he was the boat.

"It's a cold day for sitting outside and watching the harbor."

James turned to find Ben standing beside him. Ben must have been in the church and seen him sitting here, wondering what was keeping him from coming inside.

James managed a bleak smile. "There's not much to see, except for the gulls."

"The gulls never quit. They're either God's most persistent creatures or His most unimaginative," Ben said, taking a seat on the end of the bench.

"The fishermen must hate the winter," James mused. "They can't get out and do their work."

"This time of year is frustrating for

them, no doubt about it. But many don't mind some time off the water or the winter work they take in town. It's a chance to be around the house more and be with their families."

Ben sat back and looked out at the harbor. "How was your visit with the doctor in Boston yesterday?"

"Not good. But you must have guessed that by now."

James rubbed his hands on his knees and leaned forward. He didn't really want to share the news with anyone. As long as he didn't say it out loud, he could continue to pretend that maybe it wasn't really true. But he couldn't avoid telling Ben what the doctor had advised. He certainly wouldn't lie to him.

"The doctor doesn't think I've recovered enough to return to the mission. To hear him tell it, it will be several more months. If ever." James tried but couldn't keep the bitter edge from his words. "It's just one opinion, of course. He doesn't know everything."

"True. Doctors aren't infallible." Ben looked out at the water again and turned up the collar on his coat. James realized his friend must be feeling half-frozen, but his manner and tone were the very definition of patience and interest. "Why did he say you needed to wait, James? What's going on with your recovery?"

James took a breath. This was hard for him to talk about. "It's not just the malaria anymore, though my body is still weakened from the infection. My kidneys are the main problem now; they've been overworked from fighting the malaria. I have to take medication, and possibly dialysis if I don't follow the course of treatment. Any new infection now would be very dangerous. He says I can't risk it."

Ben didn't answer for a long moment. "I'm sorry, James. I know that isn't what you hoped to hear. How long did he think it would take for you to get past this part?"

James shrugged. "He was purposely vague on that point, but it sounds like a minimum of two to three months. I need to go back in two weeks to see how the medication is working."

"At least you will recover and the condition won't be chronic." Ben glanced over but James wouldn't meet his eye. "A few months more isn't so bad. You're like a fisherman, James, who woke up and found the harbor frozen over. But God still gives you these precious, brilliant days. The question is, how do you make the best of them anyway?"

James knew what Ben was trying to tell him — to count his blessings, to feel gratitude for what he had in hand, and not waste his time moping over a door that stood closed.

Still, he felt himself fixed on that door, rattling the handle, angry and unwilling to give up and turn away.

"I don't really know the answer to that, Ben. All I know is that I need to return to the mission. I've invested my entire life there. It's the work I was called to do. If the good Lord has some new plan for me, I wish He'd let me in on it."

Ben stared at him a moment. James could see that he was trying hard not to smile, though he could hardly understand what could be striking Ben as funny at this moment.

"I think He has let you in on it. In fact, I think you had a total, textbook collision with it."

James didn't catch his meaning at first or understand the teasing sparkle in his eye. Then he knew. It was Leigh, Leigh and her baby. He looked away, out at the water again.

"What if the specialist in Boston had

given you a clean bill of health yesterday? How would you feel about leaving Leigh? Would you be rushing off to catch a flight back to Nicaragua tonight?"

"No . . . of course not . . . I couldn't do that." He glanced at Ben and met his gaze. "She needs me. I promised myself I would stay until her child was born. I wouldn't leave before then."

"I didn't think you would, even if you were able to. But is it just about helping her with the baby? Leigh has a lot of friends here now. She has Vera and Dr. Harding. There are many people who would help her."

That much was true. James had told Leigh the same thing the other night by the Christmas tree. Right after he'd kissed her. He was still shocked at having done that; he wasn't even sure now that he should have acted on his feelings that way. Then again, whether he acted on them or not, the feelings were there, far deeper and more intense than what he'd told her — far stronger than he wanted to admit, even to himself.

"I care for Leigh very much. I've even said as much to her. She's changed my life, you know?" He glanced at Ben, searching for the right words to capture his feelings.

"She doesn't even realize how happy I feel around her. She thinks I help her because I'm trying to be nice, because I'm a minister or something." He laughed self-consciously. "She doesn't have any idea how much she gives me."

Ben smiled gently. "I'm glad you've found someone that makes you feel that way. It's very, very rare."

James thought that went without saying. He knew he didn't have much experience with women, especially for a man his age. He had never had much time for relationships or met women he wanted to get involved with. But, even so, he'd never felt quite like this about anyone.

"I know you've been a good friend to her, James. But she has a lot of challenges in her life right now. Is she ready for a new relationship?" Ben asked quietly.

"I'm not sure. Sometimes I think she might be. Other times, she pulls away. It's hard for me, too. I don't know where this could lead, Ben. What will happen when I am able to go back to the mission? Leigh knows I have to, someday. Maybe that's why she keeps her distance."

"Possibly. But when feelings are strong between two people, things have a way of working themselves out." Ben turned to him and caught his eye. "Be here now, James. Did you ever hear that expression? My son, Mark, likes to say it to me when I start fretting over things that haven't happened yet."

James considered Ben's words for a moment. " 'Take therefore no thought for the morrow: for the morrow shall take thought for the things of itself'?" he said, reciting from the book of Matthew.

"Exactly." Ben's expression was full of sympathy and goodwill. He reached over and rested a comforting hand on James's shoulder.

"Christmas is coming. Focus on that for a while. Only seven shopping days left. Have you bought Leigh a present yet?"

"I plan to. I just don't know what. I asked Vera what she thinks the baby would need, but she says she doesn't really remember. Maybe Carolyn could give me some advice?"

"I'm sure she can. Our house is fully equipped for Prince William, as I'm sure you've noticed." Ben smiled and got to his feet. "Come on, let's get out of the cold. I don't think the harbor is going to melt down today, no matter how long we stare at it."

James had to laugh. "I think you're

right." He stood up, gave the frozen water one last look, then turned back to his friend. "Are you hungry? I'll buy you lunch at the Clam Box."

"Fine idea. I could use a bowl of Charlie's chowder right now." Ben put on his hat, and the two men set off across the green.

Ben was a good friend, James mused. He had listened to him patiently but hadn't let him indulge his bleak, self-pitying mood. But one thing Ben said gave him pause. Had God really changed the course of his life? Or was meeting Leigh just a temporary roadblock? James knew even Ben couldn't answer that question. He needed to pray about this now, and ask the Lord to help him figure it out.

"Surprise!"

Leigh pushed opened the door to the all-purpose room, expecting to see a final flurry of work for the fair that started tomorrow. But that was not what she saw at all. Awestruck, she took a quick step backward.

She bumped into Vera, who stood close behind her, grinning like the Cheshire Cat. Then she felt Vera's gentle touch on her back, pushing her into the room again.

"Go on, dear. It's your baby shower. They're all waiting for you."

A circle of women swarmed forward to surround her, bright-eyed and smiling. Sophie Potter, her granddaughter, Miranda, Molly Willoughby and her two girls, Jessica Morgan and Rachel Anderson, Nancy Malloy, Grace Hegman, and Carolyn Lewis — all of the women on the Christmas Fair committee, as well as several more she'd gotten to know during her stay in Cape Light. Leigh gazed around, feeling stunned.

Carolyn was the first to break ranks. She leaned over and gave Leigh a hug. "You're really surprised, aren't you? We did a good job of keeping the secret."

"I was bursting to say something. I must have nearly slipped a hundred times today," Vera confessed.

Sophie patted Vera's arm. "Good job, Vera. I'm sure it wasn't easy."

Especially for Vera, Leigh thought with a secret smile. "I had no idea. This is . . . amazing," Leigh said as she gazed around.

The room had been totally transformed from its utilitarian decor. Pink and white helium balloons floated from the ceiling, trailing long curly ribbons; matching crepe paper streamers and stork decorations covered the walls. Long tables covered with pink and white cloths were set up with tea — sandwiches and salads, a huge punch bowl, and several cakes. Bunches of fresh flowers mixed with holiday greens, a subtle hint of the season, seemed to be everywhere.

A fan-backed wicker chair had been decorated as the place of honor, with more pink ribbons and baby trinkets.

"This is all so beautiful. . . . I can't believe it." She met the eyes of her eager audience and felt herself tearing up again. "You didn't have to go to all this trouble for me."

Molly came up beside her. "It's not for you, it's for the baby. Now come and sit down and start opening your gifts. *Her* gifts, I mean."

Leigh followed Molly meekly to the special chair and took her seat.

"Look what I got you," Molly said sassily, handing down a box of tissues with a bow stuck on top. "The extra-soft kind, with lotion. Remember, now that you have a baby, think *lotion*. That's all the advice I can give you, pal."

Still crying a little, Leigh had to laugh as well. She pulled some tissues from the box, wiped her eyes and determinedly got a grip on her emotions. There were so many gifts piled around her, she would be opening them from now until Christmas.

With some help from Molly and Carolyn, Leigh worked her way through the presents. There was a car seat and a portable crib, a bouncing infant seat, a feeding set, blankets, a baby backpack, a sling for carrying the infant, and mounds of clothes. There were gadgets and equipment that Leigh wasn't sure how to use or even what they did.

Finally, she came to a small carefully wrapped box. She read the card and saw that it was from Vera. She looked up to see Vera beaming at her, waiting for her reaction.

Leigh unwrapped the box then folded back sheets of ivory tissue paper. The box was filled with the most exquisite knit and crocheted baby clothes — hats, mittens, booties, a matching blanket, and two tiny sweaters with hoods.

Leigh could tell in an instant all the items were handmade. "Vera! These are gorgeous. . . ." Leigh held up a sweater in one hand and a tiny hat in the other as the other women oohed and ahhed. "When did you ever get the time to make all of this?"

Vera laughed, clearly pleased with her own stealth. "Oh, here and there. As soon as you left the room, I'd slip it out and get to work again. I hate to make such a corny joke, but I really pulled the wool over your eyes."

All the other women laughed. Leigh felt an odd twinge, realizing that Vera naïvely believed she'd pulled off a great deception. While all the time, she was the one being deceived.

Feeling a mixture of gratitude and sadness, Leigh rose and gave Vera a hug.

"Me next." Sophie stood up next to Vera and her stout arms surrounded Leigh, her hands patting her back. "You're a great gal, Leigh. Your baby is getting a wonderful mom."

Before Leigh knew what was happening, the rest of the women were taking turns giving her hugs, their good wishes, and words of encouragement.

For the second time that evening, Leigh felt stunned. She never realized she had made so many friends here, that she had won so much goodwill and trust. She felt another pang of guilt at how she had deceived them all but quickly pushed the thought aside, not wanting to mar the happy moment and the flutter of hope that suddenly sprang up inside her heart.

Maybe she had truly found a place where she could make a home for her baby. Maybe she could really stay here.

James and Ben arrived at the end of the party. James touched her shoulder and smiled into her eyes. "I heard you needed some help bringing home presents. I didn't realize I should have rented a moving van."

"You knew all about this, didn't you?" Leigh did her best to sound stern.

"I knew a little." He shrugged. "Do you like your gifts?"

"Everything's so beautiful." Leigh's voice caught in her throat as she again felt overwhelmed by everyone's generosity. "They gave me too much. Honestly."

"Babies need a houseful of things. That's what I've heard, anyway." He touched her cheek briefly with his hand, framing her face. "See, I told you you had friends here. Now do you believe me?"

She nodded, unable to speak for a moment. "Yes. I do believe you."

With the help of Molly Willoughby and the van from her store, they transported Leigh's haul. Vera didn't want her house overwhelmed with the boxes, so she directed the helpers to carry everything upstairs to the empty room next to Leigh's bedroom.

"This room could be a nice nursery, Leigh." Vera pushed aside an armchair, revealing a door that opened directly into Leigh's room. "You can keep this door open and you won't even need to go out in the hallway when the baby needs you at night."

"That's a lovely idea, Vera. I never noticed it before." Leigh opened the connecting door then shut it again.

Would she really settle in here with her baby? Though Leigh knew her time was quickly closing in on her, the idea of actually making a home with her baby still seemed far off, something she couldn't quite visualize.

Vera frowned at a corner of the floor. "I'm just going to get my DustBuster out for a minute. I know it's late and hope you don't mind, but carrying up all the boxes tracked in some dirt. I'd better catch it while I can."

"Catching" dirt was Vera's passion, Leigh had long ago learned. She was never too tired to chase after a promising specimen.

Leigh walked back into the room with the presents and started sorting out the boxes. James was still there, browsing with interest, especially in the toy section.

"What do you suppose this is for — baby bungee jumping?" James held up a small cloth sack-shaped seat with a long springy cord on one end.

"It's a bouncy seat. You hook it in a doorway. It's supposed to keep them quiet." Leigh took it from him and looked at the picture on the box.

"Of course it keeps them quiet. The child is totally terrified. What happened to rocking in a cradle?"

"That's gone the way of the wagon train, James. Infants need stimulation for their brain cells to grow."

"Sounds like you've been reading up on this." He sat in the nursing rocker she had been given and tested it out. "They can still get rocked though. I mean, for bedtime and such?"

"That's still okay, I think." Leigh nodded, fighting back a grin. He looked so cute sitting in the chair, a stuffed rabbit with floppy ears in his lap, as if he were practicing for a turn at feeding time.

"And babies need CDs of classical music now?" He picked up a CD off a stack of boxes to read the label.

"Makes them smarter, they say. Especially Mozart."

He nodded, approving. "I like Bach

better but Mozart's all right. I can go with that. Do you put tiny headphones on them, too?"

"No," she said, laughing. *But I can get you some,* she nearly added. Then she caught herself.

She was letting her imagination go too far, seeing James as the father of her baby. It wasn't hard to picture, especially lately. He would be a wonderful father, too — gentle and patient, responsible and loving. She couldn't imagine a better man for the job.

But that could never be. Not when he learned how she had lied to him. Leigh gazed around, feeling suddenly deflated — and guilty for accepting so many beautiful gifts. She hadn't meant to deceive all these good people. She hadn't meant to exploit their trust.

She sighed and pushed back her hair with her hand. James noticed and rose from the chair. "Maybe you ought to be sitting here. Want to try it? It's amazingly comfortable."

Leigh managed a tired smile and shook her head. "No, thanks. I'm ready for bed. It's been quite a night."

"Yes, a big night." He looked at all the gifts again. "Christmas came early for the baby but perhaps just in time. What does your doctor say? Will it be soon?"

"I'm really not due for at least two weeks, though she said it could be any time now."

His eyes widened in surprise. "Any time? Any time at all?"

Leigh nearly laughed at his nervous reply. "They always say that, James. They just want you to be ready. Most of the women tonight said the first baby is usually late."

"Yes, I've heard that. Well, either way, it won't be long now, will it?"

"No, not very long at all." She didn't know why she suddenly felt so blue. The thought that her baby would soon be born should have made her feel excited and full of joy, not depressed and nervous. But she couldn't help the way she felt. She was scared, for one thing. And suddenly it seemed that the sooner the baby arrived, the sooner they would have to leave here.

James seemed to sense her disquiet but didn't ask any more questions. He took her hands in his and stepped closer, then gently kissed her, a brief touch of his lips on her forehead.

"Good night, Leigh," he whispered as he stepped back. "And don't start moving these boxes around. I can help you sort it all out tomorrow night, after the fair. Maybe we can put that crib together."

"Oh . . . that would be great. Thank you." She heard herself thanking him yet again and felt silly and self-conscious.

He gazed at her, his blue eyes soft and tender. "That's what I'm here for. You ought to know that by now."

She nodded as he smiled and headed out the door and up to his room.

Leigh closed her door and got ready for bed. She waited until she heard Vera retire to her room down the hall, then she took out her phone to call Alice. She knew it was late, but Alice had left her a message during the day, saying she could call back anytime. Leigh had been so distracted by the baby shower, she nearly forgot all about it.

The phone rang several times but no one answered. Leigh finally heard Alice's answering machine pick up. Leigh hesitated, debating. Alice's husband, Pete, was a good man, but he didn't approve of his wife getting so involved in Leigh's problems, especially when it entailed snooping on her employer. Understandably, Leigh thought. She didn't want to cause problems between Alice and her husband, and she certainly didn't want to endanger Alice's job. She decided not to leave a message.

I'll call her tomorrow first thing, she resolved. She knew it might be hard for Alice to talk if Pete was around, but maybe she could just give her some idea of whatever was going on.

Leigh slipped under the covers and shut off the light. Maybe Alice had some good news for her. Maybe Martin had given up his search.

That would be a miracle. But it was funny; living in this town, miracles didn't seem as impossible as they once did.

Chapter Twelve

Dr. Harding's office was mobbed on Saturday morning, busier than Leigh had ever seen it. Christmas preparations had caused an epidemic of stuffy noses, coughs, and sore backs. Half the town seemed to be waiting to see the doctor, looking over their holiday to-do lists and quietly grumbling that they wished their turn would come.

The phone light blinked and Leigh quickly caught it. "Doctor's office. Can I help you?"

"Leigh? It's me, Vera." Vera's voice sounded shaky and far away. "I'm sorry to bother you at work, dear. But the oddest thing just happened."

"What is it, Vera? Are you okay?" Leigh sat up straight in her chair, worried about her landlady. She didn't sound right.

"Well, I suppose so. . . . This man came to the door just now. He had a picture of you. He asked me all kinds of questions."

Leigh felt her heart jump into her throat. "A man asked questions about me? Did he give his name?"

"He gave me a business card, said he was a friend of your family." Vera took a long breath. "He said some awful things about you, Leigh. I don't even care to repeat them."

Leigh's mind snapped to attention. She felt her body break out in a cold sweat. This was it, her worst fear. Martin had found her. She had to think fast.

"Vera, what did you say?" she asked sharply. "Did you tell him where I am?"

"What? Oh. No, I didn't. He asked a few times, tried to trick me. But I didn't like the man. Something about him scared me. I wouldn't even let him in the house. I told him I just washed the floor and it was still wet and —"

"Vera!" Leigh had no patience for the older woman's rambling. She felt as if her head were about to burst. "Listen, I'm sorry he bothered you. You were right not to let him in. If he comes back, I don't think you should even answer the door."

"Do you think I should call the police?"

"No, I don't think so," she said firmly. "Let's talk about this later when I get home. I've really got to run now. There's a room full of people waiting for me."

"Yes, of course. I'm sorry to bother you. But I just thought you would want to know."

"Thank you for telling me. You did the right thing. Thank you," Leigh said again, eager to hang up. "We'll figure it out in a little while. Don't worry."

Vera said good-bye and Leigh hung up the phone. Two other lights flashed on the phone, but she didn't bother to answer the calls.

She sat frozen in her seat, her mind racing. One of Martin's detectives had found her. She had to leave, there was no question about it. But how could she go? How could she leave this town and all the people who had opened their hearts to her? James, most of all. She pictured him smiling at her, his gentle blue eyes full of warmth and affection. It made her feel so good inside just to have him smile at her that way. How could she just leave him? He would never understand.

For an instant Leigh shut her eyes against the pain that was sweeping through her. She felt as if she were being cut in two. She had finally found someone she could love and trust. After Martin, she hadn't thought such a thing would ever be possible again. But it *was* possible. Everything wonderful was possible with James.

And now she had to choose between the new love she'd found by some miracle and protecting her baby. If Martin caught up with her, he would find a way to get custody; she was sure of it. So it was having James in her life or losing her baby. That was the choice laid before her at this moment. It couldn't be any clearer.

Leigh fought back the tears that were welling up inside. She had to go. Right now. She couldn't wait. The detective could be on his way here at this very moment.

She wiped her eyes with the back of her hand and took a deep breath. Lights flashed on the phone, but she didn't pick it up. Should she call James, just to say goodbye? Just to let him know how much she cared, even though she wouldn't have time to explain anything?

No, I can't. I would break down the minute I heard his voice. I'll write him a note and explain. I'll leave it at the church or mail it to him. No, I could never put all that in a note. All I could really do is thank him and say, "I love you." And he might not even believe that, once Martin's detective gets through with him.

Leigh rousing herself into motion grabbed

her handbag from the desk drawer. Time was wasting. Her heart was breaking. But there was nothing she could do. She had to go.

Nancy Malloy walked toward her, her gaze fixed on one of the patient files.

"I need to run out for a minute, Nancy." Leigh forced a steady tone into her voice. "Can you watch the desk for me?"

"Sure, no problem. Are you all right?" Nancy put the file on the desk, studying Leigh with concern.

Leigh nodded quickly, trying her best to feign a normal expression. She stood up and grabbed her coat from a rack near the door. "I just remembered I had to drop something at the post office and they close at twelve today. I'll be right back."

"Why don't you take your lunch hour? I'll cover for you. And take your time, Leigh. It's going to be one of those days."

"Thanks." Leigh gave her a brief nervous glance and rushed outside.

She walked quickly to her car, feeling tears begin to fall. Brushing them away, she opened the car door and got inside. As she pulled away from the curb, she wondered if she was being watched. Even though Vera said she hadn't told the man where Leigh worked, he could have shown her photo around and tracked her through someone else.

She took another deep breath and started driving down the street, watching to see if anyone followed. She headed down Main Street at an agonizing speed, careful to stay under the speed limit so she wouldn't get stopped. She glanced at her rearview mirror. There were a few cars behind her, but it was impossible to tell if anyone was actually tailing her.

At the village green, Leigh took a turn and the church came into view. She suddenly thought of James again, and her heartbeat quickened. He would be there right now, working at the Christmas Fair. She had planned to stop in during her lunch hour. The cars glutted the side street, overflowing from the parking lot. She could almost feel her hands pull on the wheel, steering her car into the lot. She could run inside for a moment. Maybe she could just catch a glimpse of him one more time?

A car honked, demanding her attention. Leigh turned quickly out of the way, driving past the church entrance and weaving a path through the traffic. She took several quavering breaths, feeling the opportunity pass, then turned at the first corner she came to, Providence Street, a long wide avenue with stately houses.

Again she felt the urge to turn around and go back to the church, but she pushed her foot down on the gas pedal, driving a bit faster than she should have in such a quiet neighborhood.

She had to get away. If she stopped to see James, she might be tempted to stay. The baby was what mattered most. She had to protect her, even if she broke her own heart in the bargain.

Leigh dared another glance in her rear-view mirror, checking to see if a car was following. The street was empty. She made a few more turns and found herself again on the Beach Road, headed for the highway.

She passed the turn for Meadowlark Lane, feeling her panic overshadowed by a deep wave of sadness. She couldn't even stop at Vera's house for clothes or any of the beautiful baby gifts. Well, she didn't deserve them, anyway, she reasoned, trying not to think of how hurt and betrayed everyone who had treated her so kindly would now feel.

They would never learn her true story, either, Leigh realized. They would all believe whatever Martin's detective told them. Vera might be at the fair right now, telling everyone about the detective and what he had said about her.

They might not believe it at first, but they will when they find out I've gone.

She drove on quickly, her mind on automatic. She couldn't let herself weaken. She couldn't give up. She had to think of the baby. That was her only concern now.

James could not recall ever seeing a Christmas Fair like this one, not even when he was a boy. Every inch of the building — the classrooms, the all-purpose room, and even the sanctuary — was dedicated to the purpose. Bows of greenery and satin ribbons arched over doors. Bright lights twinkled. Holiday music sounded, and the scents of pine and savory treats perfumed the air.

It seemed like half the town was there, crowded into the all-purpose room that had been magically transformed to a Christmas bazaar. The crowd roamed up and down aisles of long tables, buying wreaths, handmade ornaments, fancy Christmas stockings and candles, and homemade baked goods.

Sam Morgan manned a table with Digger Hegman, who showed children how to work the wooden toys they had made. Carolyn Lewis stood nearby, showing a customer a long table runner of deep green velvet with gold trim. James thought it looked familiar then realized Leigh had been sewing up a bunch of those one night. How different the place looked from the night of Leigh's shower, he thought. He glanced around, hoping to spot her in the crowd. She had promised to stop by around lunchtime.

He checked his watch, noticing it was just about one. A performance of the children's choir was due to begin in the sanctuary. He followed the flow of the crowd in that direction. Leigh had helped design the choir costumes, he recalled, and had especially wanted to see the kids sing.

James stood at the back of the sanctuary, searching for her once again. She wasn't there, he realized, so he positioned himself near the doorway, hoping to catch her if she came in.

The audience grew quiet as the lights dimmed. James heard angelic voices and turned to find the band of heavenly angels marching past him, two by two, down the center aisle to the front of the sanctuary.

They did looked adorable, he thought, with their delicate tissue paper wings and tilting halos. They definitely looked as if they had just dropped down from the clouds above.

Fittingly, the first song was "Hark, the Herald Angels Sing," which they sang as they climbed onto the risers and lined up in two imperfect rows. Sophie Potter's granddaughter, Miranda, stood to one side directing them. James recalled that she had been an actress briefly in New York but had decided to live with her grandmother and run the family orchard when her grandfather died. It seemed a surprising choice for a young woman, but knowing Sophie and this town, maybe not so surprising after all.

The choir sang several more songs, delighting their audience. Mostly parents and grandparents, James noticed. They finally concluded with "Silent Night."

James clapped hard as the angels took their bows. He wished Leigh hadn't missed it. She would have loved seeing the kids sing, he thought, and he would have liked watching it with her. It could be her little girl up there, someday.

He caught himself with a rueful shake of his head. So much fantasizing lately, so much daydreaming. *It's going to get you into trouble someday,* he warned himself. Still, he couldn't wipe the smile off his face, the smile that seemed to appear automatically every time he thought of Leigh.

The lights went up and the audience began to leave. Still standing by the doorway, James was one of the first into the vestibule.

Vera rushed toward him out of the crowd, startling him from his pleasant daze.

"There you are. Oh, thank goodness! I've been looking all over for you."

"What is it, Vera?" he asked. "Is something wrong?"

"A strange man came by the house. He started asking all these questions about Leigh. He showed me her picture. He said she . . . she's committed a crime and is wanted by the police. . . ."

James squinted down at her. "Leigh? There must be some mistake. That couldn't be —"

"He seemed very certain. He showed me her picture," Vera repeated. "And he said that Leigh Baxter isn't her real name."

James felt as if he had just been struck with a large wooden plank. He shook his head, as if to clear it from the blow. He noticed the curious glances of people passing by and suddenly realized that they were causing a small scene.

"Come to my office, Vera. I think we need to talk about this privately."

Vera pursed her lips and then followed. *This is ridiculous,* James told himself, *some absurd mistake. Leave it to Vera to get in a complete tizzy over nothing.*

But when he glanced over at the older woman walking silently beside him, all the bright decorations and holiday cheer that surrounded them melted away. A dark, heavy panic engulfed him. There was something about this story that made his blood run cold.

James followed Vera's car as it turned down Meadowlark Lane and then down the driveway. Leigh's car was not there, he noticed, but it was barely five o'clock. She usually didn't get home from Dr. Harding's office until six. Maybe they would find a message on the machine, a message that explained everything.

James was trying to keep a cool head and not jump to conclusions. The truth was, though, that Vera's story shook him. And it hadn't helped when he called Matt's office and discovered Leigh had left for lunch and never returned. Still, he was determined to be rational. Maybe Leigh had a doctor's appointment in Hamilton and forgot to tell them. Maybe she had gone off to the mall to do some Christmas shopping. There could be a hundred reasons why she had taken the afternoon off. There was probably a perfectly simple explanation.

James followed Vera up the path and watched as she put her key into the lock, her hand trembling. She had been so jumpy, he had hardly been able to get the whole story. He decided not to dwell on it right now. Asking more questions only made Vera more nervous and incoherent. He would wait for Leigh. That made more sense, he thought.

He hung his jacket by the side door and Vera went into the kitchen to start dinner. James felt at loose ends. He picked up the newspaper and went into the living room. The big house seemed eerily quiet, too quiet. He sat down with the paper and scanned the headlines, wondering if he should call the police and report Leigh's disappearance. No, that was panicking. But she was due to have her baby any minute. What if she was out running an errand this afternoon and found herself going into labor?

No, that couldn't be it. If something like

that happened, she would have called somebody. *She would have called me,* James thought. He was sure of it.

Every sound outside made him lift his head — a branch brushing the window or a car passing on their lonely road. It wasn't Leigh's car though, he thought, listening. He didn't hear the familiar crunch of gravel in the drive. He reached for the paper again, and the doorbell sounded.

"James, would you get the door please?"

Vera came into the hallway, watching as he went to answer a second ring of the door chimes. "If it's that man again, I don't want you to let him in." Her voice was stern and she held the frying pan at her side, a weapon at the ready.

"Don't worry, Vera. I'll take care of it." He willed his voice to sound calm while his heart beat wildly. He took a breath and pulled open the door.

The man who stood before him was just as Vera had described him: about fifty, dressed in a tan all-weather–style jacket, with a brown knit shirt underneath. His black hair was thinning on top and sprinkled with gray, cut conservatively short. He wasn't quite as tall as James but stoutly built, with broad shoulders and a paunch that hung over his belt.

"Can I help you?" James asked politely.

The man smiled at James, his face wide and soft-looking. "I'm sorry to bother you, sir. I'm looking for this woman. Have you seen her?"

He held out a photo of a woman. James didn't recognize her at first and felt himself start to relax. But as he looked more closely, familiar features began to surface through the stranger's image. It *was* Leigh, he realized, though her hair was lighter, a tawny shade, and fell straight to her shoulders. She wore a lot more makeup than he was used to seeing on her, and she was dressed in some sort of formal dress with what looked like very expensive jewelry. Still, her dark eyes were the same, as was her smile — her rare, unforgettable smile.

"You do recognize her," the man said softly.

"Who are you?" James said. "And what do you want here?"

The man smiled even wider, an unctuous grin that put James's nerves on edge.

"Walter Coleman, I'm a private investigator. Here's my card and my license." He pulled a small leather folder from his pocket and showed James his identification then handed him a business card.

What does this prove? James thought. *He*

could have made this today at a copy shop.

"May I come in a minute? Just a minute, I promise. I have something to tell you about this woman. It's important."

James stared at him a moment, then stepped aside to let him in. Behind him he could hear Vera gasp. She had come out of the kitchen and ventured as far as the staircase.

Walter Coleman smiled at her and nodded his head. "Hello again. Mrs. Plante, right?"

Vera just stared at him coldly.

"Why don't we go in here and talk?" James led the man to the living room. He offered him a seat on the couch and sat on a chair opposite.

"I'll get right to the point, sir —"

"My name is Cameron, Reverend James Cameron."

The investigator looked surprised by his title but set the photo of Leigh on the table between them.

"You recognized her," the investigator began. "I bet she looks different now, though. Changed her hair color or something?"

James was about to agree, then instinctively stopped himself from giving Coleman more information. He didn't like or trust the man. He was dreading what he might tell him, and yet he had to know. "Please, Mr. Coleman, get to the point."

Walter Coleman sighed heavily. "What I'm going to say about this woman will probably shock you. You both look like nice folks, and I know it might be hard to take it all in at first. But please, just try to hear me out." He leaned over and tapped Leigh's photo with his finger. "This woman is a con artist, sir, what you might call a pathological liar. I've been looking for her for a while now, but she's clever, always stays one step ahead of me."

"A con artist?" James practically choked on the words. "That's absurd!"

Walter Coleman showed no reaction to his outburst. "I guess I ought to have added an actress, too, an Academy Award winner just about." He gave James a pitying look. "I'll bet she told you some sad stories about herself. I'll bet she borrowed plenty of money from you, too, didn't she?"

"Well . . . yes," James admitted. "I did help her out a bit financially. Vera and I both did. But Leigh felt very bad about accepting any help. She was very reluctant. She promised to pay us back, as soon as she was able."

The investigator's mouth twisted, as if he were trying not to laugh. "Sure. She was going to pay you back, every cent of it."

"She was," James insisted. "She took a job in town even though I told her I didn't want the money back. She needed it to support her child —"

"Have you noticed any valuables missing from the house since she arrived?" Coleman asked. "Little things, silverware, say? Or small pieces of jewelry, things she could bring to a pawn shop."

"A pawn shop?" James heard Vera gasp and suddenly remembered she was also in the room, standing by the door.

James looked over at her. "I haven't noticed any belongings missing. Have you, Vera?" Silently, James willed Vera to stand tough and deny the accusation.

Vera blinked, her skin as white as paper. "I haven't really . . . but there could be. I haven't checked the silver chest in a while. . . ."

"Don't feel badly," Coleman said. "You aren't the first. She's done this before, taking advantage of innocent people like you with her schemes and deceptions."

James had had about enough of this man and his accusations; he certainly didn't need him swaying Vera.

"Leigh isn't like that," James insisted. "I know her. You've made some mistake here, I'm sure of it." But his words sounded weak and unconvincing, even to his own ears. If only Coleman didn't sound so blasted sure of himself.

"Leigh? Is that what she told you her name is? Leigh what?" Coleman pressed.

"Leigh Baxter," James answered sharply. "I've seen her license and her car registration. That's her name."

The investigator gave him another of his pitying looks, as if he couldn't believe James's gross naïveté.

"Fake identification is fairly easily to come by, Reverend, if you know where to go. Unfortunately, even a driver's license doesn't prove much these days."

James sat in stunned silence. He felt the blood drain from his head and for a moment thought he might be sick.

He couldn't quite take in what Coleman was saying, but he had an awful feeling that, without meaning to, he had given the man something that he wanted. Whatever Leigh had done, whoever she was, and no matter how she had deceived him, James still felt an impulse to protect her. Maybe because the truth — or this man's version of it — had not quite sunk in yet. Or because the two drastically different versions of her were so hard to reconcile in his mind.

And though he couldn't put his finger on it, there was something wrong with this man. James studied him a moment then asked, "Who do you work for, Mr. Coleman? Who hired you to find her? You didn't say."

Coleman sat back, his expression going blank. "Her family. Her parents, actually."

"She told me she had no family. She said she was raised by her mother in Ohio and that her mother was dead."

Coleman shrugged a beefy shoulder. "I'm sure she told you a lot of things, Reverend. That's just my point. She'll say anything to play on a person's sympathy." His condescending tone set James's nerves on edge.

"If she's such a hardened criminal, why aren't the police looking for her?" James challenged him. "Why did her family have to hire you?"

The detective squared his shoulders, his expression going hard again. "This woman is wanted for stealing money from a former employer. A great deal of money, actually. Luckily, the company didn't press charges. They don't want the bad publicity. But her family has asked me to find her, to bring her home so she can get help." He looked down at Leigh's photo again, his tone striking a serious note. "If you have any interest in her welfare at all, you ought to tell me what you know, Reverend, so I can bring her back to the people who can help her."

"Oh, James, make him go." Vera sat heavily in a chair by the doorway. She shook her head and stared at the floor.

James came to his feet. "I think you should leave now, Mr. Coleman."

The investigator stood up then leaned over and retrieved the photograph. "I know you think you're helping her. Believe me, you're only making it worse. She's in trouble, Reverend Cameron. She's on the run."

"On the run?"

"She's gone, sir. Mark my words, you'll never see her again."

James felt as if the man had just picked up the fireplace poker and run him through the heart. He was sure his expression must have registered his reaction, but he couldn't think fast enough to hide it.

"I don't think you two really understand. This woman is a criminal. You ought to check your valuables, ma'am, see if anything is missing."

Vera gasped and shook her head. "Oh, no, not Leigh. I can't imagine that."

"You're wrong," James said. "You don't know what you're talking about."

The detective looked at him, a knowing flash in his eyes, and James was certain the man had guessed the depth and nature of his true feelings.

James walked to the front door and opened it. The detective followed slowly, taking his time. He paused at the threshold.

"If I can find her, and take her home, it will be much better for her in the long run. You could tell me where you think she's gone. Maybe she mentioned someone, a friend somewhere? A place she likes to visit?"

"She never said anything like that. Now please go!" James stood shaking with rage. Even worse, he had knowingly lied. He hoped the good Lord in His mercy would understand.

Coleman was unfazed by his anger. "Think it over. Maybe you'll remember something. I'm sure this has been upsetting news for both of you, but it's better that you know the truth about her." He closed his coat and stepped out the door. "I'll be in touch, Reverend Cameron, Mrs.

Plante. Thank you for your time."

James shut the door and slid the bolt. He turned to Vera, who leaned on the banister.

"Oh, James, I don't know what to think. Where's Leigh? Why hasn't she come back yet?" Vera started crying and dabbed at her eyes with the edge of her apron.

James stood watching her, just a few feet away but feeling miles apart, as if he were watching Vera from a great distance. He felt overwhelmed himself, as if the earth were crumbling beneath his feet and he had nothing left to hold on to.

He thought of a thousand and one things Leigh had told him about herself or done. Things that didn't seem the least bit suspicious at the time, but now flocked back to taunt him. The story about being a widow and her husband passing on from a sudden heart attack. Had there ever been a husband? he wondered. And that night on the road when they met, she said she was on her way to Cape Cod — but she had been driving in the wrong direction. Her sudden decision to stay on here seemed suspect as well. There probably was no friend in Wellfleet, he realized now. All the financial help he had offered her, paying for her car and covering her room and board with

Vera; the way Vera had let that slide as well. . . . He felt the blood rise to his face, feeling played for a fool. Was it all true? Had she lied to them both so boldly, deceived them for so long?

"Mark my words, you'll never see her again."

The grim prediction echoed in his heart, like the peal of a bell, shattering everything inside him.

James pressed his hands to his head, feeling as if his brain might burst. *Dear God, this can't possibly be true. This can't be happening. Please . . . let there be some explanation and help me to see it clearly.*

James felt it deep inside, an answer to his silent cry to heaven: the knowledge that it *was* all true. He had been deceived and betrayed.

Then another voice, even stronger and unequivocal, filled him. *But the love I feel for her is still there, no matter what she's done. I love her and she's out there, all alone, running away, trying to hide from that man. She needs me now, more than ever. She needs my help and protection.*

He took a deep breath and wiped his hands across his eyes. He might have been crying, he wasn't sure. He turned to Vera, who sat silently on the staircase, looking numb and, for once in her life, dumbstruck.

"I'm going out to look for her. She can't be far. Maybe she's waiting someplace until that man goes away, so she can come back."

Vera looked up at him, as if shaken from a daze. "Come back? Come back here? Didn't you hear what he said? She's a criminal. She stole money —"

"Vera." His sharp tone silenced her. "I'm not going to judge Leigh and reject her just because of what that investigator said. We never met the man before today. We've lived with Leigh now for weeks. That must count for something. Before I decide she's a criminal, I at least want to hear what *she* has to say."

He pulled on his parka and grabbed his keys from his pocket. "I'll call you later. Don't wait up for me though."

Vera glanced at him then down at the floor again. "That isn't even her name, you know. Her real name isn't even Leigh."

The quiet comment stopped him in his tracks. He stared at her a moment, then shut the door.

James heard knocking on the window. He slowly opened his eyes, feeling as if his eyelids were made of sandpaper. He tried to turn his head, a major kink in his neck halting his progress. He had fallen asleep in his car — at the beach, he realized. His body felt cramped and sore, as if he had been stuffed into the trunk instead of curled up on the front seat.

Ben's face peered through the window, as if James were a fish in a bowl.

"Are you all right?"

James watched him mouth the words and nodded. Finally, he opened the door and slowly unfolded his aching body.

"I'm sorry I missed church this morning, Ben. . . . I tried to call you."

Ben stared at him with an incredulous look. "That's the least of it, I'd say. Did you sleep in there all night?"

James turned his head from side to side, trying to loosen the stiff muscles. "I drove around for a while, a long time actually. I thought maybe I could find her . . . stupid, right?"

He laughed at himself, at his gullibility, at his willingness to believe her and even chase after her.

Ben didn't answer right away. "You drove around. Then what?"

James shrugged. "I didn't feel like going back to Vera's. I'm sorry if she got worried.

I did call to tell her I was all right." He stared out at the ocean. "I came here around daybreak. I parked and fell asleep."

Actually, he had prayed for a long time, then fallen asleep. Ben noticed the bagpipes in the backseat of the car. "Did you play your pipes out here?"

"I just keep them back there sometimes."

Ben stuck his hands in his pockets. A light wind ruffled his hair. "Would you play something for me now? I haven't heard you in a while."

James nearly laughed out loud at the request. "You're kidding, right?"

"Not at all. Let's take a walk. It's not cold out here at the moment. We can walk and you can play."

Ben's suggestion seemed as good a plan as any. James took the pipes from the backseat of the car and slung them over his shoulder.

James fitted the main pipe into his mouth and began to play, and together they started toward the sea. Ben walked beside him, seeming unaffected by the noise level, nodding his head in time to the music. They walked for a distance, several songs' worth of shoreline. Then James stopped to catch his breath.

"That was fine. 'Greensleeves,' right?"

James nodded. "Everybody loves 'Greensleeves.' "

"A haunting melody, poetic lyrics, too." Ben picked up a stone and tossed it into the water. It skipped twice and sank into the waves. "I used to be very good at skipping stones as a boy, a real champion. You should have seen me."

"I believe you." James slipped off the pipes and sat down on the sand. "That's my problem. I believe anything people tell me."

"I wouldn't call that a problem, more like a blessing."

Ben sat down next to him and sifted a handful of sand through his fingers.

Neither of the men talked for a long time. Then James finally spoke, staring out at the sea.

"I loved her, Ben. I loved her very much and she lied to me. The whole time, she was lying." James felt his voice tight in his throat. "No wonder she kept saying I was such a good person, and she didn't feel comfortable having me help her so much. . . ."

Ben reached out and touched his arm. James stopped talking and swallowed hard.

"I don't know what went on between the two of you, James. I'm not even sure if you really know right now." Ben spoke slowly, and James sensed that he was carefully choosing his words. "But I believe that you did love her, that you still do. And from what I've heard from you and Vera and known of her myself . . . well, I'm sure that no matter what she's done, there was some good in it between you. Does that make any sense to you?"

James started to reply and stopped himself. He felt so empty and numb, as if he had nothing left to say or feel about anything.

"I don't know if this investigator's story about Leigh is true," Ben went on. "But I do know that no one is all good or all bad. Life would be much simpler if we were, but God's design is much more intricate, much more mysterious and challenging."

"I won't argue with that, but there's such a thing as the truth."

"Pinning down the truth about a person is a funny thing," Ben said. "I often find, the more I try to get my hands around it, to dissect and analyze it, the more it slips away. It eludes me." He lifted another handful of sand and let it fall through his open fingers.

"Are you trying to tell me it doesn't matter?"

Ben shook his head. "Of course it matters. Love always matters. Love is God working through us, James. You know that. 'He that loveth not, knoweth not God . . .' "

" '. . . for God is love,' " James replied quietly, completing the verse from the First Epistle of John. He sighed and stared out at the water.

Ben didn't speak for a moment, but when he did his tone was low and persistent. "Real love is indescribable and unconditional. If that's the kind of love you felt for Leigh, the love you still feel, it's a gift. It's a miracle. A blessing to you both, even though it might not feel that way right now, even if you don't understand God's purpose in this love He's given you."

"I don't," James admitted sadly. He shook his head. "I don't feel it's much of a blessing either, Ben. Truthfully, it feels more like another cross I've been sent to bear. What can it all mean? I have no idea, except that I seem to have proved myself a complete fool."

"Maybe," Ben agreed. He picked up a shell, looked it over, and tossed it away again. "Maybe being a fool over Leigh was God's purpose for you. I couldn't really say. I think it takes a long time to understand what a person means to you, what purpose they played in your life — even when it's someone close to us whom we live with day in and day out, or someone we may have lost decades ago. Every time you glance over your shoulder, the image shifts and changes meaning. Sometimes, it takes a lifetime to see it clearly."

James considered his words, thinking of people he had known. He'd certainly experienced losses and heartbreak before this one. No one can pass through this mortal life without them. But this felt different somehow. He had been blindsided. He didn't know how to handle it.

James was silent for a while, letting his gaze rest on the sea and finding comfort in its ever-changing beauty. When he spoke again, his voice was calmer.

"I've decided something out here this morning," he said. "I'm going back to the mission. I'm not going to worry about what the doctor said last week. I think he exaggerated to put a scare in me."

"I don't know about you, but he terrified me," Ben said honestly.

James bit back a smile and forged ahead with his explanation. "Look, I know you think this is just a reaction to Leigh. But it isn't, Ben . . . at least not entirely. I'm not running away. It's just that there's nothing holding me here now. I have important work to do and I've neglected it too long. I'll feel better if I'm busy, back where I belong. Work is good medicine, Ben, the best I've found. I know it's what I really need now. There's really no reason for me to stay here any longer."

Ben took a breath, looking as if James had announced he was going to run straight into the icy cold surf.

"You clearly have a calling, James. I've never questioned that. But stop a minute, think this through. You can at least wait until Christmas, can't you? I mean, it's only a few days from now."

James nodded. "I guess so. Will that make any difference?"

"It will make a difference to me — and to the congregation."

James saw his point. He had been so lost in his pain, he had forgotten his obligations. "Of course I'll stay. You're right. I shouldn't just leave you flat."

"You shouldn't leave us at all, though I know someday you'll need to. But at the right time, James, when the dust has settled and you can see your way clearly."

James didn't reply. He looked out at the water again then down the shoreline. He spotted the lighthouse, and couldn't help but recall the day he had come here with Leigh — how he had promised that they would come back and walk all the way to the light.

It was a funny feeling, realizing that wouldn't happen now. As if something precious had been stolen away from him, a golden day, true happiness, the kind you could feel seep right into every part of you, like the warmth of the sun.

She *was* a thief, he decided. She had truly robbed him.

Emily was holding Dan's hand under her mother's dining room table. She glanced at him and he gave her fingers a reassuring squeeze. He leaned forward and she saw the edge of the white envelope inside his sports coat's breast pocket. The wedding question was finally settled between the two of them, and they had vowed to stick to their solution. Now if she could only find a way to spring it on her family. . . .

"Well, that just goes to show, you never know about a person. Believe me, I've learned that lesson by bitter experience." Lillian Warwick nodded righteously, her silver fork hovering in the air as she spoke. "Everyone in this town is far too trusting. Any flimflam artist can walk right in and get away with the crown jewels."

Sara, who sat across from Emily, raised her eyebrows. "What crown jewels? I thought we were in America."

"You know very well what I mean," Lillian snapped.

Sara bit back a smile and Emily again marveled at her daughter. She was perhaps the only person in all of Cape Light who was completely unintimidated by Lillian Warwick.

Jessica spoke up before her mother could continue. "Leigh Baxter seemed to be a very nice person, Mother. Did you ever meet her?"

Lillian made a huffing sound. "A *nice* person. Now what does that mean?"

"She was . . . nice. Very quiet and unassuming." Emily shrugged. "Molly said she was great with Dr. Harding's patients, and she absolutely rescued the costumes for the children's choir. Everyone liked her. The women at church even gave her a baby shower."

"And now she's skipped town — with all the baby gifts, I'll bet. She's probably planning to sell them or something."

"Actually, I heard she left everything, even her clothes," Sara said in a more serious tone.

"Well, that's some compensation. Maybe the gifts can be returned. I wish I could say the same about my own belongings." Lillian fixed her daughters with her trademark glare. "Half my house is all over town today, thanks to that infernal rummage sale. . . ."

"The fair was very successful this year," Sam said. "The church raised a lot of money."

"Lucky that con artist didn't run off with that, too."

"Mother, can we please talk about something other than con artists?" Emily asked.

Lillian replied with an indignant sniff then smoothed down the buttons of her sweater.

Jessica sat up very straight in her chair, and Emily saw her nudge Sam with her elbow. He looked back at Jessica and smiled.

"We have something to tell everyone today," Jessica began. She was beaming now, her fair skin glowing. Emily already guessed what her sister had to say and felt a rush of sheer happiness.

"I just want you all to know . . . that Sam and I are expecting a baby."

Emily clapped her hands together. "I knew it! I could just tell by the look on your face. Congratulations!"

Lillian pursed her lips. "Well. That is news."

Emily couldn't tell if her mother was happy, surprised, or simply had such mixed feelings about motherhood, she didn't know how to react.

Dan jumped up and shook Sam's hand, then leaned far across the table to kiss Jessica's cheek. Sara hugged both her aunt and her uncle while Emily ran around the table and waited her turn.

"I'm so happy for both of you," she said.

"When is the baby due?" Sara asked Jessica.

"Not until August — if everything works out okay." Jessica sounded more subdued now, Emily thought, with good reason.

"Of course it will. August is a perfect time for a new baby."

"It seems far off. But it's going to take at least that long to get used to the idea," Sam admitted.

"The time goes by quickly," Lillian said. She cast a disapproving look at Emily and Dan. "I hope the two of you will be back from your sojourn by then."

"We'll only be gone for six weeks," Dan said. "Remind me to give you our itinerary."

"Yes, do that. I'm going to get a map and stick little pins in it to chart your progress. It will provide some distraction for the rest of the winter."

Emily couldn't quite tell if her mother was joking or not. She wanted to laugh but didn't quite dare.

"That reminds me." Dan sounded perfectly casual. "We have something to show everyone." He glanced at Emily then slipped his hand into his sports jacket and pulled out the white envelope.

Emily saw her mother's startled expression as she put her hand to her throat. "Don't tell me. You've run off and gotten married at some drive-thru window."

"It's not our marriage certificate, Mother. But you're close," Emily praised her.

Sara leaned forward eagerly, nearly tipping her water goblet. "What is it? Let me see. . . . What have you two been up to?"

Standing now, Dan seemed to be enjoying building the suspense. He held the envelope out for everyone to see. "And the nominees are . . . for Most Elegant Bride in a last-minute production . . ."

"Dan, please. Just show them what it is." Emily couldn't help it. She just wanted to get this over with.

"Sorry, You're right. Here it is, folks. . . ." He pulled out the sheet of paper and unfolded it then held it up for everyone to see. "Emily and I thought we should give you all some advance warning. This is sort of a notice, I guess, that will run on the front page of tomorrow's *Messenger.* I still happen to have some connections at the paper," he added modestly.

"Get to the point, man. What does it say? I can't bloody well read it from here at my age." Lillian shifted in her chair, looking thoroughly disgruntled.

Unfazed by her outburst, Dan slipped on his reading glasses and looked down at the page. "It says, and I quote, 'Ms. Emily Louise Warwick and Mr. Daniel Theodore Forbes respectfully request the honor of your presence at their marriage, to be performed at one o'clock in the afternoon on Saturday, January third. The ceremony and reception will take place at the Gazebo on the Village Green, Cape Light, Massachusetts. Any and all are warmly invited to attend.' "

He'd barely finished when Emily heard a loud thump from the other end of the table and the china and silver flatware rattling in response. She turned to see that her mother had pounded her fist on the table and now sat with her hand in the air, ready to do it again.

"You can't be serious! Have the two of you gone insane?"

"Mother, please, calm down. You're going to make yourself sick." Jessica rose and quickly went to her mother's side. She glanced nervously at Emily. Emily remained seated; she'd expected something like this and had even warned Dan. She wasn't at all surprised.

"Make myself sick? I'd rather go into a coma right here than die of shame on January third . . . for all the world to see." Lillian put her hand to her chest. "You've done this on purpose, to embarrass me. Admit it, Emily. I know how you think."

"Mother, please. It's my wedding. It doesn't have anything to do with you."

"I'll say it doesn't. You don't give a fig about my opinion. Or my feelings. You never did —"

"Please, just calm down a minute. Dan and I went back and forth about this for weeks. This is what we've decided to do. I think it's going to be perfect."

Dan spoke up, his tone calm and blithe, a sharp contrast to Lillian's thunderous expression. "I know it seems a bit extreme, Lillian. But Emily wasn't really going to be happy until we invited the entire town so it seemed like the perfect solution."

"Mother, please. It's our day. Don't spoil it for me."

"Oh, I won't spoil it for you, miss. Don't worry. I won't be there to spoil it. Go and make a public fool of yourself. Get married on a flying trapeze with a rose between your teeth. See what I care!"

Emily watched, appalled, as her mother stood up and grabbed her cane, then hobbled off toward the living room at a surprisingly quick pace.

Emily got up to go after her but Dan touched her arm. "Let her cool off for a while. She'll be all right."

"Dan's right," Sam said. He was doing a poor job of keeping a straight face. "But how long does it take for a nuclear reactor to cool down? Do we need protective gear or anything?"

Jessica poked him in the arm with her elbow. "Sam, please."

Sara laughed. "I'll go talk to her. You guys stay here." She touched Emily's shoulder as she passed behind her chair. "I think it's a great idea, Emily. It's really perfect for the both of you. I can't wait."

Emily smiled fondly at her, tipping back her head. "Thanks, honey. You're still going to be my bridesmaid, right?"

"Absolutely. Wouldn't miss it for the world." Sara gave Emily a quick hug, then left to check on her grandmother.

"And you'll be my bridesmaid, too," Emily said to Jessica. "I'm only going to have you two."

"We're keeping the wedding party simple," Dan said.

"And the reception," Emily added. "It's hard to figure out what to serve for so many guests. We hope Molly has some creative ideas for us."

"I'm sure she'll be totally inspired by the challenge. It's the best idea for a wedding I've ever heard." Jessica smiled brightly, then reached across and touched Emily's hand. "Don't worry about Mother. She'll come around. I predict a sweeping, dramatic, last-minute entrance — the way she showed up at my wedding." Jessica laughed quietly. It was a cherished memory now, though at the time, it had seemed like one of the most harrowing moments of her life.

Emily remembered, too. "That sounds about right. Let me know if she asks you to get her fur coat out of storage. Then I won't be worried."

Emily winked at her sister and they both laughed. Dan put his arm around her shoulder and squeezed her closer.

She knew it would be a happy day, no matter what. She was going to start a new life with the man she loved. Nothing and no one could take that happiness from her.

Chapter Thirteen

Vera rinsed the breakfast dishes and lined them up carefully in the dishwasher. She liked to put them in in a certain way, so it was more efficient when she took them out.

She watched out the window while cleaning the sink. There wasn't any activity at the bird feeder this morning. It was bitter cold outside, the temperature suddenly dipping below fifteen degrees on this last Tuesday before Christmas. The birds must have found a place to wait out this cold, she figured, though she would refill the feeders before she left tomorrow for the holidays, just in case.

She was going to visit with her daughter Gail's family in Connecticut this year. She would pick up her sister Beatrice tomorrow in Gloucester and they would drive together to beat the Christmas Eve traffic. Vera liked to have some extra time with her grandchildren before the madness began. Maybe they could bake cookies and make decorations for the table.

Although she usually didn't like to miss Christmas service at her own church, this year she felt differently. Leigh Baxter had ruined it for her. Vera was eager to leave town and get away from all the talk for a while.

She still didn't know what to do with all the baby gifts. It preyed on her mind more than it should. Leigh had only been gone three days, but Vera had called everyone from the shower and promised to return their presents. Most of the women didn't care one way or the other. "Oh, give mine to charity," they said. Now she had the job of sorting it all out, figuring what had to go where. James said to leave it until after the holidays. He promised to help her, though she knew he had even less heart for it than she did.

She hadn't been able to go in that room, the one she thought of as the nursery. The piles of boxes seemed to mock her each time she passed the open door, so she kept it shut now. Leigh's old room was still full of all her belongings, not a thing touched from the way she had left it. Just run off and left everything! It was still unbelievable to her.

It was as if someone had died, Vera thought, only worse in a way. It was as if they had died and then you found out all kinds of terrible things about them. You found out they weren't the person you thought you knew, and you had been tricked and made a fool of.

The phone rang. She dried her hands on a dish towel then walked down the hallway to answer it. It was probably Bea, she thought, calling about their arrangements for the hundredth time.

"Hello?" she said. No one responded. "Hello? Who is it?"

Vera felt impatient, thinking she'd picked up a sales call, the kind that was so hard to hang up on once they got you talking.

She moved the phone away from her ear, about to hang it up. Then she heard someone speaking and moved it back again.

"Hello, Vera? . . . It's Leigh."

Vera gasped. She felt her hand tremble. "Leigh? Why . . . how dare you? You have some nerve calling here. Haven't you caused enough trouble for everyone?"

She heard Leigh breathing hard, as if she had been running a race. She pictured her, her soft brown eyes and sweet face, so tired and pregnant. She felt her heart soften for a moment. But just as quickly, she remembered everything.

"Vera . . . I'm so sorry. Please . . . just let me talk to James a minute. Is he there?"

Vera drew in a sharp breath. She heard James coming down the back steps into the kitchen, and she quickly turned her back to the doorway. "No. . . . He's gone out. I don't know where he is. Just leave him alone now. You've caused enough trouble for us. Don't call here anymore, do you understand?"

She heard Leigh start to reply, but she reached out and slammed down the phone, as if it was suddenly burning her hand.

"Vera . . . who was that? Who were you yelling at on the phone just now?"

James stood behind her. Vera wiped her hands on her apron, a clammy feeling on her palms. "It was . . . no one. Just a salesman."

She walked past him and opened the utility closet. She couldn't remember what she was looking for and pulled out her electric broom.

James followed her. "What did the salesman want? Why were you shouting at him?"

Vera finally turned to face him. He looked awful, she thought, his complexion pale with a yellowish cast, dark shadows ringing his eyes. He hadn't shaved yet either, wasting the morning away in bed. She worried about his illness getting the best of him again over this. He was such a good man. She bit the inside of her lip. She might as well tell him. It wasn't right to lie to him about this. No matter what she really thought.

"It was Leigh. I told her not to call here anymore, not to bother us."

"Leigh?" He stepped forward, his dull expression suddenly coming alive. "Why did you hang up? Why didn't you call me?"

Vera stepped back, frightened for a moment by the look on his face. "I . . . I didn't think you should talk to her, James. Not after the way she tricked us. She probably thought she could still get around you. Maybe she was looking for some money or something. I don't know. . . ." Completely flustered, Vera let her excuses trail off.

"Oh, Vera, what did you do?" James shook his head and leaned back, staring at the ceiling. She could tell he was angry and trying hard to hold on to his temper. "Don't you understand? She's sick and broke and about to have a baby. The baby, Vera. You should have thought of the baby."

"Yes . . . yes, you're right. I wasn't thinking. I heard her voice and I just flew off the handle." Vera felt herself weeping a little but couldn't stop. "I'm just so angry at her, James. I can't help it. I treated that girl like my own daughter and she made such a fool out of me."

A bigger fool out of me, by far, James thought. He stepped over to Vera and rested his hand on her shoulder.

"I'm sorry I yelled at you. Believe me, I understand how you feel." He paused and took a deep breath. "Did she say anything about where she was? Did she leave a phone number?" he asked hopefully.

Vera shook her head. "No, it wasn't like that. She hardly said a thing. Just that she was sorry and wanted to speak to you."

James sighed again and rubbed the back of his neck. "Did you hear anything in the background? Any clue about where she was calling from?"

"It sounded as if she was outside somewhere. I might have heard cars, maybe from a road."

James walked to the phone and punched three keys. He waited a moment, listening, then jotted down a number on a pad on the phone table.

"She called from this area code," he said,

sounding brighter. "She can't be that far."

"How did you figure that out?"

"I dialed a code that gives you the number of your last incoming call — star-six-nine. See, here's the number." He showed her the slip of paper then picked up the receiver again. "I'm going to call. See where it is."

Vera followed him into the hallway. Half of her wanted to find Leigh; the other half never wanted to hear about her again.

She watched James with the phone to his ear, listening. Finally, he hung up.

"No answer. Must be a pay phone somewhere."

"Maybe the police could help you. You know, trace the phone number, like they do on TV?"

James glanced at her and shook his head. She guessed right away what he was thinking. What if the story Walter Coleman had told was true? What if Leigh really was a criminal? She knew James was the last person on earth who would let the police find her.

Not before he did, anyway.

James brushed through the kitchen and grabbed his parka and gloves from the coat tree in the mudroom. Vera watched from the doorway.

"I'm going into town," he said. "If she calls back, try to be calmer and get a number. Tell her I want to speak to her."

Vera drew in a sharp breath and nodded. "All right. If you say so."

It wasn't so hard to agree. She had a feeling Leigh would not be calling there again.

"Have you heard from Leigh, Matt? Did she call here today?"

James trailed Matt from the reception area into his office, oblivious to the other patients in the crowded waiting room.

Matt closed his office door behind them and waited until James had taken a seat before answering. "No, Leigh hasn't called. Do you think she will?"

"She called Vera's house this morning. I didn't speak to her, but I found out the number. She isn't far. I'm worried that she might be having some problem with the pregnancy."

Matt's expression was grim. "That's very possible, considering all the stress she's under right now. And she's so close to term."

"I had an idea. Maybe she's trying to find a doctor to help her. I've already called Dr. Olin. She hasn't heard from

Leigh but promised she would get in touch if she did. Could you give me a list of doctors around here that Leigh might try to visit? I thought I would call them and ask them to call me if she contacts them."

Matt nodded and walked to a bookshelf behind his desk. "That's not a bad idea, especially if you know she's still in the area." He pulled out a thick black reference book and thumbed through the pages. "Here's a directory we can start with. I can make some calls for you later. Let's look at the list and split it up."

James released a long breath. "Thanks, Matt. I appreciate all the help I can get."

James wasn't sure what Matt thought about Leigh now, whether or not he believed the stories about her. If he felt betrayed or tricked, he didn't show it. James sensed he was thinking of Leigh as a woman about to have a baby, who needed care. Doctors were trained to be as nonjudgmental as clergymen, James realized. Matt, though, was doing a far better job of it than he was. Of course, there weren't the same emotions involved for Matt — and not nearly as much at stake.

Jessica checked her watch: five forty-five. She still had fifteen minutes before their guests were due to arrive. She couldn't believe she was ready on time this year. Her guests might be late, though. A light snow had fallen during the day, which meant the Beach Road could be slow going. Everyone claimed to love a white Christmas, but no one liked to drive around in snow on Christmas Eve, she thought.

She glanced around the living room, checking things one more time. Tiny lights on the Christmas tree twinkled. An assortment of gaily wrapped boxes were piled beneath the lower branches. Sam had already started a fire, and it cast a warm golden light over the room. Pine bows and sprigs of holly were draped across the mantel; a band of carved wooden angels Sam had made for her were arranged in the greenery, each holding a long taper.

The candles. I almost forgot. She lit the candles on each angel and then some others around the room, then stood back, looking things over once again.

"Honey, you're fussing too much. Everything looks great." She looked up, wondering how long he'd been standing there watching her.

"You don't look so bad either, come to think about it," she said, smiling at him. He had just finished dressing and looked wonderfully handsome, she thought, his thick hair still a bit damp from his shower and a soft burgundy wool sweater complimenting his dark looks.

He walked over and put his arms around her. "You worked too hard today. I hope you're not too tired for all this company tonight."

She shook her head. "I feel great. I can't believe we're ready on time this year . . . well, practically."

Sam led her to the armchair and coaxed her to sit down. "You sit down and take a break. Just tell me what to do."

"Well, let's see. . . . We need to make some more room under the tree for presents. Can you move some of those boxes around?"

"No problem." Sam crouched down and began shifting boxes. "Hmm . . . this one just says 'Baby.' Who could that be?"

Jessica laughed. "You know who it's for. Sara dropped it off before she went back to Maryland."

Sam nodded. "Very thoughtful." He moved some more boxes around and shook his head, laughing softly. "Gee, there seem to be a lot them marked for 'Baby.' Okay, here we go. Finally, one for me." He held up a small box, as if finding a prize.

"That's from me, but you can't open it until later."

"I know. I know." He sighed theatrically and put the box back on the pile. "It's tough to wait, though."

Jessica knew he was joking. Well, half-joking at least. Sam could get as excited as a kid about Christmas. She knew the joy of the season had been shadowed this year by his sadness over Darrell, so she was glad that he seemed to be in a bright mood tonight for their Christmas Eve gathering.

"What's this one? Is this for Darrell?" Sam's tone became subdued as he held out a long package.

"Oh . . . yes, that's for him. Just something I saw in a toy store I thought he might like. I didn't get over to the post office this week. I guess I'll have to wait until after the holiday to mail it."

"I guess so." Sam looked up at her briefly. "If we can figure out where to send it." He stood up and brushed off his hands. "I tried to call this week at the number he gave me. The line's been disconnected, and I didn't get a chance to ask Luke about it. I just hope everything's all right."

Jessica took a breath. *I know about Darrell,* she wanted to say. Still she hesitated, wondering if it was the right time to talk about him. Luke had called her during the week at work. He had found out that Darrell was coming back to New Horizons. He wasn't quite sure when, but it would be very soon, he said. Darrell's mother seemed about to agree to put the boy in foster care. That meant that she and Sam could apply to be his guardians. There would be interviews and applications to complete, of course. A social worker would visit and do a home study, Luke had told her. "But the chances are in your favor," he said. "Sam's relationship with Darrell will count for a lot, and I'll be in your corner, all the way."

Jessica had thanked him but still felt hesitant about telling Sam the news. What if Darrell didn't come back to New Horizons? And what if his mother changed her mind again at the last minute? Luke had agreed to call her when he finally went to pick up Darrell in the city. She had waited all day and hadn't heard a word.

"Jess, are you all right?"

"I'm okay. It's just that there's something I've been meaning to speak to you about."

"Okay." Sam walked over and stood by her chair. "Something troubling you?"

"Not exactly. . . ." She sighed, not

knowing quite where to begin.

Then they both heard the sound of a car pulling up in the driveway. A few minutes later, they heard the car doors slam and the sound of voices just outside. It was Emily and Dan, along with her mother.

"Sounds like someone's here." Jessica rose and smoothed out her long satin skirt. "Do I look all right?"

"Perfect, as always." Sam gave her a questioning look. "I guess we'll have to talk about it later. You're not mad at me for anything, are you?"

"No, not at all. Don't be silly." She stood on her tiptoes and kissed his cheek. "It's nothing bad, just something that's hard to talk about. It could be a good thing for us, actually."

"Now you've got me curious."

The doorbell rang. Sam smiled down at her a second, then started off to the foyer. "But I guess I'll have to wait."

Jessica didn't answer. *Saved by the bell,* she thought. *If Luke doesn't call tonight, I guess I will have to tell him. . . .*

James turned on the flame under the frying pan and tossed in a pat of butter. He opened the egg carton, cracked open two eggs on the rim of a bowl, added a dash of milk and some shredded cheddar cheese, and beat the mixture together. A high-cholesterol dinner, but so what? It was Christmas Eve. He'd never eaten scrambled eggs on Christmas before, but there was a first time for everything, he decided.

His toast popped up from the toaster and he dropped them into a dish. A few crumbs fell to the floor and he reflexively thought of Vera's DustBuster. The crumbs could wait. Vera wouldn't be back for a few days. He would clean the house before she returned.

It was actually a relief to be alone. He loved Vera but he needed a break right now, a rest. He hadn't slept well for days, ever since Leigh had left. It was barely seven in the evening, but all he wanted to do was eat his eggs and toast, take a shower, and go straight to bed.

He bowed his head and silently said grace. "Thank you, Father, for this meal. Please bless this food and forgive me for . . . for my seclusion tonight, for indulging my low spirits. Please give me the strength and peace of mind to focus tomorrow on Christmas and your gift to the world, the birth of your son, Jesus Christ. Please give me the courage and faith to get through these difficult days. . . ."

James took a breath and abruptly ended his prayer. His talks with God were rambling on these days, he'd noticed. *God's going to think I've been living too long with Vera.*

He chewed mechanically, staring into space, his gaze falling on Vera's Elvis Santa, perched on the refrigerator. About a foot high, the mechanical music box — with Santa's outfit and beard and Elvis's sideburns, sunglasses, and a red plastic guitar — suddenly intrigued him.

He rose, set it in the middle of the kitchen table, and turned on the switch in back. Scratchy music suddenly drifted out of Santa's belly and the figure began to sway from side to side. A pseudo-Elvis voice began to croon. It took James a moment to recognize the tune. . . .

" 'Blue Christmas.' Just what I needed tonight." He let the doll sing a few more choruses then tried to shut it off. It wouldn't go off, it seemed, until the song was over. He carried it to Vera's utility closet, placed it among the vacuum cleaner collection, and shut the door. He could still hear the singing a little in the kitchen, but at least he didn't have to look at it anymore.

His eggs looked cold now, unappetizing.

He wasn't hungry anyway, just forcing himself to eat something.

The phone rang and he wondered if he should even answer it. He expected it to be Ben, checking up on him again. His friend had tried to understand when James had begged off on the invitation to spend the holiday with the Lewises. But James had a feeling that Ben, or even Carolyn, would make one last effort to get him out of the house tonight.

He stood listening to the ringing, thinking it might be best if he didn't talk to anyone right now. But finally, he reached out and picked it up. "Hello?"

"James, I'm glad I caught you in." Matt spoke in rush. "I just got a call from a friend of mine in Southport. He's on call tonight at the hospital there. He said a woman was just admitted who fits Leigh's description. He was on his way to the hospital to take care of her. . . ."

James pressed the phone to his ear, fumbling for a pencil to write things down. "Southport. Okay, what's the doctor's name?"

"Dr. Dunbar. Frank Dunbar. I told him I would call you. You shouldn't have any trouble getting in to see her. I don't know what name Leigh gave when she signed herself in, though."

"I'll find her. Thanks, Matt. Thanks a lot."

"That's okay. Good luck. . . . Call me later. Whenever you can. I'll be at Sam Morgan's house but I'll give you my cell number."

James quickly took down Matt's number and hung up the phone. He grabbed his parka and car keys and ran out the door to his car.

Southport was over an hour away, even with some speeding. He hoped there wasn't any traffic left on the highway and that everyone had reached their Christmas Eve destinations by now. He thought of calling Ben, then realized he had left his cell phone in the house. He would have to call later from the hospital, from a pay phone.

He reached the connector to the highway and headed south. His eyes fixed on the straight wide road, he whispered a quick prayer. "Please, Lord, please let everything go all right tonight with Leigh's baby. Please let me be there in time."

James talked to anyone who would listen to him, but he was still told to wait outside the big double doors of the maternity ward, where large letters on a red and white sign read NO UNAUTHORIZED ADMITTANCE.

He paced back and forth, waiting for a passing nurse or orderly who might again relay his message to someone inside. A nurse at the information desk had promised twice already that she would get in touch with Dr. Dunbar and tell him James was waiting. It didn't help matters, James thought, that he wasn't even sure of the name of the woman he was looking for and couldn't quite describe his relationship to her. It was agony to have to just wait on the other side of the doors, knowing Leigh was in there and maybe even wanted to see him.

At last the doors opened and a man dressed in green scrubs walked toward him. "Reverend Cameron? I'm Dr. Dunbar. Sorry I took so long to find you out here."

"How's Leigh? Did she have the baby yet?"

"Her labor stopped. We're trying to induce and waiting to see what's going on. The baby seems fine so far. She has some toxemia but we're dealing with that."

James wasn't sure what all this meant and felt too nervous to ask. "Can I see her?

I mean, will you ask if she'll see me?"

"I told her that you're here. She's waiting to see you. You can go in now for a few minutes if you like."

James followed the doctor into the maternity ward. Leigh was alone in a small room. There were monitors attached to her arm and to her body. Her eyes were closed, her face turned toward the window. She looked exhausted, he thought, worse than he had ever seen her, and still impossibly beautiful.

He stood at the side of her bed, afraid to wake her.

A moment later, she turned her head and opened her eyes. "James . . ." She grabbed his hand. "How did you find me?"

"I had some help, God's help mostly." The moment he said the words aloud, he knew they were true.

Leigh didn't respond at first. "I'm sorry, James. I never meant for you to find out about me that way. . . ."

He took her hand and twined his fingers through hers. "We don't have to talk now, Leigh. It's okay."

But she seemed determined. "I tried to leave — for good, I mean — but I couldn't, not without talking to you again. That first night I found a motel room, down in

Spoon Harbor. I knew I was taking a chance, but I didn't think he could find me there. I felt so sick. It was hard to travel, so I waited there. I didn't know what to do. I called Dr. Olin . . . but hung up. I called Molly Willoughby, too, but I didn't have the nerve to speak to her either."

"I'm sorry Vera hung up on you. I would have found you sooner. I had a feeling you weren't very far."

She held tight to his hand, as if for courage. "I meant to go, but I couldn't leave without talking to you. I need to tell you the truth, James."

He cupped her cheek with his hand. "It's okay. Just relax. You need to have this baby. I'm not going anywhere."

She stared up into his eyes and managed a small smile. He leaned over and kissed her. "Leigh — I don't even know if that's your real name — I know I love you, though."

She lifted her head and pressed her face against his. "I love you, too. Please believe me."

He gazed down at her. Was he fooling himself again, seeing only what he wanted to see? No, he did love her. He was willing to forgive her and accept her for whoever she was, whatever she had done. He believed that God had brought them together for a reason, and that reason would be revealed to him in God's own time.

With peace in his heart, James leaned closer and gently stroked Leigh's hair. Nothing seemed to trouble him anymore now that he'd found her again.

Hours later, James sat waiting again, this time on a different set of plastic chairs just outside another room where Leigh had been taken to recover after the delivery.

A nurse came out of the room, leaving the door open. "You can go in now."

The room was dimly lit and he walked in slowly. The first bed was empty, then behind a half-drawn curtain, he saw Leigh. She was sitting up, holding a small bundle to her chest. She looked at him, her dark eyes radiant.

"Here she is. She's beautiful, isn't she?"

James nodded, unable to speak. He moved toward the bed, wanting to see the baby but afraid to get too close. She looked so tiny and fragile, wrapped tightly in a white blanket and wearing a little pink cap.

"It's all right," Leigh said. "You can touch her."

The baby's fist was curled on Leigh's shoulder. He reached out and gently stroked the back of her hand with his fingertip. "Her skin feels like . . . like a flower petal. Look at her fingers. They're so tiny and precious. She's a miracle, isn't she?"

Leigh nodded. "It's like meeting an angel."

James nodded, speechless again. "What are you going to name her? Do you know yet?"

Leigh glanced at him. "Julia. After my mother."

"That's a beautiful name." He paused and leaned back a bit. "How about you? Do you have some other name besides Leigh I should know by now?" he asked quietly.

Leigh looked away nervously for a moment and he was sorry he asked, but when she turned back to him and began to speak, her voice was steady and resolved. "My real name is Natalie, Natalie Weber. My mother used to call me Leigh, as a nickname, so I felt comfortable using it. You can still call me that if you like. I don't mind. I like it, actually."

"Okay, I will then." He sat down on the chair next to the bed and touched her hand. "What are you hiding from, Leigh?"

She sighed and shifted the baby to her other arm. "I don't know what that private detective told you, but I have a good guess. I'm not a criminal. And I'm not a — a con artist, out to steal everyone's money."

"All right. What then? Tell me. I want to understand."

"I'm hiding from my ex-husband, James. I didn't want him to know I was having his baby. He would come after me, and he wouldn't just share custody. He would do everything he could to take her away."

To James the charge sounded extreme, but the real fear in her eyes made him hold his questions.

"About three years ago I married a man named Martin Garret. His family is extremely wealthy. They own a huge textile mill and design studio in New Hampshire. I was working there, and Martin and I started dating. He's older than me, nearly ten years. He had been married before, but he seemed to have good reasons why it didn't work out, and I believed him. Maybe because I never had a father growing up, his maturity was attractive to me. He was very charming and attentive — and possessive. It bothered me sometimes but I overlooked it. I overlooked a lot of things. It was sort of a whirlwind romance. I felt like Cinderella. At first I did, anyway. . . ."

Her voice trailed off, and James could see that it was hard for her to talk about this, hard for her to go back and remember.

He stood up and went to the window and pulled back the edge of the shade. It was still dark outside, the first rays of sunlight just coloring the edges of the horizon.

But it was already Christmas Day, he realized, a Christmas he would never forget. The light slowly grew stronger, the sun slowly rising, brightening the sky. *He is the Light of the world,* he thought.

Love is God, working through us.

He loved this woman and her child, and he would stand by her, from this day on, no matter what she had to say.

Leaning on the window ledge, he turned back to face her. "What did you do at the mill? What kind of work?"

"I'm a textile designer. I do designs for fabric and wall covering, that sort of thing."

"So what you told me about studying art and wanting to be a painter, that part was true?"

"Yes, that was all true. I grew up in Dayton, Ohio, raised by my mother, and I came to New England for college."

He allowed himself to feel a glimmer of

encouragement. Just as Ben had predicted, not everything Leigh told him had been false. "So, you and Martin were married. What happened then?"

"We were only married a few months when Martin began to change. Well, he always had a bad temper. His moods were either high or low, and little things set him off. At first it was never me he was angry with. I told myself he was just a very passionate person. But once we were married, he began to direct his rages at me. He became . . . abusive, verbally . . . and physically."

James felt a stab of shock then anger. He realized he had suspected this, yet had never let himself think it through. Even now, he couldn't bear to imagine someone hurting her.

"So, you left him?"

Leigh gave him a bitter smile. "I tried. His family hated the idea of us getting divorced. They kept encouraging us to stay together, to get counseling, to try harder. Martin was willing to do anything his parents said. He talked me into staying with him and we had some counseling. It would work for a while, and then the cycle of rages and abuse would start all over again. We finally separated and I started proceedings for a divorce. My lawyer said I could ask for a big settlement, but I didn't want anything. I just wanted to get away, to start a new life."

James came back to the side of the bed and reached for her hand. She had been through a terrible ordeal. No wonder she'd often seemed so distant, so distrustful when they first met.

"He made it hard for you to divorce him?"

"Very hard. He persuaded me to come back one last time and try to make it work again. He said he was seeing a new therapist. He promised he had changed. That's when I got pregnant. I never told him, and the first time he tried to hit me again, I ran away. I had to think of the baby."

"Of course you did."

"I didn't have any money. Martin's family kept control of our finances, including the salary I earned at the company. I managed to hide a little, though, for an emergency. A friend of mine, Martin's assistant, loaned me some, too, so I could start over. Of course, as soon as he realized I was truly gone, Martin claimed I had stolen the money from the firm. He closed our bank accounts and I wrote a bad check or two. I guess I was just very naïve and in a panic at first."

"Where did you go? How did you manage?"

"I went to Boston. I probably should have gone farther away, but I had a friend there who let me live with her and helped me get a job. Martin was difficult for a while, but he finally gave me the divorce. I don't think he wanted the abuse charges to come out. Then about two months ago, somebody told him I was pregnant. He must have counted back the months and figured out it was his child, and that started it all up again. Suddenly, it was all about *his* baby that had been wrongfully taken from him." She hesitated and took a sip of water from the cup on her bedside table before continuing. "Martin once told me he would never let me leave him. He would rather I was dead. I knew he and his family would use all their money and influence to force me to go back to him — or simply make up stories about me in court and figure out a way to take the baby."

James leaned over and kissed her forehead. "No one is going to take your baby, Leigh. That's just not going to happen."

"I know you think that's true. I want to believe it, too, James. But just think back to your own reaction. When that detective came to see you and Vera, you must have wondered about me. At the very least, you must have thought that what he said might be true. I know Vera did."

James sighed. He couldn't deny it. He had doubted her. He had let himself believe the worst. "I did, Leigh. And I'm ashamed of myself. I hope someday you can forgive me for that."

"Oh, James, of course I forgive you. I just hope you can forgive me for lying to you all those weeks."

"That goes without saying. You know," he said slowly, "there was one good thing that came out of that man visiting us. I had to face something I wouldn't let myself see before."

"And what was that?"

"That I love you. I knew it had to be love, because losing you hurt so much, and no matter what I heard about you, I still wanted you back."

"Well, here I am." She smiled and glanced down at the baby sleeping in her arms. "Here *we* are, rather." She touched the baby's cheek lightly with her fingertip, then looked back up at him. "I didn't want to face my feelings for you either," she admitted. "I was afraid I would get too close and you would uncover my secret. But you helped me, James, more than you'll ever know. Your kindness and your caring, the way you worked so hard to make me smile and laugh sometimes — you'll never know what that meant to me. . . . It saved my life."

James was so moved he could hardly speak. "I'll always be with you, Leigh — you and Julia — to care for you and make you laugh. I'll always love you, I promise you that."

James leaned over and put his arms around both of them, kissing Leigh deeply. And he knew he held a miracle in his arms, a new path, a new purpose to his life.

"Don't start yet, I'll be right in." Jessica stalled, arranging mugs of coffee and some date-nut bread on a tray. She and Sam had agreed to open their gifts for each other on Christmas Day.

Sam was in the living room by the tree, making a stack of the boxes he had wrapped for her. "C'mon, Jess," he said eagerly. "I want to see if you like this diamond tiara I bought for you."

"A diamond tiara?"

"Well, not exactly," he admitted, "but I think you'll like it anyway."

Jessica had a few presents for him under the tree, too. She didn't think he would be disappointed with her choices, though the best was yet to come.

She walked into the living room and put the tray down on the coffee table. The doorbell rang and Sam glanced at her. "Who in the world could that be?"

"One of your buddies, looking to borrow a cordless drill?"

"Jessica, it's Christmas, for goodness' sake." Sam stalked to the front door, tightening the belt on his robe.

Jessica followed him, her stomach doing somersaults.

Sam opened the door and Luke greeted him. "Hey, Sam. Merry Christmas."

"Luke, Merry Christmas! I thought you were down in the city, with your family. . . ." Then Jessica saw Sam's jaw drop in shock. She could tell that he had finally noticed someone else standing on the doorstep — someone considerably shorter than Luke.

"Darrell? For goodness' sake . . . what are you doing here?"

"Luke brought me. I'm coming back to New Horizons. He said Jessica invited me for Christmas."

Sam glanced over his shoulder at Jessica, a question in his eyes. She smiled at him and rested her hand on his arm.

"I'm sorry, Sam. I should have warned you, but I wanted it to be a surprise."

"A surprise? I'm totally . . . speechless." Sam leaned down and gave Darrell a huge hug. "Come in, you guys. It's cold out there."

"That's okay. I've got to run." Luke grinned at Sam and slapped his arm. "You have fun. Just bring him back to the center this evening by nine. I should be there all day — call if you need anything."

They said good-bye to Luke and went into the living room. Sam's gaze was fixed on Darrell, Jessica noted, as if the boy were a mirage. Darrell stood wide-eyed, taking in all the decorations and holiday trimmings. He walked toward the tree, staring up at its ornament-laden branches.

"Like the tree, Darrell?" Sam asked. "We picked it ourselves at a tree farm."

"You chopped that thing down? Like a lumberjacket or something?"

Jessica laughed at his observation. Sam was like a "lumberjacket" at times, wasn't he?

"There's a present under there for you, that big one in the back. See it?" Sam walked over to help him pull it out.

"There are a lot more, too, hidden in the closet upstairs," Jessica said, thoroughly enjoying her role as Santa. "I'll go up and get them. I just want to watch you open this one, though."

Darrell glanced at Jessica. She could see that he found her new interest in him a bit confusing but not unwelcome. This time, he wasn't resisting her attentions at all.

"Okay, here goes." He tore at the gift, eagerly ripping off the paper and bow. "A snowboard! Awesome. It's a real one, too. Look, Sam!"

"I see. It's a beauty." Sam smiled at Jessica, thanking her for finding a gift that pleased Darrell so much. He still looked stunned with delight to see Darrell here again. As happy as the night she had announced she was pregnant, Jessica realized. Yet the thought didn't make her feel threatened or nervous. Instead, she felt she was just starting to understand what Darrell meant to Sam, what he meant to both of them.

Darrell brought the snowboard over to Sam, and they examined the bindings together. "Too bad the snow isn't deep enough right now," Sam said. "I wish we could test it out."

"Yeah, me, too."

"Maybe we can drive somewhere tomorrow — to a ski run or something."

"Could we really?" Darrell asked.

"Sure." Sam looked at Jessica. "What do you think?"

"That's okay with me. Darrell doesn't have any classes for the next few days, I understand. There's a lot of fun things we can do." She paused and smiled, then slung her arm around Darrell's shoulder. "But why go all the way to a ski lodge? There's always the front stairs."

Sam and Darrell stared at her a moment. She shrugged and laughed, and finally they did, too. That was a good feeling, she thought. Maybe they had a long way to go, but this time she really felt hopeful.

Chapter Fourteen

James ran up the path and pulled open the side door to the church. A few members of the congregation who had arrived early for the service cast him curious looks, but he simply nodded and smiled in answer. It wasn't hard. Ever since he had left Leigh and the baby, he couldn't seem to stop smiling.

He'd had just enough time to make a pit stop at Vera's house, where he put in a quick call to Ben, one of several since the night before, and then rushed to shave, shower, and put on his suit. Now James tugged off his overcoat as he swept into his office. He grabbed his vestments off the coat rack in the corner, pulled the robe over his head, slung the scapular around his neck, then checked the neck piece in the mirror. The scarf was a special pattern and color today for Christmas. Every so often his mind kept slamming into that fact: it was Christmas Day. His heart was so full, his joy so deep, his relief so complete at having found Leigh, his emotions overshadowed everything.

This had to be the best day of his life, certainly the best Christmas he had ever known. Once again, he bowed his head and sent up a silent prayer of thanks for God's answer to his prayers. James knew he had been answered with a miracle, and he would live in gratitude to the end of his days.

A knock on the door startled him and he spun around. Ben stood in the doorway, smiling at him. "So, you made it. I knew you would. A full seven minutes to spare too," Ben noted, glancing at his watch.

"Miracles happen."

"So I've heard." Ben stepped forward and clasped James in a warm embrace. "Merry Christmas, my friend."

James nodded, too choked up to speak for a moment. "Merry Christmas, Ben. Merry Christmas."

He stepped back and wiped his eyes with the back of his hand. "Look at me. . . . I'm a mess."

"Par for the course, after what you've been through. I remember when Carolyn had Rachel and Mark. I felt like sleeping for a week. You would have thought I'd gone through the labor and delivery myself."

James laughed. "Pacing all night is pretty exhausting, but I still feel like I could run a marathon."

"That, too." Ben nodded wisely. "How was Leigh when you left?"

"She was great. Tired, of course, but great. The baby is so beautiful, Ben. She's unbelievable."

"I can't wait to meet her. Julia will be her name, did you say?"

"That's right. Leigh named her after her mother."

Calling from the hospital that morning, James had already told Ben the basic facts of Leigh's story. James still wanted to talk the situation over at length — Ben always offered such a wise, rational perspective — but there was no time for that now.

"I suppose you'll be running right back to the hospital after the service, but Carolyn and I wanted you to know that you're more than welcome to join us at the house today."

"Thanks, Ben. That's a lovely invitation, but I will be going back to spend the day with Leigh."

"Understandably." Ben patted James on the shoulder. "Well, time to start. I always love Christmas Day service, but this one is going to be very special for me."

The two ministers entered the sanctuary side by side, following the chorus as they walked up the aisle, singing the opening hymn. They took their seats and when the hymn was finished Ben stepped up to the pulpit.

"Merry Christmas, everyone," he began. "Before we start the service, I'd like to make a few announcements. We have the final tallies from the Christmas Fair and I want to thank everyone who gave their time and effort. It was an ambitious idea to hold it over two days, and a considerable amount of extra work was needed to pull it off. The good news is, it was a great success and we should all be proud. The bad news is, it was a great success and we'll most likely be doing the same again next year — or maybe even shooting for three days, heaven help us."

The congregation groaned and laughed at Ben's remarks, and James smiled. Yet, though only a week's time had passed since the fair, he could hardly recall it. Last Saturday seemed like a dream to him, a bad dream. It was the day Leigh had left town and his heart had been broken; that was all he would ever remember.

"The Outreach Committee and the deacons met over this past week," Ben went on, "and they have determined that this year the profits from the fair, nearly ten thousand dollars, will be donated to the Helping Hands Mission in Nicaragua."

James sat bolt upright. Did Ben just say that the church was going to send his mission ten thousand dollars? Ben caught his eye and smiled, and he knew that he had.

James got to his feet in a daze of happy astonishment. Ben urged him forward and he stumbled up the few steps to the pulpit. He took a deep breath, trying to organize his delirious thoughts into some sort of coherent sentence. "I'm overwhelmed," he finally admitted. "I don't know what to say, except that right now I must be the most blessed man on the face of the earth. I thank you all, from the bottom of my heart, for your generosity, your kindness, and your Christian spirit. I thank you on behalf of those at the mission, who will see their lives transformed by this gift, this miracle of generosity — of God's love and His spirit at work in the world."

James stood tall and looked out at the faces of the congregation, seeing their warm, familiar smiles and sensing their gentle, silent answers.

"I feel God's love in this room right now because of all of you. I guess that's what Christmas is all about. So I thank you for reminding me and for that gift, too. May God bless each and every one of you."

James bowed his head to say a silent blessing over the group then stepped back to his seat, feeling his legs weak and rubbery.

Ben returned to take his place and led the group in the first prayer. James's thoughts were spinning. How much he could do with this money back at the mission! Dozens of projects sprang to mind. Then he thought of Leigh and Julia. How could he leave them? He couldn't. Not now, not ever. Would Leigh return with him to Nicaragua? That seemed too much to ask of any woman and besides, there was so little settled between them right now. . . .

He sat back and forced his mind to put aside his worries. *Haven't you learned anything at all from these past few days and all you've been through?* Have faith, James. *Take one step at a time and have faith that it will all work out for the best. "All things work together for good to them that love God . . . ,"* he recalled. The simple verse from Romans could never have seemed any truer than it did today.

He felt relieved that he wasn't giving today's sermon — he knew he would have been too distracted — but when Ben stepped up to the pulpit James focused with complete interest, eager to hear what his friend had to say.

"Merry Christmas, everyone," Ben greeted the congregation. "You know, no matter how old we get, I think we still wake up on Christmas morning with that tingle of anticipation. Or at least, we think back to the time when we were children, or relive that feeling by watching our children and grandchildren. I guess you might say that Christmas is the season of Great Expectations.

"One year, I recall, I asked Santa for a pony. . . ." He paused, smiling in response to the laughter that rippled through his audience. "No matter how my parents tried to gently steer me toward something more realistic, like a baseball mitt or roller skates, I wanted a pony and I believed that Santa was going to deliver it to me." He shrugged and grinned. "Why not? I had been a good boy, done my chores, gotten good grades. I had only been in one scrape in the schoolyard, and the other kid started it, of course." The congregation laughed again and Ben continued. "So you've already guessed how this story ends. I didn't find a pony under the tree. I did find a baseball mitt, roller skates, a big book about horses, too, I think. Was I disappointed? Oh, you bet. But perhaps not any more so than my dear mother, who had wanted my father to buy her a bottle of French perfume — Chanel Number Five, I think it was. Well, the poor woman ended up with an electric coffeepot — or was that the year of the gardening tools? My father couldn't help himself, no matter how plainly my mother asked for what she wanted. He thought a Christmas gift should be a useful thing. He didn't know the first thing about buying perfume." Many men in the audience were grinning sheepishly, James noticed.

"Sometimes gifts are perfect, of course," Ben went on. "And sometimes they even exceed our expectations. But what is the spirit of Christmas, really? Anticipation . . . and disappointment? Expensive, jaw-dropping gifts that overwhelm us? Disillusionment when we don't find that pony and plain blindness to the pile of gifts we do receive? Fretting over our endless to-do lists and gifts lists, wondering if we've gotten the right size and color, if we've spent too little or too much? Feeling tired and empty before the party has even begun? That's the prevailing spirit for some of us, I know."

He paused and gazed out at the congregation. "This morning, we each received a gift that never disappoints, a gift that always fits, a gift that embodies the true spirit of Christmas — the very essence of the first Christmas. 'For God so loved the world that He gave His only begotten Son, that whosoever believeth in Him should not perish, but have everlasting life.' " Ben paused to let the familiar yet powerful words sink in. "God's gift of unconditional love, His love and His forgiveness. And through His love, we are connected to the world and given the power to love and forgive others. That, to me, is the true spirit of this season, the spirit we need to draw upon and put into action the whole year through.

"Think of the shepherds, guarding their flocks in the fields that dark night Jesus was born. And the wise men, how they heard of the birth and followed the star, believing the Scriptures had finally been realized. That is the spirit of Christmas, too. Great expectations that God's promise would be fulfilled. In the middle of the dark night, they went forward on faith, following a star, trusting and believing they would be led to the right place. That is the true spirit of Christmas, too, I think. To look up at the stars and see God's love and to keep moving forward on faith. That's what it means to me to keep the spirit of Christmas in our hearts every day."

He stood back and took a breath, his hands braced on either side of the podium. "May God bless you all. Now, let us bow our heads in prayer. . . ."

James prayed along with the congregation, feeling the power of Ben's Christmas message deep in his heart. These past weeks he had learned something about unconditional love — and about moving forward in faith, too.

Leigh had the oddest feeling as James drove them toward Meadowlark Lane on Sunday morning, as if her past and present were coming together. Memories surfaced of the first night he had driven her to Vera's house, after their accident. But of course, that night had been quite different — dark and snowy, whereas today was bright and clear. James had been a stranger and she had sat stiffly beside him, afraid to say a word, with no idea of where she was or where she was going. Now she sat in back, feeling overwhelming love for James and finding every bend of the road familiar — and still marveling at the strange and mysterious turns life takes.

Julia slept soundly in her car seat, swaddled in a hooded fleece snowsuit and tucked cozily under several blankets. Leigh had read that it was safer for infants to face backwards in a car, but she felt uncomfortable sitting up front, not being able to see Julia's face. James had understood perfectly and didn't mind at all chauffeuring them. In fact, he had insisted. Julia had arrived in the world only three days ago, but Leigh knew her daughter could not have found a more attentive, loving guardian if the child had picked him out from heaven above while floating around in some angelic state. Or maybe Julia had done just that, Leigh reflected with a secret smile. It would explain a lot.

She glanced over at James, catching his strong profile as he stared out at the road ahead. She did love him with all her heart. They had some difficult decisions to make, some challenges ahead, but she felt so hopeful now. She was hopeful about her life again, because he was part of it. She hadn't felt that way in such a long time; it still seemed unbelievable to her that they had managed to find a way back to each other.

"We're almost there," James said as the turn for Meadowlark Lane came into sight. "Vera was so excited this morning, she was spraying everything in sight with disinfectant. I barely escaped being sanitized myself."

Leigh laughed, though inside she felt a twinge of nerves. It was difficult to face Vera again. So far, they had only spoken over the phone — after James sat down with Vera and explained things. When Leigh had finally talked to her, Vera had sounded her usual self, asking questions about the baby and Leigh's recovery. She seemed to assume Leigh would be returning, yet Leigh still felt misgivings. So much had been left unsaid.

As the car pulled up the drive and came to a stop, Leigh saw the side door swing open. Vera stood watching them, an eager expression lighting her face.

Everyone is excited to see Julia, no matter what they feel about me, Leigh thought. Though she'd never realized it before, a newborn baby was the perfect ambassador.

Leigh started to unfasten the car seat that doubled as a baby carrier, but James poked his head in from the other door.

"You go ahead. This contraption is heavier than it looks. I'll carry the baby."

She nodded and swallowed hard then slipped out of the car and started toward Vera.

"So you're back. I can hardly believe it." Vera's voice sounded breathless and her eyes looked glassy with unshed tears. *Did Vera really care for me that much?* Leigh wondered, feeling a fresh stab of guilt.

"It's okay, I hope," Leigh started nervously. "I mean, James said it was. But I don't think I ever asked you." Leigh looked down at the ground a moment then straight into the older woman's blue-gray eyes. "I'm sorry for deceiving you, Vera, and for deceiving everyone. . . . Do you think you can forgive me?"

Vera's chin trembled and Leigh saw that she was crying. "Well, to be perfectly honest with you, I've wondered about that myself."

Vera stopped to sniffle into a hankie and Leigh held her breath. If Vera couldn't forgive her, she would have to accept that, but it made her heart ache to think she'd hurt the older woman so badly.

"I've given it some thought and prayed about it, too," Vera went on. "And I finally decided I can forgive you. And I do."

Leigh released her breath and felt her whole body relax in a whoosh of relief. "Thank you," she said quietly. "Oh, Vera, thank you."

"I was fit to be tied when you ran off, without even a word or a note to say goodbye. James must have told you how I acted. But when I heard what you'd been through . . . well, of course I understand, dear." She shook her head and took Leigh's hands in her own. "Can you forgive me for hanging up the phone on you?" She glanced over Leigh's shoulder at James, who was standing nearby. "I don't know if James ever will. You should have seen the look in his eye. Not befitting a minister, I'll tell you that much. I guess I ought to count my blessings I'm still standing here in one piece."

James's burst of laughter suddenly lightened the mood and Leigh had to smile. "We should all count our blessings, if you ask me." He stepped forward, presenting Julia in the baby carrier. She was still fast asleep with just a small bit of her face and the tip of her nose visible under all the blankets.

Leigh watched Vera practically melt on the doorstep. "There she is! Oh . . . my word. What a little dumpling! Look at that face . . . ," she cooed softly. She quickly stepped aside to usher them in. "Bring her in! Bring her right upstairs. Everything's ready."

James carried Julia inside and then up the staircase to the room that adjoined Leigh's bedroom, where they had stored the baby gifts after the shower. Leigh remembered the scene as a jumble of boxes and now stepped inside, gazing around with amazement. The walls had been painted a soft buttery yellow, the moldings and trim bright white. Tie-back curtains with an animal print in pastel colors covered the windows, and a plush area rug cushioned each step. The crib, complete with flannel sheets, quilted bumpers, and a colorful mobile floating above, was set up near the door that connected to her bedroom, and there was also a changing table, a toy chest, and a rocker in a corner.

"You can arrange it as you please, of course," Vera said. "But I thought the crib would be best away from the windows. You don't want her sleeping under a draft."

"This is beautiful, Vera. Thank you so much. James told me he put the crib and a few other things together, but I had no idea . . ."

Vera nodded, looking pleased. "It wasn't

easy, believe me. I rushed right back from my daughter's house the day after Christmas. Luckily, they kept you in the hospital a few days. I hope you like the color. The fellow in the hardware store told me parents don't go for blue or pink anymore. Yellow is sort of — equal. And cheerful, too."

"It's very cheerful. It's like sunshine. You did a wonderful job, thank you." Leigh reached out and squeezed Vera's hand.

"Somebody wants her mommy." James had the baby cradled on his shoulder and now carried her over to Leigh. Julia seemed a little fretful, but settled down again quickly once Leigh held her in her arms.

"Look at that, she knows you already." Vera's voice was hushed as she gazed down at the baby. "Does she need to eat?"

Leigh shook her head. "Not for a few hours. I think she wants to sleep some more."

"Probably. They sleep all day at this stage." Vera stood quietly a moment, gazing down at the baby, then looked up at Leigh. "I'm glad you've come home, Leigh. We missed you."

Leigh felt a lump in her throat. "Me, too, Vera."

"You put her down for her nap. I'll be in

the kitchen if you need anything."

"I guess I'll go down, too," James said. He leaned over and dropped a quick kiss on Julia's forehead; then, with a small smile, he kissed Leigh's cheek before he stepped away and left the room.

Leigh cradled Julia to her shoulder and gently swayed from side to side. She hummed a quiet tune and gazed around the yellow nursery. She soon felt the baby's body grow heavy and slack against her and knew she had fallen asleep. She laid Julia down in her new crib and covered her with a blanket. Then she sat in the nearby rocker and watched her sleep, her tiny pink fist curled up against her cheek.

This is our home now, Leigh thought. *Julia and I have finally come home.*

A short time later, she found James in the living room. He was sitting on the couch, reading a newspaper. A fire crackled in the hearth.

He smiled and looked up as she entered. "Was she fussy?"

Leigh walked over and sat down beside him, setting down the baby monitor on the lamp table. "Not at all. She fell right back asleep again."

"So far so good." James put his arm around her shoulder and she settled back against him. She gazed at the Christmas tree, which was still up on the other side of the room.

"What are you thinking about?" he asked.

Leigh shrugged. She didn't want to answer, then forced herself to be truthful. "About the night we decorated the tree."

"And I kissed you?" he finished for her.

She felt herself blush. "Yes . . . but more about putting the angel on top. I made a wish then. That was what I always used to do when I was a kid."

She had made a wish, out of habit and reminiscing for bygone days, but she had never dreamed it could come true.

He turned his head to look at her fully. "What did you wish for?"

"To be safe again. To have my baby be born healthy and to finally stop running and be able to start my life over."

James was very quiet. She tried to read his expression but couldn't tell what he was thinking. "Do you feel it's come true, Leigh? Do you believe you and Julia are safe here?"

Leigh sighed. "I do feel safe with you, James — safe in this house and in this town. But I've given it some thought and I've decided that I have to get in touch with Martin. He is Julia's natural father, and he has a right to know her. I'm just afraid of what might happen when I do."

James nodded. "I understand, and I admire you for making that decision. You do need to face your ex-husband and settle this once and for all. But you're also right to be wary, so I've spoken to a lawyer in town on your behalf, asked him a few questions about the situation. I hope you don't mind?"

"Of course not. What did he say?"

"Well, he's not an expert in the area. But when I told him your story, he thought you had solid grounds for keeping custody. Your husband's abuse was documented in your divorce, I think you said, and the way he's chased you down these past months is basically stalking. Not to mention paying these private detectives to defame your character. The lawyer thought, all things considered, the situation might never go to court. Your husband should settle without fighting it. Didn't you tell me that Martin was also having some legal problems with his business?"

"Yes, it's quite serious. There was more in the newspaper just yesterday."

"In that case, he might not want a big messy custody battle going on as well. I think the first thing to do, though, is find good representation for you, someone who really knows this area of the law. My friend in town gave me a few names. We can get some advice and take it from there." James took Leigh's hand in his own. "I know this will be very hard for you, but try to think of it as the last hurdle. We'll get through it, and you'll never have to worry again."

Leigh gazed into his eyes. It would be hard to finally face down Martin. But with James beside her, she felt her courage returning.

"I can do it. If you help me."

"Every step of the way. With the good Lord's help, too," he added. He leaned over and lightly kissed her hair.

Leigh rested her head against his shoulder. "And what's going to happen after that, James?" she asked quietly. "After you help me deal with Martin, I mean. Will you return to the mission soon?"

"Yes . . . the mission. That's a bit complicated. . . ."

Leigh lifted her head and turned to face him. "I just want you to know that I understand what your work means to you. I mean, I try to understand. And I don't want you to feel that you're forced now to make a choice between staying here with me and Julia and going back. I know how you feel about us. I believe everything you've said to me, James. But I want you to do what you need to do, whatever will make you happy. I don't want you to stay here out of some sense of — of obligation or duty. I could never be happy that way."

James touched her cheek. "Obligation? I love you, Leigh, with all my heart. You're a gift from above. The truth is, I've been unwilling to face the facts about my health for a long time. And those facts are that I'm still dealing with the aftermath of malaria, and it will be a long time before my body is sound enough to return to the kind of life I had in Nicaragua. That's the bottom line. I've just been too scared to face it. Now that I have you and Julia, though, I don't feel so frightened anymore. I think, with God's help, I can sort it all out. There are people in need all over the world. Right here in this country, in fact. I don't have to travel halfway around the globe to continue my work, and I don't have to abandon my calling entirely."

Leigh stared into his eyes, knowing there was one more truth to tell. "I don't know if I could do the kind of work you do, James. I don't know if I'm cut out for that kind of life. But I'd be willing to try, if you want me to."

James looked surprised and pleased. "All right, I may take you up on that offer someday. We'll work it out, one way or the other — but together. You know, in Ben's sermon on Christmas Day he said something that really stayed with me. He said that even in our darkest hour, we should always remember to keep our eyes fixed on the brightest star and walk forward in faith. And with God's love to guide us, we'll be led on, step by step, to the right place."

"That's lovely, James. I'll try to remember that," she promised.

"So will I. But if I forget, you remind me, all right?"

He smiled then pulled her close. Leigh melted into his strong embrace, feeling loved and secure, happy and hopeful. Finally, at peace in her heart.

"Do you think you're ready to tell him?" Sam spoke in a hushed voice as he walked over to the kitchen table where Jessica was setting out sandwiches for lunch.

Darrell was in the den, watching a *Star Wars* video. He had spent a good part of every day with them since Christmas, and just the night before, when they dropped him off at the center, Luke had pulled them aside to deliver big news: Darrell's mother had decided to sign Darrell into foster care. Jessica and Sam had already agreed between themselves that they wanted to foster Darrell, so Luke suggested they talk to Darrell and then begin the process of applying to be his guardians.

Now that everything was falling into place, Jessica felt a little nervous too — mainly because she was still unsure of how Darrell felt about her. She knew that it took time to build a trusting bond. She had fumbled things badly the first time around; she desperately wanted to get them right this time.

She thought about Sam's question. "I guess so. Luke said we ought to tell him and talk it over today, so it won't be a total surprise when the social worker comes to speak with him tomorrow."

"He hasn't asked me any questions outright, but I think he knows something's going on."

"Because I've been so nice to him, you mean?" Jessica asked with a nervous laugh.

Sam shook his head. "No, silly . . . well . . . maybe a little. I mean, I think Darrell thought you didn't like him and all this attention has him wondering."

"I understand. I just hope that over time he'll see that I'm sincere. It's hard to put my feelings into words, Sam. I don't know how to explain it to him. But I do know that, deep inside, something's really changed. It's like some switch in my heart just flipped over one day. I'm glad we're going through with this. I want us to take Darrell in and to care for him as much as I wanted a baby."

Sam stared at her and blinked. "Well, that says it all, I guess." He reached out and rested his hands on her shoulders. "I owe you an apology."

"For what?"

"I was hard on you, Jessica. When you had the miscarriage, I acted like you were the one who needed comforting and everything was fine with me. I couldn't admit that I was hurting, too, and that I was scared we might not have the family I wanted so badly."

"Oh, Sam —"

"Let me finish, please. I think — originally — maybe I did get focused on Darrell as a way of avoiding our problems. But then I really got to know him and I got attached and I just expected you to feel the same way I did. I couldn't see what was going on at the time. But I should have been more understanding about what you were going through and more considerate of your feelings, and I'm sorry for all of that."

Jessica put her arms around the man she loved so much. "It's all right. We were both dealing with a lot." She laughed softly. "Think of it this way. Now we're ending up with two children instead of just one. That's a good start, don't you think?"

"Plenty for me." Sam held her close and she rested against him. "I think this is all going to work out." His tone was soft with excitement. "I'm praying it will."

"Me, too," she admitted. She heard footsteps approaching and opened her eyes to find Darrell standing in the doorway, watching them.

"You guys kissing *again?*"

"Kind of gross, huh?" Sam guessed.

Darrell nodded emphatically. "Yuck."

"I guess that's one way of describing it," Jessica said with a grin. With one arm slung around Sam's waist, she opened her other arm, beckoning the boy forward. "Come here, Darrell."

Darrell didn't move. He looked confused, as if he didn't understand, or couldn't quite believe, that she was welcoming him into their embrace.

Sam also held an arm out to the boy. "Come over here, buddy. We just want to give you a hug, too."

Darrell gave them both a tentative smile then walked over to where they stood, stopping a few steps short of his mark.

"It's okay," Jessica coaxed him. She stepped closer to him and put her arm around his shoulder and stroked his hair. Sam slung his arm around Darrell from the opposite side, so that together, they formed a complete circle.

"We're happy to have you with us, Darrell. We really are," she said.

Darrell tolerated about twenty seconds of hugging before saying, "Uh — isn't it time for lunch?" They broke apart and Darrell rolled his eyes at them, and Jessica wondered if once again she'd done the wrong thing. But as Darrell sat down at the table he gave them both a smile that left no room for doubt — it was pure happiness.

The three of them dug into their sandwiches. Darrell combined two into a peanut-butter-and-jelly-and-ham-and-cheese hybrid, and seemed quite proud of himself when Jessica told him it was gross.

Sam waited until the boy had finished eating, then said, "We'd like to talk to you about something, Darrell, something sort of serious." Jessica felt her heartbeat pick up its pace. "I know Luke told you this morning that your mother has decided to let you live with a foster family, so you can be cared for while she's trying to get well again."

Darrell nodded, his expression suddenly serious. "Yeah, he told me that."

"Well, Jessica and I would like you to come and live here with us. We're not sure yet if that's the way it's going to work out. But we're filling out all the papers and doing what we need to do. Would that be okay with you?"

Darrell's eyes widened in shock. "Live here with you? Me? Like, every day and night, too?"

Jessica had to smile at his reaction. "Every day and night, too. You would have your own bedroom — that spare room at the top of the stairs. We'll fix it up, just for you."

"Wow . . . awesome. . . ." He stared at Jessica, then back at Sam again, looking as if he still didn't quite believe it. "Of course I want to live with you guys. What do you think — I'm crazy or something?"

Sam's grin stretched from ear to ear. "Well, we thought you might like the idea.

But we had to ask, just to be sure."

"Thank you, Sam. Thank you for working this out for me. I'm going to be really good from now on. You'll see." Darrell glanced over at Jessica, as if she was the one who might doubt his words.

Sam reached over and rested his hand on Darrell's shoulder. "Jessica's the one who really got the ball rolling, Darrell. I think you ought to thank her, too."

Jessica felt suddenly self-conscious, especially when Darrell looked at her curiously, as if he were trying to figure out if what Sam said was true.

He seemed to think it over and reach a decision. "Uh, thanks, Jessica. I'm going to be really good. From now on, I promise."

"I know you will, Darrell. I know you'll try your best. But don't worry. We don't expect perfection around here. Nobody's perfect. Not even Sam," she added with a teasing grin.

She tilted her head to one side as she caught the boy's eye. "I know our relationship got off to a bad start, Darrell. But I'm going to try my best now too. I think we can be really great friends. I'm sorry for the way I acted toward you. I think I just didn't expect a little boy in my life," she admitted.

"That's okay. . . . I was a little mean to you sometimes, too. Because Sam likes you so much, I guess. I guess I was just jealous or something."

Jessica had suspected as much but was surprised to see that Darrell could be so honest about his feelings. Maybe he was starting to trust her.

"Let's just start off again with a clean slate. And if you come to live with us, I'll tell you one thing, you never have to be jealous. There'll always be enough love to go around."

Sam glanced across the table with a loving look and she felt his silent approval.

"Guess what, Darrell," he said. "Jessica is going to have a baby in August. What do you think about that?"

"I like babies. That's cool."

Jessica grinned. "Yeah . . . I think it's pretty cool, too. I think we're going to have a pretty cool family."

Sam laughed at her and squeezed her hand. She felt his happiness, almost too much to contain. There were going to be a lot of changes for them in the new year, she reflected. But after all, that's what life was all about, wasn't it? No matter how carefully you scheduled and planned, you had to keep your mind and heart open to the unexpected ways God answered prayers. Maybe that's what she had learned from all of this, Jessica thought as she gazed fondly at Darrell. And to think, she could have missed out on so much adventure and so much joy.

It was clear and sunny out, not a cloud in sight. That was all she really cared about, Emily realized. She tilted her head to glance out the bedroom window, checking the sky for what must have been the hundredth time since dawn. She hadn't slept a wink, worrying about the weather, despite the fact that the forecasts had called for a dry, cold spell for days to come. But this was, after all, New England, what did forecasts know?

Dan had laughed at her. "It won't dare snow on our wedding day." And when that pronouncement failed to calm her, he'd added, "So we'll get hit with a few snow flakes. They say it's good luck."

She had never heard that bit of folklore and was sure he was making it up. Tossing and turning all night, all she could think about was how, if it did snow, the only one who would be happy would be her mother, who would undoubtably take it as evidence that she was, once again, right. To Lillian it would be proof that Emily's daring nuptial plan was ridiculous, sheer insanity, an event that would make them all laughing-stocks.

But the sun did shine, giving Emily great hope that her ambitious scheme might triumph after all.

She turned back to the mirror and lifted the mascara wand toward her eyes. Her hand shook wildly and she decided it was best to go without that final coat. Her hair didn't look quite right, either, she thought. The salon had made it too . . . fluffy or something. She wasn't used to the way it looked and hoped her headpiece would smash it down a bit. Her suit had been a good choice, she thought. Cream-colored wool, with a short jacket that had a nipped-in waist and a satin shawl collar, paired with a long skirt. Betty had spotted it for her; she had such a wonderful eye for clothes. Emily added a set of pearl earrings but left her throat bare.

The doorbell rang. It must be Jessica, coming to pick her up in the limo. Emily was glad her sister had arrived early. She needed help with the headpiece — and a calming presence.

Emily swung open the door, glad to see Jessica but surprised to see her daughter,

Sara, there as well.

"Is everything all right? I thought you were going to pick up your grandmother."

"I did." Sara glanced back over her shoulder. "But she didn't want to ride in my little car. She demanded a seat in the limo."

"She's in there, right now? All alone?"

"The driver is waiting with her," Jessica explained. "Though I doubt Mother will condescend to have a conversation with him."

"Oh, dear . . . well, we'll have to give him a bigger tip, I suppose. Where's Sam?"

"He's in town, helping Dan make sure everything is set up right. I told Mother to come in, but she insisted on waiting," Jessica added. She shrugged. "At least we won't be holding up everything, wondering if she's coming at all."

Emily knew Jessica was thinking back to her own wedding day, when their mother had made a dramatic, last-minute entrance.

"Good point. Well, I won't be long. I just need some help with this headpiece. Look at my hair," she moaned as she closed the door. "I don't know what happened. . . ."

"You look beautiful, Emily. Don't be silly." Sara leaned over and kissed her cheek, and Emily felt instantly cheered.

"She's right. You're an absolute knockout. Where's the headpiece? I have some bobby pins in my purse in case you need them."

Jessica and Sara followed Emily into her bedroom, and she allowed them to work on her, as bridesmaids were supposed to do.

A short time later, Jessica glanced at the bedroom clock. "That's it, Emily. We promised Dan you wouldn't be late."

"I promised him, too . . . though he might die of shock if I actually do get there on time."

Emily picked up her tiny handbag and cream-colored satin gloves. The florist had delivered their bouquets a few hours earlier, and now she handed out the flowers: cream-colored roses clustered with pale peach phlox and miniature off-white orchids. There was also an orchid corsage for her mother.

Jessica took the clear box. "I'll give it to her, though I don't think she'll want any pins in her fur coat."

Emily laughed. "It could use a few pins if you ask me. It's practically falling to pieces."

They finally left the house and walked

out to the car, where the uniformed driver opened the door and waited to help them in. Emily searched his face but saw no sign that he'd been traumatized by Lillian. Maybe her luck was holding.

The back of the limo was the size of a sitting room, Emily thought as she slid inside. Her mother looked very small, perched in one corner of the bench seat that faced to the rear. Lillian sat huddled in her voluminous mink coat and matching hat, both of which harkened back to a style decades past.

"Well, there you are. Finally. I thought you were having second thoughts in there or something."

"Hello, Mother." Emily settled herself on the rear seat, facing forward. Jessica sat beside her and Sara sat next to her grandmother.

"Well, fasten your seat belts. It's going to be a bumpy ride." Lillian cackled at her joke, a quote from an old Bette Davis movie.

Sara refused to let her grandmother get away with such pessimism. "Doesn't Emily look beautiful, Lillian? That suit is perfect for her."

Lillian surveyed her oldest daughter with a critical eye. "Not bad. Very nice lines.

I'm glad to see you chose something sensible. No use dressing up like Cinderella going to the ball at your age."

"Emily could have worn a gown if she'd wanted to." Jessica tugged off her gloves and frowned at her mother.

"What did I say? Why is everyone so touchy today? I'm just trying to pay her a compliment, for goodness' sake."

Sara laughed. "Sometimes it is hard to tell, Lillian, you have to admit."

Sara caught Emily's eye and Emily had to grin.

"I'll admit nothing of the sort." Lillian huffed and rearranged her coat over her bony knees. "I was going to compliment the flowers as well, but now I'm in fear of rubbing someone the wrong way. So I won't say anything at all."

Emily noticed the corsage on the seat between her and Jessica. She picked it up and held it out to Lillian. "Here, Mother, I almost forgot. Here are some flowers for you."

Lillian took the plastic box in her hands and gazed down at it. "An orchid. How thoughtful of you. It's not the most practical choice for an outdoor affair in this weather, however. I think I'll put it on later, so it won't freeze and then turn to mush."

Emily met her gaze but didn't answer. Her house was less than a mile from the center of town, but the ride seemed agonizingly long. She twisted her gloves in her hands and glanced out the window. The limousine couldn't travel on some of the narrow side roads, so they had been forced to take a less direct route.

Lillian cleared her throat. "I have something for you, too, Emily." Emily felt her heartbeat quicken as she saw her mother's hands flutter around the black leather clutch on her lap.

Was she going to take out the pearls? Emily wondered. Or was she just baiting her? During all the time she had been planning the wedding, her mother had never once mentioned the necklace. The wedding pearls were a family heirloom, prized by Lillian, who had been denied wearing them herself when she eloped with Emily and Jessica's father. They had come into Lillian's possession later, when both her parents had passed away. They were one of the few treasures she had inherited after her wealthy family cut her off when she married Oliver Warwick against their wishes.

Lillian had nearly denied Jessica the use of the pearls because she disapproved so strongly of Sam Morgan. But finally she had given in and Jessica had carried on the family tradition. Emily knew that, despite her barbs, Lillian actually did approve of Dan. Still, her mother nursed old grievances and had never entirely forgiven Emily for running off at age eighteen and marrying Tim Sutton, Sara's father.

Emily had to admit, she did want to wear the pearls. She had perhaps even chosen her bridal outfit with that piece of jewelry in mind. But she would never admit it to her mother. She had promised herself that if her mother didn't mention the pearls, she wouldn't either.

"I don't believe in all that 'something borrowed, something blue' business," Lillian said as the limo turned on to Main Street and approached the village green. "I had all the necessary 'somethings' on my wedding day, and little good did it do me. But, at a certain stage in life, one needs to be magnanimous, I suppose. While I disapprove of this public spectacle you've chosen to subject us to, you may as well wear the wedding pearls, Emily. I doubt you'll have another chance at them, quite frankly."

Her mother thrust out a dark blue velvet box, her face averted so that Emily couldn't see her expression.

Emily didn't know whether to laugh or cry. She took the box and opened it. There were the pearls, gleaming on their faded satin bed, probably not worth a fortune, as her mother believed, but rich in another kind of value altogether.

"Thank you, Mother. I do want to wear them," Emily confessed.

As the limo pulled up to the green and came to a stop, Jessica took the jewelry box from Emily's hands. "Here, turn around. I'll put them on for you. Just in the nick of time."

Emily turned her back to her sister and felt the cool necklace on her skin. She touched her hand to her throat. "How do they look?"

"What a question! They look perfect. A bride isn't dressed without pearls." Lillian shook her head in dismay. "If I taught you girls one thing, it had to be that."

Emily and Jessica glanced at each other, sharing a secret smile. "Yes, Mother. I do believe you're right," Emily agreed. She leaned forward and gave her mother a quick hug. "Thank you, Mother. Really."

Lillian shook her head, as if to shake off an unwanted sentimental lapse. "You're very welcome. Now, on with the show."

Emily sent up a quick prayer for courage and stepped out of the car. She felt her eyes widen in amazement. The sight that greeted her was unbelievable. The green was absolutely filled with people. Though every available folding chair within a ten-mile radius had been requisitioned for the event, there were still more people standing than seated, all of them circled around the white gazebo at the center of the park. It seemed everyone in Cape Light — and all their distant relatives — had shown up.

The gazebo had been decorated with flowers and garlands of greenery, and the town's grounds crew had set out a long green runner that stretched from where she stood to the gazebo steps.

She spotted Dan in his morning coat and Reverend Ben at the end of the aisle, waiting for her, and she felt her stomach flutter with nerves.

Sam came to greet them, looking like the leading man of an old-time movie, Emily thought, in his tuxedo and high starched white collar. He kissed her quickly on the cheek. "Happy wedding, Emily. Everything's set. We can start anytime."

Emily swallowed hard. She felt everyone's eyes on her. People waved at her and lifted their children to see. Some of the faces were close friends and some were strangers. She was used to making public appearances at parades and town events, but this was different somehow. This was her wedding day and these were her guests. She felt a certain, intangible energy rising up out of the crowd, equal parts warmth, love, and good wishes. She felt herself smiling in response, buoyed up by all the goodwill that surrounded her.

It was certainly a strange, even crazy, idea to celebrate her wedding this way, Emily thought. Her mother had not been totally off target there.

But it's the right way for me, she realized. She would look back on this day with wonder for the rest of her life.

"Sam, why don't you bring Mother to her seat and we'll start?" Jessica suggested.

Sam sketched a little bow and offered his arm to Lillian.

"Wait. . . ." Emily stepped toward them. "I have another idea. Would you like to wait up front and give me away, Mother?"

Emily had planned to bypass that tradition but now felt inspired. Why not her mother? *Even if she refuses, at least I've made the gesture.*

Lillian stared at her curiously, suspiciously even, Emily thought. "Well . . . I suppose I could do that. I am the mother of the bride, after all. I should have *some* official capacity."

Emily watched as Lillian took a firm hold of Sam's arm and allowed him to help her up the aisle. "This may take me a while," she warned Emily over her shoulder. "I'll meet you at the other end."

Finally, the music started, and the immense crowd simmered down with respectful silence. Emily watched Sara and then Jessica proceed up the aisle before her. She felt her legs get wobbly.

She pushed herself forward and began walking slowly, staring straight ahead at first, then glancing from side to side. It was so much fun spotting so many familiar faces; she couldn't resist sending a nod or a glance to so many friends and acquaintances who had come here today: Sophie and Miranda Potter, Grace and Digger Hegman, Molly Willoughby and her girls along with Dr. Harding and his daughter. A little farther down she spotted Tucker and Fran Tulley and then Lucy Bates, waving madly while Charlie stood beside her. He seemed to be smiling a bit under his usual scowl, in spite of himself, Emily thought with wonder. Had he actually abandoned his diner to see her get married?

Toward the end of the aisle, she saw Carolyn Lewis, sitting with her son, Mark. Rachel and Jack Anderson sat nearby, and next to them were Reverend James Cameron and Leigh Baxter, her newborn baby in her arms. Emily had heard the happy ending to that story and her smile grew even wider at the sight.

Finally, she reached the end of her journey. Her mother came to stand beside her, as stoic as a soldier. Dan stood on the top step of the gazebo, beaming down at her. He couldn't have looked more handsome, she thought, and she couldn't have loved him more if she tried. He walked down the steps with Reverend Ben, who stepped between them.

"Who gives this woman away to be married?" Reverend Ben asked.

"I do," her mother said firmly. She turned to face Emily and Emily saw her mother's chin quiver. Her mother touched her shoulder then leaned forward and kissed her on the cheek. "Be happy, dear. You've earned it," she said quietly.

Then she took Emily's hand and gave it to Dan. "Take good care of her. She's a jewel, you know."

Dan looked shocked speechless for a moment. "I will, Lillian. Believe me."

Sam came forward and helped Lillian to her seat, and Reverend Ben led Emily and Dan up to the top step of the gazebo.

The blessings and readings went by in a blur. Emily kept thinking she was glad she had decided to videotape the event, after all. Her mind was spinning so wildly, she couldn't take it all in.

". . . And do you, Emily, promise to take Dan, for richer or poorer, in sickness and in health, until death do you part?"

Emily stared into Dan's eyes. "I do," she said.

Simple words that somehow held all of her heart. She slipped his wedding band onto his ring finger as he had already done for her.

They stood for a moment holding hands and gazing into each other's eyes. They were married and Emily felt wildly happy, floating ten feet off the ground.

"I now pronounce you husband and wife," Reverend Ben said in his sonorous tones. "You may kiss the bride."

Dan didn't need to be told twice. He slipped his arm around her waist and planted a deep kiss on her mouth that nearly made her swoon.

The crowd cheered and clapped and when Emily finally looked up she found confetti and streamers flying through the air. Out on the dock, a cannon sounded. It was the town's cast-iron antique, usually reserved for the Revolutionary War enactments and the stroke of midnight on New Year's Eve.

What a nice touch, she thought, and wondered who had arranged it. It had to be one of her friends at the village hall.

"Ready?" Dan asked her quietly.

"I'm ready if you are."

He hooked her arm in his and they started down the steps, then down the long aisle of onlookers. More confetti, birdseed, and streamers pelted them. Friends burst through the ranks to give unauthorized hugs and kisses and to shake Dan's hand. Emily felt as if she'd just won the presidential election, the Nobel Prize, and the Miss America Pageant, all rolled into one. It was wild. It was rowdy. It was spontaneous. It was pure joy and truly the happiest day of her life.

Just behind the noise of the crowd, she heard a dull hum. She looked up at the sky and at a distance across the harbor, she spotted the plane approaching. Sam, bless his heart, obviously heard it, too. It was one of his jobs as a groomsman to make the announcement, and he now jumped up to the microphone.

"Your attention, please. The bride and groom would like a photograph with all their guests as a remembrance of this happy day. A plane is approaching in about . . . thirty seconds, and we're all going to be in an aerial shot. Please stay right where you are. Everyone on the green will be included. All you need to do is gather a little closer to the gazebo, look up, and smile."

Sam paused and looked over his shoulder, checking the horizon for the plane's progress. The group had gone relatively quiet now and everyone could hear the low thrum of the small plane's single engine.

Emily noticed people pointing up at the sky. Dan slung his arm around her shoulder and shook his head. "You didn't tell me about this."

"It was Sara's idea, a wedding gift. I couldn't say no, could I?"

Dan laughed. "I guess not. . . . But don't be surprised if it's on the front page of the *Messenger* tomorrow."

"Oh . . . goodness. I didn't even think of that!"

Dan laughed at her surprise and hugged her even closer. "Too late now."

"Okay, here he comes," Sam coached the crowd. "Five, four, three, two, one! Everyone shout, 'Good luck, Emily and Dan!' "

The crowd responded and just as the plane swooped low over the green, Emily heard the roar.

"Good luck, Emily and Dan!"

Emily looked up too, conscious only of the great shout around her, Dan's loving embrace, and the clear blue sky above. She felt surrounded by the love and goodwill of her family and friends and the joy of the day, and she felt God's love pouring down like the brilliant white sunshine.

She felt truly and deeply happy.

To live each day, aware and thankful of your blessings, that was the secret, wasn't it? Well, now she'd always have a picture to remind her.

With one arm raised, she waved as the plane passed overhead, knowing that this moment was one she'd never forget. It was etched upon her heart forever.

About the Authors

THOMAS KINKADE is America's most collected artist, a painter-communicator whose tranquil, light-infused paintings bring hope and joy to millions each year. Each painting Thomas Kinkade creates is a quiet messenger in the home, affirming the basic values of family, faith in God, and the luminous beauty of nature.

KATHERINE SPENCER was a fiction editor before turning to a full-time career as a writer. The author of more than twenty books for both children and adults, she lives with her husband and daughter in a small village on the Long Island Sound, very much like Cape Light.

The employees of Thorndike Press hope you have enjoyed this Large Print book. All our Thorndike and Wheeler Large Print titles are designed for easy reading, and all our books are made to last. Other Thorndike Press Large Print books are available at your library, through selected bookstores, or directly from us.

For information about titles, please call:

(800) 223-1244

or visit our Web site at:

www.gale.com/thorndike
www.gale.com/wheeler

To share your comments, please write:

Publisher
Thorndike Press
295 Kennedy Memorial Drive
Waterville, ME 04901